WITHDRAWN

The

QB BAD BOY
and ME

WITHDRAWN

25 SEP 1974

The
QB BAD BOY
and ME

Tay Marley

wattpad books **w**

wattpad books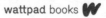

Copyright © 2019 Tayler Marley. All rights reserved.

Published in Canada by Wattpad Books, a division of Wattpad Corp.
36 Wellington Street E., Toronto, ON M5E 1C7

www.wattpad.com

No portion of this publication may be reproduced or transmitted,
in any form or by any means, without the express written
permission of the copyright holders.

First Wattpad Books edition: August 2019

ISBN 978-0-99368-994-9 (Softcover edition)
ISBN 978-0-99368-996-3 (eBook edition)

Names, characters, places, and incidents featured in this publication are
either the product of the author's imagination or are used fictitiously. Any
resemblance to actual persons (living or dead), events, institutions, or locales,
without satiric intent, is coincidental.

Wattpad, Wattpad Books, and associated logos are trademarks and/or
registered trademarks of Wattpad Corp. All rights reserved.

Library and Archives Canada Cataloguing in Publication
information is available upon request.

Printed and bound in Canada

3 5 7 9 10 8 6 4 2 1

Cover designed by Stephanie Adkison & Sayre Street Books
Images © Kiwihug on Unsplash and © Skitterphoto on Pexels

I dedicate this book to the readers.
I couldn't have done it without you.

The
QB BAD BOY
and ME

AUTHOR'S NOTE

If you've come here from Wattpad, then I'd first like to thank you for following me on this journey! You might recall Spencer and Grayson from the Wattpad version of *The QB Bad Boy and Me*. Of course, they are two very important characters, and they play a big part in this book as well—but their names are Gabby as Spencer and Josh as Grayson.

CHAPTER 1

How can an entire summer feel as if it were a mere weekend once you're back at school and time slows down again? Three months of freedom becomes an aftertaste, washed down by the bitterness of reality. I once read a quote on Pinterest that said people paint their rooms blue because it produces a calming effect—which was why I decided to lay down in the short grass of our school field so that I could stare at the sky. Strands of my long blonde hair wisped in the light breeze, and as I inhaled the fresh air in attempt not to feel suffocated, I heard my cheer captain squawking.

"Dallas! You've had all summer to lay around, get up and do laps. Now!"

It was a reasonable request; I was at an afternoon practice and Emily Raeken—or evil dictator—was my captain. And the field wasn't the best place for an afternoon snooze. I tilted my head to the side and saw dozens of white sneakers running through the green blades of grass that swayed like an ocean wave in the soft breeze.

Then and there I decided to start a petition to extend summer break for a month. Days like this shouldn't be spent in the confines of school property. They should be spent on the road, creating memories, taking beach trips, and doing whatever else one would deem buzz worthy. Personally, dancing under the sun and stars, visiting the lake, bingeing Netflix, and watching football was my idea of a summer well spent.

"Get up, Dallas! Or you can do suicide runs for the rest of the afternoon." Emily sounded as if she was at the end of her rope.

"One more year," I muttered as I rolled onto my hands and knees before getting up to jog back and forth with the rest of the squad.

One more year of cheerleading. One more year at Archwood High School. One more year in Castle Rock, Colorado. One more year before I could make my way to California and finally live the way that I'd always wanted to.

I completed the drills, agility rings, mini-hurdles, drop jumps, and wall sprints, pushing myself hard because at the end of the day, while I may have detested cheerleading and all of its preppy propaganda, I didn't do anything half-assed. If I wanted any chance of attending the California Institute of the Arts to pursue a dance career, I was stuck on the team.

Our school didn't have a dance team, and the small studio in the middle of town only offered ballet and tap. The bitter old woman who ran the studio wouldn't let me teach a class for contemporary. Who knew why. I think she was just stuck in her ways and didn't want to share. And no matter how hard I'd tried to convince the school that it'd be beneficial to start a dance team, it just didn't happen. All of the funding went toward football, cheerleading, and the academic clubs. I had to settle for cheerleading, knowing that it'd look good on my college applications.

After a grueling practice, I toweled away the sweat beads that soaked my body and winced when I saw Emily beelining toward me. The sun bounced off her auburn hair and gave her a glowing halo. She looked like an angel of terror.

"New rule," she said with boredom. "We wear uniforms to practice now. Don't show up without it next time."

"That doesn't make sense." I stared down at my shorts and sports bra. "We've always worn activewear to practice. I'll need at least a few spare uniforms if we practice in them."

"Buy another uniform or two," she said flippantly.

"They're, like, two hundred dollars," I scoffed. "Not everyone has that kind of cash."

"We practice in uniform," she ordered, her hair whipping as she turned away. Telltale signs of elation beamed from her face. I swear that causing misery gave her a hard on.

I was tempted to argue but bit my tongue. That rule had never applied, and I'd bet my life that it still didn't. Emily was intent on getting a reaction from me, and she often pressed my buttons in hopes of getting one. I think that it had a lot to do with the fact that I didn't give a damn about her "status." She put herself at the top of the pecking order, and I refused to get in line. Emily might have been our captain, but the cruel twist of fate was that her mother was our coach—except the woman was never around. I mean, never. She made a brief appearance at the Christmas party last year, breezing in on her Louboutins and self-importance. But otherwise, Emily was left to make all the calls. She decided who made the team and who didn't. Which routines we did and how we did them. She decided how often we practiced, and she did hustle. Still, her routines lacked originality, and I was sick of doing the same steps in a different order all the time.

Taking a deep breath, I snatched my gym bag from the bleachers and headed to the locker rooms on the other side of the field, where the football players practiced their drills; it was their first practice of the year too.

Most of them, if not all, probably spent the entire summer here doing those drills, but apparently there was no rest for the wicked. Our team was one of the best in the state, and Coach Finn made them work hard, ensuring that they practiced almost every day.

My phone hummed inside my gym bag. Gabby. My best friend and pretty much the only person in this school I could tolerate spending an extended amount of time with.

> Hey, so I know it's only Monday, but I'm thinking of the weekend already. FaceTime me when you're home. We'll discuss plans!

I smiled, knowing that she'd more likely than not try and coerce me into going to a party because she believed my "connections to the popular crew" should be put to good use.

Gabby adored the social life. Even though we both flew under the radar, she still liked to let her hair down and live a little. Most of our outings were for her benefit, but I tagged along because if I didn't, she wouldn't have anyone else to go with.

Typing out a reply, I was visualizing how she would bounce

up and down on the spot when she read the message when a distant masculine voice captured my attention.

"Heads-up!"

A football spiraled through the air, straight toward my face. Instinctively, I lifted my arms and caught the ball before it broke my nose, and more importantly, my pride. Because that would have been humiliating.

A well-built quarterback pulled off his helmet. "Sorry!"

He was a good forty-five feet away, but I recognized his unreal good looks immediately.

Drayton Lahey. Team quarterback. Captain of the Archwood Wolves.

His sweat-drenched light-brown locks stuck up in all directions but he still looked like a damn *GQ* model. As he began a light jog toward me, he clapped his hands together and held his arms out, signaling for the ball. His muscular frame was dominant and his olive skin glistened. How did he make sweat look good?

I saved the saliva that could have been running down my chin because while I didn't know a lot about our football team's captain, I did know that he was obnoxious, loud, and inappropriate . . . and that was just what I'd picked up without sharing any classes with him. This year we had economics together.

I pulled my arm back and stepped forward, throwing the ball through the air directly toward him. It was a perfect shot and he caught it with one hand. I saw the surprised expression that flashed briefly across his features. A few low whistles came from his teammates, and I heard the words "She-Hulk" come from somewhere downfield.

It was as if they couldn't fathom that a girl could throw a ball.

I rolled my eyes, picked up my phone and gym bag from

the grass, and continued toward the locker rooms. So much for flying under the radar. It was typical that something as simple as throwing a ball could attract attention. It was a testament to how underdeveloped teenage brains were.

The sky was filtered with red and orange hues by the time I left the locker room, like someone had smeared a paintbrush across the horizon to make a canvas transitioning a beautiful day into a clear night.

My good mood was quickly dampened when I saw my car in the parking lot and realized that it had a large dent in the back bumper, scratched with black paint. I ran my hand along the grooves with frustration. Whoever had done it hadn't stuck around to swap details, and the inconsideration made me furious.

A ding on my bumper was forgivable.

A ding and ditch was not.

My car might have been a lemon—it wasn't a fifty-thousand-dollar Jeep like what some of the kids around here drove—but it was the only one I had, and I couldn't afford for people to crash into it and not at least pony up for the damage.

I got into the car, slamming the door with a force that displayed my frustration, then drove the five minutes home with a scowl etched on my face the entire way.

The garage door was already open, so I pulled right in and jumped out with a huff, then jogged up the narrow walk to the steep steps to our front door. As soon as I got inside, I swung the door shut and hurled my backpack into the corner of the living room.

"Nathan?!" I called for my older brother, my legal guardian, hoping that he could shed some helpful light on my current car predicament.

The small open-plan living area offered no sign of the eldest

Bryan sibling, and our little two-bedroom home wasn't big enough for my voice not to travel. He was obviously not here, so I put my frustration on the back burner, walked over to the fridge, pulled out a bottle of water, and guzzled it back, quenching my thirst.

Gone for a catch with the boys. Be back later.

I wasn't surprised at the little note stuck to the kitchen counter; I came home to them regularly. My twenty-five-year-old brother was a junior coach at Arapahoe Community College here in Castle Rock, but in high school he'd been the star quarterback on a fast track to professional success. Unfortunately, he'd suffered a rotator cuff injury when he was sixteen. He shrugged it off as a minor setback and tried to heal through Cortisone injections and physical therapy alone, but he should have had surgery when the specialist recommended it instead of opting out because it was the middle of football season. He left it too long and sustained permanent damage to his joint. The specialist told him that he would never turn pro. Even so, Nathan could still run circles around some of the boys on our team. He'd accepted the end of his career with a gracious attitude, and enjoyed training his students.

The doorbell rang, startling me into spilling water all over myself.

"Great," I mumbled as I headed to the front door. I swung it open and raised a brow in surprise. "What are you doing here?"

Drayton Lahey stood before me in a fitted tank top and jeans. A flashback to that afternoon's exchange crossed my mind. Maybe he'd come to recruit me for the team.

Ha, unlikely.

"Nice bra." He nodded at the black lace that'd become visible under my white shirt, but if he thought that I was going to get flustered and panic over the fact that he could see my bra, he was dead wrong. With a bored expression, I kept my hand resting on the door.

"Are you lost?"

"Nah, I hit your car at school today." He pulled out a pack of cigarettes and placed one between his lips as he patted his pockets in search of a lighter.

"Can you not?"

I waited for him to put the cigarette away but he didn't. He got as far as finding his lighter before I leaned forward and plucked the death stick from his mouth then snapped it in half, ignoring the disbelief that contorted his features. You'd think a football player would know better than to smoke.

"That was you?" I asked, getting back to the fact that Drayton Lahey had hit my car.

"Yeah, sorry." He recovered from my assault on his cancer cane, not looking apologetic in the slightest.

"How'd you know where I live?" I asked skeptically as he leaned on the doorframe with a cavalier attitude.

"I followed you."

"Why didn't you just tell me at school?" When he didn't respond, I understood. "Oh, I see. You didn't want anyone to see you talking to me."

"What? N-o, no." He recoiled, stammering with surprise.

"Save it. Follow me. If you haven't taken too many balls to the head, maybe you can actually fix this." I stepped past him and headed down the front steps toward my car.

"Actually, I was going to give you some cash," he mumbled, jogging to catch up.

"Are you serious?" I spun on my heel and stopped in front of him. "What kind of man are you?"

I almost laughed as a wounded expression formed on his face, the blow to his masculinity clearly having an adverse effect on his bravado. I was aware that just having a penis didn't mean he'd come out of the womb with a degree in mechanics. I just couldn't resist the figurative kick between his legs.

"Look," he said with a clipped tone, ignoring my jeer at his lack of skills, "it had nothing to do with people seeing me talk to you. I was waiting on my bike for whoever owned the car and then I saw you getting . . . really pissed off. I figured I'd save a scene at school and just come here."

I glanced at his sleek black motorcycle out on the road. A sizeable dent on the side of it made me wince—it was worse than my car, that was for sure. I wasn't even sure how he'd managed to accomplish such a cock-up, but I decided not to ask.

"I appreciate you coming to own up. I think it might cost around"—I narrowed my eyes as if I was internally calculating—"six, maybe seven grand."

"Get out," he scoffed. He pulled a black cap out of the back pocket of his jeans and slipped it on backward as he wiped the sweat off his forehead.

"You're doing it wrong." I pointed at his head. "The hat serves no purpose if you don't turn it around."

"It looks better backward." He shrugged, and damn was he right. I was a sucker for a backward cap. "What do you care anyway. Here"—he slid his hand into his front pocket and pulled out a wad of cash—"get your car fixed."

I was so distracted by the fact that this dude carried stacks of hundreds around with him that I didn't notice the minivan pulling up beside the curb. I knew it was Nathan's co-worker. He had a few kids—the sticker on the back window was a family of six little stick figures.

"Dallas!" my brother called as he climbed out of the backseat. He saw Drayton as he swung his backpack on and shut the car door.

"Hey, Nathan." I smiled and slipped the money into my pocket as my brother tossed me the football he'd been cradling.

"Nathan Bryan? This is your brother?" Drayton asked excitedly. "Shit, you're a legend. Coach still has a picture of you in his office."

Nathan shook Drayton's outstretched hand, his confusion morphing into pride. "You play at Archwood?"

"Quarterback," Drayton answered as he folded his bulging arms, the muscles expanding beyond belief. His right arm was decorated with a sleeve of tattoos that had obviously been done by an extremely talented artist. They were beautiful. There was a cluster of motorcycles, faded skulls, and dead flowers. There were even a couple of hidden footballs, but they were subtle and small, and looked as if they were made out of smoke.

A road starting at his wrist ran through the art, winding up to his shoulder. At the end were the backs of a little boy and girl who were holding hands and walking into a sunset. The whole thing looked like a pencil sketch, and gave the illusion of a memory in fog and mist. I wondered what the meaning behind the sleeve was.

Don't stare.

"That's where you learned how to throw like that . . ." Drayton was talking to me, so I quickly pulled my eyes away from his biceps and tattoos.

"What do you mean?" Nathan asked.

"This afternoon at practice," Drayton said, "she would have been wiped out, but she caught a bullet and threw it back with one hell of an arm."

"Nice." Nathan regarded me with pride. "She has to put up with me using her for practice most days." He gave me a light punch in the arm and then tapped his backpack. "I bought some meat for barbecue, Dal. You're not working at the diner tonight, right? I've got some cold beers in the fridge too. Want to stay . . ."

"Drayton, and sur—"

"No, he can't!" I cut Drayton off before he could accept. "He's got stuff to do."

"Would you look at that." Drayton stared at his blank cell phone screen with a mischievous grin. "My plans just got canceled. Looks like I can join you."

"Cool. Dallas, you might want to change that shirt." Nathan headed inside, leaving Drayton and me in a stare down.

"What do you think you're doing?" I asked him, ignoring the fact that his gaze was lingering on the aforementioned shirt that I was well aware needed to be changed. But it's a bra. We all know girls wear them.

"Staying for a barbecue and beers." He shrugged, finally meeting my eyes. "What else?"

"Why? Since when do we hang out?"

"I'm actually staying to talk to your brother. I bet he has some great advice for the field." He smiled a lazy smile before leaning in close, and I could feel his breath on my neck, smell his smooth skin. "I wouldn't change your shirt. It looks just right to me."

CHAPTER 2

I'd resorted to hiding in my bedroom, FaceTiming with Gabby. Her beautiful face hung on every word, eyes wide with an eager expression behind her glasses.

"They're talking about football. Like, extensively. While they stand around the grill like a couple of pals from way back," I said.

"I don't care what they're talking about," she scoffed, wrapping a long, dark ringlet around her finger. "Drayton Lahey is in your house. Having barbecue."

"I know," I groaned. "It's like a horror movie out there."

"You think he's hot?" Gabby asked.

"Yes. That doesn't change the fact that he's a di—"

"Dallas?" The knock on my door was followed by Drayton peeking through the gap, searching the room until he found me in the corner under my window. "Food's ready."

Hands in his pockets, leaning against the doorframe with a relaxed smile, he looked as though it wasn't the most bizarre thing in the world to be standing in my bedroom.

"Is that hi—"

"Uhshutupgoodbyeseeyoutomorrow!" I hung up the call, stood up, and smoothed out the black tank top I'd changed into after the water bottle incident.

Drayton watched me with a smug smile. "Talking about me?"

"Actually, yes," I confessed. "Apparently, there was some rumor going around about you and Mara Linden."

I dropped her name because, unfortunately for me, being on the cheer team meant being ear to a bunch of meaningless gossip twenty-four seven, whether I wanted to hear it or not. I knew for a fact he'd slept with her at a Fourth of July pool party at the beginning of summer.

"She's telling everyone that your penis is tiny and your stroke game is weak." The look that seized his features was so good that I was tempted to take a picture. His arrogant expression dropped, and, in its place, mortification bloomed as he visibly swallowed. "The cheer team have been talking about it all day."

That was a half truth. They had been talking about it all day, but more in praise, because apparently, he was as incredible as he looked. Of course he was.

I gave him a sympathetic smile and tapped his arm as I walked past, ignoring the impulsive desire to keep my hand on his biceps a little longer than appropriate. "Smells good. I'm starving."

The aroma of barbecue wafted down the hallway and I followed it out the back door to the yard, where Nathan had arranged the food in the middle of the picnic table. We ate like this all the time; neither of us cooked much, and the grill was easy and convenient. What wasn't normal was the buff star quarterback of my school dragging out a seat and sitting down like he was part of the family.

Drayton had clearly recovered from the blow to his ego, and was now leaning back in the chair, taking a swig of his beer, and winking in my direction. The fact that he knew I was uncomfortable and was enjoying it made me want to slap the bottle straight out of his hand.

"Seriously, why are you still here?" I scowled, leaning over the table. "I refuse to believe that you have nothing better to do."

"Dallas." Nathan gave me a wide-eyed warning as he sat down. "What is your problem tonight?"

"My problem is that you don't even know this guy. He goes to *my* school, but *you* invited him to stay for dinner. It's weird."

"I always invite your friends to stay if they're here around dinnertime." Nathan cut into his steak. "You've never had a problem with it before."

"What friends?" I recoiled in confusion. "I have Gabby, and that's it."

"You occasionally have guys here when I come home." Nathan shrugged. "I could be a protective big brother, but instead I invite them for dinner. How rude of me."

He thought that I didn't know that he invited them to hang around so that he could interrogate them and put on the scary-big-brother-I-will-kill-you act. I exhaled and noticed that Drayton was watching me with a curious, confident expression.

The meal consisted of silence from me; I sent Gabby a steady flow of updates, and she kept demanding Snapchats of the hunk across the table. There was no chance that I'd get caught taking pictures of him, though—I'd never live it down. Drayton and Nathan yammered on about the upcoming football season and a couple of away games that the Archwood Wolves had scheduled.

Away games weren't so bad. The cheerleading squad loved

them because they meant a night away from home in a nice hotel. And while the rules would say that everyone obeyed curfew and stayed in their assigned rooms, I knew most everyone got up to no good. For me however, I slept, cheered, ate, and barred all attempts at communication. I'd never had any interest in making friends, considering how desperately I wanted to leave next year.

Drayton and I cleared the dishes. The sun had gone down, and the solar lights planted around the edge of the lawn provided a soft glow.

"Cheer, can I ask you something?"

"Cheer?" I peeped over my shoulder as he followed me into the house.

He grinned but offered no further explanation for the nickname. "Where are your parents?"

"They died in a car accident when I was nine. Nathan was seventeen," I explained with my back to him as I filled the sink with hot, soapy water. My parents' death had hurt—it still hurt and I missed them like crazy—but the topic didn't kill me to talk about. "My grandmother, Nan, helped Nathan look after me until she died when I was fifteen."

"Shit. That blows. Are you okay?" He leaned against the counter, exhaling deeply.

"I'm fine." I gave him an apprehensive look. "They've been gone a long time." It would have been comical to see his concern if it wasn't so weird. "You can go home now," I said, offering him an out so that he didn't feel obligated to hang around after he'd eaten. I always felt rude if I dashed too fast after a meal at someone's house.

I scrubbed the dishes but noticed that he wasn't moving. I

kept my head down and refused to look up at the boy whom I'd considered to be transparent. I wasn't ready to admit that he might not be such an ass after all. He suddenly pushed off the counter and I breathed a sigh of relief, thinking that he might be leaving—until he grabbed a dish towel and started drying the dishes.

"What are you doing?" I asked as he whistled an upbeat tune and toweled down the plate in his hands. "Seriously, this night has been weird enough without Drayton Lahey doing dishes in my kitchen. You are aware we've never even talked before?"

"Don't say my name like that," he ordered. "Call me Dray. And whose fault is the lack of conversation? You're antisocial as hell."

"No, I'm not," I stammered. "I'm just . . . reserved."

"Reserved, huh?" He continued toweling the dishes with a smug, disbelieving grin. "Are you reserved with the dudes here in the afternoons?"

I'd hoped that he hadn't caught that earlier dig from Nathan—who still hadn't returned from the "phone call" that he'd heard ten minutes ago. "That's none of your business."

"Come on, I'm curious," he said.

"I have a question of my own." I slipped another plate into the dish rack and hoped that that was a smooth enough transition to a new subject. "Does Emily know that you're here?"

"Emily and I aren't together, Cheer," he said. "She doesn't need to know."

"Does *she* know that you're not together?" I asked with mild amusement, watching his chiseled back as he sauntered over to the cabinet and put the plate away. "Because it seems that she's under the impression that you two are very much together."

"I just leave her to it, you know? I've never been interested, but she's got her own shit going on. Kind of feel bad for her, so if she wants to fantasize a relationship, whatever."

I wondered if he would elaborate on what she had going on but he continued with the last of the dishes and kept his lips sealed. It made me smile and I realized that I might have been too quick to judge. He wasn't as bad as his behavior would have you believe. We finished the washing up in comfortable quiet, only sharing quick glances, as if we shared a secret, which I guessed we did now. I doubted that anyone was going to find out that he'd spent the evening here. He slipped his phone out of his pocket while I emptied the sink.

"I guess I better head off," he mumbled, reading the screen before he slid it back into his pocket. He glanced around for a moment and then his green gaze settled on me again. "Tell your brother that I said thanks for dinner."

"Sure," I said.

I walked him to the front door and leaned on the frame as he stepped out into the dark night. I admired the motorcycle parked beside the curb; the incandescent beam of the streetlamp shone down on the sleek machine. I gave Drayton a once over, appreciating his toned arms, but more than that, finding myself concerned for his flawless, exposed skin. "Is it safe to wear a tank top when you ride?"

"I don't know." He grinned and rested a hand on the doorframe beside me as he leaned in. "Should we go inside and find out?"

"Wow," I laughed and gave him a light shove in the chest. "That was smooth. A for effort."

He laughed and moved back again. "My jacket is in the seat compartment. With the helmet. I *always* wear *protection*."

"Let me guess," I said, refusing to humor his innuendo. "It's leather."

"It sure is. For safety purposes," he called over his shoulder while heading down the footpath, "not because it gives me points for cool. Good night, Cheer."

I watched him pull on his jacket, which fit him like a glove, and almost wanted to question the nickname again. But I didn't. He swapped his backward cap for his helmet, and the tinted visor reflected the streetlights above as he swung his leg over the seat. The engine roared to life, loud and obnoxious. Still, I couldn't help but watch with subtle admiration as he left. The entire night had been unexpected, but I wasn't disappointed with its outcome. Not disappointed at all.

CHAPTER 3

Tuesday morning I decided not to waste any time getting the ding in my car fixed, so I took it down to the body shop first thing and asked Gabby to follow me so that I'd have a ride to school.

"What's the damage, Harry?"

Harry was a sweet old guy I'd worked for a few summers ago doing odd jobs like cleaning and sweeping for a little extra cash, before I started working at the diner.

"Well, darling," he said as he adjusted the oil-stained cap on his head while he examined the dented bumper, "I'll do it for four hundred and fifty. That's as cheap as I can go."

It was a very good deal. The repair would have cost anywhere up to a grand at any other shop. Once I paid Harry, I was left with an extra hundred, and contemplated getting myself a new outfit. But I immediately squashed the idea, knowing that I'd give the money back to Drayton.

"Thank you, Harry. You're a lifesaver!"

"You can have her back by Thursday." He patted the top of the car before signaling Tony, one of the young panel beaters, to fetch the keys and move it inside.

"Thanks, Harry!" I called as I ran across the road to Gabby's waiting car.

"Have you still not fixed the air conditioning in this thing?" I waved my hand in front of my face, gasping for some cold air as Gabby sat in the driver's seat taking selfies. "Nothing Breaks Like a Heart" by Miley Cyrus and Mark Ronson crackled through the small speakers.

The air conditioning in Gabby's little Mazda hatchback had carked it at the beginning of the summer. Even now, toward the end of the season, the need for fresh air was high. The windows were rolled down, but the breeze was just as warm, so it really didn't help at all.

"I remember why we used my car all summer now," I groaned, wiping at the sweat beads on my forehead. I gripped the front of my T-shirt and fanned it in and out.

"You think you have problems with the heat?" She pointed at her thick head of curls tied into a bun. "You know what heat does to this Afro? It gets so damn big that it needs its own area code. I have six different products going on in this situation."

I giggled. "Yeah, you migh—"

"Ahh!" Gabby cut me off with an excited squeal as she clutched the steering wheel and bounced in her seat. "I just remembered! Tell me about last night. Like, everything."

"I already have."

"No, no, no! Last night you said it was 'uneventful.' I refuse to believe that having Drayton Lahey over for dinner could possibly be uneventful."

"Honestly, he and Nathan talked about football all night. He helped me with the dishes, and then he left. He did tell me that he isn't really in a relationship with Emily."

I left out the part about his not-so-subtle flirting. I didn't need a headache right before school.

"Oh." Her brows moved up and down suggestively as she pulled into a parking space. "He made it clear that he's available, did he?"

"It's not that deep, Gabs. There was nothing to it."

We hopped out of the car and met at the tail end while she sighed with a dreamy expression. My best friend might have been overexcited and reading into things that weren't there, but I adored her enthusiasm for love.

"I can't believe you spent the evening with Drayton Lahey."

"Please don't idolize him." We linked arms and started toward the brick building. "He's a football player. He can't heal with his hands."

"I bet he can do something else with his hands, though." She nudged me and her full lips curled into a devious grin.

"I walked into that one," I groaned.

Drayton and I didn't have economics that day, so I figured that I'd wait until practice during the second half of lunch to give back his leftover cash. I sat with Gabby in the cafeteria while we ate sandwiches and she caught me up on the latest gossip. She might not talk, but she did listen and she loved it—loved high school and the dynamics and the groups and the drama. But it was all loved from afar, and she didn't immerse herself in the center of its politics. Her findings were shared with me, though, and I smiled, nodded, and responded when signaled. It didn't interest me all that much, but I humored her. Gabby was in the middle of recounting Dave Lowinski's coming-out party when I interrupted her and stood up. "I have cheer practice. Want to come and watch?"

She shook her head and waved her half-eaten sandwich. More talking meant less eating. "I'm heading to the library. See you in English?"

"Sounds good." Gabby loved the library and books. It was where all the fuel for her romantic fantasies came from, and she had a solid group of friends she sat with and read.

Yesterday was more attention than I needed from our captain, so I had my uniform for practice, to avoid Emily breathing down my neck. Once I changed, I jogged out to the field and lined up with the rest of the team who were, *surprisingly*, dressed in casual activewear.

"Why are you in uniform, Dallas?" Emily sneered, earning a few snickers from the lineup. "This is practice."

I supposed I could have argued, stomped my feet, pointed out what a sadistic and horrible bitch she was for going out of her way to humiliate me, and we were only on the second day in. Instead, I took the high road, pulling my skirt and cheer top off so I was down to my boy shorts and sports bra.

"Better?" I smiled and tossed the uniform toward my bag on the bleachers behind us.

Emily responded by barking orders for the warm-up. After twenty minutes of nonstop intensity, she finally gave us a break. Guzzling back my water, I spotted Drayton in the middle of the field, talking to a few of his friends. His black T-shirt clung to his torso and once again I found myself admiring every inch of his incredible build.

"Dray!" I called. "Hey," I said when I caught up with him, which felt awkward, but I wasn't entirely sure why. It became even more awkward when he didn't respond. His stare was blank.

"It didn't cost as much as you thought it would." I left the explanation brief so that his friends didn't find out that he'd hit my car. I assumed that's what had him so nervous. Boys and their pride. "Here's the rest of that cash."

He looked at the money but didn't move to take it as his eyes darted from the bill in my hand toward his curious buddies and back again.

"Keep it for the next batch." He grinned arrogantly, just as full of himself than ever. "It's good green, right?"

The group of brain-dead half-wits gasped, widening their eyes as they looked me up and down. Scandalous thoughts of the cheerleader on drugs were obviously plaguing their small minds. I stared Drayton down, willing him to change his story and trying not to dwell on the fact that he himself appeared to be involved in drugs. It wasn't mind-blowing information. A lot of the students around here indulged in the devil's lettuce.

"I had fun last night." He winked. "You guessed right, Maxon. She's flexible."

"Woah!" Maxon, one of the linebackers, gasped. "What?!"

Maxon and Austin slapped each other's backs, cackling and carrying on like idiots while my eyes stayed locked on Drayton's. I swear that I saw a pang of regret flash through his deep-green irises. It didn't last for more than a moment before his gorgeous features returned to stone cold.

"And I was right," I snapped. "You are disappointing."

I threw the cash at him and turned around. That was not the same person I had talked to last night, and it disappointed me to feel so let down. If that was how he wanted to behave, then so be it. There was no love lost, but I wanted nothing to do with someone so two faced. As I returned to the squad, I noticed Emily watching us, a disapproving scowl on her face. Drayton wasn't worth the hassle that she would give me if she thought that I was moving in on *her* man.

After a long and tiring practice that I was certain was ten times more intense than usual due to the chip on Emily's shoulder, I wandered out of the girl's locker room and into the gym foyer, where Drayton was leaning against the wall on the other side of the room.

"Dallas." He started toward me but I ignored him and headed straight outside and down the concrete steps.

I didn't make it far before he caught up and planted himself in front of me. "I shouldn't have said that." He put his hands on my shoulders and gazed down at me from his full height.

"Please don't speak to me"—I shrugged him off—"ever again."

"I feel like a dick." He stuffed his hands in his pockets. "I told them that it wasn't true. I swear I set them straight."

"Thanks, but I still don't want to talk to you. I'm not interested in being friends with someone who can't be the same person all of the time. And I'm also not interested in getting kicked off the cheer squad by Emily."

"She wouldn't do that. She can't."

"Have you met your ex?" I shook my head and waved a sharp, dismissive hand. "Like I said, Drayton, I don't want anything to do with you. Last night was nice, and I thought there was more to you than a hollow and shallow person. But I guess not. Good-bye."

I stepped around him but he grabbed my wrist, forcing me to turn around. "I didn't mean to hurt you. Come on, what can I say or do?"

"If you don't know the answer to that"—I pulled my wrist back—"then there really is no hope for you."

I turned around and left, and didn't look back when he called. Luckily, the rest of the afternoon went on as usual. No one whispered or looked at me as if they had found out that I was a quarterback-snatching pothead. I guess Drayton had stuck to his word and squashed any gossip. Gabby didn't mention it in English, and she would no doubt have heard if it had spread. I was relieved when I slid into her hot car that afternoon.

"Hello, hello." She grinned and started the car. I immediately rolled the window down. "We were going to talk about the weekend when I called last night, but we talked about Drayton instead."

"Waste of breath that was," I mumbled. Gabby looked at me funny. "Nothing. What are we doing this weekend?"

"We're going to Cripple Creek. There's a sixteen-plus club opening. We can't drink, obvs, but there is dancing, and we can pre-game at your house."

Putting my feet on the dash, I sighed. It wouldn't be my first choice of how to spend the night. But whatever. "How are we going to get there? It's an hour and a half drive."

"Bus?"

"How about getting home? The bus doesn't run that late."

"Bus there, Uber home?" Gabby said.

"That'll be an expensive Uber."

"Split the fare?"

"Sure. Sounds like a plan," I said.

Gabby was there for me when I needed her, so I was there for her too. There was no chance that her pals from the library would ever join her out and about; I'd asked them once before.

"I'll come over at around three," she said. "Remember, if my mom asks, we're spending the night working on that English assignment on the earliest libraries and their histories."

"Natch. At this point, I'm aware that I can't tell your mom what we're doing, Gabs. Relax."

Gabby lived with her mom, and she had never met her father. He and Camilla had been in a casual arrangement when Gabrielle was conceived, and he wasn't prepared to become a father at nineteen. Gabby no longer spared him a second thought—she used to wish that she had her dad around, but the older she got, the more she came to realize that she didn't need one. However, being alone meant that Camilla took on the role of both mom and dad, and she took it seriously. She was strict.

The lack of parental authority in my household meant that Nathan and I were both free to come and go as we pleased. Nathan did his best to enforce some rules, but he was often out himself, sleeping his way across Castle Rock, and he knew that I wasn't all that social.

"Let's go shopping on Saturday?" Gabby parked the car in my driveway, leaving the engine running as she bounced with excitement in her seat.

"Sure," I said. "Come over in the morning instead of three, then, okay? Then we've got enough time."

"Yes!" She clapped her hands. "I can't wait."

CHAPTER 4

By Saturday morning my muscles ached, my stress levels were at an unhealthy level, and my mental capacity for airhead athletes had been exhausted. School, cheer practice, and working at the diner after school was a lot, and I'd forgotten how few hours were actually in a day.

It was nine in the morning and I'd showered, dressed, and made a coffee, all thanks to Gabby, who'd arrived in my bedroom at an ungodly hour of the morning, running on the energy of some otherworldly source. She and Nathan sat beside each other on the living-room side of the breakfast bar, sharing the *Denver Post*—Nathan was immersed in the sports section—while I stood in front of the sink and attempted to wake up with the aid of caffeine.

"What are you girls doing today?" Nathan asked.

"We're going shopping." Gabby turned the page, no doubt in search of local pop-up bookstores, and earned a curt glance from Nathan. She gave me a questioning look—she wasn't sure whether or not to add that we were shopping for outfits for that night.

"We're going into Cripple Creek tonight." I sipped the coffee. "What are you doing?"

"The club opening for kids?" He sounded like an old man disapproving of the wild youth.

"Yes. It's called Illusion." I turned to the kitchen window and watched the neighbor's kids bike up and down the road. Hattie, an elderly woman who worked at the diner with me, was across the street watering the dry strip of grass in front of her pavement. Basically, I was avoiding the stare from Nathan that was practically burning a hole in the side of my head.

"How are you getting there?"

"We're taking the bus," Gabby said casually.

"The bus?" Nathan looked between the two of us as though we'd lost it. "No way, you can't take the bus at night. I'll drive."

"Nathan, it's an hour and a half out of town. The bus will be fine." I rinsed my cup and walked toward the breakfast bar, leaning on it with flat hands. "We're getting an Uber home."

"Shut up." He stood and pointed an authoritative finger at me. "I'll drive because you obviously want to drink before you go. And that's fine, but be careful. Real careful. Get an Uber home, whatever. But no bus. Weirdos live on that bus at night. It's not safe."

"All right." I smiled and wrapped my long hair into a top-knot. "Thanks."

"I've got to go." He marched over to the front door and plucked the keys from their hook. "I've got practice as usual and then a date tonight. I'll be back later to give you a ride before I go out."

Nathan and I shared our little Toyota Corolla. I used it for school and work. He carpooled during the week and then had it the rest of the time because I was either with Gabby or at home. It worked for us. He was relieved when we got it back from the shop two days ago, just in time for his weekend.

N

Later that afternoon, Gabby and I returned home with a new outfit each, excitement about the evening ahead, and an UberX booked for two in the morning. I hoped that the night wouldn't be a dive, and we wouldn't want to leave earlier.

Gabby and I lounged around the house for a few hours, having something to eat and drinking a few beers before getting ready. The kitchen was a mess after I made two enormous BLTs.

"If I eat these carbs,"—Gabby pointed an aggressive finger at the sandwich—"I'm going to bloat. The dress that I'm wearing is tight. That's a problem."

"Eat it, Gabs. Or we're not going."

"You sound like my mother."

I laughed and bit into my own sandwich. "That's an unhealthy mindset. Eat the BLT."

Whenever she went out on an empty stomach, Gabby turned into a class A booze bunny and got drunk faster than the alcoholic aunt at an open-bar wedding. Despite her protests, she ate because she knew that I was right.

While I cleaned up the kitchen, we chatted about school and our classes, and the miserable teachers we loathed and the brilliant ones that we loved. Neither of us had much love for math. Chemistry and biology could be fun on the odd occasion that we did practicals rather than bookwork. Gabby loved English. It was her favorite subject. It was my weakest one, and I'd talked her into doing my reading responses on more than one occasion because of the simple fact that she'd pick up a book and read it without even knowing what it was about. She had a major chip on her shoulder about the fact that she wasn't in economics with Drayton and me, though. Who knew what she thought she was missing.

"In econ you get to sit in class with him and stare at him and—"

"That looks amazing," I said, breaking in.

She wore a dark-green body-con dress, and I was attempting to distract her. Her warm brown skin had seen the sun over summer and her tan had given her an extra bronze glow that looked exceptional with her dress. Her figure was incredible—long legs and a slender frame. I don't think she realized how envious I was of her natural dancer's body. I was comfortable with the curves that God gave me but I wouldn't have objected to a little more height. I was about half a head shorter than Gabrielle, and that was when she wasn't wearing heels.

"Thanks!" she gushed, flattening the front of the dress in the mirror that hung on the inside of the closet door.

She popped in her contacts and ditched her glasses for the night. My little wireless speaker blasted "Youngblood" by 5 Seconds of Summer while we made up our faces in separate mirrors. Gabby sat in front of the closet door while I sat with a compact on the double bed. We sang loudly and swung our hips back and forth to the beat after we finished our makeup. It took me a fraction longer to get ready, because when I heard music, I let it carry me, moving my limbs with the beat and feeling the rhythm. There was no greater feeling than dancing as the rest of the world fell away.

"I don't know why you're so against clubbing," Gabby said as she slid into her strappy heels. "You love to dance."

"I'm not against clubbing," I told her and found my own pair of velvet black platforms. "I'm more against the sweaty, drunk, messy sea of bodies that gyrate all over you."

I took one final look in the mirror. My dress was a little shorter than Gabby's. It was a rose-gold color with a plunging neckline and pinched waist. The material was velvet and flattering. My sun-kissed tan gave me warmth where I'd usually be a little paler. I felt good, which was a promising sign, and I found myself smiling as I heard Nathan call from the living room. My long blonde hair cascaded in soft curls down my back, my eyelids were winged with a soft sprinkle of bronze shadow, and a nude lip finished off my look.

"All right, let's go."

Illusion was exactly as I'd expected it to be. When we finally made it in after standing in the line for about an hour, we entered to find a nightlife atmosphere, dark and loud with artificial smoke floating through the air, with bright flashing lights casting down from the ceiling to illuminate the large crowd in the middle of the floor. The space was huge, and about ten feet up the sides of the walls were platforms where more people were dancing, some spraying water from plastic guns down into the mass of bodies. The stage at the back of the room housed more dancers and a huge DJ booth with an enthusiastic girl inside it, pumping up the entire crowd.

"This place is awesome." Gabby gripped my arm with excitement, shouting over the Calvin Harris remix blasting so loudly I could feel my skin rippling.

She was drunk. I was drunk. We'd subtly shared a bottle of bourbon in the backseat of the car for the hour and a half it took Nathan to drive us here. It was one that I'd hidden under the seat since Nathan's twenty-fifth birthday at the beginning of July.

"It's pretty great," I shouted.

Suddenly, a tall, dark stranger appeared in front of us. He had shoulder-length hair in a half-up, half-down bun, a lanky figure, and sharp features. His eyes focused on Gabby as he leaned in with excitement.

"Gabby Laurel?"

"Yes! Tim, right? I haven't seen you in forever!" Gabby turned to me and shouted next to my ear, "Tim was my Spanish tutor at school a few years ago. He was a senior."

Now that she mentioned it, and I took a closer look, I realized that he did look familiar. He'd aged and now had longer hair and piercings in his lip, brow, and nose. He was cute, I supposed, and I didn't miss the googly gaze that Gabby was giving him.

He subtly pulled a flask out of his pants pocket and grinned. "Do you guys want a drink?"

"Yes—" Gabby said.

"No," I answered at the same time. "Don't be dumb." I nudged her and felt frustrated that I even had to tell her what the issue was with accepting a drink that was already open from a quasi stranger at a bar.

Gabby hesitated for a moment and stumbled as a group of girls pushed past us. Tim caught her around the waist.

"She's had enough. We both have," I said.

"Yeah," Gabby giggled, wrapping her hands around Tim's neck. "We could dance, though?"

"Love to." He nodded.

"Come on."

Gabby reached out and grabbed my hand, and I followed them, more than happy to assist her in getting there with a cute dude—just as long as she was safe about it. I felt like a bit of a third wheel from the heat radiating between the two of them as they ground against each other as we danced. Still, I was drunk enough to mask the bother. And the dance floor was so packed that no one would know I was alone. There were bodies all around me, hair whipping from all directions, heels occasionally stabbing my feet, and sweaty arms rubbing against mine.

Suddenly, when my hands were in the air and I was swinging my hips, a familiar, gorgeous, deep voice cut through the loud music, and I felt my mood plummet.

"Hey, Cheer."

I turned around and came face to face with Drayton, looking spectacularly gorgeous in a pair of black jeans and a casual white V-neck T-shirt that showed off his sleeve tattoo and taut biceps, not to mention the arm veins. Oh Lord, the arm veins.

"Why can't you leave me alone?" I asked.

"This is my friend, Josh." He ignored what I said and pointed at the plastered guy—or I assumed he was drunk from the way he swayed and the fact that his eyes couldn't focus—standing next to him. He was a little shorter than Drayton—still tall, just shorter. He had a nice slim, toned build and slicked-back dark-blond hair.

"Hey, Josh." I smiled as Tim's arm suddenly came around

in front of my face, offering the flask again. I shook my head and pushed his arm back behind me, all the while watching Drayton give him a hateful scowl over my shoulder. I turned to Josh and smiled. "Look, if you're anything like Drayton, then I have nothing to say to you. But if you're a decent person, then it's a pleasure."

Josh slowly nodded with uncertainty as Drayton rolled his eyes. "Ignore her," he told him, his devastating gaze piercing me. "She's kind of unreasonable and rude."

"Excuse me? You are ruining *my* night."

It was no secret that alcohol could often have quite a negative effect on me. I'd been known to get irrational, unreasonable—as Drayton so bluntly implied—and rather difficult. I shouted. Got mad. I knew it. But I couldn't stop it. He riled me up so damn much.

"I'm going to dance," I shouted again and ignored how his gaze settled on my chest before casting down to my legs. He wasn't subtle in the slightest, and I hated how it made me feel. "You need to leave me alone. Because you're two faced, and I have no tolerance tonight. Screw you and piss off."

I turned around and had the pleasure of an immediate distraction because Tim and Gabby had their tongues halfway down each other's throats. Good for her. She deserved to have some fun. I peeped over my shoulder as I began to dance and noticed that Drayton had disappeared. It wasn't like I wanted him to hang around. Because I didn't—at all.

Two hours later, I winced at the guy who had been dancing on me for the last half-hour. He was great to begin with, cute smile, great hair, nice arms, until I noticed he smelled like urine. I'd been hoping that it was someone else. But it was him.

For sure. I spotted Gabby and Tim beside the water station, still swapping spit.

I leaned in to Stank, whose name I didn't know, and attempted not to inhale. "I'm going to . . . not dance with you anymore." I didn't bother coming up with a tactful excuse because honestly, if this guy exercised so little personal hygiene that he smelled like a toilet bowl, then he didn't deserve tact.

Pushing through the crowd of bodies, I was covered in other people's sweat. My feet were fine—I was used to being on them a lot. Albeit, I usually wore more comfortable shoes. But I was managing. Finally breaking out of the thick of the crowd, I noticed that the air was clearer, making me long for the actual outside.

Gabby managed to spot me coming toward her and dashed for me, leaving Tim leaning against the bar. The humid conditions had not been kind to her hair. It had grown twice in size and the curls had gone wild.

"Dallas." She bounce-slash-stumbled into my arms and giggled with excitement. "Would you hate it if I left with Tim?"

"Wha—oh. Um." I glanced behind her and squinted. The room was moving. For sure. "I guess not."

She squealed but it was blanketed by the thudding bass of the music.

"How though?" I stumbled and she stumbled, and we gripped each other's arms to stand upright. "He can't drive?"

"No." she smiled. "He has an Uber waiting. I'll still split our fare and give you my half. Would you care though?"

It was a huge wait until two; it was just midnight.

"I'll book another one. It'll be fine. Come on, I'll walk you out."

Outside on the crowded sidewalk, Gabby thanked me, and I snapped a picture of her and Tim getting into the Uber. Then I took a photo of the license plate and waved them off with a proud smile. I made Gabby promise to text me his address. She knew it from when he used to tutor her after school. I felt like she'd be fine, but I still told her to call me when she got there.

I inhaled the fresh, cool air. The sidewalks were packed with people rolling into one another. Saturday night in Cripple Creek was never quiet. Fifth Street was lined with casinos and bars as far as the eye could see. Older men and women were dressed up, smoking, laughing, shouting. The atmosphere was alive and exciting, but I was definitely ready for bed.

I slipped my phone out of my bra—which I knew was super dangerous, but where the hell else would I put it—and opened up Uber to book another ride. I was trying to stay steady and not bump into people until I collided with a tall, firm chest.

I stared up at Drayton as he dragged on a cigarette and said, "What now?"

"Where are you off to?"

"Wherever the hell I want," I snapped, and stepped around his stupid gorgeous frame. I was being so horrible, and I knew it. But I couldn't stop. He fell into step beside me, without the cigarette, hands in his pockets. "It's dangerous to walk alone at night."

He's right.

"Leave me alone," I mumbled, still struggling with the Uber app because I couldn't see straight. "Go and tend to whatever hopeless bimbo is waiting for your attention."

"Stop." He gripped my elbow and spun me around so that we were facing each other. I stared at his angry expression. He inhaled a deep breath, his eyes moving from one end of the road to the other before he looked down at me again. "Forget about what a dick I was. Put it aside for a minute and be reasonable. Let me drive you home? Please?"

"No. I don't get into cars with strangers."

I shrugged off his hold on my arm and continued walking, collecting a few shoulder bangs as I went. He shouted through the thrum of crowded chatter. "Fine! Have it your way."

He was so arrogant and smug and stupid and attractive. That was what made it so frustrating. He was so gorgeous, and as much as I wanted to slap his mouth whenever he said something stupid, I sort of wanted to kiss it too. I had never been so confused, and the thoughts continued to rile me up while I stared at the cracked and littered pavement beneath me.

That was when I noticed that the noise had died down. The streets were emptier. Almost deserted. How long had I been walking? Where was I? There were dark and vacant tall buildings, and now the lights of the casino strip were visible, but distant.

Suddenly, I was yanked into a hard body, a hand came across my mouth, and I was dragged toward a dark, narrow walkway. My blood ran cold and my heart beat so hard that it physically hurt. Rendered paralyzed, fear seized me until the adrenaline slowed enough for my instincts to kick in. Thrashing my body and kicking my legs out, I attempted to scream. It was no use; the sound was completely muffled and there was no one around. I couldn't break out of the iron hold, and we quickly disappeared out of the public view and into the narrow walkway. The buildings on either side weren't even apartments; they were industrial buildings that would be empty until the morning. No one would stumble across me, no one would hear me.

My front was pushed against the cold brick wall and tears streamed down my cheeks as I trembled with fear, desperately clutching at any bright idea that came to mind so I could avoid becoming another statistic.

A strong hand gripped my arm and whipped me around while managing to keep one hand over my mouth. My assailant pushed my back into the wall. My vision cleared, and I came face to face with Drayton, who was looking at me with unfathomable anger.

He let go of my mouth and I let out a loud, ragged exhale harsh with gurgling sobs as I clutched my chest and almost collapsed. I was now aware that I wasn't in immediate danger, but my shoulders rose and fell at a rapid pace in time with my labored breathing.

"What the actual fuck, Drayton?" I snapped, rubbing my cheeks with the palms of my hands. "Are you out of your fucking mind?"

"Do you realize how easy that was for me!" he shouted, his body basically crushing mine against the wall. I could feel his hot breath fanning my face as he stared down at me with glowering fury.

"I don't think I need to explain how this could have ended if it hadn't been me," he said.

"You're an absolute idiot! You're the only predator out tonight!" I hissed, willing my voice to stop trembling so that I didn't sound so fragile.

"You think so?" He laughed, cold and harsh as he nodded toward the end of the alleyway. "Wait for it."

We waited for what seemed like forever, standing in silence with our bodies pressed against each other. My heart thumped at our close proximity, and I stole a quick glance at Drayton and noticed his expression morphing into frustration. He gestured at the entrance of the walkway and I watched a middle-aged man walk past. His beanie was tattered and stained a nicotine yellow. His oversized parka was covered in an array of holes and I couldn't help but feel a chill as he searched left and right. He couldn't see us, though, hidden in the confines of the pitch black.

"He was following you from the moment that you left the club," Drayton murmured, and I looked up to find him regarding me with a sickened expression. "I got in my car just to beat him here."

I swallowed hard as the extremity of the situation dawned on me. It might have been a very different outcome had Drayton not shown up, and I was undeniably grateful. I went up on my tiptoes and threw my arms around his neck. He stiffened for a moment but quickly wrapped his arms around my waist and tucked his face into my neck.

"Please, let me drive you home?" He leaned back, his hands remaining around my middle. Electricity surged through my body as his touch drowned out all coherent thought. All I could do was nod. A look of relief flashed across his face as he tucked me into his side and led us out of the alleyway.

"I called the cops and reported that guy for suspicious behavior," Drayton said. "Fucking sick."

The drive back to Castle Rock wasn't horrible. Drayton's Jeep was dark, with tinted windows, black leather seats, and lots of buttons on the dashboard. Drayton kept his hands wound tightly around the steering wheel, a look of rage still etched on his face. At first, neither of us said a word, but the silence was surprisingly not awkward.

"What's your brother doing tonight?" Drayton asked, his tone a bit more casual than his posture. We were passing all of the little stores that were close to home. The convenience store. The laundromat. The burger shack and diner.

"He's out for the night," I answered with a curious tone.

What's it to him?

He nodded and then indicated right instead of left at the next intersection that would have taken me home. "What are you doing? Where are we going?"

"My house."

"What? No! Drop me off at home," I said.

"No one's there to look after you," he said, the streetlights illuminating his flat stare.

"I don't need looking after," I snapped, growing frustrated. I'd been thrilled on the drive home when I realized that I was safe and had saved a large Uber fare. "I am capable of looking after myself."

"Okay," he scoffed. "Is that why you've been swaying from side to side in that seat for the last hour and a half?"

"Drayton, take me home," I yelled, slamming a hand on the center console. "This is so stupid. No one's going to kidnap me in my own home. The only one doing that tonight seems to be you."

"Would you just shut up and let me look after you! Damn, Dallas, do you have to argue about everything?"

"Look after me?" I shouted, outraged at his logic even though he might have been right. "I'm not a fucking child."

"You're coming home with me. End of."

CHAPTER 5

The last thing I'd expected to happen on a girls' night out was to end up kidnapped by the school's quarterback. I'd yet to determine what his motives were—for the moment, I'd given up fighting him on it.

"You are unbelievable," I said. Drayton didn't respond.

I needed to check in on Gabby. She'd promised to send me a message when they got to Tim's, and they'd left before we had. Drayton didn't snatch the phone from me or demand to know whom I was texting, so I took that as a good sign. I could have been sending an SOS for all he knew.

We drove past school. The little garden lights hidden in the stones and faux bushes illuminated the sign. It was always strange to see the school at night, so quiet and vacant. It somehow looked bigger without hundreds of students hovering around the grounds.

We drove for another ten minutes and arrived in the classier part of town. Newer houses. Prettier. In Castle Pine Village the streets were tucked away, hidden in the thick of trees and winding roads.

Drayton pulled the car into a gated driveway. He must have pressed a button or something, because the gate opened and closed again behind us. We drove up a narrow, twisted road. Trees rose on either side, and it was pitch black aside from the car's headlights. And then, among the exquisite greenery, emerged a house like I had never seen before.

It was more than gorgeous. It was sharp, made of multishade white brick, and had so many windows. Drayton killed the engine and I hopped out, still in awe, admiring what he called home and what I would call heaven. I glanced around and noted that the drive dropped off at the edges, descending into more forest. The front of the house was illuminated with spots of light glowing a soft orange fixed into the brick. It was enormous.

"You live here?" I murmured, attempting to absorb it all.

"I guess," he replied, leaning on the back of the car as he lit a cigarette. I frowned but left him to it. It was his house.

"Would it be rude to ask what your parents do?"

"My mom owns an organic skin-care company, L.E. Skincare." He took a drag on the cigarette and stared at the ground as he exhaled again.

"Wow." I nodded. "Is your mom the breadwinner or . . . what does your dad do?"

"This and that."

I was starting to see he was not one for elaborating, and I wasn't one for pressing for more details. And then I winced, considering that he might not have a father. And if he did, it might be complicated. I swallowed and hoped that I hadn't put my foot in it, even if Drayton was an ass.

He sauntered toward the house, dragging on his cigarette, the smoke billowing around him. Even the entrance was outstanding: two steps up to a landing that was larger than my bedroom, concrete urns that were almost taller than me on either side of the door, and a door surrounded by frosted windows that made up almost the entire outdoor wall. There was enough light coming from inside that I could see Drayton stubbing his cigarette out and dropping it into the urn on the left before he turned around and gestured with his head.

"Come on."

I wanted to. I so did. It must have been gorgeous in there. I folded my arms. "No, you can't kidnap people. It's rude."

"It's illegal, to be specific." He came back down the steps and beelined toward me. "But I'm not kidnapping you, I'm looking after you. Stop whining and come inside."

I refused to flutter over the fact that he wanted to look after me. This was not the real him. He was doing the two-faced thing again.

"No."

"If you scream"—he grinned and spoke in a low tone—"you'll piss my parents off."

His large hands were on me again for the second time that night. He lifted me up and threw me over his shoulder. I grunted at the impact of his solid deltoid in my stomach. There were a few disconcerting things about this situation. First, the dress that I was wearing was far too short for this and the breeze caught my bum. Second, his hands were really close to said bum. Third, I couldn't admire the gorgeous house when I was upside down.

Drayton kicked open a door after he'd walked up a set of stairs and another few feet. He set me down in the dark, disappeared, and then reappeared when a bedside lamp was switched on.

"This isn't the spare bedroom . . ."

I was far too drunk to appreciate things. His bedroom was made of neutral tones and soft carpet. A king-sized bed sat in the middle of a wall that stretched diagonally across the room and went around a corner. On the other side of the room was a fireplace, a flat-screen TV above it. Floor-to-ceiling windows on one side revealed the thick green trees outside, offering privacy and enchantment. His walls were decorated with football jerseys and other memorabilia.

"The Cowboys? Not the Broncos?"

Drayton pulled his T-shirt over his head and shrugged. "I wasn't born here."

He disappeared around the corner and I heard a door open. When I heard a tap running, I assumed that he had an en suite. I stood in place and continued to wonder how in the hell I'd ended up here. It was messing with me somewhat, but the little buzz inside my bra distracted me.

Yea fune. U jus woke me up. Foodnjght.

I couldn't help but giggle at Gabby's message, filled with typos, knowing that she was probably more drunk than I was.

"Here."

A white piece of fabric came straight for me. My face caught it—my reflexes were a little off—and when I lowered it, Drayton was sauntering toward his bed in nothing but a pair of black Calvin Kleins. His thighs were football-player thick and his torso was so sculpted that it should have been illegal.

He climbed into his bed with a lazy grin, and threw an arm behind his head as he watched me stand there with the T-shirt hanging from one hand, cell phone in the other, hoping I didn't look as brain dead as I felt.

I snapped out of it and pointed at the door. "There has to be a spare bedroom in this house."

"Nope." He grinned. "If you want to sleep on the floor, that's fine. It just won't be very comfortable."

Doubtful. Even the carpet was luxurious. There was a reason that he was insisting on having me here. There had to be. I didn't know what it was, but I was growing tired, and it was quite clear that he was just as stubborn as I was.

"I want to put it out there,"—I marched past the bed, dropping my phone on the spare side as I went—"that there will be no sex. Just so we're on the same page."

"Cheer." He leaned up on his elbow and gave me a pitiful once over. "I don't want to have sex with you. Hostile isn't really my type. Besides, I have more effective ways of getting girls into bed that usually don't require me dragging them into my house against their will."

"I'm not hostile," I scoffed, turning the corner to find the bathroom door. I left it open and pulled the shirt over my head before I slipped the dress down my body. I flicked it to the side with my foot as I shoved my arms through the sleeves of the shirt, then kicked off my heels, wincing at the cold of the tile floor on my bare feet.

"I'm annoyed because you're annoying," I continued when I returned from the bathroom and stood beside the bed.

Drayton rolled his eyes as he turned his head toward me. I was a little nervous to actually get into his bed without another invitation. As his eyes landed on me, they widened, shifting down to my thighs, where the shirt stopped. But it was momentary, and he quickly refocused his gaze at the ceiling.

"Get in."

"This is weird." I hesitated even though he'd said exactly what I had been hoping for.

"Why? It's just sharing a bed." He shrugged. "I'm not going to touch you."

"You're so arrogant." I flicked the dark-blue comforter back, exposing his body as I slid in next to him. I couldn't help the embarrassing intake of air that filled my lungs when I got another view of his sculpted frame. "I wouldn't touch you either. Ever."

He chuckled and switched the lamp beside him off, plunging us into darkness.

"Hey, what happened to your friend?" I gasped, remembering that he'd been with someone tonight. "Did you leave him in Cripple Creek?!"

"What? No, of course not," he scoffed. "He went home with some chick."

"Oh."

I rolled onto my side and propped myself up on an elbow so that I could watch and gauge his reaction to my next question. The faint light from behind him outside created a silhouette. "Drayton, why did you bring me here? I would have been fine at home. I'm not that drunk."

I'm plastered.

It was dead quiet except for his deep breathing, and I began to accept that he was, once again, not going to answer me. Suddenly, there was a ruffle of movement and then, when my brain caught up with what I was seeing, Drayton was hovering

48

above me, and I was encased beneath him. His strong arms and legs were on either side of me while his face hovered an inch above mine.

"What are you doing?" I mumbled, just able to see his smoldering expression in the shadow.

"We're alone." His voice was low and aroused a dangerous feeling in the pit of my stomach. "We're both half dressed; we're both into having a good time. No one would have to know."

My throat was so dry I couldn't talk. My gaze moved between his lips and the darkness in his eyes. I could feel the heat of his body hovering above mine. His legs grazed the outside of my thighs and his chest lightly brushed mine. His face slowly inched down, and I think he was waiting for me to say no.

Say no. Say no. Say no. Say no.

When I could feel the soft plump of his lips ever so slightly graze mine, my eyes closed. The warning voice in my head was drowned out by his intoxicating scent and his hot breath, fanning my skin. But before our mouths met, I felt his lips gently kiss my forehead, and I looked up to find him staring at me with a smug smirk.

"I just thought I'd show you that if I wanted you, I could have you."

He rolled back over to his side of the bed with a satisfied sigh, leaving me a hot mess as I rapidly breathed and processed what I'd been about to do. I blamed the alcohol.

"I actually hate you," I snapped, rolling over to face the door rather than his idiotic face.

Not for the first time that night we fell into a quiet lull, the air thick with tension. I wasn't sure what it was about him, but I felt so let down when I didn't get the sweeter side of him—the one that I'd had dinner with. I didn't mind his humor or the innuendo, or even him teasing me like that. But the smarmy-bastard attitude was gross. And it was more disappointing than I wanted it to be. The room grew quiet except for our breathing.

"Dallas, I'm sorry."

Going against my better judgment, I turned around and gave him a narrow glare. "Did you just say sorry?"

"Yes," he sighed and leaned on an elbow. My eyes had adjusted to the darkness, and I kept them trained above his shoulders, refusing to let them travel to his chest. "I shouldn't have done that just now, and I shouldn't have said what I said on Tuesday. That was messed up."

"You know what else was messed up?" I leaned on an elbow as well. "Pretending to abduct me back in Cripple Creek. I'm serious. Talk about emotional scarring."

There was a flinch in his expression and his features became cold for a moment. "The emotional scarring might have been a bit worse if you'd been raped."

"True." I swallowed, feeling squeamish under his stare. "That was cruel, though. Come on. Yo—"

"You wouldn't listen or behave like a rational human being. I did what I had to." He ran his hand through his hair. "Did it scare you? Would you walk alone at night again?"

"Yes, it did. And no, I wouldn't. But I wouldn't usually do that anyway. It just sort of happened."

"Look, I'm not apologizing for the lesson, but I do apologize for scaring you."

"The two sort of go hand in hand," I said. "Forgiveness is granted, but you're on probation. Do something stupid like that again and you'll be eating through a straw for the rest of your life."

"Damn, Cheer." He recoiled. "You're violent."

"Yep." I smiled. "I have a question."

"Shoot."

"Are you a drug dealer? After that dumbass comment on the field this week, I'm curious."

"No," he laughed. "Sometimes I have a puff at a party, but that's about it."

When I was about to ask what had possessed him to make such a stupid comment about my use of drugs, my phone flashed and vibrated. I snatched it from the comforter beside Drayton and fell onto my back, reading the home screen.

"Tinder?" Drayton scooted closer, a scandalized note in his tone. "You're on Tinder?"

"Do you know what boundaries are?" I reached out an arm and dropped the phone on the bedside table.

"You don't need to be on Tinder." His gaze appraised me again and I flushed under his stare. "You're hot enough to score without digital help."

"I don't want to date." My stomach fluttered. "And I don't want to hook up with people from school. Occasionally, when I get an itch that needs scratching, I go on Tinder to meet people who aren't from Castle Rock. No big deal. Can we sleep now?"

"Wait, wait, wait." Drayton held up a hand and then pointed at me. "You, Dallas Bryan, you do booty calls because you want a no-strings-attached situation?"

"I swear if I have to mention double standards, I will pull out your tongue."

"No, I'm not judging," he assured me. "I'm wondering where you've been all my life."

"Gross. No."

I wondered if that sounded as halfhearted as it felt. Would I ever actually do it? No. Would I fantasize about it? Probably.

"Not that I want to"—he held his fingers up for air quotes—"'scratch your itch,' but why not? What's wrong with me?"

"Aside from making me sound like a drug addict, pretending to assault me, and refusing to let me go home?"

"Yes," he said.

"The first is that you were a total dick—one person with me and a totally different person at school. Bit of a put-off. The second is that we'd have to see each other every day and that makes things complicated. No matter how much people say that it won't make things complicated, it does."

I left out the fact that I planned on moving the following June and that I didn't want to get close to anyone, hence why I kept my love life outside the town's limits.

"I understand. But in my own defense, I'm the same person no matter who I'm with," he said.

"No, you were an egotistical bastard at practice on Tuesday. Your entire demeanor changed. It's hard to explain. It was gross."

He tugged at the corner of his pillow. "I'm sorry. I don't know what that was about."

"You aren't so bad, I guess." I smiled. "I just don't want to sleep with you."

He grinned. "That's not the impression that I got ten minutes ago."

"I'm drunk," I bit. He laughed and I settled down into the pillow. "Good night."

"Good night, Cheer."

✼

In the morning, I discovered a number of things. First, Drayton slept like the dead: he didn't snore and he didn't move. At one point, I had to check if he was even breathing. Next, his bedroom was even more gorgeous in the morning. The green needles of the Douglas and White fir trees outside scratched at the window panes and it was like being in the thick of the forest. Last, I was embarrassed to recount the details of the previous night because I had been so wasted.

Bursts of conversation echoed through my mind, taunting me, growing more humiliating as each memory surfaced. The almost-kiss arrived, and I remembered how easily I'd almost given myself over to him. My hands flew over my face as I groaned quietly.

It was best to get home as soon as possible. If Nathan wasn't back, he would be soon. Reaching for my cell on the side table, I winced at the time—almost eleven thirty. My brother would have to be home. I rolled out of the bed and circled it as I dashed for the bathroom. I shut the door and attempted to decide on the best course of action. Should I walk home? No, I should call a cab. My hair and makeup were a mess. Should I wear Drayton's shirt or the dress? Had to be the dress. Leaving in his clothes would be worse than leaving in last night's clothes. I mumbled obscenities to myself as I rubbed the black from under my eyes and pulled my hair into a topknot.

When I was as presentable as I was going to get, I pulled open the bathroom door and almost died of heart failure. Drayton was leaning against the doorframe wearing just a pair of sweatpants and a mischievous grin. His bedhead was fluffy and unkempt, and if I was being honest, gorgeous.

"Morning, Cheer." He smiled. "I heard you talking to your-self. Cute."

"Shut up." I pushed past him. "Can you please give me a ride home? I was going to take a cab, but since you're up?"

"Oh, I'm up all right." I turned around and caught him staring at my legs over his shoulder.

"You are too smooth for your own good. You know, it's totally wasted on me."

"Settle down. Give me ten for a shower and I'll drive you home, Cheer."

He shut the door and a moment later the sound of water pattered from the bathroom. I spent the next ten or fifteen minutes with my thoughts going between admiration for the gorgeous property and imagining what it would be like to see Drayton in the shower. It was concerning and alarming, and I kind of couldn't stop. What was wrong with me? I sent Gabby and Nathan texts as well, to check in. Nathan let me know that he was still out, and Gabby still hadn't replied when I heard the shower switch off.

Drayton emerged in a pair of shorts, a T-shirt, and wet, tousled hair that made me sort of breathless. "Good to go?"

"Yes." I trailed along behind him as we left the bedroom, and I got a better view of the mind-blowing house. Outside of his bedroom was a living area with white suede sofas, a flat-screen TV, a kitchen space, a fireplace, and more tree-revealing windows. It was so open but so private. Among the shades of grey and white were splashes of pale blue in the decor and throw pillows. The top floor carried on around a bend but we didn't follow it. We started down the staircase, and I found that the front foyer was even bigger than I remembered.

"I need a water, want one?" Drayton asked when we hit the ground floor. He held the banister and spun around, walking a few feet up the corridor to the left of the staircase, which opened into a kitchen.

The stone floor was shades of earth tones. The cabinets and cupboards were white wood, and the countertops were black marble. The large glass sliding doors and windows at the other end of the room opened onto a deck, and I could see a deep-blue pool surrounded with rocks, like a natural watering hole might look. Lounge chairs were lined up along the concrete surround. The entire theme of this house was modern but natural. It was breathtaking.

Not unexpectedly, the kitchen wasn't empty, but it was the occupant who surprised me more than anything. Even with his back to us and the fogged memory of last night, I could tell that it was Drayton's friend. He stood in front of the fridge, scratching the back of his head. His hair wasn't as smooth and slick as it had been when we'd met.

"Hey, Josh." Drayton was seemingly not surprised to find him scouring the fridge.

Josh kept his back to us but waved over his shoulder. "Hey, man." His voice sounded tired. "I'm so hungry. All Mom buys is organic juice. Can you tell her to pick up some toaster waffles next time? Last night was wild. I need a shower." He shoved something into his mouth, chewing as he shut the fridge door. "I got stank di—"

He turned around and spluttered on the food that he'd been chewing. "Oh God."

"Hey." I waved at him.

"Hey," he replied, pounding his chest with a fist while he coughed. He gave Drayton an unimpressed glare. "Thanks for the warning!"

"You're welcome, man." Drayton laughed and slapped him on the back as he passed, then opened the fridge. "Tell us more about this stank dick."

"Shut up," he ordered with a clenched jaw before turning his attention on me. "Sorry about that."

"It's okay. You had a good night?"

"I did." He nodded, smiling. "How about you? What'd you think of Illusion? Would you go back?"

"I guess," I replied. "I'd probably drink less and be more choosy about who I dance with. I think I might have danced with half of Cripple Creek."

He laughed and pushed his hair back behind his ears. "Not me. Which is a shame. That's a gorgeous dress."

"Oh." I grinned. "Thank you."

"Hey, smelly dick," Drayton shouted. "Go and take a shower. Come on, Dallas."

In the car I took another long look at the house, just in case I never saw it again, and then turned to Drayton, who was leaning one elbow on his armrest. His other hand turned the wheel as he began down the twisting drive.

"Is he your brother?"

"Best friend. Met him when I moved here when I was thirteen. He lives with us. His parents moved to Canada six months ago and he was dating someone at the time. He didn't want to leave, so my mom let him stay with us as long as his folks were good with it. They were."

"He doesn't go to our school?"

"He used to go to Rock Canyon, but he dropped out a couple of months ago and now he works for Mom as, like, an assistant or something. He finished up his GED through the mail."

"What about the girlfriend?"

"She broke it off for some dude on the swim team at her school. It was rough for him, you know, the whole leaving-school thing."

"Your parents are great for taking him in."

"They're not bad," he said.

We pulled up in front of my house, and it wasn't like it was run-down or even in a bad neighborhood, still, it paled in comparison to Drayton's. We lived in the older part of town called the Meadows, where the land rolled and stretched. The homes sat close beside one another, and they all looked the same. We were lucky that we had the house—even if it was on the smaller side—it was our parents' first house, and they'd died before the big upgrade they had planned on.

"Gabby?" I mumbled, seeing my best friend sitting on the doorstep with her head on her knees. Her hair was back in its natural, wild form and hid her face. "Can she not see us?"

"No, the windows are too dark."

"Right." I turned to Drayton. "Thanks for last night. For your unconventional methods of looking after me."

"Anytime. Don't forget to call me if you're up for some no-strings-attached fun."

I chuckled and opened the door of the Jeep. "Sure."

"Cheer," he called before I could close the door. "Sorry again."

"It's forgotten."

I wandered up the drive, my shoes hanging from one hand, and stopped in front of Gabby, who still had her head on her knees.

"Rough night?" I teased. She peered up at me with a sarcastic glare and I gasped. On her right eye and across the bridge of her nose was a dark, swollen bruise. "Gabs, what the hell happened?"

After I ushered Gabby inside, sat her on the couch, and fetched her a glass of water and an ice pack, I dropped onto the couch beside her.

"Gabrielle?" I said. "What happened? Who did this?"

"Trust me, I deserved it." She laughed but it was humorless as she held the ice pack on her face. "I feel so stupid."

We were abruptly interrupted by Nathan, looking proud of himself as he strolled in tossing his keys up and down.

"Hello, girls," he sang, swinging the door closed before his eyes rested on Gabby's face. His expression morphed into fury, and before either of us could say anything, he stormed out of the room and up the corridor. Gabby and I exchanged confused looks at the sound of banging and thumping.

"Right." Nathan reappeared with a baseball bat in his hand. "Whose skull am I breaking?"

"Nathan," Gabby chuckled. "It was a girl. I don't think you can break a girl's skull with a baseball bat."

"Hmmm." He lowered the bat. "Does she have a car? I could smash a few windows."

"As much as we both appreciate the heroism," I told him, "Gabby hasn't even told *me* what happened. Relax for a second."

"Tim has a girlfriend," she murmured. "I had no idea. She came back to his place this morning while we were sleeping."

"Who's Tim?" Nathan tapped his bat on the ground.

"This guy that I slept with last night," she mumbled.

"Right . . . okay . . . well, I'm going to shower. You guys"— he waved the bat at us as he backed away—"can sort that out. Between you."

"What's that about?" Gabby asked when Nathan was gone.

"He thinks of you like a sister. He wants to hear about your sex life as much as he wants to hear about mine."

"Speaking of your sex life," she jostled on the sofa with excitement. "Who dropped you off this morning?"

"No way." If I told her about spending the night with Drayton, she'd read far too much into it. "You need to explain what happened."

"I did. Some bitch—okay, well, not bitch, she was his girlfriend—walked into Tim's room this morning, found us in bed, went absolutely nuts, and then socked me right in the face. I'm not even mad about getting punched," she huffed. "I'm upset because he had a girlfriend. He used me and I liked him. Remember I had that giant crush on him when he was tutoring me?"

"Gabs, you spent one night with him."

I feel a little guilty for dismissing her feelings. But really, she hadn't seen him in years; how could one drunken hookup result in anything genuine that quickly? This had always been Gabby's problem—she threw herself at the first boy who made her feel special or wanted without getting to know him first, or taking things slow, and she ended up getting hurt.

"I know you probably think that it's stupid," she mumbled. "We seemed to hit it off and I thought the potential was there, you know?" Gabby didn't wait for me to reply. "Of course, you don't know." She threw her hands up. "You're not a romantic."

A romantic? Gabby once told a kid who defended her glasses in freshman year that she was in love with him. They'd had three conversations, mainly consisting of their mutual distaste of being bullied for wearing glasses. I wouldn't call her overenthusiasm romantic. I'd call it unhealthy.

"Hey, I appreciate romance." She gave me a side-eye. "I do.

I would just rather wait until I'm in California before I find it."

"Why are you still talking about California?"

Gabby hadn't ever been shy about voicing her distaste over my choice to go out of state for college. She was completely against the idea of my up and coming relocation. There was no doubt that I'd miss her, and I'd tried to convince her on more than one occasion to come with me, but she wouldn't leave her mom.

"Gabs, if I get in, I'll be moving to California. You know I started on my application the other day."

"You could still get rejected." She shrugged, holding the ice pack on her cheek again and wincing upon contact. "I'm hoping, anyway."

"You're hoping that I don't get into the college of my dreams?"

"No, of course not." She let her head fall back onto the sofa. "I just don't want you to leave me, okay?"

"Even if I don't get into CalArts, I'm getting out of Castle Rock," I told her, smiling at her big brown, puppy-dog eyes. "But we'll always be best friends. Sisters."

It wouldn't matter how much space was between us, Gabby was my soul sister and she always would be.

"Yeah." She smiled.

We spent the rest of Sunday hanging around the house. Nathan made waffles but he didn't eat them. Breakfast for him was a protein shake, and then he went for a run. I grabbed the wireless speaker and spent a couple of hours practicing routines that I had choreographed over the summer, while Gabby lay on the couch, reading.

"I do not understand how you can do that when you are hungover," she called from behind her e-reader.

For me, dancing was a cure. It gave me release, cleared my

head, and made me feel energized and alive. That day, it was also keeping me distracted from reliving the previous night over and over again. The image of acting like an unreasonable toddler toward Drayton. And almost kissing him. I squashed the thoughts with a pirouette so that they didn't knock the wind out of me with humiliation. Drinking was not worth the hassle that it came with.

CHAPTER 6

On Monday morning, I stood beside my car in the school lot waiting for Gabby. I was nervous about seeing Drayton. Would he turn into an A1 asshole again? Would he tease me about what a mess I had been? Would he tell his buddies that I'd spent the night in his bed wearing nothing but his T-shirt and my underwear?

It was pointless to worry. He was who he was; as long as he didn't spread rumors, we'd be good.

Exactly four minutes later, Gabby pulled into the space beside me. She was trying to be late as little as possible this year. Last year, she'd had a terrible track record for missing first period because she'd be finishing chapters in her car before she'd even left the house.

"Your eye looks good," I said.

"I have, like, seventy-two thousand layers of concealer on."

"Why seventy-two?" I asked. "Why not seventy or seventy-five? Seriously, though, what'd your mom say?"

"I told her that you smacked me in the face coming out of a pirouette."

Soon we were giggling loudly and uncontrollably as people crossing the parking lot looked at us funny. The funniest part was imagining that happening for real. The dance that I did was contemporary with a strong influence of hip-hop. It was often fast paced and strong, but I did incorporate ballet steps. More so for softer, more emotional routines.

Gabby stopped laughing as she noticed something behind us. *That* Jeep. The one with dark windows and big rims. The driver's door opened and out slid Drayton.

"That Jeep," she squeaked, pointing at it with so little subtlety that she might as well have announced herself with a megaphone. "That's the Jeep that dropped you home on Sunday! Drayton? Did you spend the night with *him*?"

"Gabby." I turned around. "Shhh. He's coming. I'll tell you about it later."

She made a zipping motion across her lips. I was impressed with how well she pulled herself together—she folded her arms and her expression was neutral as Drayton stopped beside us and smiled down at me.

"How's it going?" he asked.

"Not bad," I replied.

He looked at Gabby for a brief moment and then moved his curious expression to me. "What happened to your friend?"

"Do you mean Gabby?" I asked, inclining my head in her direction.

"So you're the famous Gabby." Drayton stretched out his hand, and I could tell that she was trying not to burst at the seams with excitement. "What happened?"

The words tumbled out before I even had a chance to consider them. "She got into a fight. With this guy . . . at a bar! He told her to shake what her momma gave her . . . so she told him . . . she told him he was an inbred hick and then he slapped her. After he slapped her, Gabby beat the life out of him . . . with a barstool! It was bad . . . he's in the hospital. Don't mess with Gabby."

Drayton looked suspicious but he didn't call us out on the blatant lie. Could I not have come up with a more legitimate story? Even the one that Gabby had told her mom would have made more sense.

"Yeah, don't—don't mess with me," she laughed. "I have to go."

She turned around and almost bumped into a couple of junior girls as she dashed across the parking lot.

"That's not what really happened, is it?" he asked, walking alongside me. I couldn't help but notice the stares coming from the self-righteous shitheads Emily surrounded herself with. I couldn't help but not care either.

"Nope," I confessed. "But let her have this. The real story is . . . a little embarrassing."

"What, did she walk into a door or something?" he said pointedly. "She's not getting abused by a boyfriend or anything, is she?"

His fierce tone took me by surprise, and I ignored the light flutter in my stomach. He did protective so damn well.

"No, not at all," I assured him. "She doesn't have a boyfriend, and it definitely wasn't a domestic."

"You're not going to tell me what really happened?"

"Sorry." I shrugged my shoulders. "Girl Code. I'm legally bound to secrecy."

Drayton held the door open for me, people still watching us. "I get it, Cheer. That's actually one of the things I like about you."

I contemplated his words for a few feet until we were standing next to my locker. "There's more than one thing you like about me?"

"See ya, Dallas."

The bell rang and he strode down the corridor, disappearing in the sea of students. I was holding out for the moment when he didn't end a conversation with more questions than it started with.

I opened my locker and pulled out the books for first and second periods—English with Gabby after homeroom, and then history. I clutched the books and closed the door, receiving a hell of a fright when I found Gabby on the other side. She grinned and bounced up and down on the spot.

"Tell me everything. Are you guys, like, seeing each other? I ship it."

"First of all,"—I gestured at her happy dance—"that's cute. Second of all, *no*. We aren't doing anything."

We wove through the crowded corridor toward homeroom. She continued, "So how did you end up at his house? How did he end up dropping you off? I need to know *everything*."

"Your thirst for scandal never ceases to concern me."

"Tell me."

"Fine. I accidentally wandered off alone, distracted, drunk. Drayton found me and offered me a ride. He said that it was dangerous to walk alone at night. He was very . . . *convincing*."

"There has to be more. You slept over." We sat down beside each other at our homeroom desks. I glanced around at the surrounding students and shook my head.

"We slept. There was a little chitchat, but other than that, it was uneventful."

I also left out the fact that his spectacular, sculpted body had been on top of mine for a moment or two. It made me breathless to remember, and if I told her, she wouldn't contain herself. She'd also develop hope for something more, and that wasn't happening.

"Okay," she scoffed after a moment of bewildered staring. "That is so boring. You are so boring."

"Yeah," I sighed. "That's me."

I was an aching mess of sore muscles, and my joints groaned in protest when I got out of the car at the diner that afternoon. Cheer practice had been brutal. Our sessions weren't going to be light as we approached the new season. Nathan had sent me a text:

D, leave the keys in the car, I need to use it tonight.

After a quick sweep of the parking lot, I slid the keys under the seat. Castle Rock was a safe place, for the most part. Not perfect, but it could be worse. I tapped out a quick response as I wandered toward the diner's doors.

I don't finish until nine. Can you please pick me up?

The usual afternoon rush was in full swing when I walked into the old establishment. Our local diner—Rocky Ryan's—captured the essence of our corner of the world. The walls were painted a sky grey, the floors were stone, and photographs of mountains and the red rocks of the Garden of the Gods were all over the walls. Ryan, the owner of our little diner, loved spending time there—the views were spectacular.

"Sorry I'm late," I told Stefan, a co-worker with an immaculate burnt-orange comb-over and a posture that could rival royalty, as I rushed back from the staff room while slipping on a blue apron and my name tag.

He glanced at the clock as he accepted a ten from a customer and smiled. "You're just on time."

"Order up," Joe—our chef—called from the kitchen as a plate was slid through the window between the counter and the kitchen. I noted all of the orders that were hanging from the magnetic strip above the window and winced. It wouldn't be a slow evening.

With two plates of waffles with all of the toppings in hand, I approached a table where two of our regulars were seated. The Fishers were a couple in their eighties who came in once a week for their waffle date. It was the cutest thing in the world.

"Can I get you anything else?"

"No, dear." Mrs. Fisher gave me a pat on the arm, her wrinkles deepening with her wide smile. "You look beautiful, Dallas."

I smiled and thanked her. She told me that whenever she saw me. It was sweet. I was envious of her grandchildren. She reminded me of my grandmother—full of smiles and flattering compliments.

The orders didn't slow down. I retrieved used plates from

vacant tables, refilled coffee, and handed out pitchers of water. No one was left waiting or wanting something new when I was done with a third routine check of the floor.

"You're doing that dancing thing again." Stefan laughed as I waited at the window behind the counter for another order. I didn't bother turning around but I couldn't help but chuckle. Customers often commented on the fact that I danced around the diner while I delivered food and wiped down tables.

"Good afternoon," Stefan greeted someone with his impeccable politeness. "How can I help?"

"I was hoping that she could serve me." I heard a familiar voice. "If she's not too busy."

I turned around to face Stefan's confused look and realized whom the familiar voice belonged to.

"Josh?"

Josh looked more put together than he had on Sunday. His hair was slicked back into a little flick where it ended at the base of his neck. He was wearing a pale-blue fitted T-shirt and slim charcoal jeans. He had a little stud in one ear and a chain-link bracelet around his wrist.

"Hey." He smiled and pointed at me with a debit card in his hand. "I didn't know that you work here."

"I have for a while." I gestured for Stefan to switch places and he obliged with a smile, collecting the food that I had been waiting on. "Only part time, usually after school."

"Makes sense. I'm usually here for lunch. Their burgers are the best."

"What brings you in this afternoon?"

"Dray just finished football practice." He pointed his thumb over his shoulder, and I looked past him to the parking lot. Josh noticed me staring at the car and said, "He's on the phone with his dad. So it's just me. I'll let him know that you said hello. You're . . . together? Right?"

"No." I chortled and shook my head. "Me and Drayton? Nope."

Josh glanced behind him when a couple came in and lined up. Stefan stepped in and served them on the other register. "My bad." He turned back to me. "I just assumed."

"It happens." I gave him a tight smile and noted that his eyes were a dark blue. Almost grey. It was a nice color. "Did you want to order?"

"Yeah." He shook his head as if to clear his thoughts and glanced at the chalkboard on the wall behind me. "I'll have . . . one chicken, bacon, and guac burger, one double beef with no sauces and spinach instead of lettuce. One cola, one water, a large fries aaaaand"—he stretched out the word with a small voice—"perhaps a date to the first Archwood football game of the season on Friday night?"

"What kind of a monster wants spinach instead of lettuce?" I said quickly, without thinking. Josh was cute with his inviting smile and soft eyes. He was a bit paler, and wasn't so defined, and his presence didn't make me feel as stupid as Dra—I swallowed with shame when I realized that I'd been comparing him to his best friend. I felt nauseated.

"I'm not a date sort of girl." I winced and felt as though I'd kicked a small dog when his smile fell. "I-I'm a casual, no-strings-attached, in-and-out sort of girl. I prefer to disclose that from the get-go. You know?"

"Casual, no expectations, that's your sort of arrangement?" Josh asked.

"Yeah." I nodded and slid the debit machine over. "Seventeen dollars."

He slid the card through the machine, and I watched, feeling sort of miserable for rejecting him. Swiping left was so much less brutal than turning someone down in person.

"Well," I started before I could stop myself, "I cheer. At the games. I'm a cheerleader. But there's a big party after the game. You must know Maxon?"

"Of course." He smiled and pushed the machine back toward me.

"We could go to that together. If you don't mind casual?"

"I love casual." He slipped his debit card into his pocket. "I just got out of a relationship not that long ago. Casual is great."

"Okay." I smiled and nodded and wondered what the heck I was doing.

"We'll go from the game?"

"Do you mind picking me up at home afterward? That way I can change first."

"Sure."

I scribbled down my number on the back of one of our catering cards and slipped it inside of his to-go bag when his food was ready. He winked, assuring me that he looked forward to Friday, and I watched him leave in a stupor.

I supposed it couldn't be that different from the usual approach that I took. It just wasn't arranged on Tinder and it wasn't a total stranger. It was Drayton's best friend and live-in housemate. Oh well.

It might be fun.

CHAPTER 7

The week went along without another incident from Drayton. We talked in economics. We had a laugh on the field during practice. And I was adamant about ignoring how his laugh made me a little weak and his stupid humor made me giggle. He hadn't mentioned the fact that Josh and I had texted about Friday, so I didn't bring it up. In the kindest way possible, it was none of his business, even if Josh was his best friend.

I spent the entire week debating whether or not I should cancel the "not date" with Josh. I was at war with the decision right up until Friday rolled around and then I thought, screw it, I wasn't going to cancel on the day—that would be rude.

Gabby and I sat at the bottom of the bleachers beside the tunnel to the left of the field. The pep rally started soon, but Emily hadn't ordered us into formation. I was watching kids pile into the stands with anticipation and excitement.

My face had two thick maroon stripes on either side. A rich red lip and a white ribbon around my bun polished off the look.

Our cheer outfits weren't so bad—a maroon and white cropped tank top and a skirt with a small triangle cut out of the bottom corner. The material was soft but strong. It had to be so that we didn't tear out of our skirts when we dropped into the splits or caught a member from a tall fall.

"Are you sure you can't come tonight?" I asked Gabby for the thousandth time.

She pouted, no doubt miserable over being reminded that her mother had requested that she spend the night helping her roll dough for bread. Camilla was an assistant baker at Barb's Bakery. "I wish I could, but I sort of wouldn't want to third wheel."

"It wouldn't be like that." I nudged her.

"Dallas!" Emily stood at the entrance of the tunnel and waved a furious arm. "Let's go."

I held up a finger, signaling for her to wait. She stomped her foot.

"I have to go." I stood up and twirled a piece of Gabby's hair around my finger. A couple of freshman boys ran past and almost pushed me over.

"Have fun tonight." Gabby sighed, pushing her glasses up her nose. "Let it be known that I'm sad."

"It's known." I laughed as Emily screamed at me again. "I'll text you later. Have fun rolling dough."

"Bitch!" she called after me as I jogged across the tarmac and into the tunnel.

Inside, the lineup was being assembled. The football team had been paired up with a cheerleader each. Emily gripped me at the elbow and dragged me toward the back. "You're with Austin."

I stood beside the wide receiver and winced when he shimmied and leaned in far too close for comfort. "How's it going?"

72

His black wave of hair looked flat and full of grease, and he made an ugly noise with his nose. I sighed and turned to the side when he arched backward and started ogling my ass.

"Switch," an authoritative voice rumbled. A hand grabbed my elbow and I almost missed Aria being put in place beside Austin as I was dragged toward the front of the lineup.

Drayton looked stern as we stopped in front of the rest of the group, and I watched him with confusion as he peered behind us and scowled at his friend.

"Excuse me, Drayton," Emily snapped, marching toward us. "No, you can't just screw up the placing. I'm the cheer captain. Put her back."

"Put her back? I'm not a piece of furniture." I scowled.

"I'm the football captain." Drayton's tone was biting. "Get over it, Emily. She's with me."

His tone was final, and his expression suggested that she let it go because he was not interested in arguing. It surprised me that Emily wasn't in place beside him, what with them both being team captains and her mild obsession with our quarterback. There was an uncomfortable quiet in the tunnel as Emily retreated to wherever she'd come from, and I could sense the attention without even turning around. Drayton stared ahead of him and jostled the helmet hanging at his side in his left hand. It was sort of hard to ignore how gorgeous he was.

The silence was soon broken by Maxon. His voice echoed from the concrete walls. "Drayton, I thought you said nothing was going on with you and Cheer?"

His taunting voice caused a series of *oohs* and *aahs*, and I felt ashamed to wonder how often I'd been a topic of conversation between them. I was also ashamed of how immature half of these morons were. Drayton rolled his eyes and a small smile danced on the corner of his lips. "Yeah, because I've been too busy with your mom."

"Screw you, Lahey!"

The tension in the tunnel built as we inched closer to game time.

"What's all that about?" I whispered.

"I'm not really hooking up with his mom, Dallas." He shook his head.

"No." I rolled my eyes. "I mean, what was with switching my place?"

"You looked uncomfortable. Austin can be a douche. It's not a big deal," he said casually.

I didn't dispute the fact that his teammate was a bit of a sleaze. He nudged me with his elbow and grinned, gesturing at the tunnel opening. "Ready?"

I looked forward and realized that the freshman lackeys had taken their places in front of the tunnel, holding each end of a large banner that Drayton had the honor of tearing through.

A loud voice boomed through the speaker system, signaling our start.

"Give it up for your quarterback, team captain of the Archwood Wolves . . . Drayton Lahey!"

I jogged out beside him, adopting my preppy persona, following him as he tore through the banner and caused an uproar of praise from the student body.

While Drayton pumped up the crowd with a slow jog, I ran into a front handspring, then a front tuck, and landed with a dazzling smile with my arms outstretched. We stood beside Coach Finn in the middle of the field, Drayton on one side and me on the other, beginning our lineups. He grinned, his helmet hanging from his hand, and I forgot about the crowd as he gazed across at me. His eyes were fast and fleeting, but the moment drew me up short.

The rest of the team and squad followed behind. The girls did tricks of their own or sidestepped with a shake of their hips. It was part of our job to cheer them on with all that we had, so, with each introduction we screamed and clapped, and I pretended to care.

As far as pep rallies went, our school put on an impressive show. Coach Finn riled everyone up. "This season, like the last one, and the one before that, is ours. This team is the heart and soul of varsity football in Colorado." His voice rose with each passing moment. "Our captain, our quarterback, Drayton, is a true leader with skill and passion that he fuels his team with. And I can promise you, the green field will turn red when we defeat our enemies." Some of the cheerleaders exchanged concerned looks. Coach Finn knew how to get intense. "The Wolves will show no mercy and we will bring home the championship again and again and again because we are the predators and they are our prey."

It went on for a long time and no one could claim that Coach Finn didn't have passion. He was a bit out there, but he believed in his team.

The cheerleaders performed yet another of Emily's basic routines, which the crowd seemed to appreciate nonetheless. My position was a flyer, and I had to admit that it was one of the parts that I loved about cheering. It was a thrill, and I trusted the spotters even if we weren't best friends. The girls took their positions as if it was life and death, which it could be if I landed on my neck, so I knew that I was in safe hands. Emily was a flyer too. Thank God, since I might have had to rethink the trust thing if she was spotting me.

After the pep rally, everyone dispersed while they waited for kickoff. That night's match was being played against Greenbell Valley. Everyone was convinced that it would be an easy win because we'd given them a thrashing last time. Both the players and the cheerleaders had to stay at school between the rally and the game to reduce the risk of people being late. Surprise, surprise, Coach Raeken wasn't around. But Emily was more than willing to bark orders in place of her mother.

Of course, as usual, Emily had wandered off as well. The squad hung around beside the fence on the tarmac. Some of the girls were leaning over and chatting with their friends or boyfriends. Some were stretching. I was talking to Melissa, one of our base girls. She was tall and muscular as hell.

As it grew dark, kids from Archwood and the rival school filed in to fill the stands. The bleachers were packed with families and students from our school on one side and from the other team on the other side. Enormous spotlights surrounded the green and lit up the field as a soft chant filled the air. There were maroon banners and signs among our side of the crowd. My classmates were repping our colors, and an upbeat tune from the industrial-sized speakers kept the atmosphere alive while we waited.

Melissa excused herself from our conversation so that she could go and have a word with her sister before the game began. I turned around and bumped straight into a hard chest. As in protective-gear hard.

"Sorry, shit, I'm always running into you. Good that you've

got *protection*," I joked when I realized that it was Drayton. He looked at me funny, all gorgeous and brooding. "What?"

"Are you going out with Josh tonight?"

"Sort of. Remember, I don't do dating. It's just a casual thing. We're going to Maxon's together."

"No, you're not," he snapped. "Not with him."

"I don't appreciate that tone, you know." If he expected me to cower or back down because he was glaring at me like that, he had another thing coming. "And I am."

"No. You're. Not." He said it slower this time, as if he was talking to an idiot.

I glared at him and matched his slow tone. "Yes. I. Am."

"Why? You say you don't 'date'? You don't come to these parties. Ever. So what's the deal? Why go now, why with Josh?"

"Again, it's not a date. I made that clear and there are no expectations. We're on the same page and also I do go to parties . . . once in a while."

"Dray!" a helmeted player called from the field, signaling for him to join them.

"Don't get involved with him," he warned me. I could have been imagining it, but it sounded like he was pleading with me.

"Why do you care?"

"Because I don't want to see my best friend get hurt. Again."

His jaw twitched as he ground his teeth together, a telltale sign of frustration. I was at a loss for words as he turned around and jogged onto the field. What had I been hoping his answer would be? Nothing. I hadn't been hoping for a thing. I'd be quite content if that conversation had never happened at all.

With a few seconds left on the clock, the team assembled into formation. Drayton stood in position behind center line, and his head moved from side to side as he assessed his team. It was as quiet as a game could be, with only a low thrum of chatter from the crowd and shouts of encouragement coming from either side of the stands.

It was a moment or two before he clapped. None of us could hear what he said, but we could see him pointing at some of the defense, and then four of them moved into a spread. I could see a number of vertical seams that would allow a clean pass, but it was too obvious. Their defense would be all over our receivers.

Drayton gave a subtle nod to one of his running backs. But it wasn't subtle enough. I couldn't understand why he was butchering his play so badly. He rolled his left shoulder, crouched, and then shouted "Hut" to signal the snap. As soon as the ball was in his hands, the opposition went for our receivers. Drayton stepped back, throwing a screen pass to the wide receiver. One of our tallest players, who jumped from an attempted block by a Greenbell cornerback, caught the ball and threw a lateral to a second running back who was rushing toward the end zone.

Using two running backs in one play wasn't expected, but it must have been planned because the execution was flawless. The left shoulder roll, clever.

The running back, Derek, was almost intercepted, but performed a slick side step, just avoiding the defense, and cleared the last yards until he crossed the plane and brought the crowd to its feet. We finished the game 46-18, and the ball was thrown into the stands. Derek was swept off his feet when the rest of the team ran in for celebration.

Our side of the stands screamed. Coach Finn applauded. We

began our winning cheer routine, and I caught Drayton being pulled into the sea of muscle as I was lifted into a liberty stunt. I thought that first play was hopeless, but he was the quarterback for a reason. He knew what he was doing.

The excitement continued but as soon as the last routine was done, I headed toward the bleachers to collect my duffel, which sat beside the fence. I didn't see the need to go back to the locker rooms when I planned on going home to shower and change. As I wandered down the fence line toward the gate, I checked my cell phone for messages and saw about seven from Gabby and one from Josh.

> Let me know when to get you! Great
> cheering tonight ;)

"Dallas."

I glanced up and found Nathan leaning on the other side of the fence. His sandy-blond hair was hidden underneath a beanie and his denim-jacket collar was raised around his neck.

"Hey." I smiled and gave him a teasing punch in his good shoulder. His bad one still gave him flack from time to time. "What's up?"

"I just thought that I'd say well done and good cheering. All of that."

I laughed and adjusted the strap of the bag on my shoulder. "What'd you think of that play?"

"Brilliant," he said, proud. "Good to know that the team is still in good hands since I left."

He peered around, his expression full of nostalgia. Nathan and

I used to come to these games together before I joined the cheer squad. We'd loved watching football together since we were young. First me watching him on the field, and now him watching me. Dad would be proud of both of us following his love for the sport.

I noticed a short redhead with wild curls and little legs. She looked bored, impatient almost. I blinked at Nathan and pointed. "Did you bring a date to a varsity football game?"

He smiled but it wasn't a real smile. It was a caught-out-bare-teeth-but-wince sort of smile. "You are shameless," I scoffed with amusement.

"Hey." He pointed a finger at me. "That is no way to talk to the brother who raised you."

"Excuse you." I recoiled. "Nan raised me, and by the time she passed, I was old enough to take care of myself."

"Well," Nathan scoffed, shuffling his feet in the dirt as he folded his arms defensively across his chest, "I have nothing to say to that because you're right. Your boyfriend did well tonight."

"He is not my boyfriend."

"You talk about him so much, I figured he must be."

I do not. Do I?

"I hate you."

⚡

As soon as I got home, I showered and spent time scrubbing the paint off my cheeks. Afterward, I pulled my wet hair into a fishtail braid, leaving loose strands to frame my face, which was red and raw from exfoliant. I smeared a layer of foundation on, brushed on some contour and highlight, and then added a bit of mascara. That would do.

It was still warm enough for a cute little white playsuit. The neckline was tasteful but not totally modest, and the sleeves were long. I sent Josh a text message and sat in the living room while I slid on a pair of strappy heels. The soles were thick and gave me four inches of height.

When I saw headlights pull up outside, I peered out and saw the Jeep. I faltered for a moment, but then remembered that Drayton had his motorcycle back from the shop after having the dent fixed, and he no longer needed to drive the car that he and Josh shared. I locked the house and took care as I went down the front steps.

"You look great," Josh complimented me as I slipped into the passenger seat.

"Thanks. You too."

He did look nice with his hair in its usual slick style and wearing a blue short-sleeved button-up shirt and white shorts.

"Good game tonight, right?" He grinned, the streetlights illuminating half of his smile. "I was a little more excited for the halftime though. You looked great getting thrown around like that. Is it hard? I feel like I'd throw up. Like, you go up in the air and don't even look worried about landing on someone's hands."

"It's about trust. Even if we butcher the landing, our spotters will catch us. They're vigilant and quick. They have to be, you know? They take the role seriously. I also feel like they don't get enough credit. Those girls are so strong. The bases too."

"It looks fun."

"It's all right," I admitted. It was a serious sport, but it was fun—it didn't hold a candle to dancing, though.

He tapped the volume button on the steering wheel and bopped to an Imagine Dragons song. That was where the conversation lulled, and I stared out of the window for the next fifteen minutes until we were in Drayton's neighborhood.

When we got to Maxon's, the first thing I noticed was that it wasn't at all like Drayton's. It wasn't surrounded by the forest or facing the mountains. A white concrete parking lot–sized driveway faced the house, and a roundabout made of trimmed hedges sat in the middle of all of the parked cars. The house itself was huge and had dramatic views of Pikes Peak and the expansive rolling hills of Daniels Park.

We went straight through a living area to the upstairs, following the thumping music. Floor-to-ceiling rolling doors allowed indoor-outdoor living, and we stepped out onto a patio overlooking a breathtaking view. You couldn't even call it a backyard because the entire thing was one large space with an endless green lawn. Josh led me by the hand down the staircase that wrapped around the side of the house to the heart of the back section. Concrete bench seats wrapped around a stone fire pit. Solar lights illuminated the vast space. Students danced and drank. A dog ran around, and it was adorable.

People goofed around playing touch football on the lawn or playing a game of cards at the long wooden outdoor table under the cabana. I was tempted to send a quick video to Gabby, but that felt cruel considering she couldn't be here, and she'd be jealous.

"There's a bin over there." Josh pointed at one of seven industrial-sized coolers that were filled with ice and beer. "Want one?"

"Sure," I said.

"Want to grab us a seat?"

I looked around and spotted a free lounge chair. Josh dashed off, and as I wandered over to the lounge chair, I was intercepted.

"Drayton," I greeted him with indifference, remembering the run-in that we'd had before the game.

"I told you not to come with him."

His cropped hair was tousled, and his fitted T-shirt was agonizing, exposing his armful of ink. Did he have to be so attractive? It just didn't seem fair.

"I don't remember giving you the right to tell me who I can and cannot spend time with." I knew he was mad but I didn't stop. "What's your issue with me? Is it the fact that I use Tinder? Because I was clear with him that I'm a casual arrangement sort of person, and he was fine with that. I'm not going to hurt him. I've been honest from the beginning."

Before Drayton could answer, Josh appeared beside me and handed over a chilled bottle of beer. I thanked him and accepted it while appearing as casual as I could and not at all like Drayton and I had just been having a heated moment over the fact that Josh and I were here together.

"Good game tonight." Josh held his hand out, and he and Drayton shook with a slap on the back.

"Thanks, man." Drayton smiled. "Have a good night."

Drayton's disapproving look pierced me for a fleeting moment, and then he joined his group of friends on the stone bench seats. Becca, a raven-haired girl from the cheer team, sat beside him and rested her manicured claws on his arm, only to pull them back when Emily glared at her narrowly from across the fire pit.

Whatever. I wasn't going to spend the night dwelling on Drayton. He was being unreasonable. Accusing me of hurting his friend when I had been nothing but up front and honest. Josh and I sat down on a lounge seat and had a drink.

As we watched the scene in front of us, I said, "Drayton

mentioned your parents are in Canada." He nodded, swallowing his mouthful of beer.

"Do you spend a lot of time there?"

"Christmas and my birthday. I stay here for Thanksgiving. The Laheys do Thanksgiving really well."

I wanted to steer the conversation clear of any more Drayton. "It must be so cold over Christmas though?"

He laughed. "I hate it to be honest . . . Alberta is an ice land. But I guess I have to be glad that I don't get hauled over there more often."

"You aren't close with your parents?"

"We're close, I suppose. We talk on the phone once a week. I mean, there's no tension. We just aren't as close as some kids and their parents are. You know?"

I nodded and took another swig of my beer. He was blessed to have both of his parents at all. But I made a habit of not judging other people and their relationships with their moms and dads. It wasn't fair.

"How come they chose Canada anyway?" I asked.

"Canada chose them. Mom was offered a job as a CEO at a hospital in Calgary. She's a surgeon. Was working for that position her entire career and finally got her recognition. She took it."

"Oh." I smiled. "Good for her."

After we were done with our beer, he offered me another but I declined—one was enough.

"Should we dance?" He set his bottle down on the concrete and stood up.

I'm not sure that I would call what was going on dancing, but I let him lead me into the pile of frenzied teenagers grinding to electronic pop. The stars above us blanketed the black night and the breeze was cool enough to prevent overheating. Josh pulled me in at the waist as a remix for "Dancing on My Own" pounded through the outdoor speaker set.

"You're a great dancer," he shouted beside me, competing with the girls giggling and screaming beside us.

I was tempted to tell him that I wasn't dancing at all, just moving. But I smiled instead. "Thanks!"

His grip tightened, his fingers pinching me around the middle. I draped my hands around his neck and our bodies moved in time with the beat. It was intimate, no doubt about that. As the beat became heavier, faster, so did our movements. The rigid barrier of being unfamiliar dropped and we pressed against each other. He watched me with parted lips and a heated gaze.

The people around us increased in number and we became sandwiched between couples and groups of overexcited girls. It got hotter—both in temperature and in our demeanor. His hands traveled from my waist to my spine and up to the hair at the back of my neck.

I could feel I was being watched, the sensation of eyes on me. I was willing to bet I knew who it was, but I wouldn't look. I wouldn't give in to the desire to seek out his disapproving, stoic glare.

Josh's forehead lowered, resting on mine as he lowered his hold to my hips and pulled me in tight. His breath was ragged. So was mine, and his parted lips grazed my skin. He leaned back, just enough to gaze down at my mouth, and I could tell what he wanted. But he didn't move, so I did. I raised myself on my tiptoes and drew him into a kiss.

It didn't begin slow. It was urgent and rough, the sort of kiss that should have had me reeling, desperate for more. But I didn't feel more than just content that he was a great kisser.

We came up for air, still clutching one another. Josh let out a low laugh and exhaled. He wanted more. He bit his lip, then pulled me against him. I betrayed myself when I turned my head to the side and spotted Drayton watching me from where he sat. He stared at me, eyes full of storm.

"Do you want to get out of here?" I looked up at Josh.

His brow arched in surprise, but he nodded, eager. "Yeah. Let's go."

When I stepped out of Drayton's house two hours later, the driveway had descended into total darkness. It was just past midnight, and home wasn't that far. Still, walking down the forest-enclosed drive scared me a bit; it was like something out of *Friday the 13th*.

Starting across the large stone parking space, I heard the familiar thrum of a rumbling engine. It was distant but it didn't take long before it came closer. And then a bright glow illuminated the trees on the edge of the drive, and Drayton appeared on his motorcycle. I'd been concerned about this happening when Josh drove us here, but Drayton had hung back at the party, so I'd figured it was safe.

He stopped beside me, and I pretended that he didn't look stupid-hot in his fitted leather jacket. He kicked his stand down, cut the engine, and pulled his helmet off. It amazed me that his hair didn't end up looking awful from how often he wore headgear.

"Cheer." He rested the helmet on his handlebar.

"Drayton."

"Sneaking off, huh? All class."

"Not quite. We didn't have sex, so I wouldn't call it sneaking off."

He flinched, brows raised as he looked at the house. "Where is he? What are you doing out here alone?"

"He's sleeping. I'm leaving."

"How are you getting home? I swear, if you tell me that you're walking, shit's going to pop off."

"I'm—flying?" I gave him a tight smile and winced.

He held the helmet out at arm's length. "Get on."

"You're so demanding," I said, taking the helmet with apprehension.

His hands rested on his thighs as he sighed. "*Please* get on. I'll take you home."

"I've heard that before."

"I wouldn't bother telling you to get on the bike if I was going to drag you back into the house again."

I wasn't sure where the hesitation came from, but I didn't get on the bike. It might have had less to do with fear and more to do with the fact we'd be close, and it made my stomach flutter just thinking about it. He watched me as he kicked the stand up and held the handlebars.

"You scared, Bryan?"

It was a challenge if I ever heard one.

"I'm not scared." I took a step closer. "I just value my brain function and prefer my skin on my body, and not stuck to asphalt."

He rolled his eyes with amusement and gestured at the helmet.

"Put that on." He twisted the handlebars and kicked the starter. I flinched when the engine roared to life. "You'll be safe with me. I promise."

His words made more difference than I imagined they would. It was his tone. I could hear that he meant what he told me. He might have been hesitant to open up about some things, but when he was sincere, it was unmistakable.

I stepped on the foothold and swung a leg across the seat behind him.

"Hold on."

I was glad that he couldn't hear my heart when I wrapped my arms around his middle. Entwining my fingers in front of him, his leather jacket was cool against my arms and chest. He peered over his shoulder and I could see the side of his grin and chiseled jaw. I had never felt more betrayed, and my heart was the traitor—it pounded out of control for someone whom I was adamant not to feel anything for. It wasn't fair. I had no control over it.

CHAPTER 8

As soon as we took off, my body jolted backward. My hesitation and uncertainty was left in the wind, replaced by the adrenaline pumping through my veins. I'd had no idea how intoxicating the feeling of flying through the night air on the back of a motorcycle could be. We tore through the quiet streets, the only ones on the road, and I kept my hold tight, but lifted my head to take in the sights rushing past.

The barriers and confines of viewing the road through a car window were gone. And instead of watching the passing scenes, I was a part of them. The sense of presence was so powerful that I didn't feel the cold on my bare skin. I felt alive and free.

The engine revved and the bike lurched forward. My hold on Drayton's waist became tighter, and I could feel him laughing. I couldn't stop myself from laughing either. I wanted to throw my hands high. I wanted to shout and feel nothing between me and the wind. Endorphins took on a new meaning. Exuberance grew within me. I could feel it threatening to burst within my chest.

We passed the turnoff to my house but it didn't matter, I could have done this for hours.

We drove through the Meadows development zone. The diggers and trucks were sleeping for the night. Drayton ignored the Do Not Enter signs boarding the road. He wove his motorcycle through obstacles that a car couldn't get past. We cleared the zone and the road turned to dust and gravel. He drove across the vast rolling land, leaving a cloud of dust in our wake. Eventually, we ended up back in town, passing the cemetery and the museum. It wasn't long before we were at the bottom of Rock Park.

Drayton wasn't deterred by the steel bar stretched across the parking lot entrance. There was a narrow gap between it and the hedge, just big enough for us to fit through. The tree branches and leaves whipped against us, but he was going slowly, so it didn't hurt. He revved the engine again, and we tore up the foot trail.

Drayton killed the engine and kicked the stand down at a rest space bordered with shrubs and small trees. A wooden paling fence surrounded the cliff edge, and there were bench seats with small steel memorial dedications stuck to them.

"That was amazing," I said, pulling off the helmet. I jumped off the machine and tucked the helmet under my arm as I stood beside Drayton, full of adrenaline and excitement.

He rested his hands on his thighs and said, "Come here."

I stepped forward.

"Helmet hair." He grinned, then lifted his hands and slid his fingers through the strands that weren't woven into my braid. It sent a tingle straight down my spine. "There we go. Happens sometimes. Not that I've had a girl on the back of this thing before." I handed him the helmet with a doubtful grin. "It's true," he told me, swinging his leg over the seat and placing the helmet where he'd sat. He wasn't defensive. Just informative. "The two girls that I've briefly dated since I owned this refused to get on it."

"It's not for everyone." I shrugged a shoulder and turned my attention to the view when he ran a hand through his disheveled hair, raising more of a reaction than it warranted. "This is gorgeous. I've never been up here at night."

We wandered over to a bench in front of the fence and sat down. It was breathtaking—the infinite land, the hills in the distance that met the stars at the edge of the earth, the city that illuminated the dark with a multitone glow and headlights moving fast, like little fireflies.

"It's not bad." His tone was indifferent but the appreciation in his expression gave him away.

I was torn between wanting to admire the view and wanting to stare at his sharp jaw and soft smile. I wondered if he could sense that I was watching him, because he patted the front of his chest and then reached into the inside pocket of his jacket, refusing to look at me.

When he pulled out a packet of cigarettes, I bit down on pointing out the fact that he smelled perfect right now and he didn't need to ruin that. I stared ahead and a moment or two passed before he slipped them back into his pocket.

"I wonder," I mused, keeping my tone light, "how long your career will last before your lungs give out."

He scoffed and gave me a light nudge. "I don't smoke that often."

"Why do you do it all?"

"Nerves," he admitted with a small voice. "It's a vice, I guess.

Keeps me from fidgeting, stuttering. It gives me a focus for a moment. Sometimes, when I need it."

He'd lit up around me on more than one occasion. I noticed that his fingers were wound tight, but I didn't show him that I'd noticed.

"You don't seem like someone who gets nervous." I tried to seem cool rather than focused on the fact that he'd all but admitted that I made him nervous.

"Last I checked, I am a human being."

"I don't know about that. You do seem a little superhuman, throwing that football downfield."

"It's actually my good looks that has you questioning my species, right? You girls refer to us jocks as what, Greek gods?"

"Who's been exposing us?"

He could no longer maintain a straight face. He burst into loud laughter; the sound was unexpected, but it surrounded me, and I sort of loved it. I laughed with him and could feel the smile at the top of my cheeks.

"How come we've never talked before?" he asked. "We've gone to school together for a long time. Not one conversation."

"Well." I shrugged. "There was one. It was brief. One sided even. You tried to sit beside me on the bus for an away game last year, and I had my headphones in. I could hear. I just pretended that I couldn't."

"I remember." He twisted in the seat, his mouth agape. "You could hear me? You snob."

"I wasn't in the mood. You were loud enough from three rows back."

"I thought you were hot. I was making an effort."

My heart did a stupid flutter and I ignored it. As best that I could. "If your idea of effort is asking me if I'm wearing space pants because my ass is out of this world, then I'm embarrassed by your lack of game."

"Come on, the worst pickup lines almost never fail. Girls laugh, and it gives me an opening to compliment their smile. You didn't even flinch."

"It was so lame, it hurt."

"Tough crowd." He nudged me and turned his frame again so that he faced the view. But when he did, he subtly scooted closer, and our thighs grazed.

"I love Colorado. The views and the beautiful mountains," I sighed contentedly as he nodded. "You're the only mountain that I want to climb, though."

His mouth dropped open in disbelief and he hollered. "That was so fucking smooth, Cheer. Damn, girl."

"That's how it's done, QB. That's how it's done."

We burst into unfiltered, hysterical laughter that echoed, and as it settled, both of us were breathless.

"Just so we're clear." He grinned. "I would not oppose your offer of exploration. Climb me whenever."

"You're so much smoother without the pickup lines." I nodded, not looking at his mischievous grin. It was too alluring. "Experience much."

"Not as much as the kids at our school seem to think I have."

"People will have an opinion regardless," I said. I didn't want him to shut down if I came on too strong. "It's best to do whatever you want and let the real friends stick around."

He peered up and fixed me with piercing puzzlement. "Are people real these days?"

"Yeah," I smiled. "Once in a while."

He held my gaze for a few long moments and then his attention fell to my lips. But it was fleeting, and he ducked his head as he ran a hand through his hair. "I didn't mean to get so pissed off about Josh. It's just, he's a romantic kid. He does commitment and love, and I know that you don't. I don't want him to get hurt."

The fact that he wasn't just being a possessive bonehead made me swoon a bit. "That's fair. I understand."

"You were honest with him, though. And he said he was cool. I should have kept out of it."

"I would do the same for Gabby. You don't have to explain yourself. Anyway, I think we're better as friends, Josh and me."

Drayton seemed relieved. There was a drop in his shoulders and a contented smile on his lips. He was beautiful. We sat at the hilltop for a while longer, our bodies close and the atmosphere peaceful. Truthfully, I could have stayed there for hours. He drove me home and the ride back was just as magnificent as the ride up. I stood beside him on the sidewalk and handed his helmet over.

"I have an idea," he said.

"Uh-oh."

He chuckled. "Do you think that Gabby would be interested in meeting Josh?"

I was pleasantly surprised at his suggestion. "I doubt that she'd be uninterested."

"I just thought that it might deter any lingering thoughts that he might have for you. It wouldn't work for me, but he and I have different tastes."

I watched him pull his helmet on as I processed his confusing compliment. "Wait, what?"

He revved his engine and grinned. "I'll text in the morning. We'll get them together for lunch." He flicked the visor down and tore off up the road. Again, with more questions at the end of a conversation than I'd started with—still, I smiled as I walked toward the house.

In the morning, I rolled over in bed, smiled, and thought about how an unexpected evening had turned out to be remarkable.

My hand traveled over the top of my comforter to find my phone. It took a moment to adjust to the phone light, but when I did, I slid the unlock button and was not surprised in the slightest to see that it was nine and Gabby had sent me three texts.

> How was the party. What does Maxon's house look like in person? I've heard it's AMAZING.

> Can we please have a sleepover tonight?

> Did you bone the hottie?

I began to tap out a response and then decided to call her instead. The phone rang twice while I stared at the ceiling.

"Hello!"

"Yes, the house was amazing. Yes, we can have a sleepover, and no, we did not bone. I wasn't feeling it."

"Hmm," she hummed. "Interesting that your sex life has been dwindling since Drayton stepped onto the scene."

"What, two weeks ago?" I absentmindedly pulled my hair into the air and let it drop. I did it again. "I had three dates over summer, Gabs. I'm not a nymphomaniac."

"One might think that no one else can compare," she continued as if I hadn't spoken.

"I had a thought." I ignored her as well. "Josh, the guy I was with last night, he's super sweet. Tall. Handsome. Would you be interested in meeting him?"

"Oh!" Her shout was accusatory. "Just throw me the scraps like I'm a common street dog."

"He's not scraps. He's a nice guy. He's attractive and quite a romantic. I just thought that you might be interested. But if you're not, I'll tell hi—"

"Hang on," she snipped. "I might be interested."

"Okay, good. How ab—"

"But didn't you guys get together? How far did it go?"

"We kissed for a bit while a movie was on. It was polite. There was no touching under or on top of clothing. And then he fell asleep. I promise, nothing more went on. He's really not my type."

"All right." She sounded unfazed. "I can live with that."

"Come over then. And bring a cute outfit. You're going out with him for lunch."

"What?!"

"See you soon."

When she arrived, twenty-eight minutes later, she was frazzled. She hauled an enormous duffel into my bedroom, and I sat up, still in bed. Gabby lived on the next street over, so I wasn't shocked at how soon she got here, but I was still amused because it seemed that she'd brought her entire wardrobe. Drayton had sent me a message about two minutes earlier to let me know that he was good to go on his end, and he'd arrive with Josh at one o'clock.

Gabby had a shower and we spent a couple of hours choosing an outfit and taming her hair. It was a process that required patience, the right products, and a backup plan.

She fudged attempt number one—controlled natural curls—as it was just too hot. So I did a double French braid for her instead. Gabby sat in front of the closet-door mirror, her phone propped against it while she watched a tutorial on how to achieve a flawless face with drugstore products—of course, Gabby's products were a few shades darker—and began her makeup. On the screen, YouTube beauty guru Shaaanxo brushed on her foundation.

I lay on the bed, stomach down, and swiped through Tinder. "I love her accent. There's something about a New Zealand accent. I just want to listen to it."

"Right," Gabby agreed. She copied what she was watching. "And her dogs. Zeus and Lewie. I love them so much."

"So cute."

"I can't wait to see what she does for Halloween this year. Remember when I tried to do her deer tutorial a couple of years back? What a fail."

"True," I mumbled. I was on a roll; I'd swiped left more times than I could count. But I paused, thumb hovering when I came across a profile that I knew all too well.

Drayton Lahey.

I almost snorted at the photo. He was beside his pool, cap backward, no shirt on, and a football in hand. He was stupid hot, but it was obvious that he knew it. His location was set as Cripple Creek, and it was so on-the-nose that I smiled. But when I tapped on the info button and read his bio, it set me off.

Just putting myself on the radar of one blonde cheerleader
who may need her itch scratched. She loves it when I ride
the hell out of my motorcycle. I'm hoping she'd love to ride
the hell out of me.

I laughed so hard that Gabby peered over her shoulder mid-contour. "Just th-this video." I continued to giggle through the lie and pointed at my phone screen. "That one of the girl and um—"

"Oh, I know the one." Gabby nodded and returned to her face.

I was glad that she knew what I was talking about even if I didn't. I swiped right on the profile and we matched. I tapped out a quick message.

You've joined tinder?!

I thought I'd see what all the fuss is about. I've already had like 106 matches.

Of course you have. Any potential candidates?

Gabby looked beautiful. Her makeup was understated—soft, but enhancing her natural beauty. She stood up and smoothed her button-up sundress. It was the color of mustard and had sunflowers all over it. Her white canvas lace-ups were the perfect match. "Are you sure this is all right?"

"You look perfect." I gazed at her long legs. I was envious as usual. "He's going to be head over heels in no time."

"I might wear contacts."

"You'll look stunning either way," I told her, picking up my phone when it dinged with a notification. It was him again.

No candidates just yet. Besides I don't really trust girls that use this app. They're probably all weird looking and have cat fetishes.

I use tinder! Am I weird looking with a cat fetish?

You definitely aren't weird looking as for the cat fetish. I dunno. I wouldn't be surprised.

Shut up. Is Josh excited about the date?

Yeah, we were just braiding each other's hair and talking about how special it's going to be.

Are you always such a sarcastic asshole?

Relatively often.

"Dallas!" Nathan's voice barreled down the corridor a half-hour later from the living room. "Guests."

Gabby froze for ten seconds and then she imploded. She shifted on the spot, bit her nails, and asked me over and over again in a hushed whisper if she should change. I stood up from the bed, gripped her shoulders, and stared into her manic dark-brown eyes.

"You will be fine," I assured her. "He is such a nice guy. Even if there's no spark, it won't be a bad first date. He's just that sweet."

Out in the living room, we found Nathan standing beside Drayton and Josh. Even though Nathan was short like me, the three of them together made the room look small. Nathan had his back to us so the other two saw us first, and as much as I wanted to admire Drayton in joggers and a fitted long-sleeved shirt, instead, I appreciated how Josh's gaze widened. He couldn't take his eyes off Gabby.

"I'll leave you to it." Nathan smiled and excused himself.

We stopped in front of the boys and it was quiet. I waited for Gabby to introduce herself, but it became obvious that she was unable to. Before I could do the honors, Josh leaned in and extended his hand.

"You must be Gabby? I'm Josh."

"Hi." She giggled nervously.

When I looked at Drayton, I noticed that he was on his phone, one hand in his pocket. "Sorry." He locked it and smiled at us. "Just had to check if this girl had replied to me on Tinder."

I snorted, loudly and unattractively.

"Cute pj's." Drayton gestured at the cami and little shorts that I'd been in all morning. There had been no time to change when I'd been focused on ensuring that Gabby was content with her appearance.

It was awkward. Josh and Gabby shared a mutual attraction. There were stolen glances but there was also nervous shuffling and a distinct lack of talking. I was hopeful that things would pick up once they were alone.

"For the sake of breaking the damn tension in here,"—Drayton's voice was loud and intrusive, but it was better than the awkward silence—"Josh and Dallas made out last night, and now he's going out with Gabby less than twenty-four hours later. It's weird. For sure. Who cares? Go and have lunch."

Gabby looked horrified. Josh looked mildly frustrated but not surprised. I was impressed that Drayton managed to put it in such simple terms. It worked, though. The tension was lifted and the four of us laughed. Josh finally acknowledged that I was there, too, and his smile was polite and understanding. He went with Gabby in her car, leaving the Jeep behind. Drayton and I watched from the front step, like proud parents. I hoped that it would go well. The last thing that I wanted was to be responsible for Gabby's sadness if it was a total disaster.

"So." Drayton slipped both of his hands into his front pockets and peered down at me. Linda from two doors down walked past with her dog and stared at us with little subtlety. "Have you eaten?"

"I've had a coffee."

He wrapped his hand around my biceps and squeezed. It surprised me. Not because it was sudden, but because of how electric it felt.

"That can't be a regular thing," he stated, letting go again. "I mean, just having coffee. You've got too much muscle to skip meals."

"I like to eat," I confirmed with amusement, feeling flattered.

He peered over his shoulder into the house. "Well damn, Cheer. You sure are forward. I'm down, though."

I gave him a light slap in the chest. Gabby and Josh were long gone but we remained at the top of the front steps. The weather was warm.

"Do you want me to make you a sandwich?" I offered, wondering how he'd twist that into an innuendo. I was sure that he'd find a way.

He smiled and turned to walk inside. "Sure."

CHAPTER 9

Two weeks had passed since Gabby and Josh's lunch. It was mid-September—the weather was cooling down but their romance was heating up. They'd been talking or texting nonstop and had gone out twice since that Saturday afternoon. She was enamored of her newfound romance, and I couldn't have been happier for her.

We were sitting beside each other in the school parking lot. Cheerleaders and football players hung around, loaded their bags, and snapped selfies in front of the bus. It wasn't common for the cheerleaders to join the away games. Emily's mother oversaw the booster club that raised the funds to purchase the bus. Being involved wasn't her specialty but having connections sure was, and she'd managed to raise a ridiculous sum by simply reaching out to her elite circle and having them purchase Archwood Wolves' merchandise.

Coach Raeken made an appearance that afternoon. Her platinum hair was hidden beneath a sun hat and she wore a pair of designer shades that hid half of her face. When she arrived, I thought that she was going to be joining us. Instead, she gathered the squad, gave us a pep talk, told us she had a previous engagement that meant she wouldn't be joining us, and then left her spawn in charge. Such a cruel twist of fate.

"Fort Collins is an hour and a half from here," Gabby mentioned, pushing some loose gravel with her shoe. We were on the sidewalk a few feet away from the thick of the excitement, and there I would remain until we left. "I don't get why it's an overnight thing."

"Because,"—I retied the lace on my shoe—"one of the parents complained about us traveling so late at night. The parent council agreed that it's better for us to have a decent rest and avoid being on the road when it's dark just in case there's an accident or something."

She shrugged. "I guess there's logic in there somewhere."

I nodded and spotted Drayton sauntering out of the school gates. He was with his friends, but when he saw me he smiled and nodded as a form of greeting. It was respectful and unashamed, a vast difference from where we were three weeks ago. We'd spent a bit more time together since that evening at Rock Park—we talked on the field and he'd eaten at the diner more than once. He sort of seemed to be around even when he had no reason to be.

"Someone's thinking about sharing a room with a certain quarterback tonight." Gabby nudged me, her grin devious.

I shook my head with exasperation. "Nope."

"You so ar—"

"We should do something tomorrow when I get back?" I interrupted her accusation and hoped to distract her from her current train of thought. "Movie or bowling. Unless you have plans with Josh?"

"We have plans tonight." She smiled and pulled a curl straight, letting it go so that it sprang back into place. "So, that sounds good. Not bowling though. You're so good at it that it's not fair."

I scoffed with amusement as Coach Finn stood beside the bus doors and shouted, "We're loading up. Tick your name off the roll and choose a seat. Now!"

Gabby and I stood up. She smoothed out her skirt and I tugged on the bottom of my shorts. She pulled me into a hug and told me that she'd miss me. I was going to be gone for one night. She was adorable. "Don't do anything I wouldn't do."

"What *wouldn't* you do, Gabby?" I laughed as she let me go.

Her cunning smile told me all that I needed to know.

I was wandering toward the bus when Drayton appeared beside me. He threw an arm around my shoulders and his fragrance enveloped me. It was sweet, a softly spiced scent with an undertone of fruit. It was masculine but delectable, and it lingered.

"Sit with me on the bus?"

"Sure."

"How are our little lovebirds?" He gestured in the direction where Gabby had been. "Is she just as smitten as Josh?"

"I hope so. I haven't seen her so happy in a long time. It's cute."

He seemed surprised. "I thought you'd find it sickening." It hadn't evaded me that his firm, inked arm was still keeping me tucked beside him.

"Of course not," I defended myself. "It's sweet. I want them to fall in love and get married and have babies."

When we reached the front of the line, he dropped his hold so I could tick the box beside my name. But before Drayton could follow me onto the bus, his name was called, and we both turned around to find the principal waving him forward.

"Save me a seat," he sighed with boredom. "I have to go and receive *another* 'bring it home' pep talk."

He slipped past the last few students who were waiting to board. I left him to it and headed down the middle of the air-conditioned bus. It was nice, with wide plush seats and a bathroom at the back. There was a free set of seats in the middle. I sat at the window one and had about three seconds of comfort before I was joined by Emily, and I deflated. She was pouting, and her pin-straight auburn hair was high on her head, tied with a silver ribbon.

"As your captain, I think that it's important that we talk. Girl to girl." Pause. "It's embarrassing, your attempts to get close to Drayton. He's so nice, so he'd never say it, but you're not in the right circle. I mean, people like us come from elite families, and that comes with expectations. You come from nothing."

"Emily." I attempted not to laugh. "This is embarrassing—for you—not for me."

"Excuse me?"

"I couldn't care less about who's rich and who's not. It means nothing to me."

"That's just what a broke bitch would say," Emily said.

"I can afford school, cheerleading, food, and a car. I have a job and I have what I need. I'm just fine. Having more money than I know what to do with isn't something that I strive for. Your goals are yours. But that doesn't mean that I share the same ones. I'm good. Are we done?"

Steam practically came out of her ears. "Fall into line or lose your position on the squad. No CalArts. It's your choice."

She stood up and stormed toward the back of the bus. I hated that she could make that sort of call. She wasn't even bluffing—she'd used her mother to have cheerleaders removed before. I had a feeling that the one reason she hadn't done it already was because if she kicked me off the team, I'd have nothing to lose.

Instead of heeding her warning, I let Drayton sit beside me when he appeared in the middle of the aisle a few moments later. There were a few masculine shouts of protest from the back of the bus, but he pretended not to hear them and settled into his seat. His persistence in spending time with me was starting to mess me up a little.

The bus moved and we spent the next hour and a half sharing headphones and discussing our favorite music, new and old. We had a mutual love for Lauv. I introduced him to Drax Project and he introduced me Blackbear, and we loved our new discoveries. We also had a good laugh going into our Spotify Time Capsules and listening to all of the songs that had seen us through our youth.

When we arrived in Fort Collins, our bus stopped in front of a small, two-floor motel with a balcony that stretched from one end to the other. The rail was rusted steel and the doors could have used a paint, but it wasn't the worst. It was what our small accommodation budget would allow. Coach Finn gathered us in the parking lot while our assistant coach, Lincoln, headed toward reception to collect keys.

"Listen up," Coach Finn shouted. Drayton was still standing beside me. "The rules have not changed. No leaving your rooms after eleven. No mixing. No drinking. No drugs. No sex."

There were a number of sniggers from around the group. The rules hadn't changed, but neither had the students. Sex and alcohol were inevitable. So was mixing in the rooms at night. Half of the kids here would have plans arranged already.

"We leave for Sheridan High School at six. Do not be late. Or you will be left behind," Coach Finn continued, reading from a clipboard and scratching his mess of black hair. He always looked as though he'd received a mild electric shock. He quietly tutted for a minute as his gaze moved over the paper. "Oh. An announcement was being made this afternoon at school that would have been missed. Homecoming has been postponed."

There was a collective outcry from the girls. Some of the guys were disappointed too.

"Relax," Coach Finn scoffed. "It's being moved from the twenty-ninth of September to the twenty-sixth of October."

"But that's Halloween weekend!" Aria called out.

Maxon added, "And the same weekend as the last game of the season."

"If you make it." Coach Finn shrugged. "Some of your priorities are sounding a bit off."

"Why has it been postponed?" Becca asked, wrapping her raven hair around her fist.

"Repairs on the gymnasium," he stated. "The funding for this month is gone. Hence the date change. Now, I've had enough of discussing it. Lincoln will hand out the room cards. Find yours and go and get organized. Remember, back here at six."

It was clear that he wasn't going to talk about the homecoming dance, but that didn't stop the rest of the girls from complaining. It meant rescheduling their makeup and hair appointments.

Rebooking limousines. It might even mean that some of them had lost deposits. I felt for them.

My room was on the second floor. I'd swiped the card, pushed the door open, and stepped inside when Melissa marched in behind me and headed straight toward the single bed beside the window.

"Can I have the bed by the window?" She dumped her duffel down. "Thanks."

It didn't matter to me in the slightest which bed I got, so I didn't argue. The room was spacious enough. There was a single set of drawers, a small bathroom, and a second single bed on the wall beside the door. We'd definitely stayed in worse before.

"So." Melissa sat on the edge of her bed and pulled her legs up into a crisscross position. "I'm supposed to be, like, getting friendly with you and getting the details. You and Dray. Emily's request." She put her hands up over her head. "Honestly, I don't care who you fucking and who you ain't."

"You can report back to her that there is no fucking going on with me and Dray."

"Why not?" she scoffed.

"We're friends." I hopped on my own bed, mirroring her sitting position.

"Just friends, psssh," she said, examining one of her long, velvet-like black braids. "Heard that before."

"It's not like that with us."

"You a lesbian? Because that boy could turn a straight man."

"Let's not give him too much credit," I mumbled. "And no, I'm not a lesbian. Like I said, he's just my friend."

"Hmm." She shrugged, busying herself with her cell phone. "Whatever. I'll let Emily know you're good. I got your back.

Even if you do get freaky with him. I like you. You're a little quiet, but you're, like, one of those quiet chicks that has big balls. I respect that."

I laughed. I liked Melissa. Perhaps more so now that I knew she wasn't under Emily's thumb. It was also a relief to know that I wasn't paired with someone worse for the evening.

That night's game was at the Sheridan High School football field. The Cougars were a good team. We'd lost to them before, but our team was confident this time around, even when the game was nearing its end and the scoreboard was 28-26. We needed a touchdown or a field goal to win. It hadn't been a breeze—Sheridan had put up a hell of a fight, and both of the teams were exhausted. But it wasn't over, and we cheered in encouragement.

Drayton huddled the team. They lined up for a play. He took his place behind the center, the air thick with tension. Drayton called "Hut" and the snap was made. He stepped back as their defense went in, their protective gear crunching. He swung his arm, sidestepped, and managed to avoid losing the ball. As the defense went for the ball again, diving, Drayton twisted and threw the ball through a narrow gap of players, landing it in the hands of Derek, the running back.

Derek had the Cougars at his side and he was thrown to the ground before he could clear ten yards. The ball was hidden for a moment before it was thrown out from under the mountain of football players and into the hands of the other team. They threw the ball in the direction of their end zone. Maxon jumped and intercepted it, then threw it to Drayton. The seconds on the clock disappeared, but Drayton stepped back and threw a Hail Mary. It cleared forty-yards to Austin, our wide receiver, who caught it in the end zone. Touchdown.

The celebration was immediate. We'd won another game.

There was something about watching Drayton throw a ball that far. It was so powerful, effortless. It made me a bit weak in the knees, which must have been obvious, because later on, back in our room, Melissa pointed it out.

"Quite a man when he throwing that ball, huh?" She was in the bathroom with the door open. I couldn't see her, but I could hear her opening and closing makeup products.

It was ten. Coach Finn had performed his final round of room inspections about fifteen minutes ago. Melissa and I had both been in our pj's. Now she was wearing a leather skirt, a tucked-in tank top, and a pair of platforms. Drayton had texted straight after the game asking if I'd be joining the rest of the crew at a party by a small lake about ten minutes from the hotel. I'd declined. The last thing that I wanted to do was spend time with him while Emily was watching. When Melissa emerged from the bathroom, her bronze skin was glowing.

"He should be good at throwing a ball," I said. "He's the quarterback."

Melissa made that psssh sound again. "You were impressed. I know it." She gave herself one more once-over in the little mirror beside the bed and smiled. "You sure you don't want to come, girl?"

"I'm sure."

I wouldn't mind doing something, just not that something. I opened Messages on my phone and tapped out a message.

> Hey. I might sort of be a little bit keen to do something tonight. But it won't be drinking with those guys. No pressure. But if you want to do something else, let me know.

"Suit yourself." Melissa shrugged, swiped on some lip gloss, and then dropped the tube into her bra. "I'm gonna get my femme prowl on."

She opened the door to our room, peered from left to right, checking the corridor, and then crept out.

Drayton responded to my message faster than I was expecting.

> Come to my room. I can think of plenty to do. ;)

> You've got a one-track mind. B right there.

It was hot; the air conditioning must have been off, because when I'd finished getting dressed, I felt flushed. I'd changed into a white off-the-shoulder, long-sleeved cropped top and a pair of jeans that hugged all the right places. My hair sat in a long natural wave, and I didn't put on a lot of makeup for the simple fact that I didn't want to waste any more time.

Drayton's room was three doors down the hall. Checking for any of the adult supervisors, I knocked twice and stared at the brass number *15* for about six seconds before the door swung open. Drayton had no shirt on, just a pair of sweatpants and his signature black backward cap.

"Damn, I didn't think that you would for-real show up. Come on, come in before anyone sees you."

"I did not come here to smash. Don't be small minded."

He was cute when he pouted, but he didn't seem surprised to hear that I hadn't come for illicit activities. His room was much the same as mine. Perhaps a little bigger.

"Where's your roommate?" I asked as I leaned against the door.

He dropped backward onto the bed beside the door and threw an arm behind his head. I didn't want to stare at him. I didn't. But I did. His skin was warm. Tan. So smooth. I sort of wanted to run my tongue along the dips of his abdomen.

Wow.

"Derek's gone with the rest of them."

"You didn't want to go?"

He shook his head. "Boring. Someone texted me with a better offer."

"Dreamer."

"So, what are we doing then, Cheer?"

"I have no idea," I admitted, still leaning against the door in an attempt not to sit beside him, because then I might have actually touched his torso and that would have been inappropriate. "This was probably a dumb idea. I have no plan. Forget it."

I turned around with the intention of leaving, but he sprang up from the bed and put himself in front of me. He was so close that I had to tip my head back to look at him. His hand wrapped around mine on the door handle behind him, and it was giving me the spins. "I have an idea. Or two. Trust me?"

If this had been three weeks ago, I would have said no. I should have been reluctant now, but I wasn't. It was unexplainable. I did trust him. I pretended to be hesitant for a moment but then nodded. "Sure."

"Good. Let me get dressed."

What felt like moments later, we were in Old Town in Fort Collins. Historical buildings had been restored. The air carried the aroma of exquisite food. Music carried us through the center of town. Magical European-inspired walkways had potted flowers and Tivoli Lights stretched between the lampposts. There was a large round fountain with blue glow lights illuminating spouts of water that shot out of the ground in timed succession. Seating areas made from cobblestones were given some extra color with small trees, and as we walked farther through the throng of people, we discovered that downtown was dotted with art-covered pianos, romantic alleys, cozy restaurants, and open plazas.

We stopped and listened to a live band on an elevated makeshift stage. Their music was whimsical. I moved with it, smiling and absorbing the moment. Drayton watched me.

Moving on, we passed a small flower shop. The owner was beside the store, and there were several paint pots and brushes on the ground. There were already hundreds of random brush strokes on the concrete wall. She offered us a brush each; Drayton picked blue. I chose silver, and we left our marks.

We slipped down an alleyway. The crowded walkway was filled with excited couples and teenagers. We walked beside each other, careful not to become separated, until we arrived at a solid black door. Drayton pushed it open, and we slipped inside a narrow staircase. It descended into darkness, but he didn't hesitate, and the farther down that we went, the more I could hear the solid thump of bass music. At the bottom of the staircase, there was a curtain. Drayton held it aside. I gave him a curious look as I passed him.

A bouncer with a big, pale, bald head hovered in front of another door, watching me carefully until Drayton appeared. His expression went from hard and cold to warm and elated.

"How's it going, Caleb!" Drayton greeted the bouncer, wrapping his arm around me as he walked us forward. Under his touch, a thrill pulsed through my veins.

"Not bad. How's your dad?"

"Same old." Drayton's answer was quick and indifferent. He pulled me a bit tighter against his side. "Dallas, this is Caleb. Caleb, this is Dallas. My girlfriend."

Hold up.

What?

Dazed for a moment, I missed the rest of their little chitchat because I was unsure of what the hell had just happened.

"Behave you two, but go on in." Caleb stepped aside and Drayton pulled me into a nightclub. A real nightclub with a bar and adults and a blue hue from the lights that illuminated all of the white in the room, including my top. Drayton walked toward the bar, pulling me behind him. There must have been a different entrance because people were spilling in from a door on the other side of the room.

"Dray," I shouted over a remixed version of "Kiss and Make Up" by Dua Lipa. "I'm not dressed for a club!"

He lowered his mouth to my ear, and his breath was warm. "You look perfect."

Our fingers laced together, we squeezed through the cluster of people surrounding the bar. I'd have never made it through on my own, but his large presence got us safely to the front. He quickly looped an arm around my waist and slipped me in front of his body. I was against the bar, and his arms were on either side of me, creating a safe little cage where I wouldn't get trampled.

"We'll have a Corona and a passion-fruit martini," Drayton said to the bartender.

"That's an interesting order," I teased.

I turned around and realized how pressed against each other we were. Chest to chest. Well, chest to nose. His arms remained encased around me as he leaned on the bar, staring down at me.

"Why did you tell the bouncer that I'm your girlfriend?"

"He won't let just anyone in. You had to be someone important to me or he wouldn't have allowed it."

"Makes sense." I turned around and bopped to the beat, fingers curled on the edge of the bar while I ignored the feeling of Drayton's chest against my back. He smelled so good.

The bartender slid the drinks across the bar. Drayton picked up the beer and left me the martini. Sure, it tasted like a passionfruit slushy, but it was tainted with the taste of alcohol—the combination was awful. I winced with disgust and Drayton watched me with amusement. He took the martini and handed me the beer. I was surprised when he slurped on the straw. It was the funniest thing that I had ever seen. He was tall, muscular, and masculine, and he was sipping a frozen martini. I couldn't stop giggling.

"Thank you," I shouted with laughter, lifting the bottle. The corner of his mouth pulled into a small smile, and he winked.

When we were finished with our drinks, we ditched the glass and the bottle on the bar, and Drayton took me by the hand again, leading me through the crowd. It was effortless. He was almost impossible to ignore. He was a teenager in high school, but he carried himself with importance and confidence. It wasn't arrogant, though. It wasn't even intentional. It was just him.

We stopped in the middle of the dance floor and he placed his hands an inch from either side of my waist, hovering over the exposed skin but not touching it until I gave him a confirming nod and he gripped my hips. My hands connected at the back of his neck and we moved to the remixed beat of "Let Me Hold You (Turn Me On)" by Cheat Codes and Dante Klein. There was no avoiding the occasional hair whip or stood-on toe, but we were soon lost to the moment.

Our bodies were pressed flush; we moved our hips in time. His large hands tightened, and he watched me as we stepped. He turned me around, pulling my back into his front. I lowered. It was slow as I dropped down in front of him and came back up with rolling hips and hands in my hair.

I felt his lips beside my ear again. "I'm glad that I get to dance with you this time," he said with a raised voice. "I was jealous when I had to watch Josh doing this with you."

My stomach flipped over, and I was glad that he couldn't see me. His hands slid around, resting on my stomach. He felt me as I continued to grind against him. His grip was tight and desperate.

When I spun around again, I stepped back and danced alone. The music was the lead and the song was hot. I closed my eyes and lifted my arms. I knew the swing in my hips was sensual, even more so when I opened my eyes again and found Drayton a few inches in front of me, watching with his gaze full of longing. This was dangerous. It felt precarious. But it felt so good.

After an hour of dancing with no barriers, we agreed we needed some fresh air. Drayton also let me know that this was just the first stop of the evening.

"There's more to come, Cheer." He slid his hands into his pockets and his tone turned teasing. "You as well, if you're up for it."

He was such a shit. We walked through downtown and

found that the nightlife was still alive and in full swing. It had just passed midnight.

"You can dance, Cheer." He nudged me with his elbow and stared at the ground. "I mean, I know that most people can dance in a club. But your body. There's this flow. Like the music isn't in control. You are. It beats to your body."

I felt breathless at his explanation. No one had described my dancing like that before. No one. "It's just natural." He cleared his throat and smiled. "You can move."

"Thanks," I said, running my hands through my damp hair.

"Now, here's an observation," he mused with a knowing grin. "You don't like cheerleading. You're just doing it because we don't have a dance team. It's an alternative."

I attempted to hide how flattered I was that he had picked up on that without having been told. "You're right. Cheerleading is fun, but it doesn't do it for me like dancing does."

"That's the plan? For college."

"That's the plan," I confirmed. "I've applied to three schools: Colorado College, SMU in Texas, and CalArts in California. But I want CalArts."

"California dreams, huh?"

"Something like that. I want a change. Even if it's not forever, I want to experience something else. Something different."

"I've been to California. It's nice. I mean, some of it sucks. But I think that's the same with any place. All cities have their pros and cons."

"For sure," I agreed. "How about you. Know where you want to go?"

"I'm not sure. It doesn't bother me a whole lot. As long as I get to play football. My dad is pushing hard for Baylor, in Waco, his alma mater. A long line of Laheys attended that school. I've told him that it doesn't matter where I go. He's set in his ways though."

"Is that the reason that you support the Cowboys? Roots in Texas?"

"My mom is from Dallas. It's where they met."

"Your dad isn't from Texas?"

"Nope. Born and raised right here in Colorado. But his dad went to Baylor as well. It's sort of become a tradition to retire here."

"Oh. Retire? What did they do? Football? Is it a family tradition?"

He was quiet for a beat. "Yeah."

"Did they play in the NFL?"

There was a long pause. Drayton's hands fidgeted in his pockets. He seemed wound up. It was a long time before he spoke. "Yes. Please don't tell anyone. I've done a damn good job of hiding it."

"What do you want to hide it for?" I couldn't believe that his father and grandfather had played in the NFL.

"It's a lot of pressure when people know the truth. It's enough pressure as it is, being quarterback. My dad and grandfather both played the same position, generations of stress and expectation . . ." His laugh sounded tense. Nervous.

"How has it remained a secret though? How has no one recognized him, or your grandfather—do they live around here too?"

"My grandad died in a house fire when I was a baby, and my dad doesn't come to school. He gives me space. And besides, he retired a long time ago."

It was obvious that he didn't want to talk about it. I was surprised that he had said as much as he had. But if he didn't want to boast about his football-star father, I wasn't going to push it.

Being closed off from potential relationships and romantic connections meant that I'd never shared so much with someone before. I'd never had someone share so much with me, and I never realized how good it would feel.

We were walking and talking so easily that I lost track of time and distance, but when he eventually stopped, we were outside an exquisite Colonial home. I checked my phone and realized we'd been walking for an hour. It was one o'clock now, and the streets were dead silent.

"What are we doing?" I whispered because I was afraid to speak in a normal tone, considering how quiet it was.

"Follow me," Drayton instructed with a devious grin, and I was immediately on high alert. Whatever we were about to do, I suspected that it was not a good idea. I tiptoed behind him as we crept up the home's hedge-lined path toward a back gate secured with a high-tech lock. Somehow, that didn't deter Drayton, and without warning, he moved behind me and gripped me by my hips.

"Time to cheer," he whispered before he threw me into the air. I might have been a flyer, but his throw sort of sucked. I couldn't blame him. I was a human, not a ball. Grabbing the top of the gate, I flung myself over before dropping to the ground on the other side. Before long, Drayton dropped down beside me with a triumphant smile.

The backyard was lavish. The home must have been occupied by a family because there was a tree house that I could only have dreamed of having when I was a kid. There was a large trampoline and a swing set. All of the kids' items occupied the far side of the backyard while the rest was taken up by a large deck, a pool, a spa, and an extravagant garden.

Drayton tugged on my hand and walked us toward the swimming pool. He lifted the second gate latch as quietly as he could, and we both walked onto the concrete surrounding the water.

"Seriously. What are we doing? Are you going to drown me?" I didn't know why I was still whispering.

"Oh please." He rolled his eyes. He started to pull off his shirt, rendering all coherent thoughts extinct. "We're going to skinny-dip, Cheer."

"You're kidding." My light laugh became strangled in my throat as he dropped his pants and kicked off his shoes. "Oh wow. You're serious."

"Yep," he grinned.

"This is insane." I was panicking as he stood in front of me in nothing but his Calvins.

"Yes, it is." He nodded. "That's the point. Live a little, Cheer. And remember to trust me."

My attention moved between the house and the pool, and then back to the house again. I decided that I'd regret it more if I didn't do it. What was the use in being young if you didn't have a little irresponsible fun once in a while? I kicked off my shoes and dropped my cell phone safely into one of them so that it didn't get wet.

When I stood up straight again, Drayton winked right before he tucked his thumbs into the sides of his Calvins and pulled them down, exposing *all* of his endowed glory. I stared. I couldn't help it. I was starting to regret being so opposed to riding something that wasn't his motorcycle.

When he turned around and dropped into the pool, I felt like I needed a moment. He waved me forward, gesturing to get in. "Let's go, Cheer, the water's perfect."

"Turn around," I ordered after I'd taken my shirt off, revealing my white lace bra but nothing more.

"Hey, you got to see me butt-ass naked."

"What are we, five? Turn around."

He rolled his eyes but obliged, twisting himself in the water so he was facing the back fence. I quickly finished undressing, my heart thumping the entire time in fear that someone was watching or that someone would catch us. But I couldn't deny that the thrill of it was exciting as hell.

When I was completely undressed, I took a deep breath and slipped into the water, expecting it to be freezing cold but was pleasantly surprised to find that it was slightly heated.

"You can turn around now," I told him as I walked through the water. It was dark, only the moon and stars illuminated the sky, so there wasn't a lot to see once we were both facing each other.

"Feeling insane?" He grinned.

"I don't know what I'm feeling," I admitted as my arms swept the surface of the still water. "But it's kind of amazing."

"Feels good to let loose once in a while, doesn't it?"

"I can tell you're just itching to say I told you so," I smiled. "Go on, say it."

"You got in the pool, that's good enough for me."

There wasn't a lot of space between us. We watched each other. The breeze picked up, and it was cold against my wet shoulders and face. Drayton noticed when I shivered. He moved closer again and his legs grazed mine under the surface. "Cold?"

I swallowed and sank a little deeper until the water came to my chin. "I'm all right."

"I can warm you up?"

I was waiting for it. The joke. The innuendo. But his expression remained sincere. And then his hands settled on my hips. It startled me but I didn't move. I just felt the thudding in my chest as he pulled me through the water and into his embrace.

Our bodies touched. There wasn't an inch of space. I could feel him. All of him. His arms wrapped around me and his thumb made slow strokes on my lower back. His lips were parted. Mine were, too, and I felt short of breath.

Traffic sounded in the distance. Tree leaves rustled in the cool, night breeze. Water rippled. The filter flap in the pool opened and closed. The sounds around us were drowned out by the pounding in my chest and ears. He inched closer. When his face moved in, I saw his throat bounce as he swallowed. This wasn't the same as it was last time, when he'd been teasing me. I could tell he was nervous too. Heart beating, heat gathering in places that demanded attention, and the chill of the night long gone, I leaned in as well.

As our lips brushed, a blinding light switched on from the back deck. It was abrupt and unexpected, and we broke apart with a harsh gasp.

"Shit," Drayton snapped. He wrapped a hand around my waist and pulled me toward the edge of the pool. Both of us were panicked. I felt as if I might throw up. "Get as low as you can."

We leaned our backs against the edge of the pool and sank as low as we were able to. I kept still.

The sound of footsteps padded across the deck behind us. My hands trembled under the water. I was trying not to breathe too loudly, but it was almost impossible not to hyperventilate. A woman's voice echoed through the air.

"I can see you, Drayton."

I turned to him, my mouth agape in total disbelief. I was wound up with panic, still, but now I was also confused. Drayton hung his head in defeat, but there was a definite amusement in his green gaze.

"Hey, Aunt Cass," he called.

"There are two towels hanging on the gate here," his aunt said, sounding as if she was smiling. "Come in and see me when you're done with—whatever it is that you're doing."

When the door closed again a moment later, Drayton lifted his head, gave me a splitting grin, and then turned around to hold the edge of the pool. I had no chance to become clued in on what was going on because he lifted himself out of the pool beside me, and I got an eyeful.

"I'll get your towel," he offered, water hitting the concrete as his wet feet walked toward the gate.

A moment passed. "Here."

I turned around and found him holding a large white towel. The other one was wrapped around his waist. It sat low, exposing the defined V-line on his hips. I hesitated, glancing down at the water keeping my body hidden.

"I won't peep," he said, turning his head to the side, eyes closed tight. He was full of devious comments and sexual jokes, but he was respectful. Placing my palms flat on the poolside, I heaved myself out before dashing over to the towel. As promised, he kept his eyes closed.

When I was wrapped, the towel tucked in and my long hair dripping down my back, I said, "You can open your eyes." He looked down and let his gaze move over me slowly and appreciatively.

After a moment of blatant staring at each other, he said, "Come on."

After we collected our clothes, he led us toward the house, which was convenient because I got to watch his strong back and shoulders. His skin was pulled taut over his frame, and it was mesmerizing. He had a large, dark freckle on his shoulder blade. It was sort of cute.

Inside, Drayton closed the French doors behind us, and we were in a kitchen/dining area, where the walls and fixtures were white and charcoal. The floors were polished wood and the appliances were state of the art. A beautiful, tall woman stood behind the kitchen island. Her complexion was flawless, and her light-brown ringlets were in a fountain on the top of her head.

"I want to ask,"—she grinned, pushing two coffee cups across the granite counter—"but I'm also not sure that I want to know."

Drayton laughed. He looked nervous as he ran a hand through his hair. "Please don't tell my mom we were here . . ."

"Don't tell your mother, who's under the impression that you're tucked up in a motel bed, that you're actually halfway across Fort Collins skinny-dipping in my pool at midnight?" She pointed at the door behind us. "I don't think that's a conversation that I want to have with your mom."

Cass rinsed a cloth under the faucet and began to wipe down the countertop. She seemed young, but her hands were aged.

"I'm . . . confused," I said, feeling self-conscious. I was standing in a towel with a puddle of water forming around my feet from my hair.

"Aunt Cass, this is Dallas." Drayton pulled out a seat at the four-seater kitchen table, waving his hand between me and his aunt as he sat. "Dallas, this is Aunt Cass. She was married to my dad's brother, Noah. But—"

"They kept me and got rid of him because he's a cheating little asscrack," Cass finished with a wicked smile. She rinsed her cloth and began wiping down the stove top, which was already clean. No wonder her hands looked so aged.

"Yeah," he turned to me while watching Cass with mild concern. "Sorry you had to meet a member of my family like this."

"She hasn't met your parents?" Cass recoiled. Her expression became proud and she rolled back on her heels. "Well. I'm honored to be the first family member to meet you. Drayton doesn't bring girls home all that often. Not that this is home. But yo—"

"We're not"—Drayton cast a subtle glance in my direction—"we're just friends."

"Do you swim naked with all of your friends?" Cass teased, obviously amused. She sounded like Nathan.

"W-w-wait—" I shook my head and stared at the floor. "Why'd you let me think we were in a stranger's pool?"

"I wanted you to feel the rush of doing something bad." He shrugged. "Without getting into any real trouble."

My stomach twisted. It turned to mush while he sat in front of me giving me a heated stare. The fact that he was considerate enough to keep me out of trouble but reckless enough to do what we'd done in the first place—it was sort of perfect.

"But someone,"—Drayton broke our eye contact and turned his head toward Cass—"ruined my good deed."

"Don't look at me." Cass held her hands up in defense. "You could have texted to warn me, and I would have left you to it."

"Never mind." He stood, brushed past me, and picked up the coffee, and I couldn't help but watch. "But you've got bigger balls than me. I never would've skinny-dipped in a stranger's pool."

"Great." I grinned and folded my arms across my chest. "You're really not living up to this badass reputation you supposedly have."

"Don't be fooled by the brooding attitude and motorcycle," Cass teased. "Dray here is a big ole softie."

He rolled his eyes.

"May I use the bathroom?" I asked, gathering my clothes from the table. I needed to stop ogling Drayton while I was naked because it was winding me up.

Cass nodded and pointed behind her at the other end of the kitchen. "Through to the corridor. Second door to the left."

After apologizing for the puddle that my hair had created on the hardwood floor, I headed to the bathroom to dry off and change back into my clothes, appreciating the feeling of modesty more so than I ever had before. After toweling my hair, I quickly tied it into a French braid.

When I walked back into the kitchen, Drayton was clothed and seated at the small kitchen table, a small child perched on his knee. The little guy was dressed in an adorable panda onesie, and he rubbed his tired eyes.

"We woke this one up, apparently," Drayton informed me.

Cass tipped some powder into a bottle of hot water. "You did. He heard your voice. You know how much he loves you."

"This is Coen," Drayton told me as I sat down in the seat beside him. "My baby cousin and the best-looking kid in the family."

He started to tickle Coen's sides, causing a bubbly laugh to escape the toddler's lips. He was so cute. His light-brown hair matched his mother's, and he had huge bright-blue eyes. I watched the two of them interact with absolute awe.

"All right, Coen." Cass shook the bottle and he jumped off Drayton's lap, running toward her at full speed. "Time to go back to bed, little guy. Say good night to cousin Dray."

"Ni-night Dray-Dray." He waved his little hand and my heart turned into a puddle of goo as he and Cass disappeared through the door I'd just come from.

"Dray-Dray." I grinned. It was blowing my mind that this was the same stone-faced boy whom I felt so frustrated toward less than a month ago.

"Don't," he warned, slipping his phone out of his pocket. "Only Coen gets to call me that."

"Oh, sure . . ." I was taunting him with the fact that I wasn't going to forget that nickname anytime soon.

Cass reappeared a few minutes later. She scuffed her slippered feet and yawned.

"Are you two going back to the hotel now? I can call you a cab?"

"Nope." Drayton stood up and slid his phone into his pocket. "We have another stop to make. I've ordered an Uber. It'll be here in a minute."

"Okay," she said. "I'm going back to bed. Dallas, it was nice to meet you. I hope I see you again. Perhaps a little more clothed next time."

I laughed. She wasn't telling me off. She was actually far more relaxed about the whole thing than she had to be. "That'd be nice," I agreed.

Climbing into the Uber, I asked, "Where are we going now?" We'd gone out on a whim. How many spontaneous plans could this boy possibly make?

"You'll see."

We arrived in front of a park tucked between a museum and an enormous vintage furniture store. The trees glittered with fairy lights and solar lamps sat underneath shrubs. When we got out of the car, I noticed the projector screen at the end of the park playing *P.S. I Love You*. Couples were scattered over the grass, cuddled on blankets or beanbags. It was romantic, but I didn't point that out. Instead, I wondered if Drayton had brought us here to do something hideous like set the projector on fire or spray everyone with a hose.

"What are we doing here?"

"We're watching a movie, Cheer. We're a bit late but"—he shrugged and we stopped near the back—"I heard some of the guys talking about this place earlier. They planned on bringing the girls down."

"All an attempt to help them score?" I guessed. His grin was laced with guilt.

"That's not what's happening here." He gestured between us. "Unless—"

I gave his firm chest a shove. "Each to their own, but I'm just not into fornicating in public places."

He laughed. "Fornicating?"

"Shut up."

He sauntered toward three large baskets at the fence line and returned with two blankets, spreading one out on the ground. "I checked it over for jizz stains," he assured me as he sat down.

I wasn't entirely confident that it was the cleanest piece of material, but I sat down beside him and let him throw the other blanket across our legs.

We watched the movie in quiet for a little while. Drayton

offered to jog over to the food vendor and get some popcorn or a soda, but I declined. He began to fidget after five minutes. He twisted and moved his legs, and then he sighed and lay down on his back.

"So," he said, casually. "Thoughts on your fun-filled evening?"

I lay down as well and stared at the stars, thinking about how to answer him. So many different elements contributed to the night and I didn't think that I hated any of them. I didn't hate experiencing the enriching culture in Old Town. I didn't hate the dancing or the long walk that consisted of conversation without pause. I didn't hate our moonlit dip or meeting someone important to him.

I don't hate this.

"It's been something else, Lahey."

"Is that it?"

"I thought it was amazing, okay?" I laughed lightly as he threw his fist triumphantly into the air. "The entire night has been thrilling and exciting and I loved it. Thank you, Dray."

He smiled, watching the stars. The movie played softly in the background; the people spread out in front of us munched on snacks and murmured quietly among each other. The trees around us rustled ever so slightly in the soft breeze. This was a serene place and I was beginning to realize you could find peace in more places than just the confines of home.

Drayton moved one arm to rest beneath his head. The other was draped across his chest. I wanted to know what he was thinking about.

"It was a good night," he mumbled. I turned my head to watch him.

His hand moved. It slid down from his chest and then it wrapped around mine. It was soft and unexpected. But I didn't react. I just appreciated the moment.

"It was a good night," I agreed with him. "A great night."

CHAPTER 10

I don't think I've ever woken up to a crisp breeze ruffling my hair or the sound of birds chirping right next to my head. My eyes flew open and, for a moment, I wished I wasn't panicking, because I was curled up on Drayton's chest and his arm was tucked around my back, holding me close.

"Oh shit, Dray!" I abruptly sat up and slapped his chest as I looked around the now brightly lit park. "Wake up!"

We weren't the only ones who had spent the night here, but we were probably the only ones who were meant to be boarding a bus that morning. I couldn't see anyone else from school, and I swore if they'd seen us and just left us, I'd damage someone. I pulled out my phone to check the time when I saw Drayton sitting up in my peripheral view.

"Shit," he gasped, his head whipping from side to side. "What's the time . . ." His voice was heavy with sleep.

"It's eight!" I stood up, fretting as I smoothed my hair. I didn't even have time to admire how disheveled and good he looked after sleeping in a park all night. I probably looked like I lived in the freaking park.

"Eight?!" Drayton snapped.

Eight was late. It was super late. It was late enough that Coach would have done rounds of the rooms.

"We are so fucked."

"Suspended," Nathan snapped. We walked down the school office steps and across the parking lot, which was vacant save for one or two vehicles. "I cannot believe you got suspended."

He stopped beside the tail of our little car and leaned a hand on the trunk. His stare was hard to decipher. There was a mix of disbelief and disappointment, and perhaps an effort to refrain from shouting.

When Drayton and I had arrived back at the motel that morning, Coach Finn was in a state. He was about two seconds from calling the authorities to report two missing students. When he caught us creeping onto our floor, he'd blown a fuse and started screaming about "jail time" and "asshole kids."

Everyone assumed that we'd been off having scandalous sex. No one could imagine that we'd been doing anything else. Not to mention that if we'd wanted to have sex, we both had motel rooms for that. Emily and her minions scowled at me threateningly, although none of them uttered a word when I was with Drayton. And both of us were sat at the front of the bus to be dealt with as soon as we got back. It didn't matter that it was Saturday. The principal came in to dish out our consequences.

"I'm sorry, Nathan," I said. "I totally messed up, and I know that. Trust me, it won't happen again."

"I kind of can't believe that it happened at all." His features softened a little as he shrugged his shoulders. "You don't do this sort of thing. Sneaking out of motels with guys. Not even Gabby can coax you into a little rebellion. What gives?"

I shrugged. I knew what gave, though.

"Dallas." Nathan wore a no-nonsense expression. "I get that you like that Drayton kid. But don't mess up your schooling for him, all right? You only have this year left to make all your goals happen. Don't go off the rails. For me. Please."

"Nathan, this has nothing to do with Drayton. I've realized something—I have this one year to make memories, so when I'm older, I'll have stories to tell about the crazy stuff that I got up to. I literally have none of that now because I've wasted so much time hating people to the point that I don't want to leave the house."

"You can make those memories without getting suspended."

"I know." I nodded. It worried me that I had this on my record, but I had to hope and pray that it wouldn't mar my otherwise clean college applications. "And next time, that won't happen. I promise."

Nathan folded his arms across his chest and sighed with hesitant acceptance. "Whose idea was it to sneak out anyway?"

"It was mine."

"You risked that kid's football career for a few thrills?" He looked more upset than when he found out that I'd been suspended for being out all night with a guy. "He could have been kicked off the team."

I still wasn't sure what fate awaited Drayton. His parents hadn't arrived as far as I knew, and I'd shared a brief smile with him as I left the principal's office and saw him sitting on the floor in the corridor.

"Look, it was one night. It was irresponsible, I get that. But I had a lot of fun."

Nathan sighed with exasperation, but he couldn't stop the corners of his mouth from turning up into a small smile. "That does make me kind of happy," he admitted. "I do want you to have fun. But you're still in trouble."

"Okay."

"Seriously." I could see the wheels turning as he tried to come up with some sort of informal punishment. "You're on dishes. For two weeks."

"Nathan, I do the dishes every night."

"Yeah . . . well"—his head bopped around as his gaze became distant and wide—"while you're doing them, you can think about the fact that you're being punished, and you can be miserable about it. Seriously, don't enjoy it at all."

"Okay," I accepted my punishment with amusement. "I'll do my best not to enjoy the dishes."

"Good." His nose turned upward with triumph before he fished his keys out of his back pocket. "Now, I'm going back to the field with the boys. Try and make it home without doing something totally reckless. Seriously, you've changed. I don't even know you anymore."

I laughed at his horrified, exaggerated expression as he stumbled around to the driver's side of the car and quickly hopped in. But I admired the dramatic big brother act. He might not have it down to a fine art, but I'd be lost without him.

"Here, take this," I called as he started the car. I opened the door and threw my duffel bag in. "Thanks."

I walked over to the diner to check the new schedule. The sun was out and there was a soft breeze in the air, so a twenty-minute walk wasn't unbearable at all. I could have asked for a ride, but a walk couldn't hurt.

When I arrived, I headed straight into the staff room to look at the schedule for the next week. The roster was full and I didn't want to steal anyone's shifts just because I wasn't at school. I left a note for Ryan to let him know that if someone called in sick, I was available to cover. As it was, I didn't have a shift until Thursday afternoon, and I could use the extra hours.

I started to leave, figuring that I'd head home, when I saw Gabby in a corner booth at the back of the diner. She was curled up next to Josh. I smiled and walked toward them.

"Hey, cuties." I slid into the opposite side of the booth and the two of them startled with a little jump. There was a plate full of hot fries in front of them, so I assumed they hadn't been here long.

"You're here!" Gabby turned from Josh to give me her full-bodied attention. "Tell us everything!"

"Wait." I watched them both with disbelief. "Are you talking about the suspension?"

"Yes!" Gabby cried with excitement.

"Dray told us what happened." Josh waved his phone at me with a sheepish smile.

"He told us that *you* got suspended . . ." Gabby glanced between me and Josh. "He still hadn't seen the principal and we got no details. I'm *dying* to know. So, come on."

I couldn't help but notice the way they kept referring to themselves as "we" and it was too cute. Due to my good mood at seeing them so happy and adorable, I obliged and delved into the full-length tale of the previous night's adventures.

The entire time that I was talking Gabby's expression morphed from joy to shock to admiration back to shock and more joy. The only part that I left out of the story was the almost kiss because I didn't think the entire diner wanted to hear Gabby shrieking like a banshee. Josh looked interested, albeit a little less so than Gabby, but behind that interest I saw a small knowing smirk, and I was beginning to become intrigued by what he knew that I didn't.

"That all sounds so romantic," Gabby sighed. She rested her head in her hands with an infatuated gaze.

"It wasn't romantic," I dismissed her fantasies. "It was fun, and exciting, and that's all it was meant to be. And that's what it was."

"Oh . . . I get it." Gabby nodded with dramatic flare. "We'll talk about it later."

She jabbed her thumb in Josh's direction, assuming that he was the reason I was still denying that it was more than it was. I let her think that the conversation would be continued later, but I'd tell her the same thing then too. I was well aware that I'd developed feelings. Heart-pounding, throat-thickening, stomach-twisting sort of feelings. But I wasn't ready to say it out loud. That would make it real, and I didn't want it to be real when I barely understood it myself.

"I'm just going to run to the bathroom," Gabby said. "Sure you don't want to come, Dallas?"

I laughed and said no. When Gabby disappeared, Josh and I were alone. The fries that had been making my mouth water were finally out of her sight, so I didn't waste a moment and stole a handful.

"How's thing's, Josh?" I asked.

"Good." He smiled, but the affection he'd previously regarded me with was gone, which I was grateful for. His adoring smile was purely reserved for Gabby now. It was nice to be on good, friendly terms.

"Hey, I just want to say thanks." Josh leaned his forearms on the table in front of him. "Gabby is great and I'm glad that you introduced us."

"Really?" I bit a fry and watched him with excitement. "I know she likes you a lot."

"She's full of energy and has a positive outlook on everything. I'm glad that we told each other how we feel and didn't waste any time doing it."

His tone caught me off guard, and I looked up from the fries in my hand to notice the pointed look that he was giving me. I didn't like where this conversation was going.

"You and Dray obviously like each other," he added.

"Oh, not you too," I groaned and sank back into the seat. "Now you're a little team with your assumptions and observations."

"I don't think that they're incorrect."

"What makes you say that?"

Gabby, with ever-impeccable timing, fell back into the booth beside Josh, promptly stopping him from sharing any more information. I had the feeling that he was going to stay tight lipped on the matter anyway.

"Did you eat some of our fries?" She eyed the bowl before her accusatory glare fell on me.

"I sure did," I confessed.

We spent a few hours at the diner, chatting about this and that, eating more fries, and drinking milk shakes.

"We're going to catch a movie," Gabby said, taking off her glasses to clean them. "Do you want to come along?"

"This is as far as my third wheeling's going to take me. You guys can give me a ride home, though. Nathan has the car."

"You don't need to give me that look; of course I'll give you a ride," Gabby said. "Are you sure you don't want to come to the movies with us?"

"I'm sure. Trust me, I don't need to sit next to you guys while you make out the entire time."

"If we wanted to do that, we'd watch a movie at home." Gabby snorted as we got into the Jeep. Josh nodded his head in agreement. "Going to the movies is expensive. I want to get my money's worth while I'm there."

"*That* is a good point," I said.

When we pulled up next to the sidewalk outside of my house, I was surprised to see Drayton on the driveway, leaning on his bike with his cell phone in hand. He'd obviously gone home and changed because he was now wearing a pair of black joggers, a white tank top, a light denim jacket, and a thin silver chain around his neck. As hard as I tried, little flutters of excitement messed with my stomach, and it only got worse when he looked toward the car and smiled.

"Why is Dray here?" Gabby asked a little more casually than I'd heard her speak when she had referred to him in the past. I supposed now that she had her own hottie now, she didn't need to fangirl every time Drayton Lahey was in the vicinity.

"I have no idea." I opened the door and climbed out of the Jeep. "Thanks for the ride, Josh."

He honked the horn when he pulled away from the curb, and I waved as I walked through the gate and approached Drayton. I was surprised that he was allowed out of the house. I wondered what his consequences were.

"Hey, what are you doing here?"

"I thought I'd come see how you are." He stood up straighter and slid his phone into his pocket. "Are you upset about being suspended?"

"I feel like I should be, and usually I would be." I laughed awkwardly because the fact that I wasn't upset was startling even to me. "It was worth it. I'm trying not to think about how this is going to look on my record."

"Yeah. Same."

I winced. "You, too, huh? I thought your mom and dad might have been able to wiggle you out of trouble."

"They tried," he said, slipping his hands into his pockets. "I didn't let them, though. We deserved the same punishment and that's what I got."

"You willingly got suspended?" I stared at him with disbelief.

"Suspension isn't so bad." He shrugged with a cavalier attitude. "Expulsion is worse."

"I don't even want to think about getting expelled. No CalArts for sure, then. Do you want to come inside?"

"I do."

We headed inside and shuffled through to my bedroom so that I could ditch my shoes and open my windows. Drayton sat down on the bed and let his eyes wander aimlessly over the space.

The only other time that he'd been in here, he'd stayed at the door, and back then my feelings toward him were less than hospitable. Now seeing him in here, on my bed, looking care-free and gorgeous as always, I couldn't help but feel as though he made the room seem ten times smaller. His presence was so overwhelming, so dominating, and if I was being honest, a little bit suffocating.

"What are you going to do with your time off?" he asked.

"I went to work to put in for some more shifts, but there weren't any available." I shrugged and leaned against my dresser. "I suppose I'll study, maybe, Netflix will probably win. Definitely do some cheer and dance practice. Emily isn't going to be happy about me missing practice all week."

"She'll live." He narrowed his curious stare. "Essentially, you've got the next week free?"

"Technically, I'm not obligated to be anywhere."

He nodded his head with thought. "Want to go to California with me?"

"I'm sorry, what?" His suggestion had been so casual and nonchalant that I was sure he had to be joking. "You're kidding?"

"No." He stood up and walked toward me. "We've both got a week off school. Why not do something with it?"

"For one, I can't afford to just up and hop on a flight to California. Second, my brother is super pissed about the suspension and wouldn't even consider letting me go."

"I can afford the tickets and a place for us to stay," he scoffed with amusement as though I was ridiculous for not assuming that he'd pay for the entire trip. "Also, he's your brother. Not your dad. You're almost eighteen."

"Wait, how can you even go to California? Aren't you in trouble?"

"Not so much." He shrugged. "My parents don't care all that much as long as I'm playing ball, getting scouted, and going to Baylor."

"Why? Why do you want to go to California with me? Is there nothing else that you would rather be doing?"

"The boys still have school and Josh works. I'll be bored. You're the only one who's free."

How flattering. His life didn't revolve around me, but did he have to make it sound so last resort?

"I can't, Dray." I turned around and busied myself with the trinkets on my dresser.

"I'll take you to visit your dance college."

He knew how to get me. "I mean . . . when would we be leaving?"

"Right now. Come on, I'll help you pack."

CHAPTER 11

Flight 5367 from Colorado Springs to Los Angeles, California, now boarding. Final call for flight 5367 from Colorado Springs to Los Angeles, California.

Drayton picked up my carry-on luggage, and the two of us moved into line with our boarding passes in hand. The cell phone in my back pocket vibrated for the seventh time—Nathan again, I was sure—he had probably read the note that I'd left behind.

"Maybe I should talk to him before I get on the plane?"

"No way, Cheer, he'll talk you out of going. We'll call him when we land."

We shuffled forward so the flight attendant could scan our boarding passes before we stepped into the wide tunnel that led to the plane. I thought back to the brief message I'd scrawled after packing my bags as quickly as I could and winced with regret.

"I probably should have left a better note."

*Hey Nathan. Gone to Cali to visit CalArts. Be back in a
couple days. Love ya.*

"If you're going to call him, be quick. We have to switch our
phones to flight mode soon."

"No, you're right. I'll call him when we get there."

We found our row, and I didn't even offer Drayton the window seat. I pushed past him and dived into it so fast that he
almost tripped over his own feet. He gave me a look of concern
and then sat down beside me.

"Sorry, I've always wanted to sit in the window seat if I got
the chance," I explained with my eyes on the tarmac outside.

"Is this your first time on a plane?"

I wasn't embarrassed at the fact, but it was definitely a little
heat inducing to admit that I'd never flown before.

"Damn, Cheer," he smiled, then lifted our bags into the overhead compartment. "You excited?"

"I'm pretty excited."

"First time." He sat down and leaned in close. "Don't worry,
then, it'll be great. It always is with me."

His heated gaze turned me inside out, and being in such close
proximity to his lips reminded me how close we'd been to kissing
last night. We hadn't talked about it. And I didn't see the need
to bring it up if the unspoken agreement was to pretend as if it
had never happened.

He leaned back in his seat and got comfortable. For the dura-
tion of the flight we talked about his past flights. He told me
what it was like in a private jet and in first class. He appreciated
it, but he'd done it so much that it no longer held the thrill that
it had when he was a child.

He talked about his time in California. Now that I knew about his father's time in the NFL, he could tell me about the games that he'd attended, watching from the VIP boxes, meeting the teams, and being gifted the game ball if it survived the winning touchdown. I loved listening to him talk. He had a smooth voice and a great smile. When he told a tale, I hung on his every word.

When we arrived at LAX, it was just after five o'clock—just after six back at home. I was glad that Drayton knew his way around because I would have been lost if I was alone. The airport was huge. I had never seen anything like it before. We passed what I would call a mall, right there in the airport, and exited from just one set of electronic doors out of dozens. The sky was clouded, overcast, and it looked as if it might rain. The enormous *LAX* letters were illuminated, and there was a long line of cabs waiting for passengers.

We stood on the path and Drayton dropped his bag before he pulled his phone out of his pocket. "We'll order an Uber. It's cheaper. Where are we going?"

He looked up expectantly, his thumbs paused on the screen.

"Oh—um . . . I don't know. You're the one who knows the area."

"Well, where's CalArts?"

"Valencia."

He turned back to his cell phone again and I people watched while he did whatever it was that he was doing. There was a lot going on, but the place was too enormous to feel crowded.

"That's an hour from here," he said after a moment. "How about we stay somewhere close tonight and head there in the morning?"

I nodded in agreement and waited once again while he completed ordering the Uber. There were dozens of them close, so it only took about three minutes before we could see it inching through the line of traffic coming and going from the pick-up zone.

We greeted the driver as Drayton pushed our bags to one side of the backseat and we slid in beside them.

"What hotel did you find?" I asked.

"Fairfield Inn," he said, getting comfortable in the middle seat. "It's about a mile from here."

I was relieved because the need to eat and wind down was real. I felt like it had been forever since we were sneaking out of the hotel back in Fort Collins, but in reality it had only been twenty-four hours. In that time, I'd been skinny-dipping, spent the night in a park, been suspended, and let Drayton convince me to board a flight without a single person knowing where I was going or who I was with. It had been a whirlwind, and I could really have used a bed and some down time.

"How was your first time?" Drayton asked, slinging his arm around my shoulders, distracting me from watching the strange urban landscape around the airport.

"It was awesome," I admitted, and remembered that I needed to call Nathan. Although, it wasn't really a conversation that I wanted the Uber driver or Drayton to hear.

Taking a plane for the first time was exactly as I'd expected it to be in the best way. Yes, I did get a hell of a fright when the plane took off down the runway before it ascended. Yes, the turbulence was a little bit unsettling, and my ears became sore and blocked. Other than those two things, it was fun. The views of rolling land, green hills, and bodies of water looked so fascinating from the air. The buildings, homes, and cars that became clear as we slowly descended were so miniature, and I absorbed it all.

I did my best to ignore the intoxicating scent of Drayton's masculine musk and pulled out my cell phone, clearing the home screen of the forty-two missed calls that had accumulated during the flight. I also didn't bother to check the text messages from Nathan, but I did send him *I'm okay!* for peace of mind until I could call him. I did read the messages from Gabby.

> Where are you?! Why'd Nathan ring me saying that you've left the country with Dray?

> Oi text back.

> Girl your brother is losing his shit.

> Never mind. Just talked to Josh. He said you and Dray went to CalArts for a few days. I'm literally gonna hit you for not telling me when you get back. But as your best friend, please utilize this time and get you some Dray. Wanna hear all about it when you get back x

I quietly groaned and locked the phone, sliding it into the front pocket of my bag. I didn't even want to look at Drayton to find out if he'd seen that message. Although, my guess was, he had. I was saved from the internal pain when the Uber finally pulled up at our destination and I could untangle myself from Drayton's clutches.

The hotel was nice. It wasn't a five-star, but it was definitely nicer than anything I'd stayed in before. A light timber and blue theme ran through the foyer, with a few quirky but classy couches set up on the dark carpet. Large potted plants occupied the corners of the room and lights with intricate shades hung from the ceiling. Drayton took care of booking the room while I took a much-needed breather and sat on a couch.

When he was finished making the arrangements, we hopped on the elevator and went up to the fourth floor. We found our room around the bend of the corridor. It was much more spacious than our Fort Collins rooms. A sliding door on the far-left wall led out to a patio. What I assumed was a bathroom was on the far-right wall, and in the middle of the room was one king-sized bed.

"Why didn't you book a room with two double beds?" I asked as Drayton dropped our bags at the foot of the bed.

"Thought I'd save money where I can." He grinned as he sat down on the edge of the bed, and I resisted the urge to slap the smug smile off his face. "It's only for one night."

"Mhmm, and what about the other three nights?"

"I'll probably do the same at the next hotel too." He laughed as I rolled my eyes. "Oh come on, we've shared a bed before. You'll be fine."

"You won't be. I'm going to smother you."

He got up and walked around to the bedside table, shuffling through the drawer as he spoke.

"Your threats don't scare me. Here"—he passed me a laminated booklet—"order some room service. I'm going to take a shower. I'll eat anything."

"Mhmm." I flicked the booklet open and said in a teasing tone, "I bet."

His brows shot up and he shook his head with amusement. "You on the menu?"

"As if."

He laughed and turned around, pulling his shirt off as he left. The bathroom door closed, and I sat down on the edge of the bed, menu in hand. The tension between us was getting thicker. How was I supposed to get through almost an entire week of hotel rooms and bed sharing with him?

After I'd used the bedside phone to call reception and order more food than was needed, I shuffled through the front pocket of my bag and found my cell phone. There were more missed calls from Nathan, but before I could call him back, the bathroom door opened and Drayton sauntered out in a towel.

His body glistened from steam and water, his tattoo shone from the moisture, and his hair was in a disheveled state. I almost lost my appetite entirely as a craving for something else took over.

"What'd you order?" He wandered across the room toward his bag, seemingly unaware of the effect that he was having on me. It was worse every time I saw him like this.

"Heaps."

He waited for me to elaborate but my brain had gone on hiatus. He pulled a handful of clothes out of his duffel bag and started back to the bathroom.

"Were you about to call your brother?" he asked, gesturing his head toward the cell phone in my hand. I was reminded of the daunting task that I had been contemplating before Drayton walked out of the bathroom looking like a damn main dish.

"Oh yeah." I stood up. "I'm going to go outside and call him. You don't need to hear the inevitable dispute."

I stood on the patio and slid the glass door closed. I could see the LAX sign from where I stood. Cars moved across the highway, the lights blurring together. Palm trees lined the sidewalk below, and I did my best to soak in the nice breeze without the stress of my impending phone call bringing me down. It was still overcast and was becoming darker with grey clouds, but it wasn't cold. When I finally dialed Nathan's number, I barely heard the ringing next to my ear because my senses were flooded with nerves and my heart pounded.

"Dallas!" His voice boomed through the line before the call had rung more than twice. "Tell me that note was a joke and you're still in Colorado at the very least."

"Not exactly . . ."

"If you ran off to Vegas to marry that kid, I'll literally kill you both."

"Are you out of your mind? I did not run off to Vegas to get married. I'm in California. I'm visiting CalArts. You know I've always wanted to, and the opportunity came up, so I took it."

There was silence on the other end of the line. We both waited for a moment.

"You mean that kid with all of the money just so happened to get you both suspended and then conveniently offered to take you to California. Sounds like a setup."

"You're being paranoid. And I already told you, it's my fault we got suspended. Drayton was going to California to check out some colleges while he's suspended, so I asked him to bring me."

"You can't just take off to California and leave a note. I've been worried about you all afternoon."

"You don't need to worry. I'm perfectly safe, and I'll be home on Wednesday. I've got to work on Thursday, anyway."

"In the future, could you at least pretend to respect my authority? I know that I'm not Mom or Dad, but it's my job to keep you safe. Don't make it so hard."

"I'm sorry, I should have talked to you about it before I left."

"Can you please call me if you need me? And don't get pregnant."

"Nathan," I gasped with embarrassment. "*Good-bye.*"

When I walked back inside, Drayton was kicking the door shut with his foot, a tray of steaming hot food in each hand. Fried chicken. Fries. Potatoes and gravy, burgers, and more. But the best part of the picture was that he was only wearing a pair of low-hanging sweats and no shirt. He looked so good. He looked too good.

This is literal torture.

"Hungry?"

He grinned as he sauntered toward the table, and his biceps bulged as he carried the food.

∧

"I am literally so full." There was a thud when I slid off the chair beside the table and landed on the carpeted floor. "I cannot afford to eat like that."

"Me neither," Drayton admitted with amusement. "But it was worth it. That was good."

"You're not even bloated. It's unfair. My shorts definitely need to be undone. Go and put a shirt on. You're making me feel tubby."

"You're not tubby." He stood up and piled the plates up so that he could put them on the room-service tray outside. I helped him and after we'd left the dishes out in the corridor, we walked back inside, and I frowned at the rain pattering on the sliding door. It wouldn't last long, though.

"I need water," I said and headed for the cabinet to retrieve a glass.

"Same," Drayton said. "How come you didn't order soda or something with dinner?"

"I have no idea," I laughed, closing the cabinet behind me. I filled the glass, chugged it down, and left it in the sink.

As Drayton moved behind me to open the cabinet, I turned to walk back to the table, and we bumped into each other. His large firm body pushed me against the countertop, and I put my arms behind me on the lip of the counter to steady myself. I leaned away from him.

"Sorry, Cheer." His expression was hard to read as it moved over me.

Despite the apology, he remained where he was, his hands coming to rest beside mine on the countertop, leaving me effectively encased between his arms. He leaned over, putting himself at eye level. His breath fanned me. It was muddling me to have him so close.

There was a reason that he got who he wanted into bed, whenever he wanted them. He hadn't said a word and all I wanted to do was wrap myself around him and come undone under his touch.

"Want to play a game, Cheer?"

"Is this going to be some cheesy 'I bet I can get you to sleep with me' game?"

"What? No," he said. "I just thought that we could kill some time with a game of truth or dare. Unless *you* want to do something else?"

I knew exactly what he was thinking, and for a moment I was tempted to go along with it. No one would ever know. We could both have some fun in California, go home, and pretend as though nothing had ever happened. But even I knew that wasn't realistic. This thing between us had gone beyond physical. I could admit that much. Sleeping together would only make it worse.

I smiled with a small shrug. "Truth or dare sounds great."

"Perfect."

Our gazes remained on one another for several agonizing moments. I hadn't realized how breathless he made me. But when there was more than a foot of space between us again, my shoulders relaxed.

We sat on the bed facing each other with legs crossed. We'd searched through the drawers for a coin but had come up with nothing. That was until Drayton found an old Canadian coin from a vacation at the bottom of his duffel bag. I focused on keeping my gaze above his shoulders. It was a lot harder than it sounded when all that was in front of me was pure muscle.

We flipped the coin and I won, which meant that I got to ask first. I considered daring him to do something immature. Like getting naked on the patio. But I knew that he'd fire back some joke about how if I wanted to see him naked all I had to do was ask.

"Okay, truth or dare?"

"Dare," he responded without hesitation. Of course. He was so closed off, I would never expect him to willingly walk into potentially opening up to me.

"I dare you to call reception and ask if they have any blow-up dolls, because you're feeling lonely."

His eyes widened in surprise as he straightened up. "Dammit." He ran a hand through his hair as a light laugh escaped him. "You're good."

He moved off the bed and picked up the phone, quickly dialing down to reception. "Hello?" I heard a muffled response on the other end before Drayton met my eyes, his glimmering with amusement as he delved into the humiliating request.

"I was just curious as to whether you have any overnight companions that I can hire? Particularly of the plastic variety?

"No, no! Not a Barbie-looking prostitute." He steadied his voice, which threatened to crack with laughter. I was having a hard time containing mine. "I meant like blow-up dolls. Do you have any? I'm a lonely guy but I detest conversation. I left mine at home."

I buried my head in the pillow, my body racked with uncontrollable laughter. Hearing that entire sentence come out of his mouth without so much as a smile from his face was by far the funniest thing that I had ever seen. I regretted not taking a video, to be honest. I peeked up at him and saw that he was curled over with the phone held at arm's length.

"Okay. Thank you. No, that's fine, I understand." He adopted his serious demeanor again when he brought the phone back to his ear. "Totally fine, sir. I guess it's just me and my hand tonight. Okay. You too. Good night."

He hung up the phone and we burst into loud, side-splitting, ugly laughter. The bed bounced as he fell onto it, his gorgeous eyes curled up at the corners as they glistened with tears of laughter. I could feel the moisture in my own eyes as well, and we continued falling victim to the hilarity for quite some time before it died down.

"That was good. I'll give you that." Drayton sat back up and crossed his legs again as his laughter subsided and he rubbed his hands together. "Tomorrow is going to be an awkward checkout."

"For sure, but they've probably had weirder requests. Let's be real."

"True. My turn. Truth or dare, Cheer?"

"Truth."

"Playing it safe, huh?" I had to admit, I was a little terrified of what he would come up with for a dare. "Okay. What's your sexual weakness? What turns you on more than anything else?"

I took a deep breath. "I like being kissed with passion. Like, push me against the wall, hold my neck, tangle your hands in my hair, and crush me kind of kissing. I also kind of love having my hair pulled during actual sex."

I looked up from the bedspread that I'd been absentmindedly playing with while I spoke to find Drayton staring at me with an intense gaze and wide eyes. He shifted slightly and shook his head as he cleared his throat. The boy looked like an animal staring at his prey and I got the feeling that my description may have got his blood pumping a little.

"Y-Yeah. Sounds good," he finally mumbled and shifted his hips again. "Your turn."

I watched him curiously as he shook off the discomfort and fell back into his carefree, smug-looking, shirtless self.

"Truth or dare?"

"Truth," he responded, much to my surprise. I hadn't been expecting him to say that, so I took a minute to come up with a question.

"What's the tattoo mean?" I asked, gesturing my head toward his right arm.

His lazy smile remained set in place but I took note of the brief flinch in his features. I wasn't entirely sure what it meant—if it was sadness or anger.

"It's just a tattoo." He shrugged. "Doesn't have a meaning."

I looked at the winding road that stretched from his wrist to his shoulder with suspicion. You could say the scattered items on either side of the road weren't such a mysterious concept. Dead flowers and skulls weren't uncommon in body art. The little boy and girl at the end of the road who were walking off into the sunset, though—there was meaning behind it. I knew there was.

"Really? It means nothing? It's just something you liked so much that you got it tattooed on your skin forever?"

"Exactly." His smile was dazzling and he sat up a little taller. "All right, my turn."

I desperately wanted him to open up to me. I wished he knew that he could trust me.

"Truth or dare?"

I did my best to push the hurt aside and focused on the fun we'd been having before.

"Dare," I answered.

His smile became devious and full of intent, and I regretted being brave before he'd even opened his mouth.

"I dare you to kiss me."

"What?"

"You heard." He leaned forward. "Kiss me."

"Why?"

"What do you mean, why?" He laughed. "Because it's a dare and if you back out, I win. Which you will."

He was so smug. Smug smile. I laughed and turned my head toward the window where the rain pelted on the sliding door.

"Fine." I turned back to him with a sweet smile. "But only if we can do it in the rain."

"Why in the rain?"

"Because I've always wanted to have a cinematic rain kiss," I confessed with a light laugh. "It's not the sort of thing that gets planned. And I'm being opportunistic."

"All right." He stood up fast and gave me a light slap on the leg. "Come on."

We stood in front of each other on the patio, eyes narrowed because of the downpour. It was dark but the motel lights shone down on us.

Drayton stepped forward but I took a step back. "We need to get wet first."

"Cheer, we don't need the rain for that."

I scoffed with amusement and pushed my hair back. It was sopping now and clung to my back and neck. Droplets rolled down his firm chest. His hair caught beads and I hated how stupid good he looked in the rain. Another few moments passed, and Drayton's gaze traveled over me. My shirt and shorts were drenched and clinging to me.

Out of the blue, Drayton started shouting. His expression was etched with pain and passion, and he pointed his finger at the ground while he stared at me and screamed about sending me hundreds of letters. I was confused for a moment until I recognized it as dialogue from *The Notebook*.

"You're a clown." I shoved him in the chest and he started laughing. I wasn't sure how to feel about the fact that he could quote such a romance classic.

The rain was strong. Our eyes never wavered. He looked out of this world with his wet olive skin and broad shoulders. Water shimmered in the crevices of his sculpted torso and I swallowed, deciding to give up on this weird idea.

I turned to walk inside, but his fingers wrapped around my wrist and his other hand grasped my neck and then our wet bodies were pressed together and his mouth was on mine.

It was unreal.

He pried my lips apart and his fingertips dug into my neck, pulling at the hair behind my ears. My hands slid into his wet hair and he dropped his hold on my wrist, moving his hand to my waist instead.

Rain pelted our cheeks and our lips didn't detach, but Drayton backed me up against the wall beside the sliding door, and I tugged his hair while he held me tight around the middle with both hands. It was a great kiss. His chest was against mine, and his entire body felt so good that it made me weak.

Too weak. He was quicksand. He was dangerous and I knew that the little niggling of emotion that I felt toward him would be so much stronger if we were to go further. I savored the last moment or two, kissing him while my hands moved down his neck, onto his shoulders, and to his chest, where I gave him a light push.

He stopped and stepped back. Flecks of water showered from his lips with his heavy breaths. When I realized that my hands were still on his chest, I let them drop and they slapped against my wet sides. That was an earth-shattering, cinematic kiss; it felt as if the clouds would clear and the stars would align.

"You're a good kisser," he murmured, his gaze lingering on my tender lips for a touch longer than was subtle.

I inhaled and pushed my hair back. It had become matted where Drayton had held it, but it was worth it. I smiled and pulled the sliding door open, peeping over my shoulder as I stepped inside. "I guess I won."

He laughed, then ran a hand through his hair as rain continued to pitter patter against his firm chest and shoulders. "Game isn't over, Cheer."

CHAPTER 12

I woke up before Drayton. Once again, his sleeping concerned me on a number of levels, and I checked his pulse to make sure he hadn't died. He lay on his stomach, his tan back on full display because the sheet only just reached the top of his hips.

Last night's kiss had been playing on repeat in my mind since it happened. We'd continued playing the game, and things had ultimately returned to normal between us, but I couldn't stop thinking about it. My gaze traveled over the dips and crevices of his back, which was rising and falling deeply and slowly.

I figured that I'd use the time while he was asleep to get ready for the day. We'd decided last night that we would go to the college campus and scope out what sort of information or tour would be available on a Sunday without previous arrangement. The whole trip had been last minute, so I wasn't going to expect a lot. I got up and showered, changing into a pair of denim high-waisted shorts and a thin long-sleeved cropped shirt. I pulled my wet hair into a bun on the top of my head and put some makeup on.

When I came out of the bathroom refreshed, I found Drayton sitting on the edge of the bed, still in last night's sweats with his cell phone in hand.

I picked up my duffel and started shoving things into it. "Everything okay?"

"Yeah," he sighed, getting to his feet as he threw the phone onto the bed and fluffed his hair. "My mom's just flipping out because she saw my credit card statement online saying that I'm in California and not Dallas, where I said I was going."

"I thought that you were allowed to do what you want?"

"To an extent." He shrugged with a cavalier attitude. "I did say that I was visiting family friends in Dallas. They'll get over it."

I sighed but didn't comment. His parents, his business. "Checkout is in an hour. Want me to see how long for an Uber while you shower?"

"Sure." He sauntered toward me with a devious grin. "Unless you want to join me?"

"Ugh." I shoved his chest so he stepped back. "Go and have a shower."

The little curl in his lips and the gleam in his gaze made me weak at the knees. He was just too damn attractive for his own good.

⚡

"Maybe I should apply to this college." Drayton watched a leggy, toned girl with caramel-colored skin strut past us in a sports bra and gym shorts. She was one of the many model-looking babes strolling through the campus courtyard.

I scoffed with amusement. "Don't worry, I'll get on with

looking around so that you can go and pick up all the girls who will fall at your feet."

"Are you jealous, Cheer?"

We walked toward the administration building on the other side of the quad.

"Get a grip." Even I noticed the lack of denial.

When we'd arrived in Valencia, the first thing we'd done was book a hotel for the night. It was a lot smaller than where we'd stayed last night, but absolutely gorgeous and resort-like. Drayton had covered most of the costs so far, but I used my account for the Uber and had paid for last night's room service. I'd tucked into a little of my savings before we left, knowing that it wouldn't be right to let Drayton pay for absolutely everything. Even if he did insist.

"This place is amazing." I glanced around the administration office with awe. There were large blown-up photos all over the walls of performers, dancers, actors. The space was made up of a reception desk in the middle of the room and there were doors leading off, to other offices no doubt. A leather couch and coffee table made up a waiting area and there was an assortment of magazines on a little shelf.

"There's no one here," Drayton noted as we glanced around the deserted space.

"Maybe we can come back tomorrow?" I suggested. "There's no point looking around if I'm not getting to see how things actually operate."

"We can come back whenever you want. We've got until Wednesday."

"You don't want to spend the whole time in Valencia, do you?" We headed back out the doors we'd come through and the warm air left me with a craving for the beach—a real Californian beach.

"Not if we don't have to." Drayton slipped his sunglasses on and slung an arm over my shoulders as we walked across the quad. I couldn't help but feel a little elated at the stares that we received from a few scattered girls practicing dance or rehearsing skits in the sunshine. "If we look around tomorrow then we can go to Hollywood? It's only forty-five minutes from here."

"Ohh!" I gasped and glanced up at him. "I've always wanted to see the Walk of Fame."

"Done." He grinned. "Hollywood it is. Guess I'll have to make sure that I find us a good frat party tonight."

"Oh geez," I mumbled, quite content with movies in the hotel room for the evening.

"Think of it as getting some precollege experience in. At least you'll know what you're in for."

"I'll try anything once. Might as well do it while I have you here as a buffer."

He laughed and I watched him. How couldn't I? He had the most beautiful laugh and the crescent shape that his eyes made when his cheeks lifted was perfect.

"But I mean, now that I think about it, I've been to house parties before. It won't exactly be a *new* experience."

"You've never been to a college party though," he informed me. "Trust me, they're in a league of their own. I'll show you the ropes, Cheer."

"What would I do without you?"

"Hey, excuse me!"

We stopped and turned around to see a lean guy with chocolate-brown waves jogging toward us. He was wearing a black tank top that had *CalArts* written in graffiti font across the front of it and a pair of joggers. "Hey, sorry, are you two new around here?"

"Sort of," I answered, giving him a subtle once over. He had to be a dancer. His build was incredible, and his deep-brown eyes were mesmerizing. "I'm hoping to come here next year. We're just looking around. I'm Dallas."

"Oh, beautiful name. I'm from Dallas, actually." I thought I'd heard a mild southern twang. "I'm Cooper."

He offered Drayton his hand, who slowly unwrapped his arm from my shoulders and gave Cooper's waiting hand a sturdy shake. "Drayton."

"Nice to meet you, man," Cooper smiled a wide pearly smile, but when I looked up at Drayton, he was scowling. God, he was so rude. "I stopped you guys after I saw you coming out of administration. I'm a tour guide around here. Sort of a friendly face for the newbies. I'd be happy to show you around?"

"We were actually thinking of coming back tomorrow while the classes are going," I told him with hesitation. I didn't want to seem ungrateful. "Just so I can see it in real time."

"That's a great idea." He snapped his fingers and I couldn't help but smile at his jovial attitude. "Where are you from?"

"Castle Rock, Colorado," I informed him.

"Oh nice." He looked at Drayton and didn't seem bothered at the frown he received in return. "Are you applying too?"

"Nope."

"Drayton plays football." I glared at him before I turned back to Cooper and attempted to keep Drayton's mood from spoiling mine. "He's holding out to get scouted."

"Oh dude, UCLA is, like, half an hour away." Cooper

slapped the side of Drayton's arm with excitement. Drayton slowly glanced down at the spot Cooper's hand had just been and stared at it with boredom. "It's not a long commute at all. At least you wouldn't have to do the long-distance thing."

"Oh. No," I laughed and glanced at Drayton, who was still seeming entirely unfazed by the conversation. "Drayton and I are just friends."

"I'll be going to Baylor," Drayton said dryly.

"Oh, Baylor. Nice. My cousin went there," Cooper told an uninterested Drayton before he turned back to me. "Why don't I get your number and we can meet up tomorrow. I'll show you around, give you a little tour?"

"That sounds perfect," Drayton interjected, pulling his phone out of his pocket with a sudden peak of enthusiasm. "You can have *my* number and if there are any parties happening around here tonight, let me know about those too."

Cooper cast an uncertain glance between me and Drayton, no doubt hoping that I would interrupt before he actually had to give Drayton his cell phone. I should have interrupted because Drayton's weird behavior was doing my head in. But I couldn't. I just stood there and watched the awkward digit exchange. It might have been because I was so enthralled at the prospect of Drayton being jealous that I was rendered stupid.

"Parties, huh?" Cooper cast his gaze down to the pavement with thought as he slid his cell phone back into his pocket. "Oh, perfect." He snapped his fingers and glanced over at a group of girls doing a series of hip-hop moves. "Carrie! Anything on tonight?"

The entire group looked our way with curiosity and obvious

admiration for the quarterback standing beside me. He was sort of hard not to notice. The girl, Carrie, I assumed, nodded her fire-red head before she shouted back, "James is hosting talent week. Starts tonight!"

"What's talent week?" I asked.

"It's basically who can drink the most and still be standing at the end of the night." Cooper rolled his eyes. "Everyone goes to drink but most don't participate. There are a few guys who do it subtlety among themselves. Beer pong, keg stands, card games. That sort of thing. There's a winner at the end of the week for whoever was last man standing the most nights of the week."

"That sounds ideal." Drayton grinned and nudged me with his elbow. "I'll text you later for the address, Coop." He slapped Cooper's shoulder and then reestablished my spot beneath his arm, giving Cooper a small wave. "See you tonight."

"O-Okay, yeah," Cooper mumbled as Drayton all but dragged me in the other direction. "Nice to meet you both!"

"What was all that about?" I removed Drayton's arm from my shoulders when we hit the path outside of the college campus.

"What do you mean? I was just abiding by friend code." He lit a cigarette but I didn't bother commenting on it. I did wonder why he might be anxious. "You know, some creepy guy hits on you, and I step in to save you from the awkwardness of rejecting him. You're welcome."

"Who said I wanted to reject him?"

He turned his head toward me with eyes wide, and a large puff of toxic smoke blew directly into my face. "Him? You're into that? He's so scrawny."

"He's lean, Drayton. There's a difference." I waved the smoke away from my face and pressed the pedestrian button when we stopped at an intersection. "And he seemed really nice. It wouldn't hurt to have some potential lined up before I move here."

When the cars came to a stop on either side of the intersection and the little man signaled our turn, we crossed the road along with the rest of the foot traffic. "I'll find you better potential, Cheer. I'll wingman you tonight. Trust me. You can do better."

"You'll have time to find me a guy while you're busy chatting up all of the hot dancers who will be there tonight?"

"I'm a man of many talents," he boasted. I didn't bother to dignify his egotistical nonsense and instead stopped in front of a sandwich shop that smelled incredible.

"Should we get some lunch?"

"I could eat."

He opened the door for me and gestured that I lead. His occasional moments of chivalry never ceased to surprise me. "We can go back to our room for dessert."

His smug grin was shit eating. But it didn't surprise me.

Nor did it disappoint me. His crude sense of humor and inability to filter himself was one of my favorite things about him. It was part of the reason that I would trust him so much later on that evening.

"How do I look?" I walked out of the hotel bathroom wearing a black bandage crop top and a pair of high-waisted champagne-colored shorts. They were a silky fabric and complimented the summer tan that I'd developed over the recent months.

Drayton glanced up from his cell phone. He was sitting on the edge of the bed in his own nighttime attire. His signature look didn't differ but even I had to admit that he looked mighty fine in a pair of slim black jeans and a navy-blue V-neck T-shirt that hugged his biceps. The seams stretched as he leaned his elbows on his knees.

His eyes landed on my body and, as I waited for a little bit of shameless validation, they not so subtlety swept my frame from head to toe. A lusty expression filled his face and I felt about two feet tall.

A small grin lifted his lips as he ran a hand through his hair. "Wow," he chuckled lightly and stood up. The fluttering in my chest became even more erratic and I shifted from foot to foot. "You'll have no trouble landing a California guy tonight, Cheer."

The temptation to suggest that the Colorado boy in front of me would do just fine was real, but instead I pushed my hair behind my shoulder and smiled. "Thanks. Do you have the address?"

"Yep." He waved his phone at me while I slipped into my black ankle boots. I was surprisingly excited about tonight.

We double checked that we had everything and then headed downstairs to the Uber. The party was being held at student housing, which was about five minutes from the campus.

When we pulled up in front of the two-story house, there were people everywhere. If this was what a Sunday-night party looked like, then I couldn't even imagine how things got on a Saturday night. Red cups, beer bottles, and caps littered the entire front lawn. Broken furniture spilled from the front deck, and there was a worn-out old couch that I thought might have been doused in gas smack in the middle of the grass.

That was concerning.

The music was loud when we were in the Uber, and once we

got out, it only got worse. Or better. Depended what kind of mood you were in. Personally, I was into it.

We were greeted from all directions as we made our way into the house. It didn't seem to matter that no one knew who we were. Slurred "hello"s and "hey"s were thrown our way from drunken college kids.

"Everyone's super friendly!" I shouted over the music.

It was crowded inside the house, so making it to the kitchen looked like it was going to take a while. Suddenly, an enthusiastic boy jumped in front of us and lifted his hands in the air. "CALARTS FUCKING TALENT WEEK!"

As quick as he'd appeared, he was gone again, but I could hear him shouting the same thing over and over again as he moved through the living area.

"A participant, I suppose?"

We kept walking in search of something to drink. My small size left me vulnerable to being trampled and pushed around. Even the odd elbow got me in the side of the face. Drayton slipped his arm around my waist and pulled me against his side, acting almost as a human shield, and quickened our pace toward the kitchen. I was grateful because at this rate, I'd have been knocked unconscious before I'd even had the chance to throw back one beverage.

When we got to the kitchen, I took note of its enormous size. The actual appliance side was relatively average, but the dining area was large enough to have a beer-pong game set up, and dozens of people watched the match. At the end of the room was a sliding door that led to a backyard where, of course, there were multitudes more people.

Drayton, with his arm around my middle, leaned in close. "Beer? Or should we have some vodka shots?"

"I want to play that!" I pointed at the beer-pong table and gave him a determined nod. "Doubles?"

"I don't know, Cheer. I'm a seasoned beer-pong player. I can only have the best of the best on my team."

Just then Cooper appeared beside me and placed one hand on my shoulder, while the other cradled a beer. "Hey," he smiled. "You guys made it! Have you had a drink yet?"

"Hey! I was actually suggesting that Dray and I should have a game of beer pong. Apparently, though, I'm not worthy of his team."

"I'll be on your team." He handed me the cup of beer. I reached for it, but it was snatched from Cooper, and I turned around to find Drayton downing it behind me.

"What the hell?"

He threw the cup over his shoulder and glared at Cooper. "Don't accept open drinks from strangers, Cheer."

"If you still want to play,"—Cooper grabbed the girl closest to him, Carrie from the quad—"this is Carrie; she can be on your team, Dray."

She stumbled into Drayton's chest. She was wasted but she stared up at him with goo-goo eyes. "Yes, I can."

It would be a miracle if she could walk in a straight line, let alone throw a little white ball into a cup. I had this.

But as it turned out, it didn't matter what terrible aim Carrie had because Drayton and I became so competitive that Carrie and Cooper got pushed to the side, and the game went from doubles to singles.

We were down to two cups each. Drayton had the game in the beginning. He was so smug about it. But then I began to sink ball after ball, and it surprised me, but I think that the alcohol had a hand in that. Regardless, I was on a roll.

"This is bullshit!" Drayton threw his arms in the air when I landed the ball in his second-to-last cup. "You're cheating."

"As if!" I scoffed. "I have a good arm, remember!"

I was referring to our first meeting, when I'd almost caught a football with my face but impressed him when it landed in my hands instead. He knew it, too, and grinned.

"Drink, Drayton!" Cooper laughed from the sidelines as he cradled an almost unconscious Carrie.

"Shut up, Cooper," Drayton scoffed and poured the cup's contents down his throat after he had plucked the ball out.

He lined up his shot while swallowing his mouthful. He threw the ball at the closest cup and the entire crowd groaned in disappointment when it bounced off the rim. I jumped up and down with excitement because now it was my turn, and I was determined to sink the one that would make me the winner.

The crowd quieted. It didn't make a hell of a lot of difference because the rest of the party was still squealing, yelling, and shouting over the thumping music. But it did add a level of suspense as I lined up my shot and threw the ball, landing it perfectly in Drayton's last cup.

I screamed, my hands flew up, and I jumped up and down, cheering alongside the crowd. Drayton smiled from the other end of the table. He raised his last cup as a toast and mouthed *Congratulations* before he threw it back.

Later on, when it was quiet, I planned on rubbing the win in his face and ensuring that he ate his words of doubt. For now, I smiled back and watched as he wiped his mouth then frowned at something behind me. I didn't get the chance to turn around because I was lifted up at the waist and spun around too fast for someone who'd just drank eight cups of beer.

"That was impressive!" Cooper laughed then set me back on my feet while keeping his arms secured around my waist. We shuffled toward the sliding doors to make room for the next beer-pong match. "I had no idea that you could play like that."

"Neither did I," I admitted. I wasn't sure how I felt about the fact that there was not an inch of space between us. "That was my first time playing."

"For real? Do you want to dance?" His voice was low and his hands slid down my waist, his fingers lacing with mine. He was more confident than he had been when we'd met. I could smell the alcohol on his breath.

"No, she's good," Drayton's voice was followed by an arm that snaked me away from Cooper's hold. "Aren't you, babe?"

This was getting stupid. This had nothing to do with stepping in to save me from the embarrassment of rejecting Cooper. Drayton was just behaving like a jealous twit, and I hated that it made me feel something.

"I thought you guys weren't together . . ." Cooper instinctually took a step back.

"It's complicated." Drayton shrugged. "We're working on a few things."

"Drayton! Sto—"

"Right." Cooper flashed me a sheepish smile then turned to head outside before I could correct the situation. "That's cool. I'll see you both 'round."

He disappeared and I shrugged out of Drayton's embrace. I was a little drunk, but I was sober enough to know that he was drunk, too, and I hoped that this night didn't turn into a disaster because of it.

"What is your problem!?" I gave his chest a slight shove, which seemed to surprise him. "Why do you keep cock blocking me? First Josh, now Cooper—what's going on Dray? What's with the games?"

"You don't have a cock for me to block, Cheer," he drawled and earned a frustrated breath from the nostrils from me. "I'm not even doing anything. You don't seem that interested in him anyway. I'm sure if you were, you wouldn't let me get in the way."

"Just—just shut up and quit it!" I snapped. "I don't do it to you!"

We'd ended up in the corner of the room, shuffled slowly into it as people walked in and out of the sliding door and around the crowded space. I was backed into the corner and, not that he knew a lot about boundaries to begin with, he had truly discarded personal space from his vocab.

"You're supposed to be my wingman tonight, Dray." He was infuriating me, but at the same time I couldn't stop my heart from racing as he got closer, causing everything else around us to fade out. "You're doing a shit job. The point is to *find* someone for me, not scare them off."

"Do you honestly think any of them can make you feel the way I can?" He grabbed my waist and spun me around, pulling my back flush against his front. This was an unexpected turn of events, but the tension immediately overruled any argument that I may have been concocting. "Do you think they know what makes you feel good?"

His voice was low and raspy, but despite our intoxication, it was stable and dominating. His hands moved slowly and purposefully, traveling up from my waist and sliding across the front of my stomach, dancing tantalizingly and gently underneath my chest.

"Do you think that they know that you like this?"

He lifted one of his hands into the hair at the back of my head and tugged on it, while his other hand dragged downward to lift the bottom of my shorts as he rubbed the front of my smooth thigh. My stomach flipped as his hot breath fanned the side of my neck. I tipped my head back and allowed him access. It was too good. All of it was beyond sensual, and I could feel myself coming undone. His touch left a spark, setting fire to my mind.

"I know what you like, Dallas," he growled beside my ear.

The way my name sounded on his lips brought a soft moan from me. Embarrassment wasn't something that I had time to feel because his grip on my hair tightened in response, pulling my head back farther as his other hand wrapped around my wrists. Goose bumps covered my skin as his fingertips grazed the length of my sides and he peppered soft, toothy kisses along my bare shoulder and neck. "None of them can make you feel this way, Dallas."

He spun me around and slammed me against the wall, his face hovering a mere inch from my own, and every part of my body ached for him. I could barely form coherent thoughts around him when I was sober and right then, I didn't see any reason why we shouldn't go back to the hotel immediately and give in to each other.

"Kiss me," I mumbled, breathless with want. I needed one last, final push and I knew that as soon as his mouth found mine, I'd be done.

He leaned against the wall, his hands on either side of my head as he brought his face closer. Before our lips met, his expression dropped. He looked almost as though he was in pain, a stark contrast to the earlier lust-infused look. He studied me with an intense glare. We stayed locked in a trance of hot, sweaty, breathless energy for what seemed like an eternity.

"Not tonight, Cheer," he mumbled, lacing our fingers together. "Not tonight."

He exhaled loudly and my heart dropped when he straightened up and stepped back. The space between us suddenly felt enormous, and despite the fact that he'd just rejected me, I couldn't help but want to comfort him because he looked a little broken, and that hurt.

CHAPTER 13

"Kiss me? Ugh. *Kiss me*?!"

I slapped a hand across my face and shook my head in hopes that I could physically expel the memories of last night's fiasco straight out of existence.

"What am I? A fucking seductress? *Kiss me*!" I mocked drunk Dallas. Because that Dallas was not me. I didn't know her.

To be honest, that was pretty much the last clear memory that I had of the previous night; the rest of the evening was a bit of a blur. A hangover would seem like an appropriate aftermath, but I didn't feel too horrible, although I could have used an ibuprofen and some water.

After Drayton had politely rejected the "hot offer" to lay his lips on mine, I'd promptly drowned myself in more alcohol than I thought my body was physically capable of handling. The flashback of our little tease fest immediately caused me to flush, and I wanted to crawl into a hole every time it came flooding back to the forefront of my mind.

I peeked over at the sleeping dead beside me and remembered why it had been so easy to fall prey to his charm. He lay on his back with his bare chest on display and his head rolled to the left. Just the sight of him erupted a flutter in my stomach, and I could honestly say that I'd never felt a sexual tension like this with anyone else ever before.

The image of my intoxicated self, leaning against the wall in a hot and bothered state came barreling to mind once again, and I scrunched my features in distaste as I whispered, "Kiss me, ugh," in a taunting tone.

"I would have."

I squealed when Drayton's deep voice broke the silence around us. I was struggling with the shame before I knew that he was listening to me relive last night's nightmare out loud, and now, it was ten times worse. He turned his head and smiled at me with tired eyes.

"I'm not into taking advantage of drunk girls."

"You were drunk too. We had the same number of cups. Minus two. If anything, it would have been me taking advantage of you. You had more to drink than me."

"I'm also twice your size and can hold my booze really well." He rolled onto his side and propped himself up on his elbow, causing his pecs and biceps to flex. "But don't worry about it. I could tell you about the rest of your night, and I'm sure that might take away the embarrassment of asking me to kiss you."

"What?"

"You were a mess," he said. "I had to throw you over my shoulder and put you in a cab because you wouldn't leave."

"I don't remember that . . . I mean, I have a mantra: 'If you don't remember it, forget about it.' I don't want to hear any more."

"No, you probably don't."

Drayton saying *No one can make you feel the way I do* echoed around my head. Once again, he'd said and done all of these things to indicate that he wanted me, then turned around straight after and carried on as though nothing had happened. One person's actions had never confused me more in my entire life, and if I weren't so afraid of his answer, I would have come right out and asked what the hell he wanted from me.

"I'm going to get ready." I leaped out of bed and started searching through my duffel.

"You going back to the campus?"

"Yes," I told him. "Alone."

I headed toward the bathroom with my handful of clothes while Drayton watched me with a curious expression. I hated that I wanted him. I needed to stay focused on the future. To top it all off, we'd be living in two different states next year, which meant that he wasn't included in my next steps, and I needed to remember that. It was hard to remember anything when he looked at me with those hooded eyes and delectable lips.

After a shower, I changed into a pair of ripped denim high-waisted shorts and a tucked-in white tank top. The sun was shining and there wasn't a cloud in sight. Drayton was standing beside the door when I emerged from the bathroom. He was dressed in a T-shirt and shorts. I dropped my towel onto the end of the bed. "What are you doing? I said that I'm going alone."

I slipped my feet into a pair of flip-flops, saying quickly, "Drayton, I don't need you to come and protect me. You're so rude to Cooper. It makes things uncomfortable. I'm going to do the tour alone."

"That was a beautiful speech, Cheer. But I actually have plans of my own today. I was just waiting to let you know so that I wasn't gone when you came out of the bathroom."

Physically trying to stop a blush from smothering your entire face is literally impossible. No matter how much lip biting, breathing, and attempting to feel confident that you do, if heat wants to find its way onto the apples of your cheeks and create an ugly red rash on your neck, it will.

"Oh. My bad." I folded my arms. "What are you getting up to?"

The only way to save myself was to act cool. It was futile. He could tell how embarrassed I was. The stupid smug grin on his lips made that evident.

He tapped the space underneath my chin and winked before turning around and opening the door. "All sorts."

In that morning's frustration with Drayton, I had forgotten to ask him for Cooper's number. When I got to campus, I headed straight to the administration office, knowing that they would be able to get hold of him.

The office was no longer vacant. Three receptionists were busy behind the round desk, taking phone calls, talking to students, and assisting teachers. I'd been expecting to wait a while to find Cooper, but much to my surprise, he was sitting on the couch bopping his head along to whatever was playing on his earphones.

He lifted his head when he noticed my approach, and a wide smile made little dimples on either cheek. I wasn't usually one to fuss over dimples—I've never really understood the hype—but they did look gorgeous on his sun-kissed skin.

"Hey." He pulled out his earphones and wrapped them

around his phone. "Talk about timing. I thought you might show up today."

"Were you waiting for me?"

He was about to answer when a woman handed him a little USB. He thanked her and held it up in way of explanation. "I was waiting for this, actually. I was planning to stick around for a little longer, just in case you did come in."

"Good timing."

We walked through a door that led from the office into a wide, busy corridor.

"Since our tour has unofficially begun," he said as I took in all of the bodies walking past us, or dancing against the walls, or singing as they stared out of a window, "all of these are dance classes." He pointed at the various doors. "It's not always like this in here. People are waiting for the next class to begin."

I peered inside the doors as we passed them, admiring the dancers—ballet, jazz, hip-hop, contemporary (one class I wished I could join). We came to the end of the corridor and stepped into a sheltered walkway that traveled to another block.

He showed me everything, the entire school. The studios where producing was done. The enormous theater that was used for productions. Music classes filled with every instrument imaginable. This school had it all, and the tour took around an hour. We chatted as we walked, getting to know a little more about each other. The most important thing was that I *wanted* to get to know him more.

"I'm guessing you'd like to see more of the dance classes?" Cooper smiled when we circled back to where we'd started.

I nodded, almost unable to contain the thrill of seeing the potential classes that I could attend. As we walked, it was hard not to see myself as a student. It was hard not to imagine that I would walk these halls. I knew that I shouldn't get my hopes up, but I couldn't help it.

Cooper chuckled at my enthusiasm to his offer and we started down the corridor, which wasn't as busy as it had been earlier due to the fact that classes had started ten minutes ago. "You're in luck because my troop's starting some new choreography, and that's what the USB is for—it's got the music on it."

We walked into a beautiful studio. It was alive with about fifteen hip-hop dancers who were moving in perfect sync to a track blasting from an impressive stereo in the corner of the room. I watched in awe as we walked toward the equipment, admiring the dancers' flawless movements. The dance was sharp and precise, not to mention quick, and I felt a bit out of my league. I definitely had a lot to learn.

"Wow, this makes me extremely nervous about my audition," I mumbled. "If I ever get one."

"Do you want to jump in?" he asked as he plugged the USB into the stereo and selected a song.

"Jump in?"

"I'm about to teach these guys some new steps that I've been working on, so everyone's on the same playing field. Give it a go?"

There wasn't a lot of difference between what he was asking me to do and what I did almost every day with the cheer squad—follow along and learn the choreography. But my nerves suddenly swelled and were so strong that I contemplated heading straight for the door.

"Come on." He took my hand and led me toward the group, obviously sensing my hesitation. "Everyone, this is Dallas. She's going to tag along for the class."

I gave a small wave and made a mental note to chew him out later for the public introduction. I received a collective warm greeting, and Cooper wasted no time asking everyone to pay attention before he started the dance. I quickly kicked off my flip-flops because there was no way that I could dance in a pair of those. I noted that most people were in designer sneakers. Hopefully no one stood on my toes.

Almost instantly the entire group followed Cooper's moves and matched him step for step. He was incredible. The way that he moved was flawless and articulate. I almost forgot that I was meant to be paying attention to the routine and not watching him.

I focused on the repetition of his moves. This was obviously just the first few steps, and I kept my eyes on his feet as I copied the complex choreography. Before long, I picked it up, following along with everyone else but hardly being aware of the other dancers. As I often did while dancing, I became transported to a place where nothing but euphoria existed, and it was further elevated by the fact that I was in a real dance studio with a real class. It was so surreal and thrilling that I could do nothing but love each step, each movement, each swirl, turn, and leap. This was the dream.

Sometime later, I was sweaty and breathless, but I felt invigorated. I'd managed to keep up for however long we'd been dancing. Honestly, time was a foreign concept at this point.

"I don't know what you're worried about," Cooper said. "You're great. You'll ace the audition."

"*If* I get an audition." I fanned my face and slipped my flip-flops back on before the two of us moved away from the rest of the dancers. "But thanks. That was fun."

"If you need any help with a routine, *when,*"—he smirked—"your audition comes up, just let me know."

"Really?"

"Of course." He smiled and those little dimples made another appearance. "I'll be happy to help."

"I might just take you up on that offer."

It was about three in the afternoon when I finally started back to the hotel. I knew that Drayton and I were supposed to be going to Hollywood that afternoon, but his mysterious plans left me wondering what time we'd go. I was also itching to know what he could have been doing all day. But I was not going to ask for the simple fact that I wanted to seem less interested in all things Drayton. His hot and cold games were messing with me. At times I wanted to grab him and kiss him and tell him that I had a mild infatuation with his stupid face. Other times, I wanted to crush the feelings that I was having because I couldn't tell what he really wanted and the whole thing terrified me.

When I got back to the hotel, he was lounging in the reception area with all of our bags, his sunglasses on, and his mouth slightly parted as he stared up at the ceiling. I cautiously approached him because I had a strong inkling that he was asleep.

"Dray." I whipped his glasses off and giggled as he startled awake. His head whipped back and forth in confusion. Why was he so adorable? "What are you doing?"

"We had to check out and you weren't answering your phone." He vigorously rubbed his hands up and down his face and sat up straighter. I slipped my phone out of my pocket and winced when I noticed the seven missed calls and thirteen text messages.

"Sorry, it was on do not disturb."

He got to his feet, grabbed our bags, and threw them over his shoulder. "How was the tour?" He seemed genuine.

"Amazing," I chimed, taking my duffel from him as we started for the hotel doors. "I was able to join an actual class and learn the choreography. Cooper is such a good dancer."

I watched Drayton's mouth turn down as we stepped onto the sidewalk, and I took some sick satisfaction in watching his annoyance.

"Yeah, he's so fluid with his steps. That boy can *move*. He taught me so much and he offered to help if I needed tips for an audition. It was so much fun. I have to get accepted to that school. I need it. Cooper is so confident in my dancing that he's sure that I'll make it."

"Sounds good, Cheer," he mumbled as our Uber pulled up at the sidewalk. I waited for him to tell me about his morning. I even asked about it once during the drive, but he was vague and nonresponsive, and I wasn't going to hound him for details that he didn't want to give me.

But it was forgotten when we arrived in Hollywood. While it was not quite as glamorous as television and movies would make it seem, it was still exciting to see buildings in person that I'd only seen on the big screen. It was sort of surreal.

We spent the afternoon sightseeing and, of course, going to the Walk of Fame that I'd wanted to visit for as long as I could remember. So far, I'd had Drayton take a photo of me beside about thirty-six different celebrities' stars.

"One more! Just one more!" I begged.

"Noooooo."

"Dray, everyone does this with the stars. It's normal. Come on, take my picture."

I crouched beside the Ryan Reynolds star and gave Drayton a thumbs-up. But then I realized that Ryan Reynolds would be ashamed of such a mediocre pose, so I extended one leg behind me and knelt with the other one in the front while I held my hands up in fists.

Drayton laughed while I switched between power poses. He let me clown around for a minute or two, snapping continuous shots, before he lowered the phone.

He extended his hand and lifted me to my feet with such a strong pull that I came right off the ground for a moment. We continued walking and I read the names below us. Drayton must have noticed how I skipped with excitement whenever I saw a new name that belonged to a fave because he began to protest.

"Na-uh. Stop looking at them. Head up. You'll ask for more pictures."

Without so much as a warning, he lifted me by the waist and threw me over his shoulder. I squealed as he started to sprint. It was a blessing that he was good at football because he had to weave through crowds of people, only just avoiding colliding with the masses of tourists who lingered on the path.

"What is wrong with you?" I groaned when my stomach was finally relieved of the strong shoulder that it had been slammed into as he rushed through the streets.

"I'm starving, Cheer." He threw his arm over my shoulders and guided us through the bustling crowds. "I was never going to get to eat with the way you were going."

"I'm actually pretty hungry now that I think about it. Any suggestions for food?"

"Room service?"

"I was kind of hoping we could eat out."

"I'll eat out if you really want me to, Cheer."

I whipped my head toward his devious grin and groaned. I'd walked into that one, as I seemed to do more often than not. He was such a perv. He laughed and drew me in closer. "How about we get room service tonight and I'll take you out for breakfast in the morning? Somewhere that does the works."

"Actually, a gourmet breakfast does sound so good. People don't go out for breakfast enough. Dinner is great. But breakfast. Mmm."

We settled on our plans and went back to the room. It was a quiet night. We watched a movie. We ate too much room service. We did not play truth or dare again. And as filter-less as Drayton was, I appreciated that he didn't bring up how drunk and tragic I was at the frat party again. During the movie *Robin Hood*, Drayton fell asleep. Honestly, I wouldn't have noticed except that when his arm went around my waist and he pulled me into his body, I looked over my shoulder with confusion and found his expression soft and his lids closed. It made my heart flutter in an irregular, pounding pattern, but I didn't move. I shuffled backward a little closer and fell asleep in his hold.

N

"Wake up, Cheer!"

My eyes felt as if they'd been glued shut. I could feel the sunlight streaming through the window. The room felt hot and humid, and all I could smell was Drayton's signature scent as a soft breeze fluttered against my cheeks.

When I did manage to peep through a narrow, tired glare, I recoiled farther back into the pillow because Drayton had positioned himself on top of me. His bare chest hovered above my own. The sheets draped across his back and over either side of us.

"What the hell?" I mumbled, placing my flat palms on his firm chest and attempting to shove him. I ignored the spark that surged through me when my skin touched his. "What are you doing, you weirdo."

"We have to go home." His tone was laced with boredom but his eyes traveled my face with a brighter interest. "My mom is threatening to get rid of my motorcycle. Our trip's been cut a day short. Sorry."

I pouted but I understood. It was amazing that we could have come at all. And I was not going to hold out hope that I would win against his motorcycle.

"I'll bring you back." He grinned, still hovering a heartbeat away. "Christmas break. Promise."

His sincerity startled me. He wasn't obligated to bring me back—he hadn't been obligated to bring me in the first place—but there he was, promising my pouting self that he'd continue our adventure during the Christmas break. Why was he like this?

"Or,"—he tilted his head with a thoughtful expression—"New York for New Year's?"

"Oh, will we still be friends?" I teased. "That's almost three months from now."

His grin fell and the hurt on his face made me double back. I hadn't intended for my comment to upset him. But it was apparent that was what I'd done. "Harsh."

"It was a joke." I twisted my fingers together. I was tempted to touch his face for assurance, but that felt dangerous. "But you have friends and family to spend New Year's with, and so do I."

"Yeah." He nodded with a smile that made it hard to decipher if he was still upset at what I'd said or not. "Suppose that's true."

He hoisted himself off the bed, and the urge to touch and kiss him every time he was within arm's length hadn't let up, so I breathed a sigh of relief when he headed toward the bathroom.

"Our flight is in three hours," he called from the bathroom, sounding much more like himself. The shower started running and I sat up, combing my hands through my bird's-nest hair. "Save us some time and come shower with me."

"Keep dreaming, Lahey."

I know I will.

N

The flight was uneventful. Drayton didn't seem nervous that he'd been ordered to come home. He was relaxed and collected. We picked up our luggage from the belt and wandered through the airport toward our exit. It was a quiet Tuesday morning. Continuing through the airport, we passed stores and fast food stands. Approaching the final set of doors that opened into the pickup and drop-off terminal, Drayton stopped dead in his tracks and stared ahead of him.

"So, my mom's here." He slowly nodded toward the exit, and I followed his gaze. It didn't take long to spot the small, slender woman with dirty-blonde locks and a furious scowl etched on what was otherwise a beautiful face. She didn't look older than thirty. Dressed casually in a pair of jeans and an oversized blouse, she still managed to make the outfit look like a million dollars.

"You can run if you want." Drayton shrugged.

I considered running, especially as the woman beelined toward us, but I remained where I was because if I took off now, there was no redeeming myself from something as cowardly as that.

"Drayton Jacob Lahey," she snapped, stopping in front of us. The first thing that I noticed, after I admired how youthful she was, was her southern accent. I recalled Drayton telling me that his mom had been born and raised in Texas. "You are so damn unbelievable. What were you thinking? Taking off to California when you told us that you would be in Dallas!?"

She took a deep breath and directed her deep-green glare toward me. She wasn't my mother, but even I was worried that I was about to get grounded for life or have all of my privileges taken away. She'd mastered the art of the motherly stare down, that was for sure.

"Who's this?" She bit, still assessing me with an intimidating stare.

"This is Dallas," Drayton told her, smiling with innocence and charm as his gaze moved between the two of us. "Technically, I wasn't totally lying. I was *with* Dallas. I wasn't *in* Dallas. Well"— he winked with a devious grin—"not yet anyway."

"Drayton! For the love of God!" she cried. I must admit that while his words were obscene, I assumed she would have been used to it. Her reaction made me giggle more than anything else. "You have no tact at all, do you?"

"This is my mom, Ellie." Drayton ignored his mother, still grinning. He was contagious. I couldn't help but want to smile at the way he wound up his mom, despite the fact that I thought she was about to pop a vein. Biting down on the inside of my cheek, I turned away from him so that I didn't break my resolve.

"Nice to meet you, Dallas." She directed her attention back

to her son before I had the chance to return her sentiments. "Let's go. I'll be waiting in the car. It's out front."

"She's not always like that," he said as she walked away. "I happen to just bring out the worst in her."

"Oh, I can't imagine how."

"Are you going to be all right getting home? Need a ride?"

That car trip was not one that I wanted to be part of. "Don't worry, I'll call Nathan and ask him to come and get me."

"Safe."

I became curious as to why he was still standing there, staring at me as though there was something making the wheels in his head spin. I shifted my weight and gave him a curious smile. "What is it?"

"Here." He reluctantly slipped a bit of paper into my hand.

"What's this?"

"Cooper's number." He shrugged when I glanced up at him. "If you think there's something there, I suppose having his number will help you figure it out."

What he was doing wasn't deserving of the reaction that I felt. But I couldn't help but feel it. His flirting, the kissing, the jealousy, it all indicated feelings. But he was hot and cold. He was on and off, and while I wanted to keep clear of feeling more than I already did for him, his mixed messages were killing me. He was sucking me in just to push me away again, and it was more than I'd bargained for when I'd decided that we could be friends.

"I can't do this anymore." My voice broke when I tried to keep it even. "This thing with you and me. Friends or whatever we are. It's seriously messing with me. The lines keep getting blurred, and it's just too much. You're too confusing, Drayton."

I ignored the protests coming from my heart as my eyes met

his. It seemed that for once he was actually conveying how he felt instead of just masking it with a smug grin or a cute smirk.

"Dallas, I—"

"I need some distance from you. Okay? I'm super grateful for this trip and what you did for me, and I'll figure out some way to pay it back, but I'd appreciate it if you could just listen to me when I ask you to leave me alone."

I didn't wait for a response because knowing him, he'd say something that trumped all of my arguments and I'd become putty in his hands like I'd never been before. Pushing past him, I headed for the exit, determined not to change my mind. The smallest part of me hoped that he'd follow me.

But he didn't.

CHAPTER 14

It had been over a month since Drayton and I took our spontaneous trip to California. It had been one month since I experienced the most fun I'd ever had in my entire life. It had been one month since I finally admitted to myself that my feelings for Drayton had grown beyond control, and it had been one month since I told him not to speak to me anymore.

He'd made good on my request, and neither of us had spoken a word to each other since. Nothing drastic had changed in my life. I went to school, I cheered, I came home, I danced. I went to work, I hung out with Gabby, I played football with Nathan. These were all the things that had made up my day-to-day life before Drayton came along. However, now I felt a little emptier. It felt as if something was missing.

Not something, someone. I missed him. I missed the motorcycle rides and the quippy banter. I missed the smiles and the flirting. I missed the easygoing friendship that we'd somehow developed despite our lives being so incredibly different and having very little in common. Some days I considered giving in and asking him to forget what I'd said in hopes that we could at least be friends. But I didn't give in, because I knew that it was better this way and with time, it'd get easier.

Gabby stood beside my locker. "Texting lover boy?"

"He's not lover boy."

Cooper and I had stayed in touch since I'd left California. We texted regularly. It was platonic. There was nothing romantic about it, but the occasional "beautiful" comments on my Instagram photos or the replies to a Snapchat selfie led me to believe that if either one of us initiated it, it could develop into more.

"Oh please. How long have you been talking? Like, a month? It's okay to admit that you like him."

I rolled my eyes at Gabby and adjusted my toga.

"I thought you were Team Drayton?"

"I'm team whoever makes you happy," she defended herself. "Drayton makes you something . . . something that I'm not sure is healthy. And yes, I'd sell an organ to see you both together. But honestly, I just want you to smile more."

Gabby could be such a sweetheart sometimes. I gave her a grateful smile and chuckled at her willingness to support me despite her admiration for the school's QB.

It was Halloween. There was a big pep rally that night, then the homecoming game, and the dance was tomorrow. Most of the students had managed to survive having the dance pushed out another month, and it came faster than expected.

Much to Gabby's disappointment, I wasn't going to go. She had Josh, and I wanted her to enjoy herself without worrying about me being alone all night. Staying home, eating, and binge watching *So You Think You Can Dance* sounded a lot more enticing than going to homecoming without a date.

All week we'd had themed dress-up days leading up to tomorrow's events. Monday was wacky. Tuesday was book characters. Wednesday was sports stars. Thursday was circus, and today was the theme for homecoming this year: classic movies.

The entire student body, apart from seniors, was dressed up as classic movie characters. I'd seen about a dozen Reginas, an equal amount of Cady Herons, and a lot of Chers and Dionnes. Apparently, the only classics these kids knew of were *Mean Girls* and *Clueless*. The seniors, however, were dressed as Greek gods and goddesses. It was tradition.

I'd curled my hair in long, soft waves, and used a substantial amount of gold glitter on my eyelids, in my hair, and on my cheeks. A crown of golden leaves sat on top of my head and a snug, short toga clung to my body. All of this was paired with boots because it was too cold for sandals.

We wandered down the hall, but my steps came to a halt when I spotted Drayton about twenty feet away, surrounded by his entourage and adoring legions. It was as if he sensed that he was being watched by someone other than the fangirls in front of him, because he looked up and met my steady gaze. I didn't look away in shame or embarrassment because I was far too busy admiring him.

He was wearing a pair of white harem pants that sat low on his hips. They were secured by a gold belt, and there was a sheen on his torso from body oil. Every dip, crevice, and muscle was illuminated, glistening under the fluorescent lights. I wanted to run my fingers across the slippery surface of his abdomen and chest. This was the only day that we could get away with breaking dress code and thank God for that.

Neither of us broke eye contact, and my mind was instantly back in the rain, reliving the kiss that we'd shared in California. The memory surfaced of its own accord and left me breathless each and every time.

His somber expression didn't give much away, but the heat in his eyes was evident as they slowly traveled the length of my body. I could almost feel the tension coursing from one end of the corridor to the other, and not a single person around us could break it. However, I was contradicted when it was no longer Drayton in my line of vision but Gabby. "You guys want to get a room or something? You're, like, undressing each other with your eyes and there's not a lot of clothing on either of you to undress . . . so—"

Emily wandered past in a white silk gown that I had to admit looked as perfect and expensive as it was meant to.

"Oh, Dallas," she chimed with the fake friendliness that she had down to a fine art, "that gold crown is as tacky as your attempt to have Drayton notice you."

"Thanks! Your personality was my inspiration."

She scowled and kept walking, her minions trailing along behind her.

When I looked back down the hallway, Drayton was gone. Disappointment didn't evade me, but this was what I'd asked for. I didn't have the right to be surprised. I was, though. I'd half expected, or half hoped, that he'd ignore my wishes and pester me relentlessly, like he had before.

"Why don't you just talk to him, Dallas?" The bell rang and Gabby and I wove through the student body toward homeroom. "You obviously miss him?"

"There's no point. I'm leaving next year—why start something that's just going to end?"

"Okay, so should we stop hanging out because you're leaving next year?"

I shoved her arm with a small smile. Her point wasn't totally irrelevant, but it was different with Drayton. It hadn't taken very long for the feelings I had for him to develop, and I could see myself falling for him so hard that leaving would be impossible, and that wasn't what I wanted. I didn't want to be stuck in Castle Rock for the rest of my life, reduced to basic diner work or a teaching job, like Nathan.

"I can't fall for someone like him, Gabs. He's the kind of guy you want to climb mountains for. And he's not the kind of guy who'd meet you halfway."

"I think you might be underestimating him a little." We sat down in homeroom and dropped our bags on the floor. "If it makes you feel any better, Josh said that he's been in a shit mood since you guys got back from Cali."

"That doesn't make me feel better," I groaned and dropped my head on the desk. "That just makes me more confused. Do you know how awful it is when you want to tell someone that you care about them but there's no point because you're leaving? And he's probably not interested in anything serious anyway. It all just seems like a waste of time. You consider having some physical fun, but that'll probably just make the feelings ten times stronger, so you're stuck with no options at all?"

"Wouldn't it be better just to embrace how you feel and enjoy what time you *do* have? Graduation is months from now."

"No." I frowned. "That'd just make it harder to leave when I do go."

"I think you'd be perfect together. But that's just my opinion. I also know that you're obsessed with his attention. That's why your dress is so tight."

"Ugh, shut up."

When did I become this girl? The girl who pictured herself with the devastatingly gorgeous quarterback and became victim to an onslaught of butterflies? *When?!* When Drayton Lahey crashed into my damn car, that's when.

That night's pep rally and game were the biggest of the season. It was a huge event and it happened to be even bigger because it was Halloween. Gabby convinced me to go to Maxon's Halloween slash celebration party after the game, and I knew Drayton would be there.

My last period of the day was an independent study. I decided to go home before the pep rally and make sure that I was organized for tonight. I laid the costume that I'd chosen on my bed, along with a bag of things I'd need to take to the game.

My costume made me wince a little. I'd purchased a Dallas Cowboys jersey and had had Gabby's mom alter it a little so that it was a snug fit on my waist and long enough to wear as a dress. I'd had an *18* put on the back of it, along with my last name. I knew that the Dallas Cowboys were Drayton's favorite team.

I wasn't sure what I was hoping for. I guessed part of me wanted to wave the white flag. I wanted to initiate the first move and step toward reconciliation. As much as I didn't want to get too close to him, I knew that I couldn't spend the time until graduation fixating on how much I missed him. It'd be torture. I was in the middle of arranging my hair into a tight ponytail on the top of my head when the door thudded.

"Gabby," I mumbled. I figured the door must have been locked because I didn't think that girl knocked. Ever.

When I opened the door, the last person I'd ever expected

to see was on my doorstep, a bunch of peonies in one hand and a balloon that read "Be my homecoming queen?" in the other.

"Cooper?!" I felt like my jaw must have been on the floor. He looked incredible. "What are you doing here?"

"You said you weren't going to homecoming this year." He smiled and handed me the balloon. "I know it's a little underwhelming, but it was the best that I could do at the last minute."

I had to focus on the grip I had on the balloon's string so that it didn't float away as I stared at it in awe and disbelief. "Cooper, this is—this is amazing. You didn't have to come all the way here to take me to homecoming."

"I wanted to." He shrugged his shoulders and handed over the peonies. They weren't my favorite flower, lilies were, but the peonies were beautiful and I was seriously floored at the gesture. "You can't miss your last homecoming dance."

"I-I don't even have a dress . . ."

"Do you have time to get one tomorrow?"

I mulled it over in the cesspool of thoughts crammed violently in my head. I glanced at the small bag of luggage behind him.

"Oh, uh—" He followed my gaze, twisting his body toward the bag on the doorstep. "Sorry, the cab just dropped me off. I don't expect to stay here. I can find a hotel."

"Don't be silly." The enthusiasm with which I declined his suggestion probably came off as forced as it felt, but his expression remained sweet and polite. "You can definitely stay here. Come in. How'd you find out where I live anyway?"

He quickly picked up the bag and followed me inside. I headed into the kitchen to find a vase, stopping to tie the balloon to a barstool on my way. I felt a little flustered that Cooper had shown up unannounced and was now following me around my house.

"Don't think this is weird, but you told me where you work, so I phoned and told some guy, Stephen or something, that I had a gift to send, so could I have an address. He didn't make it easy. I had to answer a few questions, but I passed." He laughed. "I wanted to surprise you when I found out that you wouldn't be going to homecoming. It didn't seem right."

Cooper stood beside me, one hand on the countertop, the other in his pocket. He was attractive. He was sweet and we had common interests, but I hoped that he wasn't here with the intent of taking our friendship further.

"Your vase . . ." Cooper pointed at the sink, snapping me out of my own head and turning my attention to the overflowing water.

"Oh shoot." I spun the tap around and emptied some of the water before I put the flowers into the vase and placed them on the windowsill.

"I've got a pep rally and a game tonight," I explained, gesturing for Cooper to follow me to my bedroom. "Then there's a Halloween party if you—"

"Hello, hello," Nathan sang out as he opened the front door, his smile faltering when he realized that I wasn't alone. He regained his composure quickly and adopted his polite I'm-the-big-brother-so-I-don't-like-you-but-I'll-be-respectful-of-my-little-sister smile. He stretched out his hand and stepped forward. Cooper did the same.

"This is Cooper." I cut the tension and gestured at the unexpected guest. "Cooper, this is my big brother, Nathan."

"Of course." Cooper smiled, dropping their handshake. "I've heard a lot of good things. Nice to meet you."

This further confused Nathan. He looked at me and I could tell that he was curious as to whether I was actually seeing someone on a more regular basis.

"We met when I went to California—" I said.

"When you ran off without telling me after being suspended from school for running off," Nathan added.

"Thank you for that explanation," I drawled. "Yes, that's when we met. Cooper came to surprise me for homecoming. Nice, right?"

Nathan flinched. It was quiet and the awkwardness returned. After an insufferable few moments, Nathan pointed at Cooper's duffel bag beside the breakfast bar.

"That yours?"

"Yeah." Cooper kept smiling no matter how uncomfortable the situation had become.

Nathan pointed at the corridor. "Why don't you drop it in Dallas's room and get comfortable?"

"It's the first room on the right, just down there . . ." I added.

As soon as we heard the door shut, Nathan wrapped his hand around my arm and dragged me into the kitchen.

"Natha—"

"Dude, little weird?"

"What's weird?"

"That Cooper dude, coming from *California* with no warning, to take you to a homecoming dance. Have you ever watched the crime channel?"

"No. We can't afford cable."

He sighed and pinched the front of his grey T-shirt. He fanned it in and out, clearly getting worked up over the situation. "It's stalker behavior. It starts out with surprise dates, and then it turns into standing outside your bedroom window and the next thing you know, he's stabbing you to death in a parking lot because you won't accept his calls."

"Look, we're friends. I swear, if he even so much as calls me twice in a span of five minutes, I'll let you know." I gave his shoulder a pat and stepped around him.

"Be careful, Dallas. I swear, I don't like him."

"He's a nice person, Nathan, I promise. I trust him. So please relax. And be nice."

Cooper was sitting on my bed when I opened the door. He wasn't looking through my things or taking photos of my under-wear. Obviously. I trusted Cooper. We were friends and the boy didn't have a bad bone in him. He looked up from his phone. "I guess Nathan had to give the big brother talk? Be careful and all of that?"

"You weren't listening, right?"

"No," he assured me. "I just figured as much. No stress. I understand."

It was a strange sight to see him here, in my room. It almost didn't feel quite right. But I shook it off and continued getting ready for the evening, as I had been doing when he arrived.

"So, there's the game tonight and then a Halloween party afterward—"

"I remember you telling me about it," he interrupted me. He unzipped the bag at his feet and pulled out a pirate hat. "I'm going as Jack Sparrow."

"*Captain* Jack Sparrow." I grinned, standing in front of the closet mirror so that I could do my mascara.

"Is this your costume?" He picked up the football jersey, his fingers caressing the fabric. "Football—jersey—dress thing."

"Mhmm." I nodded.

The thought seemed a bit morbid now. Dressing up to attract the attention of a different boy when Cooper had come here from California to be my date. "It's a Dallas Cowboys jersey. You know, since my name's Dallas."

"Oh. You didn't want to go as an angel or Catwoman?"

"I love football." Cooper didn't need to know that I might be a little in love with the inspiration behind the outfit, not that I'd be declaring that I was in love. It was a simple white-flag gesture. I wanted Drayton back in my life.

"Are you a football fan?" I reached for the blue ribbon hanging from the hook inside of my closet. "If you're not, this might be a long night for you."

"I've never paid all that much attention, to be honest," he said.

I knew that when it came to things that didn't hold my interest, I could be a little bit of a snob, but I was fairly open minded. I loved dance but I also loved football. How could he have made it through high school and not paid attention to the most popular sport in the country? It was a minor thing, but it gave me an inkling that we just weren't compatible as more than friends.

The last game of the season was a nail biter. My heart was in my throat as I watched, knees hugged to my chest. It was 26-28, and the Porter Valley Pumas would not go down without a fight. The last few seconds on the clock ticked down as Drayton caught a snap and threw the ball to Derek. Three more hand offs were made. Each time the Pumas closed in on the Wolves, my heart leaped into my throat. But each time, the ball landed in our hands and tension crackled through the crowd. Uttered gasps and cheers built as we progressed toward the end zone. And then, without expectation, an impressive lateral was performed by Austin as the Pumas closed in. The ball spiraled backward, landing in Drayton's arms. He rushed the remaining yards, weaving, dodging interceptions, side stepping with speed and grace. I watched, enchanted, heart pounding. This determined the game. He scored a touchdown.

It brought the entire crowd to its feet.

Drayton and I might not be on speaking terms right now, but I could admit that he knew how to lead his team. His plays were cunning. His throws were prodigious. His sportsmanship was sublime.

"Good job tonight, everyone!" Emily waved her pom-poms as the field cleared. "Even you, Dallas."

Ever since Drayton and I had stopped speaking, Emily had extended a gracious attitude toward me. It was strategic and existed when we wore our uniforms only. Otherwise, she was her usual bitchy self.

"I'll see you all at Maxon's Halloween party." She waved and skipped away as if she was the most innocent little creature to grace the planet. Gross.

I walked toward the locker rooms as I needed to collect my things. I'd go home to shower and get ready for the Halloween party. Cooper had to get dressed as well. He'd been sitting in the stands with Nathan, watching the game—I'd meet them both at home. I felt nauseated thinking about the fact that he'd be with me all weekend. Once again, I hoped that he wasn't too forward with his intentions—if he had any. I'd decided to have a chat with him and make sure that he knew this was a platonic situation.

"Dallas!"

The masculine voice that had the ability to make me weak at the knees stopped me dead in my tracks, and the telltale sign of Drayton's presence got stronger as I heard footsteps approaching beside the girl's locker rooms in the foyer. Turning around, I noticed how well the maroon on his legs went with the olive of his torso. He had already stripped out of his jersey and pads, and was shirtless, and I tried not to stare. People were moving in and out of the gym foyer. The locker room doors swung open and shut. Girls giggled and guys shouted, but it was all a blur of the background. How could it hold my attention when I hadn't been this close to Drayton in over a month?

"Sorry." He glanced down at his torso after noticing my confused, likely heated, expression. "It's so hot and I was literally on my way to a shower."

"Is everything all right? Congratulations, by the way."

"Thanks. Look, I know we haven't talked in a while, but are you going to Maxon's tonight?"

"Yes, but—"

"I need to talk to you. Can you find me when you get there?"

"Sure, but—"

"Just find me, okay?" He reached out and gently squeezed my shoulder. "I want to ask you something."

Without another word he turned and strode back toward the boy's locker room. I felt light headed. My mind raced over the conversation, and my heart sped up at the warmth he'd regarded me with. No smirking. No dirty jokes or smug grins. Just sincerity behind his mysterious request. Suddenly, I felt an overwhelming sense of impending self-destruction. I had a horrible feeling that this night was not going to go down as I had planned.

N

The jersey hugged me in the right places and it was the perfect length. Nathan and I might have been Broncos supporters, but I did love the Cowboys' colors. Plus, I did root for the Cowboys from time to time. I stepped back into my bedroom after changing and found Cooper perched on the edge of the bed.

"Wow." His smile became bright as he admired the outfit. "You look great."

I accepted the compliment without giggling at his thick eyeliner. I'd let him borrow a black eye pencil so that he could complete his Captain Jack Sparrow outfit. His hat, equipped with faux dreadlocks, sat atop his head, and his pirate clothing wasn't half bad considering he'd picked out his outfit at the last minute.

"You do too."

I peeped in the mirror and assessed my look once more. My hair was still up in its ponytail, and I'd dotted a little bit of blue shimmer into the corners of my eyes. A pair of white sneakers completed the look.

Just before we left, Nathan called from the kitchen, "Where are you going looking like that?"

I was curious as to whether he was talking about the fact that I was dressed in a Cowboys' outfit or the fact that I was wearing a rather short jersey as a dress.

"More importantly," I frowned, "where are *you* going, looking like that?"

He was wearing a pink wig, green overalls, an orange long sleeve, and his eyelids were white. The red clown nose was the least concerning part of his entire outfit.

"I'm a clown." He shrugged.

"That's obvious," I scoffed. "The point in Halloween is to dress up as a character that you *aren't* in real life."

"Funny." He gave me a sarcastic smile. "Go and put some pants on."

"No thanks, Dad." I waved then grabbed Cooper's hand and dragged him toward the front door. "Have fun not getting laid tonight. You look like a nightmare!"

I slammed the door, muffling whatever comeback Nathan had been shouting and the two of us strolled toward the waiting Uber at the side of the road. I was quick to drop Cooper's hand, as I didn't want him to get the wrong idea. I needed to find the best time to casually make sure that we were on the same page. Then again, perhaps it wasn't needed. He wasn't exactly coming on to me.

Maxon's stone courtyard had been transformed into a spectacular ghoulish garden. The solar lights were wrapped with green cellophane and cast an eerie glow. The awnings and patio railings were decorated with cobwebs. There were witches on broomsticks and ghosts hovering in the air. The wire was almost invisible unless you looked hard enough, it was so well done.

Because Maxon's parents were home for this party, it was alcohol free, but the drinks that were being served sat on ice inside of large cauldrons. I didn't begrudge Cooper for marveling at the house. I reacted the same way. I imagined what his reaction might be if he saw Drayton's—it was twice the size.

"Would you believe me if I said that I need to go to the bathroom?" Cooper leaned in and shouted over a DJ Khalid song. "I'm not just going to snoop around this *amazing* house. I do need to take a leak."

I laughed and pointed at the staircase attached to the outside of the house on the other side of the courtyard. "Go up to that patio. There's a bathroom in that first living area where that group of people are. You could find a less crowded bathroom in that house, I'm sure,"—I smiled—"it's just the closest one to the party. But I doubt most of those people are waiting to use it. There's a pool table up there."

"Oh right," his shoulders dropped. "I thought that I was going to be hanging on forever. I'll be back."

"I'll be here."

He zipped through the crowd. I watched his pirate run and giggled. He did have that Jack jog down to a fine art. As I wandered farther into the crowd, a couple of the guys from the team ran past and booed at the outfit that I was wearing.

"Fuck the Cowboys," Derek, wearing an old-school cop costume, shouted.

I scoffed. "I'll leave that to you."

He scowled. The rest of the guys cackled and screamed about how glorious the Broncos were. Derek got a little too close and began to chant. He was slurring his words and stumbling. "Broncos. Broncos. Bronc—"

"That's enough."

He was pushed to the side, and I felt as if I had room to breathe again. Drayton shook his head with exasperation at the group of intoxicated team members. He gave them a series of light shoves and warnings until they headed off in another direction.

He turned around again, fixing me with an amused smile that I returned. But it wasn't long before his gaze moved and drank in what it saw: me. From head to toe, he was shameless in his appreciation. He was confident and unwavering and, as usual, I felt small but powerful.

He looked perfect as well. Of course. He was a firefighter. I think. His orange pants were held on with a pair of suspenders that fit snugly against his bare torso. I would never complain about how little he wore a shirt. He was doing society a huge favor.

"Dallas Cowboys. My team. What's that about?"

"This is your team?" I gasped with my hand over my mouth. "I had no idea. I picked it because it's my name."

"Oh. And eighteen? My number . . ."

"It was the number that came with the jersey." I shrugged. "Total coincidence."

"But," I said quickly, knowing he wasn't buying a word of what I was saying, "if this comes across as some kind of ice breaker, an attempt to clear the air and make amends, well, that could work too."

I got the sense he was relieved to hear that I wanted the two of us to be friends again. No, it wasn't easy. Yes, there were major feelings that I had toward him. But having nothing to do with him was worse. Especially when I had to see him at school every day.

"You look—perfect. Gorgeous."

My heart soared, taking on a speed that was ever-so-slightly concerning. He made my dopamine levels go haywire with the simplest words and the subtlest gestures. I wanted him to reach out and embrace me under his arm the way he used to. I hadn't even realized how much I missed that small action.

"You wanted to ask me something?"

"Yeah, but not here. Walk with me? We won't leave Maxon's, I promise."

"That's not saying much. This place is huge."

Before we'd made it a mere three feet, I stopped and gasped with embarrassment for almost leaving when Cooper was here.

"Dray." I reached for his arm as he greeted a couple of his friends sitting on the stone bench seats around the fire. He turned around and I felt disappointment coursing through me when he gave me an expectant smile. "I can't leave. Ask me here."

"What's the pr—" And that's when I knew that Cooper was back. Drayton's frown fixated behind me.

"Hey, Drayton," Cooper greeted us as he came to a stand-still beside me. Drayton didn't respond. He didn't smile or say hello. His disappointment was evident. Cooper held out a hand in front of me and offered me a pop. Which I took. "You're right. There were more bathrooms. This house is amazing."

"Cooper came to surprise me," I explained, twisting the cold bottle in my hands. I could feel the heat of the fire in the pit a few feet from us, and the glow illuminated Drayton's profile. He was so beautiful that it hurt. "He's taking me to the homecoming dance."

That's when his hard features fractured. And he flinched. I couldn't stand to see him so vulnerable. It wasn't right. I turned to Cooper, who had been sipping his drink, smearing his fake beard. "Can you give us a second. Please?"

Cooper nodded. His smile was uncertain, but he turned

around and wandered off toward one of the drink cauldrons. I could see a number of the cheerleaders who were dressed up as leopards or nurses watching him with approval. I doubted that he'd be left alone for long.

"What's he doing here?" Drayton asked.

"I just told you. He surprised me. What'd you want to ask me?" I thought deep down, I knew. But I didn't want it to be that.

"Forget it." His eyes focused on anything but me.

"You gave me his number," I reminded him firmly, but there was an obvious quiver in my tone.

"Yeah, I know. I'm glad that you've got someone like him."

"It's not like that."

But he didn't hear me. Or he didn't listen. He turned around and walked away. His back and shoulders were tense. I could see the muscles that had become rigid under his smooth skin. He approached Cooper. I worried for a minute that he was about to hit him or start a fight. But he simply said something to him, and Cooper nodded, seeming somewhat appreciative.

A beaming Gabby and Josh appeared out of nowhere. They were dressed in what could only be Damon and Elena outfits. Gabby's long black hair was pin straight, which must have taken hours. No glasses. Bootcut jeans, Converse shoes and a tight tank top—simple clothing, but it was Elena. Josh had changed up his usual slick hair for a messier tousle. He was wearing black jeans and a leather jacket. He was also attempting a Damon smirk, and it was just not working all that well for him.

"What happened to Bonnie and Clyde?"

"We were never doing that," Gabby giggled. "I just said it so that you wouldn't talk me out of doing Delena. Iconic. This ship. It's eternal."

"How'd it go?" Josh asked resting Gabby under his arm. "I saw you and Drayton talking. Did you say yes?"

"Say yes?"

"He didn't ask?"

"Ask me what?"

"Are you sure you're a cheerleader?" Cooper appeared again. His pirate hat and dreads needed adjusting. "I was just talking to those girls and they had no idea who you are."

Gabby and Josh frowned, watching Cooper. It seemed that there was a lot of confusion going around tonight.

"That's because some of the girls on the squad are enormous assholes in size zero bodies. Cooper, this is Gabby and Josh. Friends. Guys, this is Cooper."

"Oh!" Gabby gasped with realization. "Yeah. Hey."

"Nice to meet you both."

"Ah, I see." Josh said.

"See what?" I murmured. I was attempting to converse in a low tone so that Cooper couldn't hear but it wasn't immediately obvious that I was keeping him out of it. It wasn't the easiest task to accomplish.

"I see why Drayton didn't ask."

"Ask what?"

He hesitated, his mouth pursed in a tight line. He seemed at war with himself for a moment, but Gabby gave him a nudge, wanting to hear what he had to say as well. "Drayton was going to ask you to homecoming. But I think he might have flushed that plan."

"Why didn't you tell me?" Gabby swiped Josh's arm.

"Drayton made me swear not to," he defended himself. "He knew that you'd tell Dallas."

"You two should work on your communication," I mumbled as I swept the area in hopes of finding Drayton. I knew he wasn't out there though. "Seriously, you're like a month and a bit in to your relationship."

"Oh really?" Gabby bit back, folding her arms as she fixed me with a pointed glare. "*We* need to work on *our* communication. That's interesting coming from you."

Cooper stared at the floor as he tapped the bottle of soda in his hand and bopped to the music, no doubt in an attempt to save face. His dreaded pirate hat looked too cute and silly for the situation. I couldn't imagine how horribly awkward he must have felt, and I wished I wasn't about to make it ten times worse.

"Do you mind hanging here with these two for a minute?" I handed him my drink. "I just need to go and do something."

"Sure, Dallas."

I wished I was torn about how I felt. I wished the desire to ignore my instincts wasn't as strong so that I could stay right where I was and enjoy his company. I started across the court-yard. I needed to find Drayton.

Heading toward the cabana, my feet scuffed the sticky stone ground. I did my best to stretch a little taller so that I could see the faces of everyone under the canvas shelter. Pushing my way through the crowd, I kept apologizing as I was shoved into dead doctors and hot nurses, zombie brides, girls in lingerie, devils and angels, as well as the odd superhero. Crowds were a death sentence for small people.

Arriving at the other side of the cabana, having passed comfortable-looking lounge chairs and a table where a card game was taking place, I safely tucked myself into the corner, scanning the area again. A clear plastic weather surround stopped the cold breeze from coming inside. The exit was a door-sized flap. The zip was undone. When I was about to slip back into the garden, Maxon came inside, and I intercepted him before he could disappear.

"Have you seen Drayton?"

"He was out back last I saw, Cheer." He jabbed his thumb over his shoulder. He assessed me with his crooked grin and small eyes. "You're the sexiest football player I've ever seen."

"Don't call me Cheer." I rolled my eyes and pushed past him, stepping out onto the concrete patio. The space on this side of the cabana was more vacant than the other side was. The music was still loud, but as I skipped down the concrete steps and landed on the grass, the noise became dulled.

There was no sight of Drayton and I began to wonder if perhaps he'd left. I wandered through the trimmed lawn anyway, circling around the manicured hedges and following a path of concrete tiles around the corner of the house.

I sensed him before I saw him, courtesy of the stench of nicotine. The cloud of smoke that billowed into the night sky was illuminated by an outdoor lamp that served as a background, and I glanced at the brooding boy leaning against the house with his bare back and broad shoulders.

He stared at the Chucks on his feet and took another drag on the cigarette as I slowly approached him. You'd think after all that panicked searching, I would have been in more of a hurry. But I took my time, wanting to admire him before he realized that I was there and masked the raw emotion that was currently adorning his gorgeous face.

"Dray?"

He didn't react; he didn't flinch in surprise or look up. I thought

I saw a fast blink flutter his lashes, but it was dark and hard to tell.

"How's it going, Cheer?" The playful tone made me wince. All I wanted was to have a real conversation. To clear the air and say whatever it was that we both needed to say. It had been a damn long time coming. But it wouldn't happen if he was in this kind of mood.

"You were going to ask me to homecoming?" I came to a standstill in front of him, but he still didn't look at me. He twisted the end of his cigarette between his strong fingers.

"Yeah. I heard you weren't going, so I figured I'd lend my services." He finally met my eyes and took another drag of his stick before he flicked it into the grass. "No worries, though. I've got another date lined up."

"Why didn't you ask me earlier? Why did you leave it to the last minute?"

"Because I was trying to talk myself out of asking you," he said. "You told me to keep clear, and I wanted to respect that. I have respected it. Even if it has really sucked. Would you have said yes if I asked?"

"Yes."

The moonlight poured down on his face, the glow casting flattering shadows on his chest and jaw. The noise of the party resonated around us, but out here it was quiet enough that we didn't have to shout to hear each other speak. Although, right then, I felt like the silence was louder than either of our words.

"It's pointless now. You're going with Cooper." He straightened up and began to leave but I stepped in front of him, the moonlight now shining on the back of him, his face engulfed in shadow.

"I didn't even know he was coming! You gave me his number,"

I snapped. "You've confused me so many times with your actions and then you pretty much told me to pursue someone else, so what gives?"

"There was no one else that you were pursuing before, was there Dallas?" His tone was accusatory. "This was all you. You told me to stay away from you and give you space. I thought we were friends until you went and had a meltdown at the airport and told me to get fucked."

"Fr-friends?!" I stuttered with disbelief. "Friends don't dare friends to kiss them like that, and they don't flirt, and they don't get jealous when another guy comes along. For once, just tell me how you feel!"

"I wanted to win the game." He shrugged with indifference. "And as for the so-called jealousy, that's all in your mind. We're friends Dallas, that's it."

"I don't get it, your actions and words just don't line up!"

"What about your actions! You tell me you want nothing to do with me and then you show up wearing that—and yes, I'll admit that you look amazing, and seeing you in that jersey with your perfect legs out and your incredible waist is torture, but it's a contradiction, Dallas. What gives?"

I was speechless. I had butterflies in my stomach. I wanted to scream and I wanted to shout. But as well as all of that, I was ashamed. His words were like a punch in the gut. He was calling me out and he was absolutely right.

"Look"—his features softened a little—"just forget it, Dallas. Things have been easier with the space. Just keep doing you. I won't get in the way."

He stepped around me and this time, I didn't stop him.

CHAPTER 15

Gabby and I wandered through the mall the next morning. I was less than enthused to deal with crowds doing what I was doing—searching for a last-minute dress. Of course, I was far less worked up and frantic than some of the other girls who were tearing around with their parent's credit cards.

". . . so then after Josh threw up, he tried to swing at this guy he thought was staring at my ass, and Drayton literally had to pick him up, carry him to the car, and drive us both home, and oh my word, Dallas, it was hectic. He was such a mess."

I focused on the fabric of the teal dress in front of me, trying not to wince at the sound of Drayton's name or the thought of his protective heroics.

"I'm not finding anything here. Let's go try Belinda's Boutique."

Gabby prattled on about last night. After the tiff with Drayton, I'd asked Cooper if we could cut our evening short. We left Maxon's and met Nathan at another Halloween party. It was slightly less amped up and the numbers just couldn't compare, but it was fine. Unfortunately, I wasn't the best company. Cooper didn't seem to mind, though. He took everything in stride and never stopped smiling.

Gabby insisted we spend the day searching for a homecoming dress. I didn't know why she came along; she knew that I was hopeless, and we'd search the entire mall before I settled on something. Cooper had had no problem abandoning the search three stores ago; in my opinion he'd made the right decision. He let us know that he'd be in the food court drowning his male sorrows in burgers and frozen soda until we were done.

"Are you going to tell me what happened with you and Dray?" Gabby asked once she'd exhausted all of her tales of drunken adventure. I sighed as I steered us into the cute boutique. I had known that she'd ask eventually.

"Nothing happened," I said quietly as I flicked through the racks with a little more hope than I'd had earlier. These dresses were beautiful. "We're both hopeless. Neither of us will own up to how we feel—not that I actually *know* how he feels."

"I think it's obvious," Gabby said as she mirrored my movements. "He's so into you, and we can all see it."

"It can't be that obvious when he's flirting with me one minute and giving me another guy's number the next."

"Josh thought it was super weird that this Cooper guy just arrived without warning. Creepy, kind of, but sweet. I don't know. I just hope it makes Drayton jealous enough to sort his shit out."

"That's kind of evil," I laughed. Of course she'd find a silver lining.

The champagne-colored dress in my hand looked perfect. "I'm going to try this on," I said.

"Do you wonder if Dray's trying to protect himself? Maybe he doesn't want to fall for you for the exact same reason that you don't want to fall for him?" Gabby asked on the way to the change-room. "Make sure you show me once you've got that on. You guys are being so frustratingly ridiculous. You both like each other."

I lifted the straps of the dress over my shoulders and assessed it in the mirror. It looked perfect. It stopped above the knee. The fabric was satin, and the dress had a tasteful neckline that left enough cleavage visible to be alluring but not inappropriate. I smiled at the reflection in front of me. It paid to be picky sometimes.

"Gabs," I said as pulled the curtain open. She gave me an approving smile and sprang up from the seat.

"That looks incredible! Dray is going to love it!"

"You need to stop."

"You're crazy. You don't want to date the rich quarterback who could literally visit you in California whenever he wants because, why?"

"Because long distance doesn't work. Especially not with a guy like him who has a lot of options."

"Sometimes I think you don't realize how gorgeous you are." Gabby folded her arms and gave me a pointed look. My frustration diminished. I was lucky to have such an optimistic friend who loved to remind me how valuable I was. "And long distance *can* work. You're running out of excuses."

I closed the curtain again before I unzipped the dress. "How about the fact that we end up arguing whenever we talk. Doesn't really scream stable, now, does it?"

"Lovers argue, Dallas. It's just a sign of the angsty romantic connection that you both share."

I ripped the curtain back when I was finished changing and stared at her in faux disgust. She read way too many unrealistic novels and I thought an intervention was in serious order. She didn't seem concerned by the distaste, and fixed me with an innocent smile as she followed me to the cash register.

"You're just bothered because I'm right."

⚡

The dance started in a half-hour, and to say I was nervous was an understatement. I was disappointed that my plan to binge watch Netflix had been thrown out the window. Instead, I would get to watch Drayton show up looking like an A-list heartthrob with some cover girl on his arm. And I had to entertain a college dance major I hadn't expected. The entire event was being overhyped by my imagination and it was starting to make me nauseated.

I stood in front of the mirror and combed my fingers through my hair, which I'd given a natural wave to. My summer tan was wearing off so I had put a bit of tanning moisturizer on to give me warmth.

"Can I come in?" Cooper knocked on the door and opened it a crack, but he didn't appear until I let him know that it was fine. "Oh wow, Dallas. Great dress."

I smiled and gestured at his tall, lean frame. "Great suit."

Cooper looked dapper in a fitted dark-blue suit. He'd opted out of wearing a tie, but he still looked formal and handsome. The only downfall was that I felt the colors didn't look right together. Dark blue and champagne didn't fit. But there was nothing to be done about that now.

"I got you something." He smiled, walking farther into the

room with his hand behind his back. "I snuck off while you were dress shopping."

He proudly revealed the mystery gift—a beautiful corsage with a champagne ribbon and shimmering detail; the more interesting part was the lily that it was made of. He couldn't have known that my dress was going to be champagne and I had to wonder if the lily was a coincidence or not.

"How did you know that I love lilies?" I smiled appreciatively and slipped the corsage onto my wrist. Maybe I should just *try* and make an effort to feel something for him. It could go somewhere if I let it happen naturally. Maybe . . .

"Oh, I-I didn't know. I thought it looked good."

"It looks great. I love it. Thanks."

I should have felt more excited for the evening ahead, but I was anxious with a side of dread. I was stressed about Cooper. I was worried that where Drayton and I stood was so unclear. The simple fact that he and I were so up in the air left a permanent weight on my chest like I had never felt before. It was a constant ache in the back of my head.

"Shall we?" Cooper offered me his arm and I linked mine with his. We headed into the living room where Nathan was waiting with his keys in hand, watching a football game on the television.

"Aw, Sis." He smiled and spun the keys around his finger as we approached. "You look great"—his eyes moved to Cooper and his mouth turned down—"although black would have looked better," he mumbled.

"Well." I clapped my hands together as a deep heat engulfed my cheeks. He was making things incredibly awkward with his blatant hostility. "Should we go?"

"Yeah. You want a photo?" Nathan waved his phone with boredom.

His enthusiasm was outstanding. I bet if Drayton had been my date, he would have created a themed backdrop and set up his own photo shoot. I didn't bother mentioning it, and Cooper and I stood together for a few snapshots.

When we arrived at the dance, I couldn't get out of the car fast enough. The tension had been palpable; no one said a word the entire ride. Thank the good Lord that it was only a five-minute drive.

"Your brother doesn't like me, does he?" Cooper asked as we waved Nathan off and headed toward the gymnasium.

"He's just a bit of a snob when it comes to sports," I explained as lightly as I could, so that Cooper didn't take it to heart. "I think the fact that you don't worship at the altar of football bugs him. Just ignore him; it's not important."

"You guys take your football pretty seriously?" He held the gymnasium door open and ushered me inside.

"We do."

The now-transformed gym looked great, and I admired how well the social committee had done the movie classics theme. The walls were lined with famous quotes. People were taking photos with cardboard cutout characters from the films *Mean Girls*, *The Breakfast Club*, *Clueless*, *Grease*, *Sixteen Candles*, *Sleepless in Seattle*, *When Harry Met Sally*, and a slew of other favorites. Red and blue helium balloons stuck to the ceiling and streamers were cast from one wall to the other. It looked marvelous.

"Want to dance?" Cooper placed his hand on the small of my back as he leaned in with a keen smile. The dance floor was occupied with two or so dozen students, but there were more people arriving by the minute, so I supposed dancing before the floor turned into a sweaty cesspool of horny teenagers was our best option.

"Sure."

I gripped his hand and led him toward the floor to make up for the weak acceptance of his request. I was grateful that the song was an upbeat Demi Lovato tune and not a slow song that would require intimacy. I was so pathetic.

We danced for about ten minutes, during which time the gym filled up, the chatter becoming louder and the atmosphere more energetic. I did my best not to glance at the door every two seconds, but it was almost impossible. I was offered a momentary distraction from my search when Gabby and Josh arrived, looking like a couple fit for the red carpet.

Gabby's fitted dress fell to her thighs and the vibrant yellow fabric complimented her warm, glowing russet skin. The plunging neckline was decorated with a simple silver chain and pendant, and her hair was arranged into a beautiful bun on the top of her head. Josh's suit was swish, and he was wearing a tie that matched her dress. Gabby saw me from the entryway and waved, looking the happiest that I'd seen her in a long time. I decided then and there that I would drop the moody attitude so that she wouldn't worry about me.

"You look so hot," I squealed as she jostled toward me with her arms open. We embraced in a girlish, giggling hug. Now the night felt right—my best friend here, seeing her in such good spirits, admiring the way Josh grinned at her with an infatuated expression.

"You look hot." She gripped my shoulders and held me at arm's length, an adoring look fluttering her eyes before they moved toward the date behind me. "Hey, Cooper, you look nice."

"Thanks, Gabby, so do you."

"And we all know that I look amazing." Josh stepped forward and threw his arm over Gabby's shoulders. "Let's go and dance, beautiful."

A smile that met her gorgeous brown eyes lifted her cheeks and the two of them slipped away into the crowd. At least something good came from my friendship with Drayton. Two people who were absolutely perfect for each other met—they deserved so much happiness.

Cooper and I continued to dance for a while, our bodies moving in sync to the loud music. He had incredible rhythm even when he was dancing in a crowded gym and wearing a fitted suit. We danced well together, but our bodies didn't fit the way that I wanted them to. Not the way that it felt when I danced with Drayton.

"Hey, I'm just going to go and get a drink," I told him approximately three seconds into a slow song. His hands had found my hips, and I felt as though I was about to suffocate.

"I'll come."

"No, no." I exhaled and reminded myself to breathe as he waited for an explanation. "I'm going to go to the bathroom first. I won't be long."

I grabbed Melissa as she headed for the dance floor. She raised a curious brow at my hand holding her arm with an ironlike grip. Letting go, I admired her black sequin cocktail dress with shimmers of emerald that illuminated when the light hit it.

"You look gorgeous—"

"You're not my type," she laughed when I stammered then gave me a light jab in the shoulder. "What's up, girl?"

"This is Cooper. My date."

"Your date?"

"I'm going to the bathroom." I sidestepped out of his hold and patted her on the shoulder. "Chat with him for a second."

I pecked his cheek, which seemed to make him happy and beelined toward the spring-loaded gym doors, throwing them open and practically running down the concrete steps as I filled my lungs with the chilled night air.

This was too much.

It was too hard and I could feel the threat of tears as I leaned against the wall around the corner, hidden out of sight. My inability to feel something for someone else was so frustrating, so enraging that I wanted to pull my hair out.

Cooper was so sweet and kind, the sort of person that a girl would be blessed to have. But there was nothing there and I felt panicked that this was how it was going to be from now on. He couldn't make me feel the earth-shattering, euphoric, and captivating emotions that Drayton made me feel. It was so unfair that it hurt.

I was realizing that you couldn't force feelings and love to exist where they didn't, in the same way that you couldn't deny when they did. The sound of gravel crunching beneath feet startled me, and I expected to find that Cooper had followed me. Maybe even Gabby. But instead, I came face to face with a shadowed Drayton.

My heart thumped with impossible strength at the sight of him. His black tailored suit hugged him perfectly. He was wearing a crisp white shirt and a thin belt. The shirt sleeves were rolled to his elbows, stretching at the seams around his large biceps. He wasn't wearing a tie and the top two buttons of his shirt were undone, revealing his toned, olive chest. He looked beyond good. He looked mesmerizing and I couldn't describe how deep the desire I felt for him went.

"Are you okay?" He was cautious, stopping a few feet in front of me.

"Yeah," I nodded. "We should probably stop meeting like this, though."

"I saw you basically run out of the gym." He stuffed his hands into his pants pockets. "I wanted to make sure that he hadn't done anything to make you upset."

"No, Dray, he didn't," I said. "I didn't even know you were here."

"I've been here for a while." He shrugged, and his eyes moved toward the corsage on my wrist. He stepped closer and lifted my hand to inspect it, the touch sending shock waves throughout my body.

"You told him to get this, didn't you? I don't know how you knew, but you had something to do with this?"

He didn't take his eyes off the corsage. "You love champagne, you always wear it." His hand slowly moved farther up my arm, his fingers grazing my skin so gently that it raised goose bumps as he moved toward my elbow. "And the lilies are obvious. You draw them all over your econ book."

At this point, if I had been hooked up to a machine, I'd have been condemned as a medical mystery with the rate that my heart beat and my lungs worked. He had a firm but gentle grasp on my elbow. His eyes locked with mine and a vulnerability that I'd never seen before shone through his every feature, like a bright beacon of hope. If sparks of electricity were visible between two people, we'd be lighting up the entire state at this point.

"Dray—" It came out as a breathless gasp as he tugged on my elbow and cupped my neck, driving our mouths together with a hungry force that knocked the wind right out of me.

My hands wound themselves around his neck, my fingers sliding into his hair as he pushed me backward into the wall. Our tongues met and I couldn't believe that the taste of peppermint over cigarettes actually tasted good, but it did.

His smooth tongue moved expertly against my own as his hands traveled down the length of my waist, across my hips, and onto the soft satin that caressed my thighs. We clawed at each other as if we couldn't get close enough, the hard brick wall behind me no doubt creating indents on my back, but at that point a natural disaster could have taken place and I don't think that I'd have noticed.

I could feel his swollen length pressed against my stomach through the soft, silky fabric, and it drew a moan from deep within me. His pace picked up in response, his hands winding in my hair and pulling my head back to expose my throat, which he dragged his hot mouth along, kissing and sucking his way to my collarbone. "In case it wasn't obvious," he murmured, still kissing my throat. "You look so fucking gorgeous."

I stared up the starry sky, gasping in ecstasy, completely at the mercy of his touch and coming undone at his words.

His mouth worked its way back up to my own, crashing against me furiously and urgently. His arm wound around my waist, pressing our bodies impossibly close together, his rock-hard chest felt beyond sensual, and I undid another button as we continued to kiss with need. I ran my hands across his pecs and chest, something I'd wanted to do since I first saw that sculpted masterpiece. My touch drew a throaty groan from him, which reverberated right through me, igniting more need than I thought was possible.

"Come with me?" he mumbled against my mouth, continuing to pepper me with wet, hot, needy kisses.

I wanted to follow him. I wanted to follow him anywhere he wanted to go, but the reality of the situation reminded me that I couldn't. It reminded me that I shouldn't even be doing this right now.

"I can't," I gasped and leaned away from his dangerous mouth. "Dray, I can't. I'm here with someone else."

He leaned against the wall, encasing me between his arms as we both desperately tried to catch our breath. I'd messed his hair up, quite significantly, and I was sure mine didn't look a lot better. Our breathless panting could probably be heard from miles away. But it didn't seem to matter. Nothing did. Drayton's eyes flickered between mine and my mouth, and he looked as though he was going to kiss me again. I wanted that. I wanted it all, all of him, all night long. But I was there with someone else, and even I couldn't go so far as to leave Cooper at a dance where he didn't know anyone.

"Yeah," he huffed and straightened up. "You are here with someone else. I'm sorry."

He leaned back in and placed a soft, chaste kiss against my swollen lips before he caressed my cheek and walked away. I was left leaning against the wall with the spins. I'd had a lot of kisses and not one had been in league with that.

I could only feel a fraction of guilt for what I'd just done. The high was still very much in place, and Cooper was a faint thought somewhere in the back of my mind. That was until I began walking back inside, only to find him leaning against the gym wall at the corner, a sad smile on his face.

"Cooper?" I attempted to fix the disheveled state that my hair is in. "How long have you been standing there?"

"Long enough."

"Cooper, I—"

"I guess I should have seen it coming." He twisted on the heel of his foot and began to walk in the other direction.

"Wait. Ple—"

"You could have told me." He turned around and I almost bumped into him. I felt sick for being the cause of his distress. "You could have just said, 'I'm not interested. Go home. You're wasting your time.'"

"I—It—I didn't want to be rude. You came here just for me. I didn't—It would have felt—I mean, I didn't want to ruin the weekend. It didn't seem fair to brush you off when you had nowhere else to go."

I was sobbing. Not because I was scared of losing his friendship—that would be awful—but because he seemed so hurt and frustrated, and I felt terrible.

"Don't, don't be upset." He sighed and sat down on the steps. "You're not really to blame here. I arrived without warning and with how complicated things seemed between you and Drayton, I should have known that it was wishful thinking that you would be available."

"I am sorry." I sat down beside him.

"Don't be." He smiled and stared in front of him. The soft night breeze tousled his hair and chilled the surface of my skin. It was getting colder but I was well aware my anxiety over the situation was making me feel ten times worse. "I get it, you know. You guys have this thing. It's pretty obvious that you're trying to fight it."

"I'm failing," I admitted.

"I've been in Drayton's position before—I've had to watch the girl that I love move on with someone because a future wasn't in our cards. It hurts."

"Drayton doesn't love me." I quickly denied the notion, not wanting the ache in my heart to become any worse.

"I wouldn't be so sure about that." He nudged my arm with a playful smile. "The way someone looks at you can say a lot about how they feel. You both look at each other as though . . . as though no one else around you exists."

"So, what happened? With the girl that you love?"

"Her family was originally from India, really traditional. They moved here when she was young, and we went to high school together. We went to separate colleges, but we made it work. I loved her. Unfortunately, her parents had arranged for her to marry someone else when she was a child. It's not super common but it does exist in some families.

"So anyway, when it came time for her to get engaged, she tried to end things between us. But it never worked. We always found our way back to each other. It was so hard to know that her heart belonged to me. I begged her to call it off, to be with me. I was willing to marry her if that's what it took, but she knew that she'd get shunned from her family and she felt that she couldn't lose them."

His tone was almost bitter, like he resented the families involved. I supposed I would have too.

"Anyway, after they got married, her husband moved them back to India. I think he knew something was going on. We had one last night together, and I haven't seen her in over six months. If she was to show up here, right now, I'd go to her in a heartbeat."

By the end of his story he looked worn and defeated, and I swiped the tear that slipped down my cheek as I sniffled.

"I know that feeling you two share," he continued with a firm voice. "You'll always find your way back to each other because no one else can compare. And Drayton hates me—I know that because I hated Priya's husband. A lot. But I wouldn't want to come between what you have." He rested his hand on my knee. "Don't lose it. Make it work."

"I don't know if it's that easy."

"Because of the distance?"

"That," I confirmed with a small sob. "And his reputation. My inability to trust men. The fact that my feelings for him overwhelm me doesn't help. It sort of scares me."

"Communicate. Talk it over and figure out what it is that you both want. You'll never get anywhere if you don't."

The thought of telling Drayton just how much I cared about him scared me, even if what Cooper said was logical. I wasn't used to being so vulnerable and exposed. "I really am sorry for messing you around." I gently dabbed at the teardrops on my cheeks so that I didn't ruin my makeup too much. "You deserve a lot better than someone who's hung up on another guy."

"Like I already said, don't worry about it." He stood up and offered me his hand, pulling me to my feet with ease. "Would it be horrible if I said that I was kind of using you too? Trying to get over Priya?"

"That actually makes me feel better."

We both laughed and a sense of relief washed over me. Cooper said, "Look, I'm going to head home. I'll stop at your place and grab my things first."

"I'll come with you." I started down the concrete steps but was intercepted by his tall frame.

"Please stay. Salvage the rest of your homecoming dance, okay? Talk to Drayton. It's fine—I'm sure that your brother will be more than happy to see me out."

I groaned. "I'll call him and tell him to ease up."

I waited with Cooper while he ordered an Uber, the conversation taking a less heavy turn as we discussed idle topics. I promised that when I moved to California, I'd seek him out as a new friend so that I didn't have to battle being a first year alone. Things felt like they were in a good place when the Uber pulled away, and he gave me a small wave from the passenger window.

"Where have you been?" Gabby asked as I walked back into the gym. She and Josh were huddled by the punch bowl.

I didn't immediately offer an answer because I was too busy scanning the area in hopes of finding my quarterback. Cooper was right—we should at least have a conversation about what that kiss meant. Did he want to be more than friends? Did he just want something physical? I wished I knew but it was so hard to tell with him.

"Is that a hickey?" Gabby shrieked.

A slapping noise sounded as I brought my hand to my neck, covering the spot where Drayton had been devouring me not more than twenty minutes earlier. Josh and Gabby watched me while I stuttered to come up with some excuse that they wouldn't believe for even a moment.

"Were you and Cooper getting in a little quickie action in the janitor's closet?"

"I don't know a single person who'd screw in the janitor's closet. Have you been in there? It stinks, it's cramped, and it's full of cleaning supplies. We have locker rooms or classrooms that'd work far better."

Gabby rolled her eyes but what caught my attention was Josh, who was staring at me with an accusatory glare. "Drayton just came through here not too long ago." He pointed at me with a calculating grin. "He looked all scruffy and undone."

"Where is Cooper?!" Gabby sucked all of the oxygen out of the room.

"He . . . He—he left. He went home."

I explained the entire situation from beginning to end because honestly, I wanted to talk about it more. I didn't think I'd entirely recovered from the mind-blowing session. My best friend was many things—loyal, hilarious, tech savvy—but she wasn't calm, and news that thrilled her, killed her. She was doing her best not to burst into an ear-piercing scream, which I appreciated, because they did my head in.

"What does this mean for you both?" She stepped forward and folded my hand between her own. "Are you going to tell him how you feel?"

"I think I have to," I told her, taking a moment to sweep the room for the millionth time. "I suppose I'll have to find him first."

"He disappeared pretty quickly," Josh informed us. He pulled his cell phone out of his suit pocket and tapped the screen with his thumbs. "I'll call him."

"Hey, man, we're looking for you? Where'd you go?"

Josh listened for the response. He turned around and lowered his voice, which only prompted me to step forward so I could hear what was being said.

"Why can't I tell her?" he asked in a hushed tone. "She wants to talk to you about something, bro. Just come back."

Josh's shoulders rose and fell with a deep breath as he ran his hand through his hair. The conversation wasn't giving me a very positive vibe and my stomach sank when he ended the phone call, turning around with an apologetic look etched on his face.

"He . . . He wasn't feeling well." Josh gave me a tight smile.

He was lying, I knew. And he knew that I knew. The urge to press for details simmered under my tongue. But I didn't want to put him in an uncomfortable position, so I kept my mouth shut, reduced to a feeling of utter disappointment.

"Excuse me, *babe*." Gabby folded her arms with a pointed glare. "Tell us what he said."

"Please don't make me," Josh pleaded. "You know that I love you, but respect the Bro Code."

"I will do no such thing," she bit back. "My best friend wants to talk to that idiot and you bett—"

"Gabs, stop," I cut her off, placing an arm on her shoulder. I appreciated the fierce instinct to get the information that I so desperately wanted to hear, but I would rather not get between her and her boyfriend or him and his best friend. "I don't need to know. I'll just—I'll talk to him on Monday."

"No! What if something happens in that time? Like, what if

he has to move across the country? What if your feelings go away or you change your mind!"

"I didn't talk to Drayton for an entire month and the moment that he approached me, we were eating each other's faces," I said sarcastically. "I don't think another day is going to change the way I feel."

"I suppose," she pouted defiantly. "You know how long I've been waiting for you to realize this though, right? Now I have to wait even longer. It sucks."

Deep down I shared her feelings. It wasn't like I'd planned on running into his arms and declaring my undying love, but a simple confession that yes, I did have feelings for him, and, yes, it was scaring me, and I wasn't sure exactly what to do with this new, or not so new, revelation, was more of the approach I'd been planning.

My dress was draped over the end of my bed. There was a small gap in the curtains that allowed the dim light to peep through. This morning felt colder. I reached out and snatched my cell phone from the side-table drawer before I snuggled deeper under the comforter. There were no new messages from Drayton. He hadn't responded to the one that I sent him last night. I hadn't wanted to overdo it, so I kept it simple.

> Hey. Cooper's gone home. I just thought that we
> could talk. Let me know when you get time?

It was ten in the morning and there was a definite urge to send him another message. But I resisted and leaped out of bed, leaving the phone behind so that it was out of sight but, unfortunately, not out of mind. Sort of like last night's kiss. I touched the wall as I wandered down the hall toward the living room. I felt like I needed to ground myself whenever I remembered what it was like experiencing the best kiss that I'd ever felt before. Feelings made a hell of a difference during a lip-lock.

"Morning, kid," Nathan mumbled from the couch where he was sprawled with the remote in his hand and his boxer shorts on. Sunday.

I waved lazily and wandered into the kitchen in search of coffee. I realized that I should have put on something warmer before I left my bedroom. Little shorts and a tank top didn't protect a whole lot from the midmorning chill. But my robe was so far away. I'd deal for now.

"So," Nathan called while I poured milk into a cup. "Carter packed up and left lightning fast last night. What happened there?"

"His name is Cooper," I sighed. "And nothing happened. That you need to know about."

"He hurt you? I'll shiv him."

"Relax," I slid the coffee jar back into its spot beside the microwave and picked up the hot coffee. "I was the one who hurt him. Sort of."

Nathan watched me with confusion as I walked in and sat down on the single seater beside the sofa. I took a sip and he sat up. "Wait. What the hell happened?"

"And men call women gossipers. Look at you. Desperate for the details."

"I need to know," he defended himself. "You're my little sister. It's a matter of protection and all of that."

"I kissed someone else at the dance and he saw it," I groaned. "Okay?"

"Wow. What a coldhearted witch. After he came all that wa—"

"Nathan." I threw a cushion at him—being cautious not to spill the coffee—and he laughed.

"I'm kidding, who was it? The quarterback, I bet."

"It was."

He gasped. "It was?"

"Enough."

He was mocking me now, gasping and covering his mouth as if he were a thirteen-year-old gossip queen as he walked over to the side table beside the door. "Mail," he tossed me an envelope and sat down again.

"When did this arrive?" I placed the coffee on the floor beside the chair. I turned the envelope over and almost choked on air. "Nathan! It's from CalArts."

Paper tore. My heart pounded and the words were almost a blur while I attempted to read each line. Nathan stood in front of me while I mumbled under my breath.

"I got an audition!"

We both screamed. Well, I screamed. Nathan shouted with a deep voice but total enthusiasm. I stood up and we hugged while I bounced up and down. It couldn't have come at a better time. This was a blessing—the perfect way to lift my spirits and remind me of what was important—my goals and dreams.

"So proud of you, kid." Nathan held me at arm's length and smiled an enormous smile full of pride. "California here we come, huh?"

"It says the audition is December 17." I read the letter again. The paper trembled in my hand. It was going to be framed. "That's a month and a half from now."

"You're sorted." Nathan shrugged. "You've been practicing the routine tons, right? It's that one to the song 'I Get To Love You'. By Ruelle."

"That's the one." I folded the paper and inhaled a deep breath. "But it has to be perfect. *Perfect.*"

He gave me a nudge in the shoulder. "It will be. You're talented as hell. You've got this."

My dream was closer. I hadn't heard back from the other two colleges, but the fact that my dream school had allowed me an audition was surreal. Nathan sighed and picked up the television remote. "I have a date later. I should get sorted."

"Another one," I mumbled with mild distaste. I was still reading the letter over and over again. "Is this a repeat date or another newbie?"

"Her name is Alana." He grinned. "She's a new teacher's aide at the junior high. That's all I need to know."

It would have been nice if he'd suggested that we go out for a celebratory meal or at the least had a beer together. Whatever. It was what it was. I'd almost forgotten that I had a coffee. So I picked it up—still clutching the letter—and sipped it while Nathan flicked through the television channels. We'd just sort of come to a standstill in the living room, as if moving or sitting back down could shatter this dream state that we were in.

But when I heard the sound of a motorcycle engine tearing up the road, becoming louder and louder, we both looked at each other and I felt as if my stomach was in my throat.

"Give me that." Nathan took the coffee cup and we continued

listening as the noise slowed down outside and then stopped. "One guess who that is."

"I'm not prepared." I swallowed.

"Prepared for what?"

Nathan didn't know the entire series of events from last night. Such as Drayton disappearing and making zero contact after we'd almost had sex on the side of a building.

After another moment of quiet—save for the thumping in my chest and ears—there was a knock on the door. There was no reason to be so panicked. This was what I'd wanted. I wanted to see him and talk to him. But it was the thought of admitting how I felt that was making me a bundle of nerves. I had never been such a mess around men before. I didn't like it.

Nathan headed toward the front door. I stood where I was and watched as he opened it and revealed Drayton. He was wearing a fitted pair of sweats and a hoodie. It was effortless and perfect on his muscular build. His hair was tousled from his helmet, and he nodded a polite greeting at Nathan.

"How's it going?" Nathan shook Drayton's hand and pointed a thumb over his shoulder. "Dallas, it's for you."

Funny bastard.

Drayton looked past Nathan, who beelined for the corridor, and found me standing in the middle of the room.

"Cute pj's."

"I got an audition." I held the letter up. "At CalArts. I got an audition."

His entire expression brightened as he stepped inside and closed the door. "Fuck yeah." He beamed pure elation. His excitement was sincere. "That's—that's so damn good. Knew you could do it."

He was in front of me now, his arms flinched, and it seemed as if he wanted to give me a hug. He must have decided that it was necessary in his congratulations because he wrapped his arms around me and pulled me in tight. It was intoxicating. His firm arms and chest. I was in far deeper than I'd thought. He let me go and while there was an abundance of unresolved tension between us, it didn't feel awkward. It felt right.

"I'm sorry about last night." He slipped his hands into his pockets. "Not about the kiss. I can't even think about that kiss when I'm in public."

I laughed. It was strangled and weird. But I laughed.

"But about after." He shrugged a shoulder. "Can we go and talk? Please?"

I smiled. "Sure. Let me get changed first."

"Wrap up," he called after me. "It's cold out."

He was right. It was cold out. I was wearing a pair of faded blue jeans, a cute turtleneck sweater, and a pair of knock-off Doc Martens, and I still shivered when we stepped outside. I followed him toward his motorcycle and noticed that there were two helmets resting on the seat. One of them was smaller. It was sleek, a glossy black with a clear face guard. It looked brand new.

"That's yours." He pointed at the helmet, then picked up his own.

"Mine?"

"Yeah. I was almost here and I realized that we can't ride around with one helmet in the middle of the day."

"So it's mine? As in, I can keep it?"

"You seem confused."

He pulled his helmet on, still watching me with the visor up while he laughed. I shut up because I didn't want to keep repeating myself. But it was a little bit startling that he would go and purchase a brand-new helmet for me. How often did he plan on having me on the back of this thing? My heart jumped a beat.

When we arrived at Rock Park, the same place that we'd come the first time we rode together, we left the motorcycle in the parking lot, which was no longer vacant, and walked the trail.

There were more people than just us there. It was a popular spot but it wasn't overcrowded. We walked. Small talk passed between us. And then we came to a trail that had a chain and sign across the path. It warned that it wasn't open to public thoroughfare. But of course, I wasn't surprised when Drayton swung his leg over the chain and gestured for me to follow him down the small, narrow path flanked by two tall thin sheds holding supplies for park rangers. It wasn't long before the shrubs and bush parted in a small clearing. A clearing so small it was almost the edge of the cliff. There was just enough room for us both to sit with our legs out in front of us.

"You wanted to talk." He leaned back on his hands and gave me a side-on glance.

"So did you."

"You first." He nodded at me. "Unless I can guess. You don't think that we should kiss again. It was a mistake. Etcetera, etcetera."

"No," I scoffed. "I like you. More than I want to. I want to kiss you again. And more. You're an idiot, but apparently I'm super into it because . . . because I really, *really* like you."

I was afraid to turn and look at him. My fears could be realized—he might be interested in something physical only. He might have changed his mind entirely after last night. All I knew was that my heart was hammering and I was nervous about what was to come next.

"Last night," he started, "Emily cornered me outside of the dance. She saw us, and not by accident. She followed me and she made some threats. She doesn't want us to spend time together, and if I don't go along with it, she said that she would have her mom put in words with CalArts. And SMU. Because that's near Baylor."

He rolled his eyes. He was so casual about it, as if Emily's scheming psychotic ass wasn't totally insane and unreasonable.

"What the hell?" I gaped. "I mean, I'm not surprised. But I am. She's . . . what the hell?"

"I'm crazy about you, Cheer." He ignored my rant and sat up straighter, directing himself toward me. "The moment you caught that ball and threw it back, I was interested. And the more that we talked, the more I felt. You're direct and honest. You don't stand for bullshit. You are who you are, and you don't apologize for it.

"When I took you to California, it wasn't because I had nothing better to do. It was because I wanted to spend time with you. Watching you experience new things, it's the fucking best. You have appreciation for detail. You don't take things for granted. You don't have your head up your ass, and when I dared you to kiss me, it wasn't so I could win the bet. It was because I was too much of a coward to be up front about what I wanted. Because I was scared that I'd end up giving you my whole heart, and you would leave and take it with you."

I leaned over and kissed him. He cupped my neck and wrapped an arm around my waist, pulling me onto his lap so that I was straddling him. Each time that we kissed, it got better and better. There was nothing to hold us back now. And it was evident in the way that we grabbed at each other and did whatever we could to close the distance between us.

"Wait," I leaned back, breathless and dizzied. "What does this all mean? I'm—I'm going to California next year. I don—"

"You don't want a relationship." He nodded, breathless as well. His hands still had a tight hold on my middle. "I know. But I like you and you like me. Can you trust that I won't hurt you and let's see where this goes?"

His movements were restless as he clutched me. His green gaze was still fixed on my mouth and while it was something that I wanted to avoid, I couldn't help but nod. Because I wanted to see where this could go as well.

"As long as you trust that I won't hurt you either." I shifted my hips and we kissed again. He had such soft lips, but he was so fierce and dominating.

"Wait." I leaned back again. "Emily? I mean, she's what? Out to get me?"

He dropped his head and exhaled. "Full disclosure, I don't think that she'll go that far. I think it's an attempt to keep control over the situation. She'll make life miserable, but I can't see her messing with your college plans. She wouldn't risk pissing me off to that extent. She's lucky that I put up with her bullshit now."

"Why do you put up with it?"

He frowned, holding me close while he watched the view behind me. "Because I've seen what her home life is like. I'm not saying that it's an excuse to be a bitch. But . . . it explains things."

I wanted to ask. But at the same time, I didn't feel that I had the right to know. Or needed to know. I hated Emily, but this sounded personal.

"Her parents are pieces of shit," he explained without prompting. "Her dad doesn't acknowledge her. Her mom is more interested in pretending that she's still a teenager rather than an adult with responsibilities. Their money and his career are more important than their daughter. I don't know, seeing it in person is so much worse. It's cold."

I felt genuine empathy for her. I wasn't a total monster. When my mom and dad were alive, Nathan and I were their entire world. We had the real deal. And the fact that Drayton was understanding of Emily and patient, and felt for her, it made me feel all that much more for him.

"We can keep this between us for a while." I shrugged, running my fingers through his hair. "We don't need to flaunt it all over school."

"I shouldn't have to hide you." His hands moved down my spine, slow and tantalizing.

"We're not hiding. We're just not throwing it in anyone's face. I wouldn't mind a bit of time to figure this out myself. It feels as if it's all happened so fast," I said. What I didn't say was that while it felt incredible, and I was happy and full of butterflies, I was aware of what the two of us were like. It might not last.

He watched me, his gaze moving across my face with a soft expression, like he wanted to absorb the moment. "All right, for now."

And then we kissed.

CHAPTER 16

Over the course of the next week we abided by what we said and kept this new romance between us, under wraps. Gabby and Josh knew, and of course, she'd been beside herself with excitement. But other than that, we were discreet.

It was hard sometimes. We both had to resist the urge to kiss whenever we were close at school. We watched each other, and even that could be dangerous because Gabby was quite clear about how obvious it was when we gave each other *the stare*.

We stole a kiss here and there, when we were 100 percent alone, and he came over in the afternoons if I wasn't working. That was when things grew more heated. The tension between us was reaching a boiling point. I almost couldn't handle it. But it felt so good to be open with him, or as open as we could be while we were hiding.

On Friday evening, I had a shift at the diner. The third one that week. It was as crowded as it was most Fridays. I hadn't worked a Friday in quite some time due to cheering at the football games, but now that the season was over, I was back in rotation.

Nathan drove me to work and swore that he would pick me up afterward. He didn't have to tell me what he was doing, I knew that he had a date. It surprised me that there were girls left in Castle Rock he hadn't slept with. Nevertheless, at the end of the shift, I wandered out to the parking lot. We'd had our first major snowfall that week, and it had been dropping white powder ever since, so the ground was like ice, and it was freezing.

Nathan was nowhere in sight although he'd promised me until he was blue in the face that he would be here. I walked down the sidewalk, pulling my coat tighter while I slid my phone out of my pocket.

Whoever he was with must have been a damn good distraction, because he had never forgotten to pick me up before. I dialed his number, hand trembling, nose stinging, lips quivering. If I had been preparing for a walk, I would have worn gloves and boots, not black lace-ups that were already soaked through.

No answer. I groaned, a cloud of white air billowing in front of me. My thumbs were stiff and rigid, but I managed to tap out a text. It was short because I didn't have the strength for a long one.

Pick me up!

It occurred to me then that the roads were icy tonight, and it had become slippery and dangerous. I swallowed and tapped out another text message.

If I hadn't been so distracted with frustration, I would have hung out at the diner or asked someone for a ride. Hindsight. I was almost frozen, and was losing the feeling in my feet and hands when a car went past me and abruptly slammed its breaks on. It was a miracle that it didn't lose control.

When I noticed more than just its glowing red lights against the black night, I realized that I knew this car. This Jeep, to be precise. The driver's door opened and Drayton stepped out. I almost didn't notice how furious he looked because he was wearing a fitted button-up coat with the collar up and a pair of white-washed jeans. He looked perfect. But he also looked furious.

"What the hell are you doing?"

"It's nice to see you too, babe."

"What are you doing, Dallas?"

"I'm—" I twisted, looking around behind me because I felt as though I was missing something. "I'm walking home."

"Why? Where's your car?"

"Nathan's got it. He was supposed to pick me up, but I think he forgot."

"Get in the car." He turned around and stormed back to the driver's side. His attitude was frustrating, and usually I would tell him to sort it out before I spent time with him, but I might have ended up with frostbite if I didn't get into a heated vehicle.

Tension radiated from Drayton, which made the sixty-second trip undeniably uncomfortable. His knuckles turned white from gripping the steering wheel so damn hard. When we pulled up in front of the house, I was barely out of the car before Nathan swung the front door open and flew out of the house in a panic.

"Dallas, I'm so sorry!" He waved the keys in his hand. "I was literally on my way. I forgot for a sec. I got distracted."

It was safe to assume that his date was inside. That was literally the only distraction that could possibly keep him from remembering something so simple. I was glad to see that he was alive though.

"It's fine, Nath—"

"You forgot?" Drayton snapped. I hadn't even realized that he'd hopped out of the car. "How the hell do you forget your own fucking sister!"

"Drayton!" I held my hand up to suggest that he stop. "Calm down. It's not a big deal."

"The hell it isn't," he shouted. "Don't let your sister walk home in the middle of the night. What the fuck is wrong with you, man? Take some responsibility!"

I was completely floored at the outburst and when I turned around to look at Nathan, he wore a similar expression to my utter shock.

"Fucking man up," Drayton snarled as he stormed back toward his Jeep. He hopped in and tore off down the road, leaving Nathan and me on the front lawn wondering what in the hell had just happened.

"Sis, what is wrong with your friend?" Nathan blinked as Drayton's taillights disappeared around the corner.

"I have no idea," I mumbled.

As I passed him, I snatched the keys and ran inside. No surprise, there was a girl on the couch. I didn't even wave. I went straight to my bedroom, changed out of my wet socks and shoes, pulled on some jeans, a sweater, and my snow boots, and then I left again.

I wasn't a huge fan of speeding. I never had been. But I didn't hesitate to hit the gas. Of course, speeding when it was snowing was going, like, ten miles an hour, so it wasn't exactly *The Fast and the Furious*, but I managed to make good time.

When I pulled into Drayton's driveway and shut off the car, I saw the Jeep. He must have seen me coming because the front door opened and he stepped outside, closing it behind him.

"Yeah, Dallas, I know," he grunted. "I flipped out at your broth—"

"You need to tell me what the hell that was about," I ordered, marching up the front steps.

"It wasn't about anything." He shrugged. The fury had faded but there was still a distinct hostility in his attitude. "Leave it alone."

"No." I stood in front of him, refusing to back down. "I deserve an explanation. This isn't the first time you've flipped out at me for walking home alone at night. And if you're going to yell at my brother, then I want to know why. Dray,"—I stepped closer and lifted my hand to the stubble of his jawline, gently caressing the sharp structure of his face—"let me in. Tell me what that was really about. I know there's something you're keeping from me. You can trust me."

I didn't want to think about the fact that we'd only been seeing each other for one week and we were fighting. He was unresponsive for what seemed like minutes. Total silence enveloped both of us but it wasn't uncomfortable. Silence never had been with us.

I was relieved when he encased my hand in his own and turned to lead me inside. I'd been willing to let the secrets slide for so long, knowing that everyone has them, and his could be for a good reason. But after tonight, I needed to know, not just out of casual curiosity, but because I couldn't stand to think of him being tortured by this burden. Whatever it was, I wanted him to know that I was there.

After I removed my boots, we sat down on the three-seater sofa in one of the living areas. It was a beautiful space, aesthetically decorated with decadent art pieces and the same stone theme as the rest of the house. The modern features, like the tinted windows and built-in television, were remarkable, and there was a faux lick of flames coming from the electric fireplace that cast a light mood throughout the room. But all of this was an unfocused image in the background because Drayton dominated all else. He outshone everyone and everything in any room he entered. To me at least.

I shuffled toward him as he took a deep breath and rubbed his hands together, almost as if he was amping himself up for the conversation, mustering all of his courage and strength.

"I haven't told anyone this before," he stated with his eyes on the ground. "I haven't even really said it out loud."

"I'm here," I offered. I didn't want to push him, but he needed to know that he could tell me anything.

"I haven't always been an only child," he told me with a voice so heartbroken that it almost shattered my own. "I had a twin sister. Her name was Abigail. Abby for short. She was—she was my best friend. We did everything together, you know? Dad was always taking us on these football fields and carting us around the country, but it was awesome because we always made the most of it."

He smiled at the floor, his memories lifting his lips.

"When we lived in Texas, we had this group of friends who

lived a few houses down from us. We were twelve and our friend was turning thirteen, so he was having a big party, minus alcohol, ya know? It was games like air hockey and pool, that sort of thing. A bunch of kids were invited so we all went together.

"Anyway, I got pretty tired around eleven. We lived down the street, so we walked back and forth all the time. It took us about thirty seconds to get home. I told Abby I was heading home and that I'd come back and get her when she was ready. She just had to text me."

His head fell, hanging low as a sob racked his body. Watching him in so much pain was beyond unbearable. I'd seen him open up to me, I'd seen him express emotion, but nothing like this.

"The next morning I woke up and realized that I'd slept through a bunch of calls and texts. The last one said that she thought someone was following her."

He took a moment to steady his voice and wiped his face with the back of his hand. Sniffing before he exhaled, he tried to gain composure. I didn't need him to finish the story—I knew where it was headed—but I didn't stop him when he continued.

"They found her body two days later, in a ditch about thirty miles from home. Naked, beaten, and assaulted. They caught the guy. He was just some sick pervert who happened to stumble across her. There was no association. My dad retired from the NFL and we moved here a few months later, in hopes of a fresh start."

"Drayton, I'm so sorry—"

"Don't!" He sat up straighter and turned to me with a firm expression, his eyes rimmed red. "Do not tell me you're sorry. What happened to her is my fault."

"No, it isn't," I argued, picking his hand up and lacing our fingers together. "Drayton, it isn't your fault."

"I should have walked with her. It's my fault."

"Stop! You were just a child," I told him with a firm tone. "What about your parents? They should have been picking you up and dropping you off themselves. You can't shoulder that kind of blame."

"My parents left a sitter with us. Stupid airhead was obsessed with her boyfriend and not much else," he growled with disapproval. "They were in Miami for a game."

"Dray, please, you can't carry around guilt for something that wasn't your fault." I squeezed his hand and didn't take my eyes off his face. "It'll make you sick. You didn't do anything wrong."

"Sure feels like it."

A thought occurred to me and I lifted the sleeve of his T-shirt to reveal his shoulder, where the little boy and girl walked into the sunset. "This is about her isn't it?" I asked, grazing my fingertips along the surface of his skin, a field of goose bumps forming in my wake.

"Yeah," he mumbled, his eyes focused on the hand caressing his shoulder.

"Drayton, if you don't believe anything else I say, believe this: you are not responsible for what happened." I tucked my hand around the length of his jaw and caressed his cheek with my thumb. "This isn't on you. But I understand why you hate seeing me walk home at night now."

His facial muscles quivered, and it hurt to see him in so much pain.

"That night that you walked away from me in Cripple Creek was—it was—shit. I felt like I was reliving a nightmare. Reliving that night and I couldn't let it end the same way. Dallas, I don't like seeing any young girl walking alone,"—he swiveled his body toward me—"but especially not you. Promise me that you'll always call me if you need a ride. That's what I'm here for. You mean too much to me. Promise me?"

"I promise."

His shoulders relaxed and his features smoothed at the verbal agreement. I wished I'd known about this sooner. It brought him into a whole new light. I understood him better than I ever had. He'd been battling this demon on his own for so long, with no one to tell him that he shouldn't feel the guilt that he did. No one to comfort him when the memories became too much. He pulled me into a hug, and I relaxed into his side, resting my head on his chest. We leaned back into the couch and remained like that for a while. It was quiet. Shadows danced on the dark walls from the faux flames. He smelled different. He smelled the same—intoxicating and alluring—but the nicotine wasn't lingering. I hadn't seen him touch a cigarette in a while, and after how wound up he'd been earlier, I would have expected him to turn to his vice. I kept the observation quiet, but I felt hopeful.

After some amount of time, I wasn't sure how long, his hand began to caress my arm. "Thank you," he murmured.

"What for?"

"For listening. For understanding and for not making me feel worse."

"Dray, I would never. I meant what I said. You aren't to blame, and you don't deserve to carry around that sort of guilt."

Our eyes locked and my heart started to race when I felt his hot breath fan my face. A current of electricity surged between us, becoming stronger as we moved closer. I'd always been impossibly attracted to Drayton, but now that I knew him on a deeper level, a level that opened a wider understanding and a more intimate connection displayed by trust, I was certain that I loved him.

He closed the distance between us, and our mouths met, erupting so much need from within me that I couldn't move fast enough to wrap my arms around his neck. I couldn't get him close enough as I threw my leg over his lap. His hands slid up my thighs as we kissed with a passion so strong that I could feel my head spinning because of his touch, his mouth, his hands as they came around to the backs of my thighs.

Traveling up the length of my spine, his hands tangled in the hair on the back of my head as he pulled it back and exposed my throat. He worked his way down my jaw and neck as I ground my hips into his. He groaned, a loud, carnal groan that only added fuel to the burning fire that was flaming all around us.

"Do you want to go upstairs?" My breath was ragged and harsh.

He leaned back, staring up at me with awe and lust. Without giving a verbal answer, he cupped my ass and jumped to his feet, swinging my legs around his waist.

"Fuck yes, I do," he growled.

Being with Drayton was different. Better. The way that he watched me was tender, but his hands were rough. His touch was driven by affection, but his grip was fueled by desire. The words that he whispered beside my ear, hot breath on my neck, were dirty and carnal but his tone was emotive. Between us existed more than just lust—we knew each other. We were vulnerable and our hearts were on our sleeves, and it was a difference that I never knew was missing. But moving with him, in perfect sync as we'd always done, naked, exposed in more than just a physical sense, I'd never felt more connected to another person before, and it was a sensation that left me undone.

CHAPTER 17

I was on cloud nine.

I needed a shower; my hair was probably a wreck and I wasn't going to walk right for a day or two, but I had literally never felt more satisfied in my entire life. It had been a while since the last time I woke up in Drayton's bedroom. Flecks of light peeped through the trees on the other side of the window. The fireplace was on a low heat, keeping us warm.

I stared out the window and smiled at the feeling of Drayton's naked chest pressed against my back, his arm slung over and clutching my waist. I was being spooned and it was as perfect as I'd imagined it would be. Happiness wasn't even the right word for my current state of emotion.

"Morning," Drayton's raspy morning voice startled me out of my reverie. His arms tightened around my waist and he softly pressed his lips to the skin behind my ear.

"Hey." I chewed on my lip as his toe-curling kisses traveled down the side of my throat. It took very little from him to erupt that carnal need that burst under his touch. I was mildly disappointed when his lips stopped and he turned me around to face him.

"Last night was perfect, Cheer." He brushed his fingers along the length of my forehead, tucking my hair behind my ear as his eyes traveled my face.

"It was perfect," I agreed, enraptured by his presence. I knew that I was in trouble when my heart felt as if it was going to come out of my chest when he watched me. "So, just for curiosity's sake, what were you doing last night? Following me?"

"Dreamer," he scoffed with a grin. He sat up and leaned against the headboard with one arm behind his head. The sheet draped across his hips, revealing his V-line. He was mouthwatering. "I was at Maxon's. Got bored. I was on my way to see what you were doing."

"Ah." I smiled and nodded.

He mimicked me. He wrapped his arm around my middle and pulled me in so that I was on top of him. It was one swift, effortless movement, and his hand tangled in the hair on the back of my head.

"What ar—"

The door opened and we both turned our heads to the left. Standing in the doorway was his father. Drayton lifted the sheet up as I dipped lower so that my chest wasn't exposed. Even under the cover, I was mortified.

"Dad." Drayton sat forward and gestured with frustration. "Knock. What the hell?"

His father appeared unfazed. He was tall, like his son. Well built, young with dark hair and stubble—the spitting image of Drayton but with a much more indifferent expression and a suit

253

clinging to his muscular frame. He rested a hand on the door-knob. "You have a phone call with the coach and the head of the sports department at Baylor this morning."

"I haven't forgotten."

"Hello." He let go of the handle and tugged on the cuff of his sleeve. "I'm Leroy."

"It's nice to meet you." I nodded, horrified that I was meeting Drayton's father for the first time with nothing on but a sheet that probably cost more than my car, but that was irrelevant. He acknowledged me with a brief tip of his head, then turned back to his son with the same no-nonsense expression that he'd regarded him with before.

"Eleven. Be organized, dressed, and alone."

When he was gone, Drayton relaxed again. He fell back into his pillow and threw an arm across his face. I was disappointed to have met both of his parents under less than ideal circumstances.

"Do you realize that I was naked when I met your aunt and now your dad?" I clutched the sheet and frowned. "How does that happen to a person twice?"

"Lucky bastards. The most I got was the see-through shirt. Where were the naked meet and greets when I knocked on the door?"

I scoffed with amusement and peered over my shoulder. Drayton was still hiding beneath his forearm. "You okay?"

"He used to be cooler," he mumbled. "I give him grace because losing my sister nearly killed him, but, man, he knows how to push me."

"He's pretty set on which college you attend?"

"Yep. He won't stop hounding me about my letter of intent. I was offered six scholarships. *Six*. And I'm not even allowed to consider another school."

Six was impressive. He had options and part of me was desperate to ask if he was offered one near CalArts. But I didn't. Because I didn't want him to base his decision on me. It was too big.

"Let's not talk about it. It pisses me off."

"Feeling wound up?" I asked, snuggling into his side. "You need an outlet?"

He rolled over me, my body pinned beneath his. "Are you offering one?"

His grin disappeared as he leaned in and trailed soft kisses under my jaw.

⚡

On Monday afternoon, in the last ten minutes of lunch, I leaned against my locker in the corridor and swiped through Instagram. Gabby had gone to the library so that she could catch up on her reading but I'd hung back, knowing that my next class was down the hall and there was no point wandering farther off. I scrolled through videos of dance teams that I followed and admired their routines, read announcement posts on new competitions, and marveled at still shots showing the sheer power that it took to move their bodies the way that they did.

I was so immersed, with my lip pinched between my fingers, that I didn't notice someone coming up behind me. But when a strong pair of hands went around my middle and soft lips touched the side of my neck, I smiled and almost forgot that Drayton and I were meant to be keeping our situation a secret.

"What are you doing?" I turned to face him and swept my

eyes along the corridor. There were a few freshmen hanging around near the staircase, but that was it.

Drayton stood tall in front of me and rested a hand on the wall as he backed me into it. "I cannot see you and keep on walking. It's impossible." He dipped down and kissed me, softly and gently.

Or it was soft and gentle until his free hand moved to cup my neck and his thumb drew circles on the edge of my jaw. I melted into it and held a fistful of his shirt. My insatiable need to taste and touch him was overwhelming, and putting a hand to his chest to stop him was almost impossible.

"This is way too public," my voice hitched as my tongue swiped across my bottom lip. I loved the taste of him. "You'll get us caught."

He exhaled with one hand still on the wall beside me and his gorgeous face just an inch from mine. Before I could react, he wrapped his hand around mine and dragged me into the closest classroom. With the door shut, he pressed me against the wall beside it and kissed me, hard. The posters crinkled and crunched behind me.

Desk legs scraped along the floor as Drayton lifted me under the thighs and propped me on top of the wooden tables. The sound of our mouths smacking and our ragged panting echoed around us, and when he moved his mouth to my neck and I threw my head back, legs clenching, I finally noticed that we were in the sex-ed classroom. The irony. A girl with a wide smile and her thumbs up looked down at me from the wall. The speech bubble next to her said: *A condom is cheaper than a child.* I almost laughed but Drayton's hand clutched a fistful of hair and tugged as he pressed his hips into mine and I gasped.

Our mouths met again and we became so frantic, grabbing, touching, and kissing, that I thought we were about to do it right there in front of the Sensible Sarah poster. But the bell rang, and we both knew that this would not be an ideal time to take our clothes off. Drayton groaned and his head fell into the crook of my neck as he remained between my legs with his hands on the desk.

"We should get out of here," I said. I could hear the corridor getting busier. He nodded and stepped back, which made me slap a hand over my mouth because his arousal was blatant, standing to attention in his pants.

"Yeah, I know." He ran a hand through his hair and gave me a devious grin. "Want to help me get rid of it?"

"Nice try." I stood up and smoothed my hair down. "Just wrap your hoodie around your waist. The arms will hide it. Maybe."

He sighed and dropped his backpack before pulling his hoodie off. It pulled his T-shirt up and I admired the brief peek of his firm torso. After he'd sorted himself out and we were safe to leave, I opened the door and stepped into the hall to find Emily about six feet away. I panicked and pulled the door shut, smacking Drayton's arm with it before he could follow me. We should have been leaving separately, anyway. I heard him curse, but from the unbothered scowl on Emily's face, I assumed that she hadn't heard it.

"What?" She stopped beside me when I remained in front of the door, smiling.

"Nothing."

"What's with the dipshit smile?" She rested her hand on her hip, impatience in her tone.

"I was just so happy to see you that I couldn't help but smile."

She narrowed her glare, her pillowed red lips curling down. "You're being very suspicious. What do you *think* you know?"

Now I was just confused. I didn't let her know that, though. If she was the one squirming, I wanted to keep it like that. "We should hang out sometime. Get a coffee. A movie. Perhaps we could torment some small children together. You do that for fun, right?"

She scoffed and barged into me with her shoulder as she passed. I watched her leave with amusement, but when I looked around and noticed how packed the corridor was, I frowned. Still, Drayton couldn't hide in the classroom forever. I opened the door so that I could tell him to give me a five-minute start. But when I peeped through the crack, he was nowhere to be found. That was when I noticed the open window on the other side of the room.

I laughed and closed the door again. This secret thing was kind of fun sometimes.

CHAPTER 18

Traditionally, Nathan and I spent Thanksgiving with Camilla and Gabby. But things were a little different this year. Josh and Gabby were dating. Drayton and I were together, even if it still hadn't become public knowledge. Nevertheless, Drayton insisted that Nathan and I join his family's Thanksgiving celebration. Josh had invited Gabby and Camilla as well. At around eleven Thursday morning, the four of us pulled up at the Lahey mansion and Camilla couldn't contain her enthusiasm, "I bet the kitchen is beautiful!"

She was out of the car first. Her dark hair, much like Gabby's, was in a braid that fell over her shoulder. We'd been told to dress in blue—for the Dallas Cowboys—but Camilla said that the color didn't compliment her and opted for a green long-sleeved dress underneath her thick coat. Nathan still looked miserable because he knew that we were here as Cowboys supporters that night. He tugged at the blue beanie on his head, the only blue that he'd agreed to wear, and lingered behind Gabby and me as we went up to the front-door landing and rang the doorbell.

Ellie, Drayton's mother, greeted us. She was head to toe in blue cashmere, and perfect dark-blonde waves framed her face.

"Come in, come in." She was all smiles and Cartier bracelets jangling as she waved us forward. "Dallas, hello again."

"Hey, Mrs. Lahey." I was pleased to see that she was more relaxed than she had been the last time we'd met. We stood in the immaculate foyer, tiles gleaming and the water feature drizzling. "This is Nathan. Nathan, Mrs. Lahey."

"Ellie," she corrected as she and Gabby exchanged cheek kisses. Weird, but not unreasonable, I supposed. Gabby spent a lot of time here. "Lovely to meet you, Nathan. Drayton has told me so much about your history at the school. And you must be Camilla?"

Nathan seemed proud and Gabby's mom snapped her head toward Ellie. She'd been immersed in the perfection surrounding her. "Yes. Hello. Your home is sensational."

Ellie touched a hand to her chest with appreciation and wrapped an arm around Camilla's. "Let me show you around."

That left the three of us, and we wandered through the first living area, which led to another living area that was twice as large with two huge sofas and armchairs. The flat-screen television was theater sized and had Nathan salivating.

A catering table was laid at the back of the room, and there were more snacks to choose from than at a convenience store. Leroy had an old school–looking blue football hoodie on. It had his name and number across the back of it. He had a beer in hand and was focused on the sports highlights on the television until he heard that he was no longer alone. He turned around and regarded us with his usual flat stare. We hadn't spoken since he walked in on Drayton and me in bed, and it seemed that his impression of me wasn't great.

"The kids are in the dining room," he said.

Gabby piped up with a nervous appreciation. "Okay, thanks."

She gripped my elbow to drag me out of the room, but I didn't want to ditch Nathan. It was a misplaced concern, though, because Nathan walked toward Leroy and offered his hand. "It's nice to meet you, sir. Nathan Bryan."

Leroy shook his hand and I could tell Nathan would be happier here, talking with an adult rather than hanging around with the teenagers. Gabby and I went back the way that we'd come, past the kitchen where we could hear Ellie and Camilla, and entered the dining area.

It looked beautiful, sure. A long table was elegantly decorated with rustic placings, little pumpkins, floral designs, and expensive china. But my focus went straight to the corner of the room where Drayton, Maxon, Austin, Emily, and Becca were standing beside a table of chilled beverages.

"Oh, is Josh upstairs?" Gabby asked.

Drayton nodded but he watched me.

"Ew," Emily sneered when she saw me. Her scowl moved over my outfit—a simple blue hoodie that was snug, a white beanie, and a pair of black jeans. No matter how hard she tried, she could never make me feel inadequate—I would have to care for that. "What is she doing here?"

Drayton stared at her with so much hatred that if the other three hadn't been watching me with interest, they would have known that there was something going on.

"She came with me," Gabby interjected with a small voice, pushing her glasses up her nose. I appreciated her defense, despite being nonconfrontational. "I'll be upstairs, Dal. Want to come?"

"No." I smiled at the group of athletes in front of me. "I'm good here."

She left and Drayton mouthed *Sorry* before the rest of them could notice. I tried not to stare at his muscular frame underneath his blue shirt—the sleeves rolled up to his elbows—and jeans. He leaned against the wall with a bottle of beer in his hand and watched me approach the drinks table.

"Come on, Becca," Emily ordered as I stood beside her and poured a soda into a glass. "This event just got kicked from classy to crap."

I kept my head down but laughed at her pathetic attempt to insult me. She and Becca wandered off arm in arm, and I quietly hoped that they would leave altogether.

"How's it going, Cheer?" Maxon gave me a teeth-baring grin, and out of the corner of my eye I saw Drayton stiffen. "Nice blue nails. Spirited."

"Please don't call me that."

I saw Austin's devious stare move to Drayton, but I didn't look or give it mind. "Only Dray gets to use that name, right?"

"No one does," I snapped. I wanted to know what they were doing here in the first place, but I was the new one. This was probably a long-standing tradition, and I had no right to get upset.

"Excuse me." I turned around and left the room, hearing the sniggering male voices behind me and Drayton telling them to shut it.

The afternoon just became duller from there. Everyone else was having a good time. We all sat around the exquisite table and the food was five star, but I'd come with the idea in mind that

Drayton and I would be able to relax and be ourselves. Instead, it was as if we were at school. Nathan and Gabby sat on either side of me. They were both immersed in conversation, though. Leroy and Nathan had been chatting all afternoon, and Gabby was focused on Josh. Drayton sat on the opposite side of the table with Maxon on his right and Austin on his left.

As hard as I tried, I couldn't stop looking up at him, and he was always watching me first. His hands clasped in front of his chin, his leg shook. His movements were restless throughout the entire meal and at one point, he pulled his cell phone out of his pocket and tapped the screen.

"Drayton," Ellie scolded with a spoonful of soup hovering in front of her mouth. My phone vibrated in my pocket while she was talking. "No phones during the meal. We talked about this last night."

His bored stare was directed at his plate as he ran his hand through his hair. It was obvious that he'd sent that text to me but after watching Drayton get scolded for using his phone, I wasn't about to check mine. He gestured with wide eyes but I subtly shook my head and pushed beans around on my plate. This hiding thing sucked, but it was for my benefit, and I was grateful that he didn't just come out and expose us in front of the she-devil at the end of the table.

After the meal, Leroy let us all know that the Cowboys game against the Miami Dolphins would be on in the theater room. I thought the television in the living room was large enough. Gabby and I helped Camilla and Ellie wash up.

Gabby stood at the island and wrapped leftovers. She whispered, "Josh said that Becca and Emily weren't invited. Maxon and Austin brought them."

I smiled and nodded with understanding as I scraped scraps onto one plate. I supposed I could check the text now, but I finished with the washing up first. The moms poured themselves some wine, and Gabby and I went and found Josh in the rec room, where there was gaming and a pool table. The girls were nowhere to be seen, and Maxon and Drayton were playing pool while Austin gamed.

I sat down on a single armchair and checked my phone. I could feel Drayton watching me as I opened his message.

> I didn't invite them. Mom always invites Maxon and Austin. They brought the girls. I'm real sorry. Go upstairs? I'll come up after?

I closed the message and leaned back in the seat. The game would be on soon, at four, and I wasn't upset with Drayton. We could wait until everyone was gathered in the theater, and no one would come and look for us. I met his piercing stare and shook my head but smiled. He looked frustrated. Gabby and Josh excused themselves and disappeared, again. After a few minutes, Austin looked over at me.

"Come and tap in to a game, Ch—Dallas?"

I stared at the bloodshed on the screen and frowned. Gaming didn't interest me, but I shrugged and stood up, wandering past Drayton, who leaned over the pool table with his cue lined up. I bumped into him and quickly apologized.

"It's all good," he said. I hoped that I was the only one who could hear the teasing in his tone.

Austin showed me the ropes of the game but it was still hard.

Each time that I died, it affected him because we were on a team or something. I honestly had no idea what I was doing. I was just tapping buttons and attempting to aim the gun. Each fail that I made, Austin became more restless, his tone shorter, and I was sure that the pace at which he was sinking his beers was not helping.

"Fucking hell, man." He shot up out of his seat and dropped his controller. I watched him with amusement. "It's not that hard to get. Are you stupid?"

"Dude," I said. "Calm down. It's a game."

I looked at Drayton and Maxon, who were watching their friend throw a tantrum. Drayton's knuckles went white as they twisted around the pool cue.

"Exactly, it's a game. Not rocket science, you idiot."

I stood up. "Get a grip. Childish brat."

"Shut the fuck up," he scoffed and sat back down. "Dumbass."

"Bro, relax," Maxon said, amused.

"Quit talking to her like that." Drayton sounded dangerous, like he was attempting to keep in control.

"It's fine," I said.

"Fuck off, Drayton." Austin started setting up a new game, without me in it. "She's an idiot. The hell are you even doing here? Piss off back to the diner, grease girl."

I exhaled, jaw clenched, and leaned down to rip the controller out of his hands before storming over to the console and switching it off.

He stood up fast and stormed straight for me. For a moment, I wondered if I'd taken things too far. "You fucking bitch. That loses progress."

He stopped in front of me, towering over me, and I couldn't

believe it when he shoved my shoulder. Was he seriously this worked up over a game? He opened his mouth, no doubt to spill more insults, but he didn't get the chance because he was grabbed around the back of the neck and shoved into the wall.

"Did you just touch her?" Drayton held him by the throat and my heart sped up at how fast things had taken a turn.

Sort of hot, though.

Drayton looked so angry. I hadn't seen him like this before. Not even after the incident with Nathan. He shoved Austin back into the wall. "Don't ever put a hand on her again, Austin. I swear to God—"

"Dray." Maxon stood beside them and tapped his shoulder. "Come on. Ease up. She's all good."

"That's not the fucking point." Drayton shoved Maxon back with his free hand and pointed at Austin, who was struggling against Drayton's grip, staring at him with rage. "Talk to her like that again, *touch* her like that again, and I'll fuck you up."

He let Austin go and stepped back. Austin rubbed his neck and the two of them locked in a menacing stare as Austin wandered off. He passed me and raised his hands with a taunting wave before he gave me a light shove in the shoulder again. It wasn't aggressive. It didn't hurt. But testing Drayton's promise wasn't the best idea.

Drayton took one step forward, gripped Austin's shirt, and punched him so hard in the jaw that he went straight down, collapsing on the floor.

"Bro." Maxon knelt beside Austin and started helping him up. Drayton watched them, unfazed.

"You can fuck off out of my house."

Maxon supported Austin, who looked dazed as a red welt started forming on his cheek and jaw. "I'll drive him home."

"Bye."

The two of them were gone before Drayton turned to me and his anger morphed into a splitting grin.

I shook my head with amusement. "I'm sort of aroused."

I wasn't sure where Becca and Emily were, but I was relieved that neither of them had seen that. Drayton approached me, fast and swift, and pulled me in at the waist. "Well thank fuck we're alone."

He kissed me and I raised myself on my tiptoes to deepen it, sliding my fingers into his hair. The way that he handled himself never ceased to amuse me. He was so protective and fierce. It made me swoon and feel safe. We heard someone clearing their throat behind us and turned around to find Gabby and Josh.

"Just saw Austin and Maxon leaving," Josh said, his mouth lifting at the corners. "Looks like we missed something."

"Something." Drayton shrugged as his hand slid down my spine and came to rest above my bum. "We'll be fine when he's sober and apologizes."

Gabby looked confused but didn't ask. I would tell her later. "Where are the girls?"

Josh gestured behind him. "Flirting with Nathan in the theater. It's embarrassing. Want to watch?"

I nodded and went to step forward, but Drayton kept his hold tight and tucked me into his side. "We'll be there in a minute."

They left us in the rec room and we reveled in a little time alone before we joined the others to watch the Thanksgiving game. It was one of the best holidays that I'd had.

CHAPTER 19

On the afternoon before my audition at CalArts, Nathan and I were sitting in the hotel restaurant eating an early dinner. The hotel that we were staying at was the Hilton Garden Inn. It was nice and just six minutes from CalArts. Palm trees covered the grounds and there was a pool—although I doubted that we'd use it. The outdoor court was nice at dusk. Blue fairy lights wrapped around the palm-tree trunks. There was a small gym as well, which I considered using for a light workout before the audition.

Nathan sat across from me in the cozy establishment. The carpet was a patterned brown, the room was long, and dark wooden tables sat in rows. Windows stretched along the left wall and offered a view of the enchanting outdoor court. I glanced up from the open-faced steak sandwich in front of me and found Nathan grinning at his phone screen.

"What?"

He snapped his head up.

"What's so amusing?"

"Oh," he chuckled. "Nothing. I have a date tonight. That's all."

My shoulders fell and my glare narrowed. "We've been here for four hours. How?"

"I'm prepared."

"You're a ho," I mumbled, shoveling a forkful of focaccia bread and steak into my mouth.

His laugh was disbelieving. "A ho?"

"I have to be at the school first thing in the morning. Are you going to be there?"

"Yes." He seemed confused that I would even ask.

I was disappointed that we'd come to California together and he had already organized himself to go out and leave me alone. We finished our meal with a significant drop in conversation and he suggested that we wander the grounds for a while. The Christmas lights were festive. It was light-sweater weather. I was wearing a long-sleeved shirt and jeans. No snow was a serious reprieve from home. A text from Drayton popped up.

> It's so cold here. My balls need their own tea cozies. Come back and cuddle me soon. Okay? Good luck for tomorrow. You'll nail it. Just like you nail me. HAHAHA. I'm done. I swear. Miss you x

The message made me giggle. He was such a goof. But it warmed me all over to know that he was missing me as well. I knew that I'd messed up the no commitment plan—not that we'd talked titles—that I had in place. But with Drayton, I sort of had no choice. He was impossible not to love.

"Is that Drayton?"

I nodded.

"How's that going? King and queen of the school yet?"

"No." I gave Nathan a brief side-on glance as I tapped out a response to Drayton. "No one knows."

"What?"

"We're not out. Or public. Or whatever."

"Why?"

I groaned. "Because my cheer captain is a huge bitch who wants to dictate the happiness of others. That's all."

The conversation came to a pause when we arrived back at the hotel reception. We headed through the reception area and out into a square court. Our room was on the bottom floor of the two-story hotel. The room was nice. Clean. There was a narrow space between the end of the two double beds and the dresser. A desk, a computer chair, and an armchair sat at the end of the room beside a small window. It was enough for one night.

Nathan closed the door behind us and I fell back onto one of the beds. It groaned in protest, but it wasn't uncomfortable, which was a relief. I needed to be well rested for tomorrow.

Nathan sat down on the corner of his bed beside the window. "What's the deal with the cheer captain?"

"She's a bitch," I mumbled, staring at the ceiling. "She'll screw my chances of getting CalArts if she thinks that I'm dating Drayton."

"Really?"

"Yes." I sat up and began shuffling through my duffel bag. There wasn't a whole lot of space in the room but I'd use what I could to practice for the audition. "I need to get CalArts since, you know, I didn't get an audition for SMU or Colorado College."

"You didn't?" Nathan almost followed me into the bathroom until he realized that he was following me into the bathroom. He seemed somewhat distressed.

"I didn't," I continued talking from behind the bathroom door, pulling off my jeans and shirt, and pulling on the shorts and T-shirt. "I'm not sure why. But it means that I need this to go well tomorrow."

"How come I didn't know about this?"

"You've been sort of distracted. You're out a lot. Plus, it's not news worth talking about. If I don't get accepted into CalArts, college gets pushed back another year. I'm focusing on the positive."

"What do you mean I've been distracted?"

"It means that you've been distracted." I tied my hair back. "You're out all weekend. You're late home after work. Like, damn, I sound like a nagging wife. But whatever. You're dating a lot. It is what it is."

Nathan didn't like being cornered. He didn't like being called out, but when I opened the bathroom door, I noticed that his cheeks had turned dark red. After Drayton shouted at him for forgetting me at work a month and a half ago, he apologized. But for a week or so, he also brought it up in conversation whenever it seemed "natural." He wanted to know if Drayton was still upset with him.

"You've never seemed to have a problem with it before?"

"Yeah." I started stretching. "Because I don't have a problem with it. But planning a date on our first trip to California together seems a little shit."

"You could have said something."

"Why should I have to?! Why wouldn't you just give it up for *one* damn evening so that we can hang out and experience this together?"

"I thought that you'd be practicing all night," he defended himself, waving at the room and my outfit in a frantic state. "I figured that you wouldn't want me hanging around."

"Well . . . I do!" I shouted. "I need my brother. For two days. That's all. But if you're too obsessed with your dick, forget it."

"That's a bit uncalled for." He rubbed the back of his neck.

"Is it? Is it uncalled for? Why don't you just get sorted and go."

"I can't go now."

"Yes, you can."

"No, I can't," he argued. "You're upset."

"Fantastic observation skills." I straightened up from a calf stretch and stepped into a side lunge. "I'll be fine, Nathan. Like you said, I'll be practicing all night. And then I suppose I'll need some sleep. I'm not panicking over my future. I'm super calm. I don't need support *at all.*"

"Dal," he sighed and ran a hand through his hair. "I didn't realize. I didn't know that it made you so upset."

The springs squeaked and the white comforter wrinkled as he sat down again. "You're independent as hell. You always have been. If I'd known that you . . . well . . . needed me, I would never have arranged a date. I mean, is this just tonight? Or all of the time?"

"I mean, the fact that you've slept with half of Castle Rock and never had a follow-up date is a little gross. You know, being served groceries as well as looks at the store because you didn't call the cashier back is a bit shit. But that's not the point."

"What's the point?"

"Sometimes, when it's important, think about someone else. Is it that hard? It doesn't seem that hard to figure out, Nathan."

We didn't argue often, but it did feel good to get that off my chest. I wanted him to know how I felt. But I didn't want him to feel bad.

"It's not hard." His smile was tight and he stood up from the bed. "I'll cancel tonight and we ca—"

"You don't have to—"

"I want to." He slid his phone out of his back pocket. "I'm here. We're going to embrace our evening in California. Even if we don't leave this room."

I laughed.

When I was born, Nathan was eight. When I was eight, he was sixteen. He suffered his shoulder injury that year. And when he turned seventeen, just after accepting that he wouldn't play professional football, our parents died. He went from being a teenager without a care in the world who had the freedom of college at his fingertips to the caregiver of a child. He had to learn balance and maintain an identity. He'd done well. I was proud of him.

And it seemed that he was proud of me too, or so he told me while I practiced my routine for hours on end. He convinced me to take a break at one point. We had a hot coffee from a quaint cafe near our hotel. We snapped a few photos and selfies, and when we got into bed at eight, we talked. The lights were off. Our beds were side by side and there was a low but persistent thrum coming from the small bar fridge.

"Nathan," I said, "have you ever been in love? I mean, I know that you date around a lot. But have *none* of them caught your interest further than just a one-night stand?"

There was no response for a moment. I wondered if he'd fallen asleep faster than should have been possible. But then he sighed. "Sort of. Well . . . it could have gone there. But she didn't reciprocate the feelings. She didn't see it working out long term, anyway."

"Who was she?"

"Just a girl I went to school with, I'm over it now."

"Sure about that? You do a lot of sleeping around for someone who's over heartbreak."

"I'm over it." I could hear his mattress as he shifted around. "Anyway, how about you? You in love?"

While the thought of being in love terrified me, it also turned me inside out. "Yeah. Which is sort of something that I wanted to avoid, but it seems to be happening."

"Why would you want to avoid it?"

"Because." I tucked the sheets up around me. "I guess things are sort of uncertain at the moment. We're on different paths to different colleges, and we haven't even talked titles. How can I transition a discussion about long-distance relationships into that conversation when we haven't even defined what we are?"

"You're overthinking it." Nathan sounded tired. "Long distance works. You're obviously in love. Don't make things more complicated than they need to be. Just go with the flow. You'll be happier if you embrace whatever happens."

What he was telling me made sense. A lot of sense. But it was easier said than done.

The theater was enormous. It was intimidating and the seats

weren't even full. There were three women and two men sitting at a panel in front of the stage. Red velvet curtains were raised. A single light illuminated the spot where I stood, feeling as if my heart was going to beat out of its chest.

I had never felt pressure like this. I couldn't remember the names of the five judges. My stomach was in knots, my future a moving mirage that could slip straight past me if I didn't perform the correct steps, lost forever.

The first notes from "I Get to Love You" flowed from the speaker and I counted down in my head. Focus was something that I worked hard to maintain for the first few steps. And then I slipped into a trance. A state of bliss and ease. My heart didn't feel as erratic as it had when I'd walked onto the stage. What had been a feeling of anxious dread moments earlier had turned into euphoria.

My movements were in time with the soft rhythm. My toes were pointed, arms moving through the air weightlessly. The smile on my face was natural, nothing artificial about it. The lyrics about unplanned love resonated in my head as I danced. It was true. I could never have planned to feel this way. I had chosen this song for its grace and its subtle power.

The rhythm pulsed into me. It was in my veins. It was electric, setting my nerves alight and moving my limbs. With each step that I took, I forgot. There were no concerns about the future, about what was going to happen after graduation. I was free; free to move and feel and express how I felt without fear.

I was free to feel the love in my heart.

As I neared the end of the routine, I knew that it was the best that I'd performed it to date. The emotion that existed within each step was pure, unfiltered and raw. When I first choreographed the routine, I was just a dancer. I knew the steps and understood the music. But not the feelings behind them.

I knew how to invoke emotion on the stage, how to portray those emotions on my face and in my movements. But feeling it, truly letting the exquisite gratification of being in the deep end flow within me was what I believe carried me through the performance without a single slip up.

CHAPTER 20

When we were kids, Mom and Dad made Christmas magical. And when our grandmother was around, we'd eat a beautiful meal at her place. She made the best pork belly ever. Christmas and New Year's had been quiet in our home for a long time.

The magic was gone, and the food was average; it was just another day. Except we ate a lot of sugar and watched Hallmark Channel Christmas movies. In the past, I'd been to Gabby's for dinner. But Nathan didn't want to go this year, and I didn't want to leave him. So we spent time together and reminisced about when our parents were alive.

Nathan headed out for New Year's Eve this year. He wasn't gone all night, which surprised me. It seemed as if our conversation in California had made a difference. Whatever the reason, it was nice to have his full attention until he dashed off to the bar to count in another year.

I'd tried to convince Gabby that we should do something together even if it meant going to one of the many countdown parties that our peers were throwing, but her mom wanted her at home.

The night was uneventful because as luck would have it, Drayton was in Texas over the break. He said that his mom had family and friends there. He didn't let up with the texts while he was gone. It was never ending . . . and sweet and super inappropriate sometimes.

When we went back to school, the snow was thick. It was cold—an inconvenience to everyone. White covered the grounds and glittered in the setting sun. The parking lot had to be plowed before, during, and after the cars had left. All sports practices had to remain indoors. Drayton and I made discreet plans in the gymnasium to meet each other after school. We were still being cautious around the cheer team, although I thought that after Thanksgiving, some of his teammates had a fair idea about what was going on. He and Austin were civil again after Austin had apologized for being so unhinged. "Sorry for being a dick when you pissed me off."

Not exactly the most heartfelt apology that I'd ever heard, but I accepted it and let it go.

While it was torture to go the entire six and a half hours of school without a kiss or cuddle after being apart for almost two weeks, I looked forward to a proper hello when I went over to Drayton's house later. He'd informed me earlier that he'd have a few hours alone before his parents were back, and he wouldn't object to making use of the privacy.

Gabby and I walked through the halls later that afternoon. We had both hung back to work on an assignment for English. The chosen novel for our current read and review was *My Sister's Keeper* by Jodi Picoult. It was sadder than I cared for—forced trauma on pupils should be illegal.

The students had all gone home. The corridors were quiet, and it was getting colder and darker outside. Gabby was filling me in on how Josh's Christmas in Canada with his parents had gone. It sounded cold—colder than what we experienced here.

"I think one day I might go to Australia or New Zealand for Christmas break," I mentioned, sliding my phone out of my pocket when I felt it vibrate. "It's summer there. Could be a nice change to experience."

"Christmas in the summer," she mumbled with amusement. "It's hard to imagine."

There was a text message from Drayton. I read it while Gabby continued to weigh the pros and cons of experiencing a different season over our winter break.

> Are you still at school? I left my folder in the locker rooms. I have a bunch of dumb quiz question things to fill out for Coach. Can you please grab it for me if you haven't left?

> And drive safe please x

"I have to run over to the gym and grab something for Drayton," I said, slipping my phone away as we pushed open the school doors and stepped into the white, cold parking lot. It was getting dark and Gabby frowned.

"I'll come."

We both reached into our bags and retrieved our gloves. "No, Gabs, it's fine. I'll be quick. It's so cold. Go home."

Gabby dropped her bottom lip. "But it's getting dark."

"I'm going to the gym and then back to the car. I'll survive."

"But—"

"Gabs." I walked backward, slow and careful on the slick concrete. "Go. I'll probably see you at Drayton's, hmm?"

She grinned. "Yeah. I'll be with Josh."

I didn't let her keep arguing. "Good. Go and keep warm. I'll see you later."

I carefully jogged over to the gym, a cloud of white air billowing with each breath that passed my shivering lips.

The locker rooms reeked. I'd never been into the boys' one before, but the odor was foul. The wall of sweat-smell hit me the moment that I opened the door, but I didn't plan on hanging around. I headed toward the row of cubby holes in search of Drayton's.

As I passed Coach Finn's office, I peered at the large window and came to a standstill.

Because Emily and the assistant coach, Lincoln, were going at it. He had her bent over the desk. They still had their clothes on, thank God, but I'd seen too much. I'd been afraid that I might stumble on a pair of dirty underwear or an athletic cup while I was in here, not my cheerleading captain and the twenty-five-year-old assistant coach having a bone.

Before I could run, Emily shrieked. There was a series of panicked gasps and flustered hand gestures while the two of them put themselves together. Lincoln smoothed down his brown hair and wiped a hand across his damp brow as the two of them emerged from the office.

My feet had remained planted to the spot. I was in a state of shock and disbelief. I mean, I wasn't entirely surprised at Emily—she's the sort of girl you'd find screwing someone's uncle at a family brunch—but more so at the fact that I'd managed to snap a photo or two and I might just have a one-up on this witch who wanted to ruin my life for some unknown reason.

"Give me the phone." She held out her palm and used the other hand to fix a loose strand of her red hair. "Don't screw with me, Dallas. Phone."

"Yeah . . . no, I'll leave the screwing to Lincoln." He was flustered and blubbering, but he made no move to snatch my phone. I slipped it into my coat pocket and did up the zip.

"She's eighteen." Lincoln let out a strangled noise. "It's not illegal."

"I don't know if the board would see it like that." I narrowed a calculating stare at him. "She's still a student."

"Give it up." Emily's throat sounded as if it was closing over. "Linc, just get out of here. You're making it worse.

"Dallas." She was attempting to be calm but her voice trembled and her smile looked more Joker-like than friendly. "Please give me the phone or delete those photos."

"So you can keep threatening me and making the rest of the semester total shit?" I scoffed. "No."

She stared at me, then her lip began to quiver and soon after her entire frame began to hum with the realization that Drayton had told me about her attempt to keep us apart. It was sort of like watching the countdown on a microwave—you know that the beep is coming and you can count the seconds until it goes off. There's an anticipation. She finally exhaled loudly and collapsed on the bench seat outside of the office.

"You could ruin his career," she sobbed. She was crying actual tears. I watched her with marvel. "You can't do that to him. Don't ruin his career."

I almost didn't want to take the bait—she might be the best actress this county has ever seen. "You know that he's taking advantage of you, right?" I sat down beside her. "He's practically a teacher and almost a decade older, Emily. What are you doing?"

She turned and stared at me through tear-filled eyes. "He loves me!" It was hard to decipher her words through her blubbering, but I worked hard to keep up. "I love him. He really cares, Dallas. People never fucking care. He does."

I remembered Drayton telling me that her home life was terrible. That her parents didn't care and had never given her the time of day; consequences that followed such actions were often too dire to reverse. It explained her need to keep in constant control. Looking for love in place of parental affection was almost never going to end well either.

"I won't need to use the photo if you just leave me alone," I told her, spotting Drayton's cubby. I stood up and collected his folder, aware of Emily watching me with tears slipping down her cheeks. "Drayton and I are . . . together. We're happy. Don't call CalArts or whatever it is that you were going to have your mom do, and I won't show that photo to anyone."

"Fine." She stared at her feet. "Whatever. You always manage to get what you want."

"I really don't know what your issue is. You're obviously happy with Lincoln. What's with the need to keep Drayton off limits as well?"

"Because you piss me off," she snapped, standing so fast that I flinched. But she didn't move again, she just wiped her wet face. "You don't even make an effort with people and they still like you. Everyone likes you."

She almost sounded . . . jealous.

"I might not make an effort to make lots of friends or whatever, but I'm polite, Emily." I shrugged a shoulder. "Treat people with kindness and respect. That might sound like an overused Tumblr post, but it makes a difference. If you ever need someone to talk to," I told her, "I'm not a terrible listener."

She wiped her nose and the sound of her sniffling echoed as she squared her shoulders and glared. "I don't want to talk to you."

I turned around and started out of the room. "The offer is there."

"You're late." Drayton met me at the car when I arrived at his house fifteen minutes later. It was dark but the drive was illuminated with spotlights. Some of the trees along the edge had twinkling lights in them as well. It was such an enchanting property. "I was getting worried."

"Here's your folder." I handed it to him, and he threw it back into the car. He slammed the door shut and pushed me against it as his warm lips were on my cold ones.

It was abrupt and intense, and I melted into him despite being pushed up against a freezing-cold car. We kissed a kiss that made up for the winter-break absence, and when his mouth left mine, I felt breathless. And it had nothing to do with the freezing temperatures.

"Couldn't keep waiting," he mumbled, his smiling lips coming back in for a series of quick pecks. "Missed you."

"I missed you too," I admitted. The forest of trees that surrounded his home were almost buried up to their branches in white powder. It was sprinkled on the twigs and coated the ground.

"My baby cousins will be here soon. For dinner. You should stay."

"If you want me to. Is there an occasion?"

He shrugged with an indifferent nod, kicking the snow with his foot. I watched him, admiring his fitted long sleeve, vest, and sweatpants. I wondered how he wasn't colder. I was wearing tights, a skirt, a coat, gloves, and a hat, and I was still cold.

I leaned down and started scooping the snow into a ball. "So," I said in a casual tone as he began to help me with a small snowman. "We don't have to hide at school now. I caught Emily and Lincoln . . . in the coach's office . . ."

Drayton raised a brow and shook his head. "I'm surprised. But not," he commented, snapping a couple of twigs to create arms. Our snowman might not have a face at this point as we were lacking material. "She's bold when she's going after what she wants. Man, the texts that she used to send me."

He let out a low whistle and I refused to ask for details. The wince in his expression was more information than I needed. We stood up and assessed our little masterpiece. It was faceless, aside from a few finger holes that Drayton made for eyes, but it was cute. "I sort of feel bad for her."

Drayton wrapped an arm around me and we headed for the front door. "You feel bad for her?" His tone was disbelieving. "She's been a huge asshole."

"Yeah, but I didn't understand her as well befor—"

"Mhmm," he interrupted. "I get it. You know her more now. You see more and you understand. All of that. I just didn't take you for such a softie."

"I'm not going to let her push me around," I declared, shuddering at the mere thought of going back to square one, where I'd felt helpless under her thumb. "But I don't hate her. I don't hate anyone. I just—I feel bad that she hasn't experienced parental love and all that. I was young when my parents died, but I won't ever forget how special it was."

He was quiet. The only sound was our feet crunching in the fresh snowfall and a soft breeze rustling the tree branches. He smiled and peered down at me, his arm holding me close beside him.

"Sounds like my mom is home," he gestured with a subtle nod toward the drive behind us as we walked up the front steps. The stone was slippery, so we were careful. I guessed the incident with Emily had taken up more time than I'd thought, and we no longer had the house to ourselves. "We can watch a movie, eat food, and I can play with your hair?"

He'd come to discover that I was weak for people playing with my hair. Before we could go inside, though, headlights illuminated the snow and a white Mercedes with tinted black windows pulled in beside my dinky little car. His mom hopped out. She was stunning, as usual, the epitome of winter grace in a mid-length cashmere coat and a matching set of gloves, hat, and scarf.

"Dray," she called, "come and help me with the groceries, please."

Drayton sauntered toward her, so I followed along, figuring that I'd offer my assistance.

"Hello, Dallas," she greeted me with a chipper smile. I hadn't seen her since Thanksgiving. After she'd found out about Drayton hitting Austin, she'd let him have it in front of the entire dinner party. "How have you been darlin'? I'm not in a foul mood this time. Unless Drayton here has been doing something he shouldn't."

She raised a brow toward her son, who was currently leaning into the trunk of the car. He rolled his eyes and proceeded to pick up the entire ten bags with ease.

"On the straight and narrow, Mom." He grinned as she closed the trunk.

"Good," she cooed. "Dallas, you should stay for dinner. We're having homemade burritos for Drayton's birthday."

"It's your birthday?"

Ellie looked at Drayton but didn't give in to whatever confusion she was feeling, just turned around and disappeared inside. Drayton and I followed behind her.

"My birthday is next week," he explained. "We celebrate early because my mom and dad go away on the actual day."

"Your parents won't be here for your birthday?"

"I haven't spent my birthday with my parents since Abby died." Sorrow filled my chest and I watched as he toed off his boots at the door, still holding the ten bags with ease. "Don't worry about it. I obviously shared my birthday with Abby, and it's hard for them. It doesn't really bother me. Josh and I usually throw a party. They go away to grieve, to remember her in their own way. I like to honor Abby by getting blackout drunk, and I don't think they want to see that."

We walked into the kitchen and I admired the stone theme and shimmering appliances once again. Drayton's house never ceased to amaze me. There was a frosted cake in a glass case on the marble table. Cushioned leather barstools lined up along one side of the island. It smelled clean and cozy, like citrus and coffee.

"Your parents are so young," I commented, leaning on the edge of the island to look at a photo of them. Drayton set the groceries down on the other side. His mom was nowhere to be seen.

"They are, I guess." He shrugged a shoulder, shuffling through the bags. "They had just graduated from high school when they found out that they were pregnant. First night that they ever met. Boom."

"Gold medalist, huh," I laughed.

He dug through the groceries and found a protein bar. "Do you like burritos?"

"Of course." I rolled my eyes as if it was the most ridiculous question that I'd ever heard. "I've never had them homemade, though."

"My mom doesn't do a lot of cooking," he explained as he leaned one hand on the lip of the bench and chewed on his snack, which was in the other. "But she makes fucking awesome burritos."

"Language," Ellie sang out, swiping the back of Drayton's head as she came back into the kitchen in a more casual outfit of sweatpants and UGG boots with a warm sweater. "Where are Josh and Gabby? They were here when I left."

"I don't know," Drayton pulled some orange juice out of another bag while his mother tapped her foot impatiently behind him. "Probably pounding it out in his room."

"Drayton Jacob Lahey!" she shouted, giving him another swipe, which he managed to avoid as he moved toward the cabinet then pulled two glasses from the top shelf. "Don't be foul!"

"You asked," he muttered, pouring a drink into each. Drayton was probably on the money, though. I wouldn't be surprised if that was exactly what Josh and Gabby were doing.

"Come on, babe." Drayton picked up the glasses and signaled for me to follow him as he rounded the kitchen island and headed for the entrance. "Let's go and stop those nymphos from making babies."

"Drayton!" Ellie hollered but we were already halfway up the staircase.

I was aware that we weren't going in search of our friends. We were going to his bedroom where the bed was made and the fire was going. I loved his room; it was a dream. He set our drinks on a bedside table and spun around, pulling me into him. His hands went south and as he grabbed my bum, his gaze became wide and his mouth popped open. "Damn, Cheer. You're soaked. That was quick."

I reached around behind me and felt the back of my skirt, which was indeed wet and cold. "It's from crouching in the snow." I gave him a shove in the chest. He laughed.

"Take it off," he casually ordered as he sauntered over to his dresser. "I think I have a pair of sweats in here that I wore when I was, like, seven. They might fit you."

I unzipped my skirt, thankful that my tights weren't wet.

"Dammit," he mumbled, pushing clothes from left to right. "No pants. This hoodie might be long enough, though."

I stripped off my shirt as he turned around with one of his football hoodies in hand. When his sights landed on me standing beside his bed in tights and a bra, his gaze lingered on my chest and then it moved, slowly, up and down as he drew his bottom lip between his teeth.

"Damn, if we were eating alone tonight, I'd be having your burrito for dinner."

"You are too damn smooth."

He grinned and tilted his head to the side as he walked forward. He handed the maroon hoodie over with a sigh of disappointment. "You're lucky that I care about your comfort."

"Thanks." I pulled the hoodie over my head. It smelled like him—masculine but fruity. There was a very real chance that he wouldn't be getting this back anytime soon. "It's huge."

"Why, thank you." He winked. "So I've been told."

"You can't be stopped."

"Nope. It looks good."

The number on the back was his *18*, and *Lahey* was written across the shoulders in big, bold letters.

"I'm keeping this by the way," I told him as I sat on the edge of his bed.

He knelt in front of me. "Is that so? Going to sleep in it every night?"

"Maybe."

His hands slid up my legs, tantalizing and slow, as he went higher.

"Would it be weird if I got a little jealous over that hoodie," he mumbled with a low voice, getting up and trapping me between his arms. He leaned over me so that I had to fall back onto the mattress.

"No, not weird." I barely managed to finish my sentence before his mouth met mine and his tongue pried my lips apart. He reached back and his hand gripped behind my knee as he pulled my leg up so that it was wrapped around his waist. He lowered his hips onto mine and I gasped at his hardness. His kiss became rougher and one hand slipped under the hoodie, grazing my skin.

"Oh sheesh, you two," Josh's voice chortled from the door.

We broke our kiss but Drayton kept his position, hovering between my legs as he glanced to the side where Gabby and Josh stood. "Get a room."

"We're in a room," Drayton bit back. "Get out."

"Mom wants your help with dinner," Josh said.

"You go and help her."

"I am," Josh replied. "She wants us both downstairs. She was very specific."

"That's probably because I told her you and Gabby were making babies in your room."

Drayton huffed with a pout but got up and helped me to my feet. As disappointing as it was to be interrupted, I tried to calm down and stop the throbbing between my legs. It wasn't as if we could have gone further in a full house anyway. The four of us headed downstairs. Drayton kept his arm around my shoulder. It felt safe being tucked beside him.

"You know," I said as I peered up at him, "you made this sound like a casual thing. Why didn't you tell me it was a birthday dinner? I would have come more prepared."

He leaned forward and looked me over. "You look like a main course to me," he grinned. "For real. That hoodie looks good on you. We should skip dinner."

"Ow!" he exclaimed as I nudged him in the side. "I didn't want to scare you. You're so anticommitment. I thought you'd freak out."

"Fair enough. Don't stress about that though, tell me next time."

He wore a surprised but pleased smile as we walked into the kitchen and found Ellie in an apron, ingredients spread across the countertop. "Where have the four of you been? I need help. And you need to keep the bedroom doors open."

We offered our assistance to avoid the scolding.

"Gabby, put this on the table for me, please." Ellie handed a stack of condiments across the kitchen island to Gabby, who proceeded to place them in the middle of the large marble dining table.

She put Drayton and Josh to work cutting up vegetables. Honestly, I think there were more crude cucumber jokes going on than anything else. As for me, I was at the stove top, flipping the soft, homemade tortillas after Ellie had rolled them out.

She was in the middle of explaining her business after I'd asked her about how it all came to be. "It was the plan from the get-go." She cut off a handful of dough and threw some flour over it. "I wanted to get into skin care from the time that I was young. My mom and dad weren't that supportive, but that's a whole other story, we're only just on speaking terms again. Anyway. After I got pregnant, I moved in with Leroy's parents—sweetest people ever—and they actually left me a small-business starter fund in their will."

"Sounds like they really believed in you," I said, watching her wipe some flour off her cheek with the back of her hand.

"They were wonderful people," she said as she nodded, her expression distant. "The name of the brand, L.E. Skincare, was a play on my name—it sounds like Ellie. It's mine and Leroy's initials and it's Leroy's mother's initials. Eleanor Lahey. I managed to work all of the importance in there."

I flipped the tortilla in the pan and smiled. "That's so nice. And clever. I'll have to get some of the products. Are they online?"

"Don't be silly," she responded in that southern accent of hers. "I'll give you a cleansing set. We can figure out your skin type after dinner."

"Really?"

"Of course. The products are affordable anyway. When I was growing up, we struggled financially, a lot. I wanted a decent skin-care set to be accessible to people who didn't make a lot of money."

"She also donates a ton of her products to refuge centers and shelters, right, Mom?" Drayton towered over her and kissed her cheek. "She's big into charities too."

Ellie blushed and gave her son a pat on the shoulder. It was sweet to watch. Their family had experienced so much pain, losing a sister and daughter. I knew how loss felt, so it was heartwarming to see what a tight unit they were. How much love, care, and respect existed here. It was a stark difference to the Drayton that I'd met all those months ago.

"Hello," a masculine voice greeted us, and I turned around to find Leroy strolling into the kitchen. "There are a lot of teenagers in here."

"It's Drayton's birthday dinner, Leroy." Ellie grinned while she power grated through a block of cheese. "You know Dallas and Gabby of course."

He slipped out of his designer suit jacket to reveal a fitted shirt that accentuated his large shoulders and massive arms. Good bodies must have run in the family. "Where's the rest of the team?"

"Oh please," Ellie scoffed. "I wasn't going to host the entire football team. It'd cost us a small fortune in food."

"Probably for the best after what happened the last time Drayton's team members were here." Leroy gave his son an amused but disapproving stare as he headed for the fridge and retrieved a beer. Drayton shrugged.

Josh and Gabby were sitting on a small two-seater sofa beside the floor-to-ceiling glass patio doors at the end of the kitchen, and I was about to join them when we heard a cluster of footsteps, the door closing, and a sing song of hellos from the front passage before Cass and two children appeared.

"Hey, Cass," Ellie rounded the kitchen island and took the bottle of wine that Cass held out. She pecked Cass's cheek and greeted the two young children. I recognized Coen but I hadn't met the little girl. She was a spitting image of her mother, with tight ringlets and bright-blue eyes. Two of her front teeth were missing as well. She must have been around seven, and it was obvious that she was going to be a heartbreaker when she was older.

Cass said hello to Leroy before she gave Gabby and Josh a quick wave. I took the last tortilla out of the frying pan and added it to the plate in the warming oven, proud of myself for completing such an important task. It wouldn't be dinner without the tortillas. Drayton laced our fingers together and we strolled over to the other side of the island where he embraced his aunt in a one-armed hug, still keeping his grip on my hand.

"Hello, you two." Her smile was warm. She slipped an envelope into his hand. "How are you both? Good to see you again, Dallas."

Drayton dropped the envelope onto the countertop without opening it.

"When did you meet Dallas?" Ellie asked with furrowed brows as she dropped a package of ground beef into a frying pan.

The three of us exchanged wide-eyed, cautionary glances. Drayton's parents were aware of our away-game antics, but we hadn't gone into specifics about what we had actually got up to.

Drayton was usually so quick with his wit that I'd expected him to cover for us, but he was at a loss for words.

"At the away game," Cass finally answered with a convincing smile. "In Fort Collins. I went and watched the game. That's where I met her."

"You went and watched a varsity football game?" Leroy questioned her with an arched brow and a doubtful tone. "Since when do you watch varsity football?"

"Since it was my nephew playing, and I was being supportive."

Cass smiled a that-was-close grin and changed the subject. "How are things between you,"—her eyes flickered toward our joined hands—"two who are 'just friends.'"

"Things have changed a little since then," Drayton declared with pride. I glanced up to find him regarding me with an affectionate gaze and, as always, my response to his adoring looks was an erratic heartbeat and an eruption of flutters in the pit of my stomach.

Our moment was adorably interrupted by a little Coen, who was bouncing up and down with outstretched arms and twinkling fingers. "Dray-Dray!"

"Hey, little dude." Drayton scooped the toddler up and perched him comfortably on his forearm. Coen wrapped his arm around Drayton's neck and grinned with significantly greater energy than he'd had the last time I'd met him. The young girl, who'd been quietly chatting to Leroy, skipped toward us with a small grin.

"Draaaaay," she sang.

"Yes, Lucy?" Drayton gave her his undivided attention while he continued to bounce the little boy on his arm. I'd never seen him more domestic. Or more gorgeous, for that matter.

"Coen wants to know who that girl is."

She pointed a finger at me with a shy, toothless grin. It was adorable, and I believed I used to use the same tactic to get answers to questions that I didn't want to ask.

"Oh, that's Dallas," Drayton smiled, putting Coen down again. "My baby momma."

Tension seized the entire room. Silence was all that followed his statement. It was so quiet that I could hear the groan of the fridge and the beating of my own heart. Ellie stopped grating. Leroy's shoulders became rigid. They both stared at me with bewilderment and a touch of outrage. Lucy looked more confused than anything.

"What's a baby momma?"

"You better be kidding," Leroy snapped, his thunderous glare moving between the two of us.

"Excuse me. *Teen father*"—Drayton pointed at his own chest—"I'm the evidence. Don't be a hypocrite."

"Touché," Cass laughed.

Gabby and Josh stared at the floor, attempting to smother their laughter. Ellie gave her son a warning stare. "Dray—"

"I'm kidding." He rolled his eyes and waved his hand flippantly. "I wrap it before I tap it. You're on the pill anyway, right, babe?"

Ellie forced a laugh while her husband muttered obscenities and Cass sniggered, pouring herself a glass of wine. I slapped Drayton in the chest with a backhand.

Drayton chuckled. I slapped his arm again for good measure. "Rough. I like it."

He kissed my neck and although it made my toes curl, I leaned forward and attempted to move out of his hold. There was only one person who could possibly annoy and turn me on at the same time.

"Stop," I whispered. "Not while there's so many people around."

"I don't care who sees." He turned me around and cupped the nape of my neck, locking our lips in a tasteful, gentle kiss. It had such a whirlwind effect.

"Food's ready."

The kitchen became a flurry of frenzied bodies, scraping chairs, and loud inhaling as people took in the aroma of the delicious meal that was laid out on the table. My mind wandered to Nathan, and I felt a little guilty that he'd probably fix himself toast or noodles because I hadn't let him know about my plans. He'd no doubt texted me, but my phone was in my coat upstairs, and I wasn't going to check it now. I was almost certain that Drayton would follow me, and then we'd never get to eat. Well, not burritos anyway.

During the first half-hour of the meal, there wasn't a lot of chitchat as everyone was too busy devouring the delicious food that Drayton's mother had made, which, to make no exaggeration about it, was mouthwatering.

But as the rush to eat settled, the conversation picked up. Gabby, Josh, Drayton, and I were on one side of the table. Cass, Ellie, Leroy, and the kids were on the other. Gabby talked with Ellie for a while. She spent more time here than I did, so it wasn't surprising that she was close to Drayton's mom.

Cass chatted to us when she could, but she did spend quite some time taming her toddler, who didn't want to be at the table. And then Leroy decided to pick up the conversation. He leaned an elbow on the tabletop and clutched a cold beer.

"Good New Year's, Dallas?"

"It was good, thanks. Quiet, but nice. I spent it with my brother for the most part."

"Parents?"

"Dad." Drayton paused with his burrito midway to his mouth in front of him. "Come on. I tol—"

"It's okay," I interrupted and smiled with assurance that it didn't bother me to talk about. Of course, his loss was different, so his reaction would be too. "My brother looks after us. My parents died when we were kids."

Leroy nodded and there was a subtle flinch of empathy on his face before he continued. "So you don't plan on going to college?"

"No, I do. I've been saving up for college for a while now. I want to major in dance. I've got a part-time job at Rocky Ryan's in town, and my brother is going to help too. Plus, I've applied for financial aid, and I think I have a good shot at getting it . . ."

"What colleges have you applied to?"

"My top pick is CalArts." I nodded and noticed Drayton, sitting with his elbows on the table and his hands clasped in front of his chin beside me. His shoulders were tense and his thumb grazed back and forth across his bottom lip. "I just had an audition for their dance program."

"CalArts as in California?" Leroy asked, watching me as he drank his beer. It was startling to see how alike he and Drayton were.

"No, Dad," Drayton interrupted when I began to nod in confirmation. "CalArts as in Caledonia."

The rest of the table were eating and immersed in their own conversations, but I caught Ellie checking out of her chitchat with Cass once in a while, watching the three of us with particular interest, more so when her son piped up with something sarcastic and irritating.

"You didn't want to apply for SMU? They have a commendable dance program."

"Can we not do this right now?" Drayton snapped.

Leroy watched me, waiting for an answer. I looked at Gabby and she was focused on anything but the subtle drama that was unfolding. I wished that she could save me right now.

"I did apply at SMU, but I didn't get an audition. If CalArts doesn't accept me then . . . I'll probably try again next year. I don't really want to go anywhere else."

Leroy shrugged after a moment of deliberation. "Long-distance relationships work. It's not the end of the world if you and Drayton end up in different states."

"Dad," Drayton warned.

Ellie leaned in closer beside her husband, her soft features contorted with concern. She placed a hand on his forearm and murmured for him to drop it for now.

But he didn't. "Drayton is attending Baylor. Close to SMU. That school has seen generations of Laheys graduate. I just get the feeling that something is holding him back from writing his letter of intent."

Drayton's palms slammed down on the tabletop and his chair pushed back, scraping the stone floor. He stood up and offered me his hand while his glare remained fixed on his father. "Couldn't leave it alone for one fucking night. It's my damn birthday for fuck sakes."

Ellie watched him, inching out of her seat while her gaze glimmered with concern. "Dray—"

"Come on, Dallas."

I stood—mostly because he had a hold on my arm, but also because I knew that he needed someone right now. Before we could disappear, I turned and looked at Ellie. "Thank you for dinner. Loved it."

In Drayton's room, I closed the door and watched him in front of his window. His shoulders were broad, and his jawline could cut the tension that had been felt in the kitchen. Even though he was still, looking into the night, his frame hummed with restless irritation. Relationships between a child and parent were never something that another person should weigh in on; all families were different. But I felt pissed that Leroy chose tonight to grill me over college. It was meant to be his son's celebration, and he spoiled it.

From that one interaction, it was obvious to me that Leroy was smooth when he was getting his point across. He didn't need to shout or get upset because his delivery was calm, intimidating, and calculating. I knew what he meant without him saying it once. He didn't want me influencing Drayton's college choice. Not that I'd ever attempted to.

Drayton's sigh was low and exhausted. He didn't even look this drained after a grueling three-hour practice. I sat down on the bed and waited until he wanted to talk. He knew that I was there. He pulled his hoodie off. It pulled up the T-shirt underneath, exposing his firm torso.

I knew that I shouldn't drool over his unreal muscle definition at a time like this, but I couldn't help it. He pulled his shirt down and dropped the hoodie on an armchair beside the fireplace. When he sat beside me on the bed, his familiar scent surrounded me.

"He thinks that I'm going to choose you over Baylor," he told me.

I wasn't sure what Drayton had told his parents about our . . . relationship. Had he told them that it was the real deal? Hell, he hadn't even told me that. There had been no talk of titles or labels, even if I felt it. I was still uncertain about what our future held.

"I talk about you a lot," he answered my thoughts. "And a month and a half is longer than any of the other girls have lasted."

I let out a breath of laughter through my nose and nodded. "I get it. This is new for me too."

"I've obviously dated here and there." He shrugged, still watching the soft charcoal carpet beneath his feet. I noticed that his socks had little footballs on them. "But most of them dip after one evening in our house."

"Can't handle the embarrassment?" I nudged him, referring to the earlier baby momma comment.

"You say that like it's a joke, but it's pretty much how it is. I put my cards on the table. I don't hide much—with the exception of my sister—but most of them want the surface and not the rest of it. They see who I am. Who I really am. And they complain. Nitpick. Freak out that I say whatever I want."

He turned his head and watched me with that gorgeous green stare. His lashes were thick and framed his almond-shaped eyes.

"You don't take shit," he murmured, his gaze sweeping my face, focusing and absorbing all of the details that he saw. "But you've never made me feel like I shouldn't be exactly who I am."

"With the exception of telling you not to be a jerk to me at school in front of *the boys*." I leaned in and pressed a kiss against his soft lips. "I like all of who you are," I whispered.

"You're not going to run?"

It was hard to know what would happen after school. Falling in love with someone before I moved was the reason I'd avoided it for so long. And it still scared me.

"No running," I promised.

This feeling could become so strong that it broke me. But I didn't want to turn back now. I loved being in love.

CHAPTER 21

I was not a book person. I was more of a doer. I didn't love sitting down to read pages and pages of someone else's life when I could have been living my own, or, even worse, analyzing and writing an entire essay on whatever book the teacher had chosen—not even a book that I'd chosen. It was just . . . tiresome.

"This is stupid." I kicked the couch behind me. Gabby and I were sprawled on her living-room floor working on an assignment together. "What does it matter what color the author uses to describe the walls? She probably just picked something and went with it."

Gabby rolled from her back to her stomach. Long strands of her wild brown hair curtained around her as she stared at me with disapproval. "We've been over this a million times."

"Still don't get it."

"Do you want me to do it?" She'd finished her assignment a while ago.

"No, I don't." I stared at the paper below me.

"Give me the paper. I'll do it."

Full disclosure: my grades would sink if it weren't for Gabby. She held out her hand. I could feel her stare boring into me. She happened to love doing the work, so I didn't feel too awful sliding the paper across the carpet.

"This will be your students one day."

"What?"

"When you're a professor at some swanky college and your papers are full of intellect and challenge. This will be your students."

She shook her head, giggling as she stared at the paper. While she got to work, I checked my cell phone. It was Drayton's actual birthday tomorrow. His parents were out of town. I wasn't sure where; I hadn't asked. Josh and Drayton were out getting supplies for tomorrow night's party. Food. Alcohol—I wasn't sure how they would manage that one—cups, soda for the sober, and whatever else a house party required. Eight new text messages.

Cheer, should I get blue or purple ping pong balls? Both?

Should I get a rainbow selection of ping pong balls?

I found flavored condoms. You hate cherry, I know this. What about orange?

I got strawberry.

Josh has a Richie Rich haircut. Noticed that? He works it though. Should I do that to my hair?

Na fuck that.

You're busy huh? English? I'll see you later? I'll pick you up from Gabby's when I drop Josh off. He's super-excited to have dinner with her mom tonight.

Sarcasm.

The messages made me laugh. I didn't want to derail Drayton's plans for his birthday. He had his own traditions. But I did have something planned for the two of us that night while Josh and Gabby were having dinner here with Camilla.

"Drayton will be here soon," I mentioned, sitting up. I'd been sprawled on the floor for too long, causing my ribs to become sore. "I need to get dressed."

Her absentminded smile lifted. She was thinking about the fact that she'd get to see her man soon. I felt that.

Gabby continued the assignment so that I could get dressed. I had a duffel bag with me for the weekend. I'd be at Drayton's that night and the next, so I figured that I would save a trip home and pack what I needed for both. My outfit was nothing special. An oversized turtleneck, boots, and black jeans. My hair was down and straight, so I slipped a beanie on. I was excited about this evening. I was nervous as well. The gift that I had planned for Drayton was a little different, but I hoped that he would love it.

The transition from Gabby's bedroom to the rest of her house was such a change that you could forget it was the same building. She once worked an entire summer at the bakery with her mom so that she had enough cash to decorate her room. The walls were lavender and the furniture was white. It was simple but sweet.

The rest of the house was older, with patterned wallpaper and couches. Colorful quilts hung from the walls, rugs covered the carpet, patterned vases and wrought iron figures lined the shelves, and there was an enormous square mirror above the fireplace.

"All right." Gabby stood up from her spot on the floor fifteen minutes later. "I'm done. Mine's an A. Yours is a B plus. I had to keep it real," she said. "Do you think Emily will be at Drayton's tomorrow night?"

"Who knows. It doesn't bother me. We're on . . . civil terms after the whole Lincoln thing."

"It is killing me that I can't tell anyone the most scandalous thing that's happening at our school."

"Don't even think about it," I warned her. The last thing that I needed was Emily believing that I'd spread rumors about her. Not that rumors was the right word. Nonetheless, no one was going to find out. "She's got it harder than we thought. I feel bad for her."

"Don't show her that you care."

"No, I wouldn't. That'd make her furious. I think the charity game in February is the last game that we cheer for together and then I'm done." It was a relief just muttering the words out loud.

The Archwood Wolves and the Kenner Valley Bobcats were having their annual charity game to raise funds for homeless and troubled youth. It was a freezing-cold, extra-long night—longer than our usual matches—but it was for a good cause. Most of Castle Rock attended.

Emily hated it. She made a fuss about cheering in less than ideal conditions and never put effort into the routine. I used to think that it was because she was a soulless shell of a human being. Now I was beginning to think that the whole cause hit her a little close to home.

The front door opened and closed, and then Josh and Drayton sauntered in. Drayton had never been to Gabby's before, so he looked around the living room for a brief moment before he found me draped across the sofa, scrolling through Instagram.

"Hello, beautiful." He pulled me up and gave me a kiss.

Josh fell into an armchair and nodded. "Smells good in here."

"Mom's cooking chilli," Gabby informed him, falling into his lap. "It'll be hot."

Josh smiled and nodded, then ran a hand through his slick hair. Drayton picked up my duffel and kept me tucked under his arm as he pointed at our friends. "Do either of you want to tell me what the fuck I'm in for tonight? I don't like being left out of the secrets."

Gabby frantically waved her hand, her brows pulled tight. "Don't swear! My mom is here. Are you insane?"

Drayton gave her a blank stare before he shrugged and tried again. "No one? No one's going to tell me?"

"You are such a baby," I laughed. "You'll find out soon."

He pulled me toward the living-room entrance, waving over his shoulder. "Come on, then. I'm hoping there will be nudity involved."

The sounds of Josh's and Gabby's protests were silenced by the door closing behind us. We made a fast dash for the Jeep. It was cold out as usual, but I hoped that the snow would hold off for a few more hours.

Drayton had been attempting to extract information from me since he'd found out that I had a surprise for him. Josh had been kind enough to lend some assistance—I needed the patio on the second floor set up. I couldn't do it myself, so he did it for me.

It was the first place that I went when we arrived at his house. Drayton carried my duffel bag.

"I just need to go to the bathroom," I announced and slipped out from under his arm when we hit the second floor and stopped in front of his bedroom door.

He stared down at me, finger pointing at his room with his lips parted, no doubt to suggest the en suite. But before he could, I spun around and beelined down the hall. The second-floor living room was warm; the electric fire cast a moving shadow on the off-white walls as I moved across to the patio doors.

It was too cold to hang around outside, and it was a rather inconvenient gift, considering the weather, but it was all in place. Sitting on the ground beside a two-seater outdoor sofa draped with rugs and pillows was a lantern, a silver gift box, and a paper bag of snacks. At the edge of the patio, in front of the stone railing was a telescope.

The space was enchanting. There had been a light snowfall since Josh had put this together, but the roof extended far enough that the patio was protected. White powder coated the tree branches, and the railing was illuminated with twinkling white lights that glowed a soft blue against the crisp white.

There were times when I considered the coating of Colorado in ice and snow a total disadvantage, but without a doubt, it was magnificent. The snow appeared so soft, and flurries of snowflakes danced in the wind. In those moments it was easy to forget just how destructive the snow could be.

My appreciation for the scene in front of me was interrupted when I heard the glass door being tapped behind me.

"What's all this?" Drayton asked as he came outside.

"Your birthday present."

"You didn't have to get me anything," he said as I scuttled over to the sofa and picked up the gift box on the ground. "What's that?"

"Questions," I drawled with boredom and shoved the box into his hand. "Open it."

His curious stare remained on me while he lifted the box lid. I could feel the pom-pom on the top of my hat bopping while I bounced with anticipation. It seemed that I was more excited than he was. He discarded the lid and inside of the box, among blue satin lining, was a framed certificate issued from the Star-Name-Registry.

Abigail Eleanor Lahey

The gift came with its own coordinates and a letter of confirmation. He read the certificate over and over again.

"You had a star named after my sister," he murmured.

"I swear that it's there." I turned around and stared up at the clouds. "It's just . . . not the best night for stargazing. But the telescope is here, so we can hang out and hope that it clears up. I also bought this lantern to light in her honor."

Drayton told me that he usually got blackout drunk on his birthday. It was a coping mechanism and I hoped that I wasn't overstepping. My heart beat a bit harder when I picked up the lantern and realized that he might hate this entire thing.

"We need a lighter," I said, aware that he was unresponsive. I was afraid to look at him now. I was afraid that he'd tell me I needed to butt out. "I know that you don't smoke a lot now, so I brought one with me. We ca—"

My sentence was halted and the perpetrator was his warm mouth. The lantern almost slipped from my grasp when his large hands cupped my neck and his body crushed mine. Drayton ran warm no matter the weather, and the winter chill dissipated as I melted into his kiss.

"You know this is the best thing that anyone has ever done for me?" He sounded breathless as he held my face.

"Really? I was worried that you would be upset."

"Up-Upset?" he stammered. "No, Cheer. Not a chance. This is so fucking thoughtful. It'll be as if she's right here."

His hands continued to hold me while he stared upward. I wasn't going to complain about the human heater keeping me cozy. If he didn't want to let me go, I wouldn't object. His tortured gaze glistened. It was as if the universe was in his orbs. Dark but so bright.

"She was always meant to be a star."

"Do you want to light this?" I asked, holding out the lantern.

He dropped his hold on my face and nodded. We wandered over to the railing. Not all aspects of the gift were going in our favor tonight—we couldn't see the star because of the clouds—but there were no leaves to hide the lantern when it went up. And the snow wasn't falling.

I handed Drayton the lighter, and the flame glowed, casting a shadow that flickered. There was a cute surprise when the lantern candle was lit—the paper casing had silhouettes of a little boy and girl on all four edges. Each edge had a different action.

The boy and the girl were holding hands.

The boy and the girl were flying a kite.

The boy and the girl were throwing a football.

The boy and the girl were hugging.

Drayton was quiet as he turned the lantern in his hands. There was a small tremor. It was almost unnoticeable, but it was there. Still, he smiled. Even when two or three tears rolled down his face, he smiled.

This was his moment, so I remained at his side but kept

quiet as he lifted the lantern into the cold, dark sky and let it go. He wrapped his arm around my shoulders and tucked me into his side. He smelled like cologne and the leather seats in the Jeep.

We sat down on the sofa and watched the lantern. It was a speck now. A beautiful, glowing speck among the miserable-looking clouds. Sort of like Abigail's memory, I imagined. The circumstances and devastation around her death were wretched. But remembering her was enough to make Drayton smile, and that was a testament to what a light she was in his life.

The throws and pillows provided shelter against the light wind that picked up. I cuddled into Drayton's side. We chewed on chips and sour worms.

"She used to tell me that she was going to end up marrying one of my friends," he said. His arm held me close. "She said that it was obviously going to happen because she'd be at all of the football games and all of the practices."

"Naturally," I chuckled.

Billows of white air were expelled with each breath.

"I didn't approve. We were, like, eleven and she was talking about her future wedding. I hated it. We used to argue, and she'd get in the shit with me."

Pain tainted his words, tarnishing memories with the inevitable hurt. But his light laugh made it a little less heartbreaking to listen to him reminisce.

"But we had this thing," he told me. "We didn't have to talk. We could just . . . communicate. She'd run up to me after a fight, hug me, and it was good again. She hated the fact that I was so protective of her."

The end of his words were bitter, like he didn't think he'd

been protective enough. I didn't want him to do that to himself. "Did she look like you?"

"Same eyes. Similar nose. Hers was smaller. Girlier, I guess. I have photos on my phone."

He reached into his back pocket. The chip bag slid off the blanket and onto the ground, where I left it. The sour worms had been forgotten as well.

"There's a whole room dedicated to her downstairs," he said, excitedly tapping his screen with his thumb. "Mom and Dad agreed not to have photos of her around the house when I started bringing friends home. No one wanted to answer any questions."

"Here." He held the phone out in front of me. It was a portrait shot. One that would have been done at school. "That was taken three months before she died."

She was beautiful. Olive skin like her brother. Long light-brown hair pulled into twin braids. Looking at her smile, seeing the innocence of a child who had experienced nothing but good in her life and knowing that her end was so evil and brutal, my stomach churned into a nauseated knot.

Abigail had had her entire life in front of her. A smile like hers was impossible to fake. It was in her eyes, shining like the sun should have on all of her long living days. I could feel sorrow swelling in my chest, which was tight and filled with regret over something that I could never have controlled. But I didn't want to spoil the moment. "She was gorgeous."

"She would have been *too* pretty," his voice hitched as he locked the phone again. He pulled the blanket up farther around us. "I can just imagine all of the attention she would have had. I would have ended up in so many fights," he laughed.

"I *should* have ended up in those fights," he said quietly. I let my head rest against his chest. He wrapped both of his arms around me. "You would have liked her too. She had attitude. It made my dad real proud."

"They were close?"

"Closer than he and I ever were. I think he still blames me for what happened."

I didn't know what to tell him. I didn't know anything about Leroy apart from the fact that he seemed mildly controlling. But even Drayton said that he used to be cool. Perhaps the father that he once had was hidden beneath grief. A parent should never have to bury their child.

"How did you guys celebrate your birthday?" I kept steering the conversation back to topics that I hoped would make him smile to remember.

"We had the same group of friends." His cheek rested against my head. "We didn't split up our parties. Mom and Dad did something pretty cool every year. Themed parties until we were ten and then it turned into big sleepovers with games. Spotlight and capture the flag. That sort of thing."

"That sounds fun."

"It was."

There was relief again when his tone was lighter. I wasn't sure how long we spent outside. Drayton talked about Abigail for hours. He laughed and I listened to his stories. Perhaps this was what he needed—someone to encourage remembering in a way that didn't have to be so painful. It would always hurt. Loss was a wound that never totally healed. It left a scar. And time didn't mend the damage; it just changed the pain. It became different. But honoring a loved one's memory was remedial.

Which was why I found it so heartwarming when Drayton asked me about my mom and dad. He took his turn to listen to the memories that I had. We offered each other strength. An ear. A shoulder to lean on.

When it got too cold, we went inside. The fire crackled in his bedroom, casting an ambient lighting and we lay beside each other, still sharing tales of a time that was different. We did that until we fell asleep, and I had never felt more in tune or connected to Drayton than I did that night.

CHAPTER 22

In the morning, I cooked breakfast for Drayton. It was his birthday, so it seemed appropriate to deliver it in bed. We ate together. We kissed, we cuddled. He was in a good mood.

He politely asked that I give him a bit of time alone so that he could go to his sister's memorial room. I obliged without hesitation and let him know that I'd be showering.

Josh and Gabby appeared from his room in the middle of the afternoon. They must have come in late last night. The four of us spent a while getting the house organized for the party. We hid valuables in a spare bedroom that could be locked. And not just valuables. Vases. Ornaments. Whatever could end up broken or damaged.

By nine the house was crawling with not only Archwood students but students from some of the other schools in Castle Rock. Music thudded through the built-in sound system. Voices competed with the songs. The main area of congregation was the rec room downstairs, but there wasn't enough room, so the first floor was crowded as well.

People were gathered around the pool table; others had set up a beer-pong match in the kitchen. There was dancing, and the amount of alcohol that flowed through the house was insane—Maxon's older brother had bought everything for tonight. No one was supposed to know who it was because of the implications, but I was trusted with the information.

"Hey," Gabby latched onto my arm the moment I came back from the bathroom. She was wrecked and it wasn't even ten. "Can you come to the bathroom with me?"

Never mind the fact that I had told her that I was going two minutes ago and she told me that she didn't need to.

We held hands and attempted to get up the staircase, which for some unknown reason had turned into a gathering point. Not to sound like that annoying mom who was constantly reminding everyone that microwaves were cancerous and cell phone towers were going to kill us, but I really didn't understand why people chose to hang out on the staircase. It was dangerous and it was narrow, hardly the most convenient social setting.

The bathroom was empty, much to Gabby's relief. Not that it would have mattered because there were three on this floor alone. I shut the door behind us and she ran in, her heels clacking against the tiles.

"I am busting. Holy shit," she stumbled as she hiked up her pink satin dress and fell onto the toilet. A satisfied sigh left her glossed lips.

I stood in front of the mirror and assessed my hair and makeup as if it could have changed in the minutes that had passed since I was in here last. The new long-sleeved black dress that I'd found on clearance last weekend was fitted with a low-cut neckline and a zip at the front that went from top to bottom. Pairing the short dress with a pair of black platforms gave the illusion that my legs were a hint longer. Silly little stumps.

Gabby flushed the toilet and stumbled toward the basin with a slurred smile.

"You look so-o-o-o-o hot," she gushed, banging on the top of the soap dispenser with a careless thwack. "I'm drunk."

"No shit," I laughed, turning the tap on for her because she'd forgotten to do that before her hands got all slippery with soap.

When we left the bathroom and headed downstairs in search of another drink for me and a water for Gabby, we bumped into Emily, who was beautified to perfection in a blood-red chiffon dress. She looked down at me as if I was a peasant, unworthy of her presence. What else was new?

"I was hoping that I might see you tonight," I said, remembering an idea that I'd had that morning while I was flipping eggs for breakfast. She raised a brow and I let Gabby's arm go so that she could escape to the kitchen. "I have a favor to ask."

"No."

"Come on, hear me out."

She pushed her perfect auburn curls over her shoulder and checked her cell phone. "Maybe on Monday. I'm leaving."

"You've been here for like fifteen minutes."

"Yes. That's long enough. Believe me." Her lips curled with distaste as she peered around at all of the excitement. "You're new to this, but let me explain how it goes. There's drinking. More drinking. Perhaps a fight. Too much PDA and then Drayton gets so drunk that he can't stand and it's embarrassing. But one of these girls is hoping to be his chosen birthday screw. Just be aware."

I exhaled and attempted not to laugh at how ironic it was that our roles had sort of switched. I would have been the one leaving in the past. I'd still prefer a quiet night in. But this was about Drayton.

"Let me guess, you used to be the chosen birthday screw."

She looked at me and pursed her lips. "I've never slept with him," she admitted with a small voice. Somehow, she still sounded confident. "He never wanted to."

It was hard to determine how serious her crush on him was, but for a brief moment, she seemed hurt, and I once again felt sort of bad for her. It was an unnatural, unwelcome feeling. And then I felt relieved to know that she'd never touched him.

"Anyway." She lifted her head and gave me a tap on the shoulder. "I'm leaving. Lincoln is waiting. See if I care about this favor of yours on Monday. You never know."

I watched her leave and figured that going an entire conversation without an insult or the urge to throw down was progress.

The kitchen was bustling. The large glass doors were shut, but the windows were cracked open because despite the fact that it was freezing outside, the copious amounts of bodies inside were causing a claustrophobic heat. I didn't love having my phone jostling around against my boob, so I switched it off, dropped it in the utensil drawer, and snatched an unopened bottle of vodka from the cupboard.

"Dallas." Gabby shoved her phone in my face, recording a Snapchat while I poured a shot. "Do a keg stand."

"You do a keg stand," I scoffed and threw back my shot. The

afterburn made me wince. Gabby recorded me pulling the same face that a baby makes when they eat a lemon wedge.

"No, I hate beer," she argued, still filming the conversation. "You're one of those weird people who actually likes the taste of beer."

"Hey, Maxon," I called to the linebacker who was currently manning the kegs. He wasn't wearing a shirt and he was well and truly off his face.

"What's up, Cheer?" he shouted.

"Don't call me that. What's the current record?"

"Mitchum!" He pointed at one of our defensemen, who was slouched in a corner, I don't even think he was conscious. "A minute fifty-six."

"That's a long time to be drinking beer." I winced. I'd wanted to do it for a challenge, but I also valued having a functional liver.

"Come on, Cheer." Maxon lifted the hose and started gyrating around the keg in some sort of disturbing ritualistic dance. "You know you want to."

I stood in front of him and scowled. "Call me Cheer again, and I'll be shoving that hose up your ass."

He recoiled and lifted his free hand in surrender.

"Come on, Dal," Gabby whooped. "You can do it. I really do believe in you. If Mit*chump* can do it, you can too."

We peered over at the boy who was now throwing up. With the help of his girlfriend, it was being directed into a bowl rather than all over the wall and floor.

"If I end up in that state," I pointed out, "you're looking after me."

"Absolutely!"

"Fine." I laughed at her intoxicated enthusiasm. She clapped her hands and stepped back, familiarizing herself with her phone again as she began to film.

"All right, usually you'd need two guys to lift a dude onto the keg,"—Maxon stepped behind me and put his hands on my hips—"but I think I can manage you by myself."

"Good attempt." I stepped out of his hold. "I'm a cheerleader. I can manage a handstand just fine."

"Sheesh. Fine." He rolled his eyes but stepped back, giving me the space I'd ordered. I put the tap in my mouth, rested my hands on either side of the barrel and kicked off the ground.

"Yes, bitch!" Gabby shouted as I started swallowing beer. I paced myself, knowing that if I didn't chug it too fast, I might be able to stay up longer. Eventually, the blood rushing to my head became an unbearable weight. It hurt, blurring my vision and making me feel ill, so I dropped one leg at a time and spit the hose out.

"Forty-seven seconds." Maxon slapped me on the back, hollering with excitement along with Gabby and a few other watchers. I wiped my mouth with the back of my hand and did my best to stop the kitchen from spinning.

I'd just had *a lot* of beer.

"What a legend!" Gabby screamed, standing next to me with the phone in front of us. She was recording a Snap video. "Forty-seven seconds. How do you feel, babe?"

"Like I'm going to throw up." I hiccupped. It was aggressive. "I need water."

I headed for the fridge and found a bottle. I wasn't sure how, but I finished the entire thing and then I felt worse. "I want bread," I mumbled and began to go through the cabinets. I found a loaf of gluten free and decided that I'd rather chew on cardboard.

"Maxon!" someone, maybe Austin, shouted from the kitchen entrance. "Drayton's birthday present is here."

Maxon's expression became alight with smarmy glee. He dashed across the kitchen, disappearing as he literally rubbed his hands together like a creep. I was curious to know what required such devious and excited behavior.

"Come on." I tugged on Gabby's wrist and we followed them, pushing through the crowd to get downstairs. It was harder than it had been earlier.

When I finally made it through, it wasn't hard to find Drayton. He was in the center of the room, sitting on a chair while some bitch gave him a lap dance. Loud shouts of approval almost drowned out the sound of Little Mix coming from the ceiling speakers.

I watched, aggravated, hating every second that I saw another girl all over him. He was smiling an awkward smile and his hands were at his sides. Instead of watching the massive set of boobs that were bouncing around in front of him, he was scanning the room and I wondered if he was looking for me.

"Hey." Josh tapped my shoulder. I hadn't noticed him approaching, so I turned and attempted not to take my frustration out on him. "This wasn't his idea. It's something the guys do to each other at birthdays sometimes. He was hoping they wouldn't do it to him this year."

"Some warning would have been nice," I mumbled before I turned to leave, ignoring the pitiful expression that Gabby threw me.

I was drunk. And history revealed that I wasn't the most level-headed when I was under the influence. The best thing that I could do was leave and calm down. I was proud for realizing that before I pulled someone's fucking weave off . . . although it was tempting.

"Where do you think you're going?"

I stumbled when I was intercepted. It took me a moment, but I realized that it was Melissa with her gorgeous skin and intimidating stare. Why did I feel like I was in trouble?

"I'm going upstairs."

"Ain't that your man?" She gestured her head behind me but I didn't need to turn around to know who she was pointing at. "You know what I'd do if I were you? I'd go do her job for her."

"What?"

"Girl, you can dance. You're hot as hell and he's damn near obsessed with you. Go and take her place. Give him a dance."

"In front of all these people?" I slurred and stumbled forward. She couldn't be suggesting what she just suggested. I couldn't be considering it either.

"You cheer in front of people all the time."

"This is a little different."

"I wouldn't put up with that shit. Show him how a real woman does it."

I was considering it. She pointed an orange manicured finger at the stripper. "Full disclosure: that's a real woman. She's fine. I'm just giving you hype."

"You give good hype." The room swayed. I was sure it was the room. Not me.

"Go." She gave me a little push.

I turned around, and the girl was wearing even less than before. Mustering up the few fucks that I actually gave and throwing them out the window, I adopted confidence and bee-lined toward them.

Drayton saw me over the girl's shoulder. I ignored the guilt-ridden grin on his gorgeous face, palmed Barbie's shoulder, and pushed her off Drayton's lap. She landed in a heap on the floor.

She shouted something about doing a job. Which was cool. She could earn that coin—there was no shortage of people in this room who'd accept her services—but before she could stand up and attempt to continue, I slung a leg across Drayton's lap and straddled him.

"Cheer?" he murmured. I held his shoulders, kept a straight back, and rolled my hips. It was slow and sensual. "Dallas?"

"Happy Birthday," I shouted, encouraging the crowd to join in. A symphony of slurred happy birthday songs began. There was a cloud of cigarette smoke in the air, bottles clinked, and people shouted. Whenever I closed my eyes, I lost all sense of surrounding and Drayton's hands had to stop me from toppling over more than once.

I giggled and decided that I had better remain eyes wide open. I lifted my leg straight into the air and spun around so that my back was to him. Still grinding against his crotch, I slowly unzipped the front of my dress, earning enthusiastic encouragement in the form of clapping and cheering.

"Dallas."

I stood up and bent over, hands on the carpet, ass in the air. I whipped my hair and slowly stood up with rolling hips. It felt good to be appreciated.

I circled the chair that Drayton was sitting on, dancing seductively as I strategically dropped the dress from my shoulders. When I'd come full circle and was in front of him again, I was in nothing but a thong and bra. The dress landed on the floor just as the stripper had earlier.

The crowd was loud.

"Take it off!"

There wasn't a lot left to take off, but it didn't matter because Drayton bolted up out of the chair. His hand wrapped around my biceps and he dragged me through the den, picking up my dress as we went. A collective sound of protest and disappointment followed our departure. I turned around and saw *a lot* of people watching. There hadn't been that many there before. I swear.

Drayton acted as a bodyguard, shielding me as he pushed through the crowd. Shoulders bumped mine. Feet were stood on. Sweat joined the stench of cigarettes and alcohol.

"What the fuck are you doing?!" He pushed me into his room and slammed the door. "What was that?"

"It was a lap dance," I mumbled. He tossed the dress at me but it fell to the floor before my arms registered that they needed to catch the object flying at my face, and that was when I started to feel a rage of my own. "Oh, so that artificial bitch that they got from the back pages can dance on you, but not me?"

"Do you think that's what this is about?!" he yelled, walking toward me with rigid movements and a thunderous glare. "Do you think that I'd rather have her than you?! That's not the fucking problem!"

"What is the problem, asshole!?" I shoved his chest but he barely moved. This was not a conversation that we should have been having right then. Both of us were far too drunk to be arguing. It wouldn't end well. "Ya know what, fuck you."

He bit his lip with frustration. "*That* would be more preferable," he muttered under his breath. He exhaled and locked me in a piercing stare. "Look, the problem is that I don't want those perverted assholes staring at my girlfriend while she dances around in her fucking underwear." He clenched his jaw and pointed at the door behind him. "I know how their sick heads work."

"Your—your girlfriend?" I stammered.

His gaze narrowed as he stared down at me. "*That's* what you got from that?"

"Yeah."

He sighed, and ran his hands down his face. We stood in front of each other and I knew that I was wobbling. Life would be so much easier if I just didn't feel how I felt. He let his fingertips travel the length of my arm. His hooded lids fluttered as he looked me over. I was still half naked.

I don't even know what's happening.

"I didn't mean to be an asshole. I'm not going to tell you what to do. But I've heard how they talk, Dallas. Fucking Austin and Derek. Even Maxon. They are filth. I can't stand the thought of them seeing and thinking and being just fucking—gross."

He'd just called me his girlfriend and I knew that it seemed like a bad time to get hung up on such a minor detail, but I was feeling some sort of way and I couldn't stop it.

I swallowed. "You're not that drunk, are you?"

"No. Not *that* drunk."

"Why? Wasn't that the point in tonight?"

"It used to be," he said as his hand came to rest on my hip. I shivered when his thumb circled. Somehow, we'd backed up and I felt the wall, cold, behind me. "I found a more effective source of comfort. She's a damn good dancer."

His lips brushed mine. Warm as usual. There was alcohol on his breath but no cigarettes. What he told me was true. I'd become a vice. Not one that gave him a buzz or helped him to forget. But one that he could trust, talk to, and relax around.

He kissed me. It didn't start out slow. It was hot and desperate, and I was burning with need. His hands lifted mine and pinned them against the wall above my head. Desire budded, pulsated, and began to consume me. His mouth was fast and wet, tasting and taking. But he was so giving.

He gripped either thigh and hoisted me into the air. My lace thong didn't protest when his fingers slipped past the thin fabric. My legs became tight around his waist as his mouth dragged down my jaw, throat, and chest.

"You shout at me like that again," I gasped, feeling his fingers. "I'll slap you back to birth."

He chuckled and nodded, the top of his head tickled my neck. "I'm sorry," he mumbled between our kisses.

We collapsed into a heap on the top of his bed. Who knew if we'd make it downstairs again? It wasn't even a concern at this point—not when he discarded his clothing and removed what was left of mine.

N

The morning brought a headache. It brought cotton mouth and most notably, embarrassment. I should never have done that keg stand. It had all gone downhill from there.

Melissa. She'd convinced me that doing a striptease in front of the entire grade and more would be a good idea. Melissa and I would be having words on Monday.

Drayton and I brushed our teeth and got back into bed. Morning breath was never pleasant, but after a night of alcohol, it was even worse. We snuggled naked under the throw, swimming in soft sheets. We were on our sides, Drayton's arm draped across my middle, his fingertips creating tantalizing circles on my waist.

We'd been discussing the events of last night's party and there had been a significant amount of cringing going on, mostly from me. We'd both apologized for our part in the drama that had unfolded, but when we came to the fact that we'd ditched his own celebration to argue and have make-up sex, he frowned.

"I'm sorry for the way that I made you mine." His biceps flexed as he ran his hand up and down my back.

"It doesn't matter." I leaned forward and gave him a quick kiss. Without missing a beat, he grabbed my waist, rolled backward, and lifted me so that I was straddling his firm torso.

"It does matter," he mumbled, his fingers gently massaging my hips. "I should have asked you properly."

"What's properly?"

"Well," he sat up and leaned against his headboard. "I should have said 'Dallas, I think you're gorgeous, you're funny'"—he leaned in and pressed a soft kiss to my neck—"'you're beautiful'"—another one—"'you're strong and smart'"—another kiss—"'and you make me happier than I've been in a long time. Please be my girl?'"

"And I would have said 'Sure, babe.'"

Suddenly, the door swung open and hit the wall with a dull thud. Drayton pulled the sheet up behind me, creating a protective curtain. I looked over my shoulder to find Gabby and Josh at the threshold, throwing dollar bills into the air.

"Ayyyy-oooo!" they sang, shimmying into the room while they continued to make it rain. If I hadn't been naked, I would have dived out of bed and stolen the cash.

"What the hell are you two doing?" Drayton asked as I repositioned myself beside him.

"Dallas left too fast last night," Gabby laughed, throwing a handful of paper over the bed. "She didn't get to collect her tips."

"I wasn't actually there." Josh shrugged, his hands resting on his hips. "Gabby made me leave when you started unzipping your dress. I'm just here for the aftermath. The regret must be killer."

"I'm blessed with great friends," I said sarcastically.

"You are," Gabby sighed with satisfaction as she dropped onto the bed, earning a curt glance from Drayton.

"Well." Josh began to back out of the room just as I noticed that he was wearing satin boxer shorts and a matching T-shirt. It was a *Star Wars* pj set. "I'm going to eat leftover pizza for breakfast."

"I'm coming." Gabby jumped to her feet. Just watching the movement gave me second-hand nausea. "By the way, Dallas, your dance last night was *hot*! It wasn't what you'd expect from someone who was so drunk. But you actually looked great. If all else in your life fails, I think you'd be a very successful showgirl."

"She's not wrong," Drayton agreed once she was gone. "You definitely gave the stripper a run for her money."

"Did she get paid? I feel sort of bad."

"She would have been paid when she arrived. Don't stress."

I nodded and sank farther down. The sheets smelled like lavender and pine, but after last night, they were going to need to be washed.

"What are we doing today?" He pulled me into a spoon. His elbow kept him propped up so that he could feather kisses along the side of my throat.

"Hmmm." I contemplated our options for a moment. "What about a ride?"

"Sounds perfect," I felt his smile against my skin. "Then later, we can take the motorcycle out."

N

Monday was interesting. Until someone at school could top the striptease that I'd performed at Drayton's party, I was going to be the subject of teasing jeers and suggestive comments. It was a good thing that I had thick skin and the childish drama rolled right over me. At lunchtime, Drayton and I stood in the gymnasium before practice. The cheer squad had to get a routine together for the charity game next month, but knowing Emily, she'd recycle one that the entire team could do in their sleep. Whatever she could do to lighten her workload—that was why I was patiently waiting for her to show up, so that I could ask her the favor that I'd mentioned at Drayton's.

He stood behind me with his chin on my head and his arms wrapped around my middle. I was a small girl, below average height, and when he held me, I felt like he could wrap right around me and I would disappear. It was such a safe feeling. I loved how well we fit.

"What up, Cheer," Derek sauntered past us with his fingers wrapped around a football. "What's the going rate? You makin' good coin?"

As if I hadn't heard that one this morning. I rolled my eyes but felt Drayton straighten up behind me. I held on to his arms and squeezed. It was futile. If he wanted to get past me, it wouldn't be hard.

"What's your going rate, Derek?" Drayton's chest rumbled as he spoke behind me. "Enough to fix that face when I rearrange it?"

Derek scoffed and tossed the ball into his other hand. "Relax."

He wandered over to join Austin, Maxon, and Mitchum, who were warming up. Austin might have been the only person who hadn't said a word to me about the dance. I had a feeling that he'd learned his lesson.

I turned around and looked up at my man, who was scowling in the direction of his friends. It wasn't as if I didn't love how protective he was—I did—but even he had his limits. There was only so much trouble that his parents could keep him out of.

"It doesn't bother me," I reminded him, fingers clasping at the back of his neck. His taut shoulders were tense. "At all."

He pushed a piece of hair behind my ear and his gaze moved over each inch of my face. Seeing me. Hearing me. He was so present. "I know. But I'm not letting anyone talk to my girl like that."

My stomach turned over itself and then flew into my throat.

"Drayton." We both looked over at the other side of the room, where Lincoln was gathering the football team. He shot us a warning look—likely because I had been about to mount my boyfriend—and gestured that Drayton join them.

That was when I saw Emily slipping in from the foyer where the office was located. I sighed and went on my tiptoes to plant a kiss on his cheek. "Got a little scruff there." I ran a hand across his jaw before I backed up. He had the faintest shadow of stubble.

He grinned. "You like it?"

"Love it." I winked and spun around so that I could join the squad. I beelined straight for our captain.

She folded her arms and began the conversation. "I heard

that you and Drayton had sex in front of the entire party after I left. Gross."

"It was a striptease," I sighed. "We did not hav—forget it. How are you?"

"What's it to you?"

"I'm being nice."

"Gross. Don't. Get on with this favor request and don't hold your breath."

"Fine." I couldn't keep up with her moods. "I was wondering, hoping, actually, that I might be able to captain the team for the charity game. I have a routine. I have ideas. It would be a little different. More dance, but still cheer. I would really love to give it a go."

"Are you going to use that photo against me if I say no?"

"No, Emily—otherwise I wouldn't be asking for permission. I would just tell you that I'm going to do it. I prefer not to resort to blackmail."

She shrugged. "Okay, fine. Takes the pressure off me."

I tried to keep the shock from my face. That might have been the nicest thing that she'd ever done for me.

CHAPTER 23

The game was that night and both teams—football and cheer— were in tip-top shape for the end of February. It had been a great experience over the last few weeks, acting as the captain for a while. Emily had a little bit of trouble in the beginning—she'd bark orders during practice or attempt to correct the steps even though the routine was new to her as well.

Keeping with the theme of miracles, we managed to get through the last month without blood being shed, threats being made, or hair being pulled. It was progress, albeit small. It was still preferable to the total hate and resentment that had existed between us before.

Nathan and I were sitting in the living room after school. I was on the floor, staring at our threadbare carpet and promising myself that I'd have the cash to replace it one day. Nathan was on the sofa with his leg propped on his knee while he read his phone.

We were watching *Supernatural* reruns. Gabby was in

love with this show. She drooled, I mean *drooled,* over Dean Winchester. She had an obsession with her television heroes, but she argued with the use of the word obsessed.

It's not an obsession, she'd say in defense. *It's dedication.*

Our old sofa groaned when Nathan shifted. He dropped his leg and put the other one up. "You get that letter?" he asked, biting on a thumb nail. "The acceptance one?"

"Still waiting."

It was nice that he asked if I'd got an acceptance letter rather than simply asking if I'd heard back. It felt as if acceptance was all that it could be. The audition at CalArts had gone well but I was trying not to get my hopes up.

"I'll have to get a roommate when you leave." Nathan's phone bounced when he tossed it and the spring in the couch squeaked. "It'll be too quiet without you dancing around all the time."

"Nathan, get married. Have a couple of kids. Settle down. You're twenty-five, dude."

"This is prime time. This is when I'm meant to be doing the bachelor thing."

Dust danced when I dragged my feet across the carpet toward me. Knees to my chest, I hugged my legs and rested my chin on top. "And that would be fine if I believed that it made you happy. You hate being alone. That's the reason that you—"

"We're not doing this again." He stood, stretched, and strolled into the kitchen. "Dallas, you are not a shrink. I do not need *advice.*"

"It's not advice. It's an opinion."

The cupboard doors opened and closed in the kitchen. Before long, there were frozen berries and fruit spread across the countertop. Nathan held the blender cup in one hand and peered over at where I was still sitting on the living-room floor.

"Smoothie?"

"No thanks."

I was about an hour from game time and the last thing that I needed was to be thrown around with dairy in my stomach, which reminded me I should have been going. Standing up, I slipped my cell phone into my bra and ran a hand through my ponytail while I deliberated if I needed to remember anything else.

"Dallas," Nathan snapped. "Quit doing that."

I stared. "Doing what?"

"Putting your cell phone in your bra. How many damn times do we have to go over this?"

He stormed toward me. There was milk on his black T-shirt, and I laughed at how childish it seemed, until he pinched the bottom of my phone and pulled it out of its hiding spot.

"Nathan." I swatted his shoulder and snatched it back. "I don't need your *advice.*"

"It's not advice, dipshit. It's called cellular radiation and it's a real thing. Use a pocket."

My big brother had been health conscious for as long as I could remember. It went further than his diet and exercise. Putting my phone in my bra was a bad habit, so I slipped it into my pants pocket and smiled with sarcasm.

"Happy? Can we go now?"

"Hang on, let me put this stuff away."

He went back to the kitchen to finish his smoothie and pack up the ingredients.

"Yeah. And, Nathan, change your shirt."

At school, the chaos was unreal. The parking lot was congested with cars that honked and drivers who leaned out of their windows, cussing when their spot was stolen. Bumpers touched bumpers and the traffic crawled at a snail's pace. This was the specific reason that Nathan and I had caught an Uber. It astounded me that people did this every single year and refused to learn that driving was not worth it.

The stands had filled up. There was a near-constant cloud of cold breath above all of the heads. People were huddled with blankets and wore hats. Little children were in sleeping bags. Noses were red and hands were hidden in gloves. But the atmosphere was so positive. It was inspiring that so many people supported such a good cause.

I was sitting on the track with Melissa. We were underneath a big blanket covered in a picture of Lady Gaga. We had fifteen minutes before kickoff, and I was excited to see Drayton play again.

Our cheer uniforms were sleeveless, but we'd all agreed to wear a maroon long sleeve underneath our tops because of how cold it was. The days were no longer filled with permafrost, but nighttime was still cuddle weather.

There was a sudden pause in the elevator music that had been humming in the background. It wasn't loud, but the abrupt stop was enough that the crowd became quiet in anticipation. The field was vacant. It couldn't be time for the game to begin.

Melissa and I stood up and wandered, along with the other curious cheerleaders, toward the edge of the field. A new song began. The sound was louder than it had been before and I recognized the song was "I Like Me Better" by Lauv.

As soon as the first verse began, six of the football players emerged from the left tunnel. They cradled a football each and lined up in the middle of the field.

The first player stepped forward and kicked his football into the air. It exploded into fireworks. It was loud and I startled, but it was so beautiful. The crowd gasped with marvel and awe as bursts of color popped against the canvas of black. The second player followed with his ball.

And so it continued in quick succession until the sixth player had kicked his ball. The impromptu display was such a unique beginning to the game. I was so fixated on figuring out how those footballs were engineered that I almost missed Drayton walking onto the field.

He was in his uniform but with no helmet, just his maroon and white colors, his chest gear and a football under one arm. He sauntered toward the head of the setup, and I watched him, curious as to why he hadn't mentioned that he was doing some sort of pre-game performance.

"Baby," he cupped his hand around his mouth and shouted. "Catch!"

Without giving it a second thought, I stepped forward and noticed that the cheerleaders stepped back. He evaluated his aim and then sent the ball with a strong arm, letting it spiral straight for me.

Much to my relief, I caught the ball, feeling triumphant because the crowd was huge and missing would have been embarrassing. I glanced down at the ball and almost dropped it when I read the words that were scrawled across it in thick black font.

You're the greatest catch that I've ever made, Cheer.
Touchdown at prom with me?

It was a promposal. He'd planned this entire thing for me, and I'd had no idea.

I was still staring at the ball, reading the words and semi-ignoring the fact that thousands of people were watching me. The sheer thought of that would have killed me once upon a time. But I no longer cared. I looked up just in time to see that Drayton had run across the field and was a few feet in front of me. As he swept me up, the ball slipped out of my hold and I wrapped myself around him, hooking my legs around his waist as he spun in a slow circle.

He held me up under the bum, the maroon in our uniforms blended together, and we kissed. I held his face, gripped his hair, and attempted not to let it go too far in front of all of the families that were there. Our lips parted and met again over and over. Closed mouth kisses. To keep it appropriate.

He leaned back and I was met with that green gaze that turned me inside out. "Is that a yes?"

I bit down on a smile and shrugged. "Sure."

His grin widened, touching the corners of his eyes, and that laugh, it could melt butter. The crowd was applauding. There were congratulations and a lot of *awws* going on.

Coach Finn's voice boomed through a megaphone. "All right, good job, lovebirds. Now let the girl go, Lahey. We've got a game to win."

Drayton let me drop down in front of him. He loved his sport but I knew him well enough to know that he wouldn't mind disappearing right now. He began to back up, still holding one of my hands. "You look beautiful, Cheer."

"Good luck tonight."

He winked, and then he won.

After the game, there was a celebration at Maxon's. Gabby was given a direct invitation from Maxon himself. She'd become closer with some of the team and their extended group thanks to her relationship with Josh. She could drink most of them under the table, and it appeared that they loved it.

"Dallas," she called from her spot around a round glass table, low to the floor, where a bunch of people were sitting for a drinking game. "Come and join."

I was perched in Drayton's lap on a suede recliner. We'd come to the party out of obligation to the team, but both of us were eager to leave. "No, it's all right," I called back, raising my voice above the loud music. I didn't want to join a game only to leave in the middle of it.

Maxon's second-floor living room was an open space with a lot of seating, hardwood floors, and enormous windows that allowed a view of the town's lights. That was one thing that I loved most about these elite houses—they had so much spare space that excessive windows weren't even an issue. I loved a good view.

"Bro." Maxon slapped Drayton on the shoulder as he circled the chair with a Bud Light in his hand. I wanted to tell him to get a real drink. "You've done us all wrong."

Drayton's thumb rubbed small circles on my hip. "What are you on about?"

"Becca's been talking about the prom since we started school. Now I have to top that damn promposal."

A couple of the guys who were close enough to hear agreed. Their complaints made me laugh. It was true that it would be a tough act to top, but that was Drayton. He was an extra-mile sort of person. A promposal hadn't even occurred to me, but I wasn't surprised that he'd gone all out. It gave me butterflies whenever I thought about it.

"You couldn't top it if you tried," Drayton scoffed, and I giggled at his "humble" attitude. He started to stand up, so I climbed off his lap and let him wrap his hand around mine. "We're off. Good game tonight. I'm going to go home and do a victory lap."

There was a series of laughter as he looked down at me with amusement. Idiot. He kissed my head and tugged the hood of his football jersey so that it bunched around the back of his neck. I did the same with mine. It was cold outside and we were bracing for the frostbitten air that would blast us the moment that we stepped outside.

We said our collective farewells. I knew that Josh and Gabby would be back at Drayton's at some point that night.

"So what did you think of that surprise?" Drayton asked when were in the car. His headlights illuminated the dark road and he leaned over, holding my hand.

"I loved it. I didn't see it coming. At all."

He tipped his head back on the headrest as he kept watching the road, a devious grin lifting his mouth. "You'll see me coming tonight."

"Wow."

⚡

In the morning, well, sort of morning—it was almost lunch-time—the four of us were sharing a booth at the diner. It was quiet. It smelled like onions and coffee. Outside, it was dark, the sky filled with grey clouds that threatened rainfall, and the diner lights felt bright and harsh against the gloomy backdrop. I stood at the counter while Kenzie scrawled down our order. "That was such a cute promposal last night," she said, tearing off the order slip and sticking it to the magnetic strip

I smiled and watched with amusement as her gaze darted toward the booth where Drayton leaned back in the seat with his hands clasped behind his head. I couldn't blame her for having a bit of a stare. I was used to the fact that he was admired a lot.

"I'll bring the order over when it's done." She tucked a strand of her shoulder-length copper hair behind her ear.

"Thanks, Kenz."

I slid into the booth beside Drayton and tucked into his side. Gabby and Josh were hungover. They were wearing sunglasses even though the weather was overcast and we were inside. They leaned against each other on the other side of the booth and suffered.

Drayton's arm rested around my shoulders. His muscles ached and whenever I shifted, he winced from all of the bruising around his biceps I told him more than once to move his arm, but he insisted on keeping me tucked in beside him.

"Gah, where is this food?" I murmured after fifteen minutes, staring at the kitchen where I could see our chef, Joe, checking his cell phone. "I'm starving."

"Don't lie," Drayton laughed. "You just ate."

It took me a minute to understand what he was talking about. Then I remembered what we'd been doing before we left his house and I smothered a snort.

"Can you not?" Josh frowned, catching on as well. His head

was tipped back, leaning on Gabby's and both of them had a flattering double chin happening.

"Can I not what?" Drayton scoffed, tapping the tabletop with his spare hand. "Can I not talk to my girlfriend about our sex life?"

Josh groaned and I wondered if Gabby was asleep or if she was just avoiding the conversation. "You're obsessed."

"I'm obsessed?" Drayton leaned forward with disbelief. His hoodie pulled tight against his chest. "Your room smells like dick all the time. You have jizz on your headboard."

Gabby was definitely awake. Her chapped lips parted in horror.

"Why are you so fucking loud?" Josh seethed.

"How did you even achieve that?" Drayton laughed. "Learn how to aim. You damn spaz."

I twisted the hoodie string around my finger. "Better on the headboard than in Gabby's uterus."

She remained quiet but slowly lifted a hand and rested it on her face, as if she was hiding. Drayton's loud laugh further irritated the hungover couple. Both of them cringed, their lips pursed in protest.

We were provided with a distraction when Kenzie delivered our nachos. The plate was huge. Cheese, salsa, sour cream, and of course, a mountain of chips. It was mouthwatering, and Drayton and I wasted no time digging in.

Gabby and Josh hesitated. It must have been the thought of stomaching food that was making them reluctant. Usually they wouldn't be so shy. I pushed the plate farther into the middle of the table and both of them gagged when the aroma wafted toward their noses. So dramatic.

"You're not usually this tragic in the morning," I said. "Exactly how much did you have to drink?"

"It's not about how much," Gabby groaned, her body draped across the tabletop as if she couldn't hold up her own weight. "We had poisonous tequila shots."

I had to agree with her there. I didn't touch the stuff.

"Gabs," I clapped my hands together to dust off chip powder. "Your mom was asking me about your college applications. Like, she doesn't know where you applied? I'm getting kind of worried."

She remained head down on the table, ignoring me. Josh's eyes were hidden behind his shades but his lips pursed. He knew something.

"You're almost a straight-A student," I continued. "What is the issue? Did you really not app—"

"I did. Shut up," she interrupted. The door jingled, piercing our now-silent group as new customers came in and out. "I applied at the Arapahoe Community College. Mom didn't want me moving far and Josh is here. Okay? Happy?"

I looked at Josh, confused, as well as Drayton, who shrugged. "Why wouldn't you just tell me that, Gabs?"

She slowly sat up, wincing and breathing through her movements. "Because you always go on about how smart I am and how I could go anywhere, and I chose *people* over college. You would never do that. I didn't want to get harassed about it."

"I haven't been pushy, have I?" She didn't answer me. "I didn't mean to make you feel pressured. I just want the best for you, Gabs."

"Someone's in a grump," Drayton mumbled, mouth full of food.

"I'm happy if you're happy," I assured her.

She didn't respond, but she did smile. A small smile. I attempted to encourage her to eat again—it was no doubt what she needed—but when I pushed the oversized blue plate farther toward her, she scowled and shoved it back.

"Hey, remember when you two made out once?" Drayton waved a finger between his best friend and me. Even behind their sunglasses, I could see Josh's and Gabby's brows furrow.

"What the fuck?"

Drayton ignored Josh. "Dude, I wanted to cut off your tongue when I saw that shit. Baby, I'm so glad that you didn't sleep with him."

If the fluorescent lights and white noise of the diner weren't making our friends throbbing headaches worse, Drayton sure was. Gabby's chest visibly expanded and her feet shuffled under the table.

"Ignore him," I told her, folding a napkin into a triangle.

"Josh, who's the better kisser?"

Josh turned his palms upward, a sheen of sweat shining under the light.

"Drayton, I do not need to know the answer to that," I said, a side-on glance expressing my disapproval. "None of us do."

"I do."

"Why are we talking about this?" Gabby croaked.

Drayton shrugged. "What else would we talk about?"

"Anything!" Josh cried. "Literally *anything* else."

Josh had known Drayton a lot longer than I had, but even I knew that ignoring him was the best way to make him stop. He loved winding people up. He was a child.

"Come on," he coaxed. "Or I'll assume it's Dallas."

"If I say Dallas, I hurt Gabby. If I say Gabby, you'll chew me out for insulting Dallas." Josh clenched his jaw and banged a fist on the table. "I can't win so I'm not answering."

"Good idea," Drayton nodded. "Safe."

"It's Gabby." I winked at her, biting another chip loaded with salsa. I chewed and swallowed. "We've made out before. I know that it's her."

Drayton recoiled, his head whipping between both of us so fast that I expected it to snap. "Pics or it didn't happen."

I nudged him with my elbow. He wasn't done, though. "Should we have a foursome?"

It didn't even surprise me that he said it. It was the volume at which he said it that might have been responsible for Josh standing up and leaving. Gabby watched him pull the door open, a gust of cold air and the jingle of the bell following.

"I should go." She stood up, slow and fatigued. "He's just tired."

When she was gone, Drayton sighed. "Finally."

"You did that on purpose?"

"Of course, I did." He shrugged, settling farther into the seat. He hissed when my shoulder bumped his biceps. "So that we could be alone."

"We could have left, Dray. Or just told them that we wanted to spend some time alone."

"Nah," he grinned. "That was more fun."

"You don't really want to have a foursome then?"

"Fuck no. Some couples can do that. Sweet. I couldn't deal watching someone else put their hands on you. I'd slip and murder them. Why? Do you want to have one?"

"No."

"Sweet."

The vibrating on the tabletop clattered the salt dispenser and startled me. Drayton chuckled, pushing the plate away from his reach so that he couldn't eat any more. I picked up my cell and read the email notification on the screen.

It was from CalArts.

I'd been waiting for this moment since the audition. I'd imagined where I'd be and how I would respond to this email. And now that it was here, I had no idea how to proceed. Drayton leaned over and read the unopened email notification.

"Cheer." He sat up straighter. "Read it. Babe? Open the email."

"I'm scared."

"Should we go somewhere private?"

"No."

"Well . . ." he sounded apprehensive, cautious, as he shifted beside me. "I'm not sure what else to do here."

"Open it." I shoved the cell phone into his hand. "I can't do it."

My heart was hammering, pounding so furiously that I began to feel lightheaded.

"Okay." He started to put in the passcode, his gold thumb ring shimmering in the diner's lights. Before I even realized that I'd done it, I snatched the phone back. His now-empty hand hovered open. "Okay."

"Sorry, I just—no. You do it."

I handed the phone back.

"Is this a thing? Are we going to keep passing the phone back and forth?" he said. "If so, we should go home and do it in the nude. It'd be more interesting."

"Shut up." I backhanded his chest but managed to laugh. His unapologetic humor grounded me, and I calmed down a little bit. "Open it. I'm good. I won't snatch it again."

"You kids need something else?" Hattie, an older waitress who did shifts on the weekends, picked up the plate of nachos and smiled, red lipstick smeared across her veneers. "Drink? Snacks?"

"No thanks, ma'am." Drayton gestured the cell phone in my direction. "Got a whole meal right here."

"No thanks, Hattie," I answered quickly, attempting to keep the impatience out of my tone. "We're good."

"Okay." I inhaled. I exhaled. I nodded. "Do it."

Drayton unlocked the phone again. I looked up at his face instead of watching the screen. His eyes moved to mine for a second and he grinned. "Fuck, you're cute." He returned to the phone and I could hear the soft tap of his thumb pads getting closer and closer to knowing just what the future held.

The reflection was in his green gaze, but I couldn't read what he was reading. I just knew that when his brows pulled together, for a mere millisecond, my heart stopped. I didn't get in.

"You did it, Cheer," he looked at me and smiled so bright that he could have outshone the sun. "You did it. You got in."

"I got in?" I snatched the phone. It was hard to read the screen as adrenaline pumped through me and I felt dazed. "Where, where, oh there! Ah. Dray! I got in."

The phone clattered on the tabletop as I dropped it and dived on top of him. He tumbled into the corner of the booth but didn't fail to encase me in his strong hold. He buried his face in my neck and congratulated me over and over again. We hugged for a while. I read the email again. We kissed and he decided to make an announcement.

"If you know this girl right here," he shouted, "give her a congrats. She just got accepted to her dream college."

The entire diner didn't know who I was, but they all clapped regardless. It was sort of embarrassing, but sweet as well. Hattie, Kenzie, and Joe gave me a more personal congratulations, and after about fifteen minutes of reveling in success, I sighed in contentment and relaxed back into the seat. The email was still open.

"Dray." I peered up at my man, who was sipping a pop that Kenzie gave me on the house. "How come you seemed . . . disappointed when you read the email?"

"Disappointed? What are you talking about?"

"You sort of frowned when you were reading it."

"You're imagining things." He put the drink down and leaned both of his elbows on the tabletop, as if he was putting his back to me.

"I know that you frowned." I was gentle with the words. "Is it because I'll be going to California for sure now?"

"Cheer." He looked over his shoulder. "I didn't frown. I'm not disappointed. I was probably concentrating or looking for the paragraph. I don't know. I'm not disappointed. Why are you trying to start an argument?"

"I'm not."

"Stop with the accusations, then."

His leg bounced under the table as we fell silent. What the hell did I do that for?

"Have you written a letter of intent?" I asked when I couldn't handle the quiet for another moment. "Like, I don't even know where you're going to college."

His hands came together in front of his chin and he shook his head.

"So you don't know where you're going to college? Dray, you'll miss the deadline."

"Can we go?" He turned his knees toward me, wanting out of the worn leather booth.

Despite the fact that he was being a bit shut off and I'd unintentionally spoiled the good mood, he held my hand in the car.

"Dray, where are you going to college?"

He stared out of the windshield, turning the wipers on when a light rain began to fall. "I don't know. It depends on whether I can convince my dad to stop being a dick."

"Okay. Where do you want to go to college?"

"UCLA. It's a good school." His hand dropped mine so that he could turn on the blinker and the lights. The rain was getting heavier. "And it's close to you."

"Please don't choose a college based on me. It's too big. I don't want to change your plans."

He ignored me and drove with one hand on the wheel, his other fist resting in front of his mouth, elbow on the door. When we arrived at Drayton's house, we stood on the front patio. He watched the snow melting. Small clumps of white ice washed down the drive.

"Why shouldn't I pick a college that's close to you, Cheer?" He didn't look at me. "I want to be with you. It's a good school. It's in California. Not a lot of downfall that I can see."

"Because I wouldn't choose a school to be close to you." I stood in front of him, but he stared over my head. He looked hurt, biting the inside of his cheek. "I have a plan. I've had that plan for a long time and it's happening. I wouldn't change that, and you shouldn't have to change your plans for me."

"I didn't have a plan. I've never given it that much thought at all." His eyes met mine. "I was going go to Baylor because that was how it had always been, and I didn't question it. But I don't care where I go to college. As long as I get to play the sport I love, what does it matter? My dad is the one with the fucking problem."

"That fight isn't something that I want to get in the middle of."

He scoffed and turned around. "Sounds like you really couldn't give a shit what happens to us."

"Excuse me?" I snapped. He didn't turn around. Rain fell on the awning, the pattering loud and in time with the pounding in my chest. "What the hell? Of course I care. But things don't have to change. And even if they do, it won't change how I feel."

He didn't respond. He kept his back to me, hands in his pockets. The college conversation had always been a bit of a sensitive subject because it had always been possible that we'd be apart. But if I had known that it would turn into this, I would have had it sooner.

"I'm leaving." I turned around and started down the steps, but then I remembered how much he hated it when I walked alone. I was mad, but I wasn't cruel.

It didn't seem to matter though. He stormed into rain and blipped the button for the Jeep. Unbelievable. I opened the passenger door and climbed in, my wet jeans squelching on the leather seat as I sat down. He drove in desolate silence. I was itching to continue the conversation, but I didn't have a clue what to say.

I didn't even know what he was so upset about. I wanted him to choose his own path and his own future without the influence of others. What was so awful about that?

He didn't even pull into the drive. He stopped at the curb and I got out. This was stupid. More ridiculous than I could even comprehend. But it seemed that we needed some space before we could talk this over.

I made it as far as the mailbox before I heard his door open and close. He flicked his hood up to shield his eyes from the rain.

"You seem to have a big opinion for someone who wants me to make my own choice." He threw his arms open and shrugged. "Thought it was up to me where I go to college."

"It is!"

"So what the hell is the issue if I choose UCLA?"

Drops of rain rolled over my face. My hair was sopping, clinging to my neck and chest. I held a hand above my brow so that I could look at him without blurred vision. It didn't help much.

"It's not an issue. Just don't do it for me."

"I can choose you if I want to, Dallas. I can still have a good education, a good future if I choose you."

"But what about your dad?"

"I'll worry about my dad," he shouted and stepped closer. The rain had drenched his maroon hoodie, darkening it. "Stop making excuses. Because it feels like you're pushing me away right now. I know that you didn't want a relationship, and that's what happened. Do you not want to be with me now that you're going to California?"

"Of course I want to be with you. That's the point that you're missing. We can be together no matter where either of us are."

"Sure, we can, but if I want to choose UCLA because the thought of living near my girlfriend makes me happy, then why shouldn't I?"

"Would your dad even allow that?"

The drain beside the sidewalk gurgled, our clothes were soaked, and it hurt to argue with the same person who made me feel whole.

"I don't know," he confessed. "I'm working on it."

I said nothing.

"I don't want to fight, Dallas. I'm going home," he told me quietly. I almost didn't hear him over the rain. He watched me through the thick fall. "There's nothing wrong with being in love, Dallas. There's no weakness in making space for it in your life."

His words hit me. It was brutal and truthful, but it was something that I'd been in denial over until I was watching him climb into his Jeep. He drove away, and the farther that he got, the more that I wanted him to come back.

We hadn't said I love you, but what he just said was an admittance of its own. As I ran inside, I thought about the fact that all I'd ever wanted was to stand alone. To be strong and accomplished without a man holding me down. I'd thought that it was weak to make a relationship as important as a career. Drayton had never held me down. He'd lifted me up.

"Hey." Nathan sat on the couch with a beer and his boxer shorts on. The football highlights were on television. Sunday. "Bit wet out there, huh?"

"CalArts emailed. I got in."

Nathan stood up, eyes wide and pride beaming in his smile. "Dude. That's so damn cool. Man. I am so proud."

He gave me an awkward hug. I was still dripping after standing in the rain and he wasn't wearing a lot of clothing. But I knew that he was overwhelmed with pride.

"Thanks, Nathan."

"We should celebrate? Let's . . . go out for dinner? Invite Drayton and Gabby. Whoever."

"I think that we should celebrate just the two of us." I smiled and headed toward the corridor. "I'll shower and dress first."

"I better put on some nicer clothes."

I knew that I had handled the argument all wrong. It had left me with a small bout of nausea, and I used the shower to disguise a few fallen tears. It felt wrong to know that Drayton assumed I didn't want him for the simple fact that I was off to a college in California. Did he believe that he was so disposable? And as much as I believed that we would be fine in separate states, his desperation to be close worried me. The whole fight left me upset and confused. I needed a bit of time to clear my head before I saw Drayton again. The next time that we spoke, I didn't want it to end in argument. Or worse.

Driving home from dinner, the road was slick. Nathan clutched the wheel and drummed his fingers along to the song coming from the stereo. It crackled. It was old.

"I know that you don't want to talk about it," he said and I sighed, letting my forehead press against the cold passenger window. "But I have to say something. Just one thing and then I'll let it go."

He'd figured out rather fast that I was having relationship issues when I stared at a plate of fries and garlic bread and refused to touch it. "Fine." I rolled my wrist. "What is it?"

"I wasn't a good example while you were growing up." My head whipped toward him. "I wasn't. I didn't hide my habits. There was nothing discreet about the girls I had coming in and out. There was no example of exclusivity, and I think that I unintentionally gave you this impression that relationships were the worst thing in the world."

"You can't take that sort of responsibility, Nathan. You were seventeen. No one expected you to be perfect."

He looked at me for a moment, shaking his head. "No, I could have done better. I should have. You took on the same habits that I had and I didn't want to admit it, but I knew that it was because of what you'd watched from an impressionable age. But, Dal, don't be afraid of your relationship. It's a good one. I can tell."

I watched him as he frowned, staring in front of him. "Nathan, I am who I am, and I've never considered that a bad thing. Drayton and I are having a . . . rough patch. But it hasn't changed how I feel about him."

"Who you are isn't a bad thing," he said. "But don't push him away out of fear. I know you, Dallas. I see more than you realize. You might not even realize that you're doing it."

The streetlights illuminated the car, casting shadows. I stared out of the fogged-up windshield and felt my stomach drop. "Can you drop me off at Drayton's, please?"

He didn't look at me. But he did smile.

When we pulled up at the gate, I handed Nathan my swipe card and he opened his window, allowing a burst of freezing-cold air to blast through the warm car. The gates opened and he drove slowly, careful until the enormous and luminous house came into view. Drayton's bedroom light was on.

"Thanks. I'll be back later. Maybe."

"You have school tomorrow," he warned me as I got out of the car. I shivered and gave him a quick wave before I jogged over to the front door, which opened before I could touch the bell.

"Dallas." Drayton encircled my wrist and pulled me into the warm house. His cap was on backward and he wore a snug long sleeve and sweatpants. He watched me with panic. "What's wrong? Are you okay?"

"I'm fine." My heart swelled at his concern. "Can we please talk?"

He nodded. I took my boots off and he wrapped his hand around mine and led me upstairs. His room was so warm that I pulled off my coat and scarf while he sat on the corner of his bed. The fire crackled and the flames flickered. I was more at ease than I'd been all afternoon. His presence, the familiarity of it, made me feel at home, and that was how I knew what I wanted. It was how I knew that it was okay to want it.

"I'm sorry for how I handled things this afternoon," I said, standing in front of him. I folded my arms and then unfolded them. I tugged on the long sleeves of my oversized sweater. I couldn't stop fidgeting. "I know how I feel. But you don't know how I feel unless I tell you. And I could do better with that. With verbalizing. I guess I was putting up a bit of a wall without realizing it. Because how I feel does scare me sometimes, Dray."

He rested his elbows on his knees, hands clasped as he looked up at me. "And how do you feel, Dallas?"

I felt breathless. "I love you."

His lips parted and his gaze grew wide. He stood slowly and cautiously. "Tell me again," he murmured. He stood so close that I had to tip my head back to see the enamored expression on his face.

"I love you, Drayton. And it does scare me. Because this is new. But I feel it and you need to hear it. Of course I want you close when we go to college. The closer, the better. But I love you enough to know that if we aren't dealt the cards that we want, I will still love you."

His hand cupped the nape of my neck and he pushed our mouths together. There were times when his lips had a language of their own, one that I could understand. One that I could speak. I felt it before he said it. "I love you too." He held my face, his forehead on mine. "So much."

"No matter what happens," I said, raising my arms to clasp my fingers behind his neck.

He spun us around and I fell backward onto the bed. He crawled over me and looked down with so much love that it was electric. His touch ignited me. His kiss reminded me how to breathe even as it stole the air from my lungs. Loving Drayton had never been hard. It had happened on its own. It had taken the wheel and I never wanted it back. But for a while, I'd focused so hard on what I wanted that I forgot to focus on what I deserved. The perspective was breathtaking.

"Please tell me again," Drayton murmured against my throat as his hand popped the button on my jeans. "I love you, baby. Tell me that you love me."

"I love you, Drayton."

Drayton had always been supportive and celebrated my success, just as I'd done for him. I was wrong to assume that a relationship would make me weak. I could still achieve everything that I'd ever wanted. Having him there beside me, cheering me on, lifting me up, that was a privilege. I loved him and I knew that he loved me too. We'd be okay.

CHAPTER 24

Prom night started at Gabby's house. We had our makeup done by a freelance artist who did an exquisite job. We looked flawless with contour, highlight, and brows that could have been sculpted by an angel.

Josh and Drayton arrived while Gabby was standing in front of the mirror in her living room, running her fingers through her pin-straight hair. It was parted in the middle and tucked behind her ears. She'd used a picture of Kim Kardashian West when we went to the salon that afternoon. I'd opted for a curled updo. A bun sat low at the back of my head and wisps of hair framed my face.

Drayton and Josh strolled in wearing hoodies and jeans. But like us, their hair had been done. Drayton's was its usual crop on the top of his head. Product kept it still and the sides had been cut shorter. Josh wore his signature slicked-back style.

"Don't you look fucking beautiful," Drayton hollered as soon as he walked into the room. He went in for a kiss, but I pointed at the nude lip color on my mouth and offered him my head instead.

Josh and Gabby went straight into selfie mode and began snapping a few photos.

"Did you guys remember to pick up your suits from the dry cleaner's?" Gabby asked, assessing her brand-new nails after Josh sat down on the corner of the coffee table. "Or do we need to go and get them?"

"Nah, we're fucking dumb and forgot," Drayton drawled with sarcasm. Gabby rolled her eyes in the mirror, watching his reflection.

Camilla appeared from the kitchen wearing a floral apron covered in flour, her long dark hair in a tight braid. The plate of brownies in her hands steamed. The delicious morsels were powdered with icing sugar, and the aroma of homemade baking was mouthwatering.

"Ahh." She nodded when she saw Drayton standing beside the sofa. "I thought it must have been you when I heard all of the cussing."

He put a hand across his chest and graced her with a sincere apologetic smile. He was so damn charming. "Sorry, Ms. Laurel."

She smiled but he should have counted his blessings. If it was me or Gabby dropping f-bombs, we'd be six feet deep.

"Brownie?"

"This is the reason that my clothes are getting too tight." Gabby pointed at her mother, finally tearing herself from her own reflection. Not that I could blame her, I would stare at myself if I had her face as well.

I passed on the brownie as well. Not because I was concerned about my clothes, but because there weren't a lot on the plate and Josh and Drayton were inhaling what was there. Gabby complained about the injustice of men eating whatever they wanted and not putting on weight. In their defense, they did put in the hours at the gym.

When we arrived at Drayton's, Gabby was devastated to find that there was even more food there to tempt her than there had been at home. Ellie had laid out a spread in one of the sitting areas downstairs. The coffee table was covered in cakes, cookies, club sandwiches, and cupcakes.

The four of us separated to get into our outfits. The girls were upstairs; the boys were downstairs. Ellie arranged it that so that Gabby and I could descend the staircase in our dresses. Her excitement was contagious.

The spare bedroom smelled like fresh linen and lilies, which I didn't think of much until I saw the bouquet sitting in a vase on the bedside table. The ribbon around the stems had a card attached to it and Gabby watched—and obsessed—as I tiptoed across the soft carpet to read it out loud.

> *Favorite flower for my favorite girl. Love all of who you are. I love what you love. I want to be who you need. Will never stop trying to win you over. Every day is the first day.*
>
> *—Your QB*

"Well," Gabby's voice quivered. When I looked at her, she was fanning her face. "How he can be such a shameless idiot and the most romantic man on the planet, I will never know."

"You and me both." I read the note again.

She walked off, her shoulders slumped. It was a bit dramatic, but she sniffed and started to pull her romper off. "Josh needs to step up. He didn't even compliment my hair! Not one word. It looks so good right now."

"It does. It looks beau—"

"You've told me! It looks beautiful. I know. I want him to tell me that."

"Gabs," I stared at her with bewilderment. She was one foot stomp from a full-on tantrum. "Don't compare them. They're two different people. Josh adores you. Stop being so dramatic."

We were standing in our floor-length ball gowns, unzipped and shoeless. I was right; Gabby was a model. The silk fabric draped, flowing from her figure like honey being poured from a jar, soft and seamless. The dress was dark blue with thin straps and a ruched neckline that sat low and exposed her smooth chest and sharp collarbones.

She turned around so that I could zip up the back. It was tighter than I expected it to be. It was a perfect fit when it was undone. The zip did go up, but it was snug. Gabby stared in the mirror and frowned.

"This fit me three months ago. Remember? We bought this together and it fit."

It had fit her three months ago. Now her boobs looked about ready to burst.

"Whatever, I just won't sit down all night."

"I bet Ellie has something in her closet," I suggested, looking behind her at the full-length mirror. Her bum looked fantastic. "We could ask?"

"Nope." She held my shoulders and swapped our positions so

that she could zip me up while I looked in the mirror. "I'll wear this. If it zips, it fits."

My dress hadn't decided to change its measurements. It fit just as it had when I'd tried it on three months ago. It was strapless. The top half had corset-like boning, and it was fitted and flattering, accentuating my curves and chest. The material was white with rose-gold bordering. From the waist down, it flowed into sheer white waves of soft fabric that felt like a cloud kissing my legs. I felt beautiful.

Gabby was leaning on the wall beside the door. Her platforms were on. So were mine. But she was making no move to leave. Her forehead was a bit shinier than it had been earlier.

"Are you feeling okay, Gabs?"

"Just a bit hot. Sort of ick. It's just warm up here, I think. I'm worried about my hair."

If it was warm, I would know about it. I felt the heat harder than she did.

"We should go downstairs, then," I offered and stared at her stomach. It couldn't be what the little niggling voice in the back of my head was suggesting. It couldn't be because she would have thought about that first.

"Mhmm." She pushed herself off the wall and her heels raised her ten stories tall. "I need water."

Click clacks against the stone floor followed our footsteps toward the staircase. Voices chattered from below. Ellie was onto something when she'd suggested that we meet our men at the bottom of the staircase. I felt like a princess.

I saw him before he saw me. His suit was divine. It was tailored to his tall frame. Snug. His tie was the same color as the rose gold on my dress. His soft leather shoes were something that would be seen on a red carpet. I was used to seeing him in casual street wear and Converse. But he pulled this off so well.

He looked up and his mouth dropped open. "Fuck. Me."

I laughed and noticed Ellie watching him with disapproval.

"Someone's taking a picture, right?" Drayton shouted, his gaze never leaving mine. "Because I'm in the moment but someone better get a photo of my girl."

"All right, we get it," Gabby's monotone complaint droned behind me. "Drayton is obsessed with Dallas and he shows it. Cool."

I peeped at Josh who was wearing a similar suit to Drayton's but without a tie, and the shirt underneath his jacket was the same dark blue as Gabby's dress. He frowned at Gabby.

"Gabby, you do look beautiful."

When I reached the floor, Drayton's hand took mine. It was warm, as usual. Butterflies caused havoc in my stomach due to his no-holding-back smile. It was the best one of all. Bright and bold.

"You look perfect." His hold moved to my waist, the rest of the room forgotten.

"*You* look perfect." I stored it to memory. His figure in this outfit. His perfection. The fabric of his suit was like butter beneath my fingertips. It was Armani—I'd been with him when he bought it, and while the thought of spending so much on one outfit made me sweat, I couldn't deny that it was worth it.

Ellie was snapping photos, the flash reflected in Drayton's soft green stare of admiration. "You girls look gorgeous," she cooed.

The four of us stood in front of the water feature in the foyer. The sound of its fall was whimsical while we posed for Ellie, who was an enthusiastic photographer. We took group photos, couple photos, friend photos.

Ellie mentioned that she wanted to do a photo with Leroy and Drayton. Before she could run off to find Leroy, she showed me how to operate her big Canon camera, which I felt afraid to hold for the sheer fact that it was the equivalent feeling to watching a stack of cash burn in my palm. If I dropped it, I was going to die.

"Drayton!"

We all looked up at the entrance at the far end of the corridor, where a disgruntled and frustrated voice came from. Leroy appeared a moment later, holding a piece of paper in the same hand that his Rolex watch was on. If looks could kill.

Drayton watched his father approaching him with boredom. His hands were in his pockets and there was not a crease of concern on his face.

"You told me that you sent that goddamn letter of intent to Baylor." He shoved the paper into his son's chest but Drayton didn't touch it. "The deadline has been and gone. You didn't get the fucking scholarship. What the hell is—"

Ellie stepped between them and held a palm up to her husband. "Don't talk to him like that. You need to calm down."

My throat felt thick watching the tension. Drayton appeared calm but his chest was rising and falling and his jaw fluttered. Gabby and Josh discreetly pointed at the kitchen and tiptoed across the foyer. It would be preferable to follow them. And perhaps I should have, because this seemed personal. But I didn't want to leave Drayton.

"I'm not going to Baylor," Drayton said. His lips barely parted.

"Apparently, you're not going anywhere now," Leroy snapped. He took a step back and threw the paper at the ground. "I will talk to the coach and you will do a walk-on tryout."

"No. It's not happening. I told you. I'll go where I want. Or I'll go nowhere."

Ellie remained between them. She was smaller than both, but determined to keep them apart. Leroy and Drayton glared at each other with identical scowls.

Leroy looked at me. "This is your fault."

Somehow telling him that I was in favor of Drayton choosing the path that he'd planned to begin with seemed like it would make things worse. I didn't know what to tell him. I stood tall and attempted not to crumble under his harsh glare.

"Leroy," Ellie warned.

"There was not one issue until she arrived." He pointed at his son. "I thought you were smarter than that. But well done. You screwed up your own future over a girl."

"Don't talk about her like that." Drayton's breathing became heavier, his hands were restless in his pockets. "You don't know what you're talking about."

"Please, can we do this later," Ellie said desperately. "The kids have to go. The limo will be here soon."

"You screwed everything up."

Drayton moved past his mother, stood in front of me, and squared his shoulders. "You're fucking pushing me, man."

"Enough," Ellie shouted, once again intercepting and putting herself in the middle of a standoff. "Leroy, enough. You need to go and cool off. Now."

Her face was flushed and her hand trembled as she pointed at the staircase. Without another word, Leroy turned around and went upstairs.

"Mom," Drayton said.

"He doesn't mean it, Drayton," she mumbled.

"Didn't mean to what? Force me into his old school because he's on a power trip?"

"It's where his father wen—"

"Yeah. I know. Where his father went and his father. I get it. But I can choose a new path, Mom. I don't have to do the same thing as them. UCLA is a good school."

"I know." She nodded and leaned against the bannister as if she couldn't hold up her own weight. "But it's more complicated than that. You know that Grandpa Lahey died in that house fire when you were a baby, right?"

Drayton nodded.

"Well, before he died one of the last conversations that your dad had with Grandpa was about college football. He told Grandpa that you'd attend Baylor, their alma mater. It was a casual conversation over lunch. It was light and cute, but it was the last conversation that they had, Dray. He died that afternoon. And ever since then, your dad has been trying to keep his promise."

Leroy had suffered so much loss. He might be cold and harsh, but it was unimaginable that he'd lost his parents and his daughter so tragically. The commiseration that I felt was immediate. I knew exactly what it was like to lose both parents.

Drayton exhaled and ran a hand through his hair. "Why did no one tell me this?"

"He didn't want to use guilt tactics to encourage your choice."

"Being an asshole was his preferred option?"

"I know that he's gone about this all wrong, but he felt panicked. He knew as soon as Dallas stepped onto the scene that this might happen"—she looked at me and smiled—"which doesn't put you at blame, honey. But Dray, you've never cared all that much about the college itself. He knew it was possible that being in love would have some pull on what you chose."

"I still should have known the real reason he was so insistent on where I went to school."

"I told him that. But would it have made a difference?"

Drayton's gaze moved around the room, thoughtful for a moment until he shrugged. "Maybe. Maybe not. At least I would have understood, and we could have saved ourselves all of this fucking bullshit."

"Language."

"Sorry, Mom."

She inhaled a long deep breath. I couldn't imagine the toll that it would take watching her husband and son fight with so much vehemence. "Forget about it for tonight if you can. Just have a nice prom. I'll talk to Dad and we can attempt a civil discussion tomorrow."

"Yeah." He pulled his mom into a hug, his chin resting on her head. "Love you, Mom."

N

Silver and pale-pink balloons full of helium dotted the entire ceiling. The hotel had opened up three separate banquet rooms to create a space large enough for our prom. A polished wooden floor was at one end of the room, along with a booth for the DJ.

The other end of the room was made up of square tables draped in black cloth. Individual pink electric candles flickered in the middle of each table, and the chairs were silver steel.

It was dark but light was provided in the form of the afore-mentioned candles and twinkling lights zigzagging from one side of the ceiling to the other. It was elegant and enchanting. Beside the sliding door, which went out to a large patio, was a backdrop for photographs. Couples and groups were lined up, and the air was alive with laughter and upbeat music. The dancing was energetic, and although the start of the night had been less than ideal, the tension was slipping. The more that Drayton relaxed, the easier it was to be in the moment. Gabby and Josh disappeared in search of food the minute we arrived.

"Hey." Drayton tugged on my arm as I absentmindedly headed toward the dance floor. I turned and let him pull me into a tender embrace, his hands fanning out on my hips. "Have I told you that you look beautiful? Like, breathtaking. The most stunning girl that I've ever laid eyes on."

I giggled at the soft pecks he laid on my cheeks between each compliment. He was being careful not to smudge my makeup. I could feel a multitude of envious eyes boring into the two of us. People had accepted that Drayton and I were in a relationship, but that didn't stop the girls from pining and wishing for what was mine.

"You've told me about"—I narrowed my eyes, tilting my head from side to side as I pretended to think it over—"a thousand times."

"And I'm going to keep telling you because I cannot get over how damn incredible you look." He stepped back and lifted my hand above my head so that I could do a twirl.

He kept his hand around mine and pulled me in close again, his sigh content. He led us onto the dance floor. A relatively slow song was playing, allowing us to dance intimately. His free hand rested on my lower back, just above my bum, and I held his shoulder. As we moved, slowly and sweetly, to the song, I looked up and felt inexplicably grateful for finding a love like his. He was so appreciative of all that he had, and it was uplifting. I rested my head on his chest and felt the beat of his heart. It was in time with mine.

"You know," he said, "I remember the first time that I realized how gorgeous you are."

"You do?"

"I mean, I always knew you were attractive. Even when we didn't have anything to do with each other. But the moment that you first took my breath away, the first moment that you floored me was the night that I kidnapped you and took you back to my place. You came out of the bathroom wearing my T-shirt and I swear I almost lost it."

"That was the moment?" I laughed. "Not when I was dressed up in my club outfit?"

"You looked hot as hell in that little rose-gold dress"—my heart skipped a beat at the fact that he remembered what I was wearing—"but there was just something so damn gorgeous about seeing you in my shirt, seeing you dressed down and comfortable. Seeing you in my clothing is a huge turn on, and I knew right then and there that I wanted to see it more often. It was definitely hard keeping my hands to myself that night."

"Why did you?"

"You'd been drinking," he stated with a lopsided smile. "Call me crazy, but I knew you were special, more special than a drunken hookup. I couldn't leave you alone after that, though. But I wanted you to want me too."

I laughed. "I can't believe we didn't just get it all out there in the beginning. We both felt the same way. Talk about a lack of communication."

"I wasted so much time," he said with a slightly more somber expression than before. "I fucked around, playing games and waiting for you to want me back when I should have just told you how I felt."

His knuckles gently grazed the nape of my neck as his fingers fanned out and he locked me in an intense stare. "I'm doing my best to make up for that lost time, Cheer. I'll tell you all day, every day, just how much you mean to me. Because I'm an idiot and it took me way too long to say it in the first place."

I watched him, breathless. "I love you, Drayton."

"I love you too."

His hands, tender and gentle but powerful, held my face. As if I wasn't close enough, he moved one hand a time, repositioning them on my back so that he could hold me tight. He was almost lifting me off the ground as his tongue lapped at mine and I wrapped my arms around his neck.

"Excuse me, you two."

Drayton and I broke apart and found Miss Fowler's disapproving glare. She towered over even Drayton, and she scowled behind her thin wire-framed glasses.

"Enough of that."

The middle-aged woman *tsked* before moving back through the crowd of dancing teenagers. Drayton and I shared an amused laugh and continued to kiss as though we provided the air to each other's lungs. If anyone wanted us to stop, they were going to have to physically keep us apart.

Good luck to them.

We danced for a while, never letting go of each other. Drayton studied me with a heated gaze, worshipping my every move with the most admiring expression that had ever adorned his face. Later, we found Gabby and Josh, and danced with them for a while before we all headed off to the photo area. We took group shots, friend shots, and couple shots. The poses ranged from cute and romantic to wildly outrageous and possibly somewhat inappropriate . . . but I hadn't expected anything less from my man.

I let him go for a little while so that he could take photos with the team and his friends. Those photos ended up taking the longest, I thought. Everyone wanted a picture with their captain. Even I got in on a few of the photos with the cheer team. Emily looked beautiful. She didn't care when I told her that, but when she turned around and didn't realize that I was watching, she smiled.

"Should we go and wait for him on the balcony?" Gabby suggested while we sat at a nearby table, watching Drayton with his team. "I haven't been out there yet."

Josh and I nodded, and we got up, pushing our ribboned seats back under the table.

I was amazed at how big the patio was. It stretched from one corner of the building to the other and extended at least thirteen feet out in front. The railing had been wrapped with fairy lights that twinkled in a timed pattern, and there were a few scattered two-person tables and seats that were all occupied by various students who, on closer inspection, looked as though they were sharing a blunt.

Of course.

The night air wasn't warm, but it was a welcomed refresher.

I hadn't realized how suffocated I was beginning to feel inside until I was able to inhale some of the fresh oxygen outside. We stood by the railing and looked out over central Castle Rock. There wasn't a lot of traffic, but a couple of car roofs were idle at the red traffic lights. Store lights illuminated the footpaths.

"How is Drayton doing after that whole thing that happened earlier?" Gabby asked. She held her hand out to Josh, who seemed confused for a moment but then reached into his jacket pocket and retrieved a flask.

"He's fine," I answered, pointing at the object in her hand. "Where did that come from?"

"Josh had the flask." She pointed at her boyfriend, who leaned an elbow on the railing, watching the street below. "He filled it up with something from the liquor cabinet at home. What is it?"

"Bourbon," he answered.

I watched her unscrew the lid and felt weird about it. She drank all the time. That wasn't what the problem was. I looked at her dress, tight. I looked at her boobs, huge. I stood up straight, stepped forward, and slapped the flask out of her hand. It splashed a potent-smelling liquid and narrowly missed my dress as it flew over the railing and disappeared out of sight.

"What the . . . ?" Gabby leaned over and I was worried that her addiction had got to the point where she'd jump to her death just to save her precious poison.

"You can't drink," I yelped, but lowered my voice as she and Josh stared, not able to understand what the issue was.

"Why can't she drink?"

"Yeah, why?" Gabby threw her hands up.

This wasn't the gentlest way of telling someone that you thought she might be pregnant. Hell, I shouldn't have had to tell her at all. Surely, she'd suspected it herself. Surely? No, she wouldn't have been drinking if she thought it was possible, which just brought me back to the disbelief I felt at the fact that she hadn't even considered it.

"Can we talk?" I grabbed her wrist. "In private. Josh, find Drayton. We'll be—around."

"Okay?" He followed behind us, looking like a lost puppy as we stepped back into the stuffy banquet room. I felt a pang of disappointment because "I Like Me Better" was playing and I'd have loved to dance to it with Drayton. But I saw that he was still busy with photos and the team, so we split off from Josh and I dragged Gabby into the corridor and into the elevator.

"What. The. Fuck. Is. Happening?" Gabby banged her head against the lift wall while I aggressively smacked the ground-level button.

"I think you're pregnant!" I blurted.

Her forehead remained on the wall, but she stared at me from the corner of her eye, her mouth open. Her chest rose and fell rapidly, and when the elevator doors opened with a bell, breaking the piercing silence, we both jumped in fright.

"Where are we going?" she mumbled as I once again grabbed her wrist before dragging her through the hotel lobby.

"We're going to get a pregnancy test from the convenience store across the road."

"I can't be pregnant."

I brought us to a halt on the sidewalk outside and turned to face her. She looked beyond lost under the hotel lights, like her brain had up and left, and she was just a shell that continued to exist.

"Are you sure that you can't be pregnant? Have you had your

period recently? Used a condom? Every. Single. Time?"

Something on the pavement must have been fascinating because she stared at it. "No," she mumbled.

"No what? Which question were you answering?"

"No."

"Okaaaaay." I spun on my heel, my dress billowing around me as I shook my head in bewilderment. "Let's go."

I was a woman on a mission. The pregnancy test was slammed on the store counter within a matter of minutes. Gabby was still dazed and confused behind me. She really was something else.

"You can wipe that look off your face, Jeremy," I warned the obnoxious seventeen-year-old sales clerk who'd been working there for years. He was a chubby, greasy perv, and he was in no position to judge. "Just bag it and mind your business."

I pushed Gabby inside the women's restroom on the lobby floor of the hotel. There was a plush waiting sofa and a wall of stalls. The marble floors gleamed and the white sinks were immaculate. There was nothing worse than hotel toilets that weren't cared for.

"You take this and go pee on it, now," I ordered, pulling the test out of the paper bag and aggressively discarding the plastic film that surrounded the box.

I let the rubbish fall to the floor and practically threw the box over my shoulder before I uncapped the stick and placed it in Gabby's hand.

"There, I've done everything I can, save for pissing on the stick myself. That's all you." I steered her toward a stall, but she stopped at the threshold and turned around with wide eyes.

"What if I'm pregnant?"

"We'll talk about the what ifs when you know for sure, okay? There's no point talking about it when you can get a definitive answer right now."

She nodded and took a deep breath before she slipped inside and shut the door. I felt a little dizzy when I finally took a minute to be still. The whole situation was overwhelming, but I'd shut out the reality of it while I whizzed around and babied my best friend. Pun intended.

I picked up the discarded wrappers and paper bag, throwing them into the bin before I sat down on the sofa. I remembered that I'd felt my phone vibrating while I'd been in the convenience store, so I fished it out of my cleavage and unlocked it, seeing a message from Drayton.

Everything okay baby? Josh said
you two took off.

It's all good. Just helping Gabs with something
downstairs. I'll explain later. Be back up soon.

"It's negative." She shrugged her shoulders and dropped down beside me. She grunted when the silk of her dress pulled taut around her middle.

I watched her, wondering why she wasn't throwing a damn party. Her life could have been turned upside down in a matter of moments. I was a little surprised that I'd misread the symptoms, but I supposed there could be other reasons for nausea and barely there weight gain.

"You're happy about that, right?"

"Yeah—I mean, it wouldn't have been ideal." She sat forward, resting her chin in her hand and her elbow on her knee. I was worried about the seams of her dress splitting. "But it's weird. I feel—almost disappointed."

"I get that," I admitted, smiling at her confusion. "I've read about lots of woman who say that even if they absolutely didn't want it to be positive, they feel disappointed when it's negative. It's a weird emotion. Especially considering you aren't the most maternal person I know."

"That's why it's even weirder to feel disappointed. I don't know what to do with kids. But maybe it would have been different with my own."

"You'd hope so."

"You would," she huffed and stood up, the test swinging from her hand.

"Wait, give me that," I snapped, standing up. I rushed toward her before she could discard the test in the bin.

"Gabby! You said this was negative!" I practically screamed, staring at the white stick in my hands. "This has two lines! Two very red lines!"

"I thought two lines was negative," she shouted back, ripping the test out of my hand so that she could stare at it.

"No! Two lines is positive. You're pregnant!"

"I'm pregnant?"

"Yes!"

"Yes?"

"Yes!"

She gasped. "Holy shit!"

"Holy shit," a third, more masculine voice joined us and we whipped our heads in the direction of the door, where Josh watched us with ghost-white skin. Drayton stood behind him, similar shock on his face.

Josh looked like he was going to throw up. He stared at the test in Gabby's hand and she stammered with panic, not able to get a coherent word out.

"You two should talk." I walked toward the door, my heels clacking on the marble floors, providing the only noise among the awkward silence.

"This is the women's restroom?" Gabby mumbled as I pushed Josh into the bathroom, giving him a shove so that he snapped out of his stupor.

"Who gives a shit," I told her and pulled the door shut, shoving Drayton out of the way with my butt. "Talk!"

Emily won the crown for prom queen. Drayton was announced as king and I was named a princess. There was no king and queen dance, and I did not end up on stage to get a tiara because we weren't there. Emily didn't care about her first dance. She was just pleased to have the crown.

Instead of being at the end of our prom night, Drayton and I were consoling our friends who were soon to be parents. We found out all of this information about winners and dances from

Melissa, who called me at midnight last night to fill me in.

"Ooh, girl you should have seen her up on that stage, acting like she won a damn Golden Globe . . .

". . . The whole damn room was out with their Nancy Drew sleuth kits looking for Drayton. You better know what conclusion was made, girl. You two were getting smack on in a hotel room. Nasties. That's what they said. Not me . . .

". . . I didn't set them straight, though. I thought so too . . ."

The conversation went on for quite some time, but I didn't once mention the real reason that we weren't there for Drayton to receive his crown. I let her believe that we were doing what we were accused of.

Which, once we had safely delivered Gabby and Josh to her house, we did do. In the back of the car.

And then again when we got to his house.

Gabby knew that she needed to tell her mom. As terrified as she was to have her ass handed to her, she knew it was what she had to do. Josh refused to let her go it alone, which made me proud.

Drayton and I were in his kitchen. His parents were out for the day, which I was quietly relieved about. The midmorning sun was coming through the glass doors and it was relaxing to sit on the sofa and absorb the beams of vitamin D without enduring the chill. My hair was still curled from the salon, but it was up in a knot on top of my head and I was wearing shorts and a camisole.

Drayton sat at the other end of the sofa in nothing but his boxer shorts. The sunshine illuminated his olive skin. He glowed. My feet rested in his lap and he ran his hands over my legs while I read a text message from Gabby.

Been up all night with Mom. She's cried SO MUCH.
Threatened to murder Josh. Apologized for being
violent. Cried some more. Told me I'm a dumbass.
But we pulled through. Still a lot to figure out. I'm
buzzing. But we're doing this.

"I can't believe Gabby is having a baby." I put the phone
down and picked up the coffee beside the couch. I rubbed the
inner corner of my eye to get out the morning sleep.

Drayton nodded. "Josh sent me a text. He's shitting bricks
but he's in it."

"So he should be." I stared at the black goop on my fingertip
and winced. I could have sworn that I'd washed my face properly
last night. I swiped under my eyes. "He had a part in it. If he
ditches her, I will beat him the fuck up."

"Damn," he laughed. "You know how to turn a man on."

My lips curled upward as I wrapped them around the cup rim
and sipped on hot caffeine. What a long night.

"You want to do that one day?" He rested an arm along the
back of the sofa and watched me. His stubble was coming in; he
looked good with a bit of scruff.

"Do what?"

"Have my babies?"

"I wouldn't mind having a couple of little athletes." We stared
at each other and I wondered if he felt as confident as I did. Or
if he was just messing around.

He slid over, and his hand moved up my thigh as he half lay
on top of me. "We should practice. A lot. Just to be sure that we
get it right."

"Sure," I murmured, smiling, as he shifted so that I was
encased beneath him. He held the back of the sofa and knelt on

either side of me. His kiss was soft and gentle as his free hand slipped under my back and pulled me upward.

"Cheer," he mumbled against my mouth. "I mean it—it doesn't matter where we go from here. I see a future with you."

I leaned back, tingling from head to toe as his hips moved against mine. "I do too."

"Even if I end up at Baylor? You'll still love me? Call me every night? Let me sleep on your little dorm bed when I come and visit? Get naked on FaceTime?"

I scoffed with amusement. "We'll talk about the FaceTime." I held his neck, my fingers clasped at the back of his head. "But of course, Drayton. I said that before. I'm in this."

CHAPTER 25

Gabby was twelve weeks pregnant, to the day, when we graduated. She was due at the beginning of December. So far, her top complaints were weight gain, nausea, the fact that she was going to have to push a human being out of her vagina, and that she could no longer drink.

Perhaps not in that particular order.

Ellie, understanding of what it was to be a teen parent, was quick to offer whatever help she could. Much to Josh's disappointment, though, Ellie would not be the one to break the news to Josh's parents in Canada. That was up to him. But, even though Josh wasn't her son, she welcomed Gabby and offered that Gabby live with them.

But Camilla wasn't in favor of Gabby leaving home. She wanted to support her daughter through the pregnancy. Not that it was surprising—she had never been in a rush for Gabby to move out. She was handling it all better than some mothers would, but she was still upset. Camilla had given Gabby her freedom and trusted her because Gabby was intelligent, and then Gabby went and got herself knocked up.

All of those involved had sort of adopted a what's-done-is-done attitude.

"What about Han for a boy?" Josh tapped the edge of his beer bottle, the condensation sliding down the glass edge and falling into the swimming pool. "Like Han Solo? From *Star Wars*."

Gabby, living out *the last days that she'd get to wear a bikini* in the water beside him, glared at his beer while she scowled at the suggestion.

"We are not naming our child after an alien."

Josh fretted. He stuttered and waved his hand in disbelief. "An alien? What—are—have you even been watching the movies when I've put them on?"

"No," Gabby said. "Sort of how you don't watch *The Vampire Diaries* with me."

Drayton looked at me with boredom. We were sitting on the edge of the pool. He was in his swim shorts, dark blue, with his cap on backward. I was in a bikini and lace beach shorts.

We'd graduated that morning. The three of us. No more school. No more cheerleading. No more homework. It was a surreal feeling, knowing that we wouldn't be back. But I was excited for the next chapter in what life had to offer.

Drayton was kind enough to offer up his home for a graduation pool party. His mom was super pleased—sarcasm—but it was sort of a bargain in exchange for Drayton agreeing to a walk-on tryout at Baylor. Things had been tense between his father and me. In truth, I hadn't spent a lot of time around the house, and if I was here, I was upstairs.

Students from school were all over the back garden. In

the pool. In the cabana. Ellie might not have loved the idea of her home being used to celebrate—she was none the wiser to Drayton's birthday antics—but she would never risk being labeled as a bad hostess. There were tables on the deck, catering tables covered in hot food, cold beverages, and dessert platters.

Before Drayton could suggest that he and I bounce and leave these two parents-to-be arguing over which names were awful and which were worse, his teammates demanded his attention.

"I'm just suggesting that we consider Luke or Leia. Those aren't super unusual names, Gabs."

I sighed and stood up, my feet padding through puddles beside the pool edge as I wandered toward the deck. Inside, I chewed on a piece of watermelon that I snatched from the table and wandered through the kitchen. It was quiet in here. No one was allowed in the house unless it was to use the bathroom. I was the exception of course, and I found Ellie on a barstool with a glass of wine.

"Keeping guard?" I sat down beside her, tossing my curled hair behind my shoulder.

She swallowed her Cabernet Sauvignon. "Mhmm. I know that girls like to go the bathroom in groups. But seven at once seems excessive."

I laughed.

Ellie looked beautiful in a floor-length maxi dress. The pattern and colors were peacock. Blues and greens. Her sun-kissed shoulders were freckled and her green eyes were the same as Drayton's.

Suddenly, Leroy appeared. He wandered in, dressed casually in a T-shirt and shorts. Ellie smiled as he stood behind her and kissed the top of her head. I might not have seen them, but he must have had some loveable qualities. Ellie was successful. She had her own income. She wouldn't have remained married to this man if he was a total asshole.

"You look beautiful," he mumbled beside her ear as he leaned around her and picked up the wine from the countertop. I didn't think that I was meant to hear him. But I did.

He filled her glass while she grinned and then he looked at me. "Hello, Dallas."

"Hey."

He set the bottle down. Ellie sipped on her fresh beverage and he slipped his hands into his pockets. "Can we please talk for a moment?"

I quickly stood up. "I'll leave you two alone."

"No," he almost chuckled. Almost. "You and me, Dallas. Can we please talk for a moment?"

I stood, staring with uncertainty. Ellie didn't offer much in the way of assurance, but she did smile and nod when I looked at her for help. It wasn't that I hated Leroy. I wasn't scared of him. I just preferred not to be shouted at.

But I agreed with a timid nod and followed him out of the kitchen. We didn't go far. We crossed the foyer, passing the staircase and front door. He stopped in the living room, his shoulders rising and falling with a deep breath.

"I want to apologize," he stated. It was matter of fact and to the point as he stared out of the front window. A new car full of graduates pulled up. "I said things that I'm not proud of. Things that I would hate to hear another adult saying to my son. Or daughter if sh—"

There was a hitch in his voice, and I felt more awkward than I knew how to deal with. But I also felt a pang in my chest at the pain that crossed his features.

"The point is," he continued, a quick shrug in his shoulders brushing off the sorrow. "I shouldn't have blamed you for Drayton's choices. What I said was out of line."

Part of me wondered if he was just apologizing because he'd got his way.

"I hope that you can forgive me, and we can move past this." He finally turned to look at me. "Drayton's happiness is what is most important to his mother and me."

Don't say it. Don't. Don't do it. "Must help that he chose Baylor." *Well done, Dallas.*

Instead of scowling or shouting, he laughed. I had never seen him laugh like that before. He seemed so amused. "You're perfect for him."

"Uh—"

"Enjoy the party, Dallas."

He nodded and stepped around me. I twisted, watching as he left the room and Drayton entered. His attention moved from his father to me and back again, the level of confusion growing deeper with each passing moment.

They came to a stop in front of each other. Drayton's frown was intimidating as he watched his dad, not that I could blame him for being cautious. But Leroy laughed—he was doing that a lot this afternoon—and gave him a slap on the bare shoulder. "It's fine, Son. Relax."

Drayton was so protective of me.

When his dad was gone, Drayton sauntered toward me and pointed a thumb over his shoulder. "What was that about?"

"He was apologizing."

"Ha." Drayton folded his arms. His chest was delectable. "Took him long enough."

"It's fine." I waved off his mild frustration. I didn't see the need to hang on to the argument. Some things still bothered me. The fact that he hadn't stopped throwing a tantrum until *after* Drayton chose Baylor was one of them. But I didn't voice it. It wasn't worth putting back whatever progress Drayton had made with Leroy.

"Come upstairs." He nodded his head upward and held his hand out. I took it. "I have a graduation gift for you."

"What!" I attempted to plant my feet flat so that he couldn't pull me upstairs. It didn't work in the slightest. "Dray, we said no graduation gifts. I didn't get you anything."

"Are you well today? Feeling okay? Are you happy?"

"Yes," I mumbled, not entirely sure where the twenty questions had come from. "To all of it."

"Then you've given me everything that I need."

I don't think that he realized that he couldn't just spit that sort of stuff out and then leave me to deal with the fact that I was a swooning mess. He kicked his bedroom door closed after us, and I was attempting to focus on the fact that we'd come up here for a reason, because after that adorable confession, I was feeling all sorts of aroused.

He left me beside his bed and rummaged through the top drawer of his dresser. I admired the back of him and grinned. "You have a juicy booty."

He peeped at me over his shoulder and laughed. "Give me ten and yours will be too," he mumbled, returning to his search. He made me weak.

"Turn around," he ordered. His hand remained inside of the drawer, but it seemed as though he had found what he was looking for.

When I'd turned around so that I was facing the door, I heard the sound of his feet against the soft carpet and within a few moments, an object came down in front of my face, a cold chain settling around my neck.

I looked down and picked up the key that hung from the chain. There was no doubting my confusion while I stared at the item in the palm of my hand. I started to turn around, still staring at the foreign object. "What's the key fo—"

Drayton was holding his phone up when I turned around and on the screen was a picture of a stunning black motorcycle. It had purple detailing around the trim and handlebars. It wasn't an overwhelming purple. It was deep and rich, but tasteful and appealing.

"This is being kept in a warehouse in California." He looked eager and excited, and sported an enormous grin. "It's yours."

"You bought me a fucking motorcycle!" I squealed, snatching the phone out of his hand so that I could get a closer look. I was in utter disbelief. I knew that he was insane, but this was on an entirely different level.

"Yep!" He slid his hands into his swim-short pockets. They hung low on his hips. "Thought you could use some transport, and I know that you love to ride my bike. When you're not riding me, of course." He winked and I didn't even have the wit to respond. I was too far floored at the outrageous gesture.

"This is too much!" I cried and threw the phone onto the bed. "I didn't even get you anything. That must have cost a lot of money. You can't jus—"

I was silenced by his mouth on mine. His arms encircled my waist, pulling me in close and tight, then he kissed me for a long time, his tongue exploring mine and his hands traveling the small of my back and waist. When we finally broke apart, I was breathless. I was a panting, wound-up mess. He didn't release his hold, just gave me that seductive grin that caused my insides to turn to over.

"I love you, Cheer. And the fact that you love me, too, is enough. I don't need anything more than that. I've got the money to buy whatever I want." He leaned forward and gave me a chaste kiss. "What I *need* is you. As long as I have that, I'm good."

"Well—me too," I pouted. "You didn't have to get me a motorcycle."

"I wanted to." He bopped me on the nose. "And I could. And I did. So shut up and tell me that you love me."

I playfully rolled my eyes. "I love you."

✦

"Wow." Nathan stared at the phone screen as I swiped through the photos of the motorcycle with him. "That was generous."

"Tell me about it." I nodded. The graduation party had lasted long into the night. But Nathan and I were due some time together, so we had plans to get lunch and throw some ball down at the field.

"You'll have to get a license, I suppose?" He handed the phone back across the restaurant table and I lifted my bum so that I could slip it into my back pocket.

"And I'll have to learn how to ride one. I can get proper lessons or something. He said that he's going to cover them."

"You seem embarrassed?"

"He does too much for me." I shrugged a shoulder, pinching

the soda straw between my fingers as I sipped on the iced beverage. "I need a job when I get to California."

Nathan pushed his fork around the plate, shifting beans and salad. "One thing at a time. Get settled in first—you don't know what the homework will be like."

"I need a job," I said. "It doesn't matter what the homework is like. I'm not going to survive without one."

He tilted his head from side to side. "I guess. I don't like the thought of you burning yourself out."

"I'll be fine." I smiled at his concern. "I might put in a few applications next week when I go and sort out the dorm room though. A job before I get there would be even better."

"No one can accuse you of being lazy."

"I just need to be prepared. I don't want to fail."

"You've got this. Don't even stress."

Drayton and I were headed to California for a little summer vacation. It was also so that I could organize a few final things at the college, but we figured that we'd make the most of it and hang around for the week.

I was a little bit nervous about spreading out time so that I made the most of it with everyone. Gabby and Josh and Nathan. Melissa made me swear that we'd go and see a movie or take a pole class together. That sounded sort of fun.

I knew that despite the fact that I was living the dream that I'd had for as long as I could remember, I was still going to miss the people I loved. It'd be hard when it was time to leave, and I had a feeling that I wouldn't feel the full effect of it until I was gone.

"All right." Nathan put his hand behind him and reached into his back pocket. "I can't compete with a motorcycle, it's just not going to happen. I should have given you my gift first. But whatever. Happy graduation."

He slid a velvet box across the wooden tabletop. It was small, the size of a ring box. I picked it up and gave him a curious smile as I lifted the lid.

I almost burst into tears. "Nathan!"

It was an heirloom locket that had belonged to our mother. It had been in our family for generations. It used to hang beside Mom's vanity. I had begged her to let me wear it, over and over again, but I wasn't allowed. Its value was too great, and Mom didn't want it to be at risk. She did promise me that it would be mine someday, though.

After she died, I looked for it, but it was gone. I assumed that Nan had it and didn't want us to know. But now, upon opening it and finding new photos, I knew that it was Nathan who'd had it.

Inside of the locket was a photo of Nathan and me taken back in February. We'd gone out for a simple dinner for my birthday. I wasn't interested in something over the top. But we did take a selfie beside a window and it had been developed down to the perfect locket size. On the other side of the locket was a photo of Mom and Dad just a few months before their deaths. It was summer. Mom was holding her hat down, Dad was holding Mom.

Their love was undeniable.

"They would have been so proud, kid." Nathan smiled when I looked up at him through blurred vision. "You've come so far. Achieved so much. I can just imagine how much that would have meant to them."

I tapped at the corners of my eyes, wiping at the tears that would ruin my mascara in a minute. "Why did you do this to me in public?" I chuckled and sniffed.

"I've been holding on to that for ages." He leaned forward and put his elbows on the tabletop. "Thought it'd make a good graduation gift."

The gold had been polished. It shone as I turned it over and opened and closed it. "I was looking for it for so long. You must have had a good laugh, watching me search the entire damn house."

"You were nine." His stare was blank. "You looked for a few days. And not that well. But it was sort of entertaining."

I fastened the locket around my neck. Nathan tilted his head, watching and appearing as though he wanted to get up and help when I struggled for a moment. But the clip clicked and the cold piece of jewelry sat on my chest.

"Very nice."

"Thank you, Nathan."

"'Course, kid."

I refused to keep sobbing in public. This was the sweetest gift that I'd ever received, even if Drayton had lost his mind and bought me motorcycle. Nothing could compare to something so sentimental.

A waiter passed our table, plates of hot food in his hand stirring up a new appetite, and I decided to peep at the dessert menu. I couldn't read the words Molten Lava Chocolate Cake and not order it, so we had dessert and then we drove to the park near home. Nathan snatched his football from the backseat then we wandered out into the grass. The sun was warm. I felt that familiar content that came with summer settle over me while I waited for Nathan to send me the ball. "What's the plan this summer? Aside from California. Should we do some camping?"

I caught his pass and gave him a puzzled smile. We had to raise our voices a bit but he wasn't too far from me. "You want to go camping with me?"

"I love camping."

"Yeah." I threw the ball back and he raised an arm, catching it with one hand. "But you usually go with your friends."

"We should go together." He wrapped both of his hands around the ball and shrugged before he sent it back. "You can invite Drayton if you want. Gabby. Whoever."

"Gabs will just complain that she's too pregnant to go camping," I sighed with amusement.

"How is all that going? We talked a bit at graduation but I didn't want to bring it up in public."

"She would have appreciated that." I nodded. "She's fine, I suppose. Just taking it one step at a time."

"Not going to lie, I'm glad that wasn't you. Damn."

"It won't be for a long time," I laughed.

"So." He caught the ball. "Make the most of this summer. Live it up. Be good to your best friend but do not hibernate with her because she doesn't want to leave the house. Don't spend the entire three months crying over the fact that you're going to a different state than your boyfriend for college."

"Nathan," I sighed.

Of course, it was a bit of a bummer that Drayton and I would be apart. I was going to miss him, more than I could comprehend.

I'd miss late-night cuddles in bed while we watched Netflix docuseries about sports or cute romantic movies that Drayton teased me for appreciating. I'd miss how he played with my hair. How he tucked me in when he thought that I'd fallen asleep. I'd miss him picking me up for spontaneous dates—bowling, food, the movies. I'd miss going to the gym with him, even if I did watch more than I lifted. I'd even miss the embarrassment—the moments that we'd be strolling in the mall and he'd hear a song that he loved so he'd pull me in and spin me around and I'd have no choice but to dance. Or his R-rated commentary in stores in front of whoever was listening. He had no filter and I loved every single thing about him.

All right, I might sob a little bit when I left. But we'd survive. I knew that we would. We'd make the most of the summer that we had left and figure the rest out later.

And that's what we did.

✈

This is the final boarding call for flight KO3348 from Colorado Springs to Los Angeles. Final call for KO3348 from Colorado Springs to Los Angeles.

"Dal." Gabby gave me an apologetic smile. "You have to go. You'll miss the flight."

"But he's not here." I stared at the door and then I turned around and looked at the air hostess who knew that I was her last passenger to board. I needed to leave but he wasn't here. "He said that he would be here."

"Yeah bu—"

My phone vibrated in my hand and I read the screen so fast that I had to go over the words once more in order for them to make sense.

Cheer, baby. I'm sorry I couldn't make it. Traffic. Fuck. I love you. I'll see you soon though okay. This wasn't going to be good-bye so think nothing of it. Have a safe flight.

"He's not coming." I swallowed; there was a burn behind my eyes. My nose stung. But I gave Gabby and Nathan a wide smile. "I better go. But I'll be back again so . . . this isn't good-bye."

"Don't be a cheese." Nathan jabbed me in the shoulder but I could see a distinct shade of red rimming his eyes. I didn't want to make it worse for him.

"You better be back." Gabby had a cute little bump now. She suited it. "As soon as I go into labor you have to get on a flight and come home. I need you there, holding my hand."

"That's Josh's job."

"You would handle the hand holding better." She nodded, her dark curls bouncing. "Trust me. You'll come right?"

I swept her into a tight hug. "Of course I will. My hand is yours to break."

"Good."

"As long as I can send over my assignments for you to do."

"Deal."

Both of our bums were sticking out a bit due to the fact that there was a lump between us. I loved it, though. I leaned down, gave my future niece a quick kiss through the thin tank top and then moved over to Nathan.

"Go." He gave me a big hug. "You'll miss the flight and I'll be stuck with you. Can't wait to have the house to myself."

"Mhmm, sure."

I savored one more squeeze from him and then I picked up

the backpack that I'd brought as carry-on and ran over to the gate. The flight attendant looked frustrated, but she smiled regardless and scanned the boarding pass. Once more, I turned around and waved. Gabby and Nathan stood beside each other, waving—one with more enthusiasm than the other.

The seats were full when I emerged from the tunnel and onto the plane. I was in row D. Seat two. The numbers were on the overhead compartment doors so I stared up at them as I moved through the aisle. When I stopped beside my seat, I shrugged off the backpack and put it beside another in the overhead compartment. I contemplated getting a hoodie out of it. I was in a romper because it was hot as hell outside, but the flight could get cold.

I decided against it and looked down at the seat to find a familiar set of green eyes watching me, his smile as devious as ever.

"Wh—Dra—what the fuck?"

He was here. On the flight. He was in the seat beside mine, with his cap on backward. His powder-blue T-shirt hugged his shoulders.

"You should sit down, Cheer." He gestured at the seat. "The flight attendant looks kind of irritated."

I fell into the seat beside him, still watching his face because I couldn't believe that he was here. "What's going on?"

"Thought we should catch the same flight? We can share an Uber. I mean, we'll have to split off once you've settled into your dorm because I have to settle into mine at UCLA, but it's not that far."

"UCLA?"

"Yeah." He nodded, smiling as if I should understand this in clear context without so much as an explanation. "The college that I'll be attending. UCLA. In Califor—"

"You're going to UCLA?"

His smile softened as his gaze moved, traveling across my face. "I am, Cheer."

"What the hell?" I punched him in the arm and he recoiled.

"Damn, can we save that shit for the bedroom?" He rubbed his bare skin. "Or the dorm room?"

"Why didn't you tell me? I mean, how is this possible? I thought that you didn't write a letter of intent?"

"I did. To UCLA. Months ago. It was risky but I pulled it off. Dad changed his tune after the whole prom night bullshit. He agreed to let me do a walk-on wherever I wanted, but I'd done the letter of intent."

"You did it months ago?"

"Mhmm." He picked up the hem of my romper and absent-mindedly toyed with the fabric between his fingers. "Dad gave me the green light to choose which school I went to, but he flipped one last time when I told him that I'd already sorted UCLA. We're fine now, though."

"How come you didn't tell me? All of that . . . tension over it. You could have said something."

"I didn't want to get your hopes up just in case it didn't happen or I couldn't change Dad's mind."

"You're going to be so close," I mumbled as his hand spread out on my knee and slid under the romper hem.

"So close." He didn't bother waiting for the flight attendant to pass as she finished closing the overhead compartments. His hand held my face and he kissed me.

We would have been fine in separate states. I believed that.

But the fact that we didn't have to be in separate states, the fact that he'd be half an hour from where I was and we could see each other whenever we wanted, it was the hope that I never wanted to have, fulfilled and more.

Being in love with him, sharing a future, and succeeding together was more powerful than I could have imagined it would be. And realizing that I didn't have to choose one over the other, that I could have the dream school and the goals while being in love at the same time might be the most valued lesson of all.

I couldn't wait to see where the road took us.

EPILOGUE

DRAYTON—TWO YEARS LATER

There she was. The woman I loved. Her hair, soft like silk, draped around her shoulders. She clutched a stack of books close to her chest as she bounded down the dorm building stairs. She wasn't alone. There were dozens of girls heading in the same direction—classes started in fifteen minutes—but she was all that I saw. I leaned against my motorcycle parked beside the curb and watched her smile breathe vibrance into the world. Nothing could be as bright as her.

As she saw me, her smile became wider, and it floored me. No matter what, her happiness gave me peace. She ran forward, her thin sundress whipping in the warm breeze and clinging to her gorgeous curves.

"What are you doing here?" She fell into my embrace and I kissed her head. "I have class. Where are you supposed to be?"

"Right here." My hands slipped down her spine as I stared down at her. She grinned and went on her tiptoes. I still had to lean down to reach her lips. "But in an hour and a half, *we* have to be somewhere."

She shifted from one foot to the other and frowned with confusion. "Where?"

"It's a surprise."

She was getting used to surprises. Because I surprised her all the time. But she still dropped her bottom lip and frowned. "Go on." I gave her a tap on the bum and gestured. "Class. I'll be waiting in your room. I love you."

She smiled and pulled me down for a quick kiss. "I love you too."

While she was in class, I hung around in her shared dorm room. Lennon—Dallas's roommate—allowed me to be in here as long as I didn't go near her side of the room or touch her things. Which wasn't an issue. I lay on the little bed, which had seen more action than mine, and pulled out my phone. Dallas and I spent most of our time in her room since Lennon went out a lot and I didn't like the way that my roommate, Oliver, looked at Dallas.

It was part of the reason that I couldn't wait to surprise Dallas this afternoon. My girl was only on her second year in and she was already doing the most incredible things. She'd starred in three music videos as a backup dancer. She'd done a few live concerts for various artists around California. She was getting her name out there, going to school, and working in a sporting-goods store part time. She made me so proud.

We'd been talking about moving in together more and more since we'd spent so much of the summer apart because of our schedules. I had gone home and she was back and forth between Colorado and California. I missed her. We figured that it was time.

When Dallas came back, she rushed in and dropped her things. It was my surprise, but somehow she managed to be the one forcing me out of the room when I tried to get her into bed. I couldn't help it. She made my dick twitch. We went downstairs and stood beside the motorcycle with our helmets. She rode hers all the time but she still loved being my passenger.

"You should let me drive," she said, lifting her visor after she had pulled her helmet on.

"This bike is too big for you," I said, amused as her dark-brown gaze narrowed. "You're scary enough on your own bike."

"Bullshit. I'm an excellent driver."

It was true. She'd picked it up damn quick. I swung a leg over the seat and gestured for her to get on behind me. I loved the feeling of her body behind mine. How she'd slip her hands under my leathers and run her fingers along my lower torso. She flicked her visor down and zipped up her jacket. She hated wearing her leathers when it was hot, but like hell would I let her risk her safety. She wrapped around me, just as she'd wrapped herself around my entire life, and squeezed.

"You're the one who has a higher crash count than me," she added, shouting over the rumbling engine. "You might recall how we met. Crashed into my damn car."

"Yeah, but that was on purpose," I shouted over my shoulder. "It doesn't count."

"What?"

I laughed, flicked my visor down, and tore off down the street before she could continue interrogating me. Fifteen minutes later we arrived at an apartment complex in Panorama City. Dallas climbed off the bike and pulled her helmet off. Her hair stood up and I reached out to smooth it down while she stared at me.

"You crashed into my car on purpose?"

I took my helmet off and we both started pulling our leathers off. "Yeah, I had to get your attention somehow."

She tipped her head back and stared at the clouds as she exhaled a loud breath. "I shouldn't even be surprised. That is such a Drayton thing to do. Far be it for you to talk to me like a normal person."

"You made me nervous."

Her lips pursed with amusement. "I love you."

Hearing that still made my heart beat faster. "I love you too."

She let out a breath and finally took a look at the building. It was white and red brick. Square edges and white steel railing on the patios. Tall trees were spread out around the front parking lot. She looked at me, confused.

"What are we doing here?"

"Looking at an apartment. Perhaps one that we can share."

Her mouth fell open.

"There's one available and it's in our price range. I want to take care of it, but I know you. You'll want to chip in with costs—"

"You're damn right."

"Fine." I smiled and tucked her under my arm after I'd stashed our leathers in the seat compartment. We wandered toward the building entrance. The round concrete arch read *Sunset Terrace*. "We can sign the lease today if you like it."

"I love it."

"You haven't seen it."

"You have, though. Right?"

"Yeah."

"I trust you." She stopped and peered up at me, squinting at the sun pouring down on us. "You have good taste and we'll be living together. That's the main thing."

"Fifteen minutes to CalArts. Twenty to UCLA."

"You've got it all figured out."

She giggled as I grabbed her waist and drew her in. "So, you're in?"

"Always." She cupped my jaw and her thumb made circles on my skin. "As long as you're there."

The End

ACKNOWLEDGMENTS

My dream to become a published author came true and there are so many people to thank. First and foremost, Wattpad. I stumbled upon this app one day, and it was love at first sight—a community for reading, writing, and interacting with authors and readers. It was heaven and it was where my passion for writing was reignited. *Marley Meets Josh* and *Never Met a Girl Like Her,* my first and second stories, introduced me to so many loyal readers who are still with me to this very day. Their comments and feedback and encouragement were the motivation that I couldn't have lived without. By the time I started *The QB Bad Boy and Me*, I had a collective of one hundred thousand reads and two thousand followers. Not bad. However, *The QB* changed all of that, and suddenly I was looking at millions of reads and tens of thousands of followers. My readers are the best bunch of people I've ever encountered. Their positive comments, messages, and support has never failed to amaze me. I'm here today because of this app, the community, and the best people that I know.

I want to thank God. All things are possible through him. My Nana and Grandad. Wow. I'll never forget how often I would go and visit after I'd dropped the kids off at school. My nana and I would sit in her kitchen all day, talking about writing. She was an author for Mills & Boon in the seventies and we could spend hours talking about the differences between writing now and writing then. My grandparents were so encouraging, always asking how my books were coming along and how many reads I'd reached and what my next project was. Their faith in my abilities was more heartwarming than I can ever accurately describe. I love you guys. Thank you for believing in me.

My mum and sister. They've been reading from the beginning. They offer their feedback. They tell other people about my stories. And they bounce ideas around with me. If I was suffering from writer's block or a chapter or an idea, Mum would be right there, giving me ideas that ultimately helped progress the story. I love sitting with them and hearing them discuss a storyline—what they loved about it and what they found funny. Sometimes my sister would catch up on a chapter while I was sitting with her, and when she'd laugh out loud or express frustration or love for a character, it would warm my heart. I knew that I was doing something right if I could get my sister hooked on my books, considering she was never a reader. Love you guys.

Ashley. This girl has played a huge role in my Wattpad journey. I started reading her books on Wattpad, and we became fast friends with so many common interests. When I posted my very first story she created the cover and the rest is history. She's made all of my covers, my aesthetics, and any graphics that I've requested from her. She's always available to bounce ideas off. We brainstorm about each other's books. We rant over writer's block. We talk every single day and she's one of my very best friends. One day I'll make it to Canada and we'll get to meet! I'm looking forward to it.

Jess. Twenty years of friendship takes this girl from best friend to sister status. I would be lost without her. She's my soulmate. She's been reading my books from the get-go. She's believed in me. She's cheered me on and given me her wholehearted support. She and I are two halves of a whole. Love you forever and ever.

Isaac. My husband. If it wasn't for his hard work none of this would be possible. He allowed me to remain at home and dedicate my time toward writing. I promised him that I could succeed, that I could make a career out of it with a little bit of time. And he believed in me. It paid off. I love you.

I want to thank Deanna and Alysha for changing my life when they called me with this opportunity. These women have been so wonderful to work with, so encouraging and supportive. It amazes me that they can work with so many different authors and have a personal relationship with each one. They are responsive and never delay to answer my many, many questions. I've felt so blessed to have been able to work with such wonderful ladies. I want to thank Adam Wilson for his help in the beginning of the editing process. I would never have known where to start if it weren't for his wonderful edit letter and notes.

And of course, thank you to the readers. Thank you to Alyssia and Sharlene and Hayley, three of my earliest readers. Thank you to Lina. Thank you to Isabelle Ronin for advice that I didn't even realize I needed! Thank you to the ones that I wish I could name individually with personal messages, but that would require a separate book, there are so many of you! Where I am couldn't have been achieved without your votes, comments, and reads. The Instagram conversations and the laughs. It made all of the difference. It made *The QB Bad Boy and Me* the most-read Wattpad book in 2018. It put me on the map, and it made my dream come true. Thank you. I can't say it enough.

ABOUT THE AUTHOR

Tay Marley wears many hats: bibliophile, entrepreneur, wife, mother, and featured Wattpad author. Her whirlwind journey on Wattpad began in 2017, and led to one hundred thousand dedicated followers, a five-part series, and three stand-alone books—including her breakout story, *The QB Bad Boy and Me*—which have amassed over forty-one million reads. She resides in New Zealand with her husband. When she isn't writing about confident women and their love interests, she's teaching her three small children how to be the leads in their own epic tales.

Buy the stories already loved by millions on Wattpad

Collect the #OriginalSix Wattpad Books

Now available everywhere books are sold.

wattpad books

Where stories live.

Discover millions of stories created by diverse writers from around the globe.

Download the app or visit www.wattpad.com today.